Worlds Away

by Alexa Land

The Firsts and Forever Series

Book Thirteen

Cover Photo

Model Quinn Biddle

By Christopher Correia

CJC Photography

http://www.cjc-photography.com/

Books by Alexa Land Include:

Feral (prequel to Tinder)

The Tinder Chronicles (Tinder, Hunted and Destined)

And the Firsts and Forever Series:

Way Off Plan

All In

In Pieces

Gathering Storm

Salvation

Skye Blue

Against the Wall

Belonging

Coming Home

All I Believe

Hitman's Holiday (short story)

The Distance

Who I Used to Be

Worlds Away

A Firsts and Forever Family Tree is located at the end
of this book

Dedicated to:

Kim W.

I'm so grateful for your friendship,
the time you've devoted to
making my books the
best they can be, and
your ongoing support, Kim!

Special thanks to:
Ri and Ish
You're Amazing!

And to every single person
who's ever taken a chance
on an Indie Author and bought
one of our books:
Thank you from
the bottom of my heart!

Contents

Chapter One

"You remind me of my pinky toe, because I know I'll be banging you on my coffee table later tonight."

"Oh my God."

"No? Okay, how about: did you get those pants on sale? Because they're a hundred percent off at my place."

I grinned a little and said, "That's even worse."

"Then go with: I'm no weatherman, but you can expect a few inches tonight." My new friend River smiled at me and wiggled his eyebrows.

"Those lines are going to get me a restraining order, not a date."

"He'll be into it if he has a sense of humor, and if he doesn't, you don't want him anyway. What about this? There must be a mirror in your pants, because I can see myself in them."

My grin got wider. "You need to stop."

River exclaimed, "But I'm just getting warmed up! Hey, go over there and ask him: on a scale of one to America, how free are you tonight?"

I actually laughed at that one, despite myself, while River's friend Yoshi groaned and asked him, "Have you ever actually gotten a phone number using any of those lines?"

"Absolutely," River said.

Yoshi rolled his eyes. "You have not."

River pushed his sun-streaked brown hair behind his shoulder and said, "Okay, not me personally. I don't need pick-up lines, because come on!" He held his arms out to the sides and shot him a cocky look. He was cute, in a rumpled California surfer kind of way. "But our new pal Sawyer here and that blond, British guy across the room have been making eyes at each other all night, and he still hasn't made a move. It's my patriotic duty to help a member of our armed forces in his mission to invade Britain, again and again and again, all night long!"

"Former member of the armed forces," I corrected.

"Whatever."

Murphy joined me on the couch and handed me a beer as he asked, "Who's invading Britain?"

"Sawyer, hopefully. He's interested in that tall blond in the pink shirt on the dance floor," Yoshi explained, "but River's trying to make sure he strikes out by loading him up with sleazy pick-up lines."

"His name's Alastair," I said. "Do you know him, Murph?"

He nodded. "Al's a good guy. I've met him at a few parties."

"He doesn't go by Al, does he?" I asked.

"Nah, but he should. Alastair is kind of a mouthful."

"Aw see," River said, "Sawyer here would love to find out whether Alastair's a mouthful, but none of you are helping! Murphy, what's your best pick-up line?"

"Now, do I look like I need a line?" Not even a little. Murphy was a big, handsome African-American guy with dreads, tattoos, and glasses, all of which I found sexy. He probably had men falling all over him, despite his inexplicable fondness for bad pun T-shirts. He'd worn a nice dress shirt to our friends' wedding ceremony earlier that day, but for the reception, he'd unbuttoned it to reveal a tee with a drawing of two bucks rubbing noses, along with the caption 'deerly beloved'. Apparently the shirts were a thing with him.

"Sawyer doesn't need them, either." Yoshi turned to me and said, "Dude, you're hot as hell! If you take your sexy, muscle-bound self over there and just say hello to that guy, he'll probably dissolve into a puddle."

"I'm no good at the whole flirting thing," I said. "Plus, I already know he's not interested in me. We met a few months ago at Kai and Jessie's wedding, and he didn't give me the time of day."

Murphy told me, "That's because he was crushing on Zachary back then, but that was before my man TJ came along and sealed the deal. Alastair's moved on."

10

I glanced over my shoulder and across the crowded living room, and spotted my friend Zachary dancing with TJ, his husband of about eight hours. They'd gotten married in a simple but beautiful ceremony at City Hall. It was followed by the informal reception where we were all gathered, hosted by TJ's son and son-in-law, Trevor and Vincent, in their swanky Russian Hill Edwardian.

The grooms looked perfectly happy and in love, and so did my best friend Kai. He was slow-dancing with his husband Jessie right beside the newlyweds, even though Ash, the lavender-haired DJ, was playing upbeat dance music. Meanwhile, Alastair was pretending it was 1975 and doing what looked vaguely like the hustle. His partner was a guy with overgrown dark hair, thick Clark Kent glasses, and a T-shirt printed to look like a tuxedo. They were both terrible dancers, but I admired their enthusiasm and commitment to partying with abandon. "I think Alastair's here with a date," I said as I turned back to my companions, "so it'd be tacky to hit on him."

Murphy waved his hand dismissively. "That's not a date, that's Rollie. They go to college together, and they're just friends."

"Are you sure?"

He nodded. "I'm sure about this, too: every time Alastair catches you looking at him, he gets all flustered. He's interested, Sawyer. Make your move!"

A slender teenager named Darwin perched on the arm of the sofa next to me just then and said, "Hey, guys. What's up?" He was cute, transgender, and possibly Goth, though the latter could have just been a byproduct of his jet black hair, pale skin, and tendency to wear dark colors. He always struck me as a bit self-conscious, too. At that moment, he was adjusting and readjusting the lapel of his black dress shirt.

I gave him a friendly smile. "River was just treating us to his horrifying collection of cheesy pick-up lines. Do you have any?"

His hands stilled, and Darwin grinned a little as he said, "You mean like, damn boy, are you my appendix? Because this funny feeling in my stomach makes me want to take you out."

The color rose in his cheeks when we all laughed, but he seemed pleased by our reaction. "Exactly like that," River said.

Darwin asked, "Who's trying to pick someone up?"

River pointed at me. "Sawyer wants to get busy with that British guy, Alastair, but for some reason he won't make a move. I figured I'd help him out with some sure-fire opening lines."

The teen considered that for a moment, then said, "Or he could just go over there and say hi."

"That's the best suggestion by far, but I'm not trying to 'get busy', whatever that even means," I said. "River just saw me looking and got me to admit I think Alastair's attractive. Somehow, that led to a crash course in how to repel a guy in two sentences or less."

Yoshi turned to me and said, "You know he keeps looking over here, right?"

When I glanced over my shoulder at Alastair, we locked eyes and grinned at each other. He was gorgeous. He was also flawlessly pulled together, in a way that made me want to do something about it. I could just imagine how irresistible he'd look with tousled morning-after hair.

Alastair colored slightly, as if he could read my mind, before leaning in and saying something to Rollie. I turned back to my new friends and said, "We're probably freaking him out with all our staring."

"That look wasn't freaked out, it was 'do me now, big boy!' I don't get why you're still sitting here," River said.

"I'll talk to him later, when I don't have an audience," I muttered. "It's hard enough without worrying about you guys evaluating my performance."

River considered that for a beat, then leaned back in his chair. "That's a good call, actually. I would have recorded it on my phone, then come back at you with charts, diagrams, and an instant replay. Just out of love, you understand. I'm here to help, bro."

He flashed me a smile, and I asked, "How many beers have you had?"

"All of them."

"That's what I thought."

Darwin glanced at Yoshi and asked, "Not to like, change the subject, but is it okay if I look at your tattoo?"

"Yeah, of course." Yoshi held out his left arm, which was sleeved with an exquisitely rendered cityscape. Entire stories played out in that intricate grid, tiny people interacting amid the cars and buildings.

The teen gingerly took hold of his wrist and studied the tattoo as he said, "This is incredible. Who did it?"

"Thanks. I did," Yoshi said. "I own a tattoo studio in Dubose Triangle. It's called Artifact."

"Oh my God, you're Yoshiro Miyazaki!" Darwin's eyes went wide.

That made River chuckle. "Your first fanboy, Yosh. It's a big moment!"

His friend fought back a grin and tried to look haughty as he informed River, "Not the first, thank you very much."

"I've seen your work in national magazines," Darwin said. "I also remember when you opened a second studio near my parents' house a couple years ago, but it shut down after six months. I never understood that, because you're the greatest tattoo artist in the city!"

"Thanks for saying that," Yoshi said. "The second location was just a bad business decision. My studio got busy when somebody famous wore one of my T-shirts in an interview, so I thought I should expand. But in typical San Francisco style, one week you're trendy, the next you're old news. At least the original location's still keeping its head above water, thank God."

"Someday, when I can afford it, I plan to come to you for my first tattoo," Darwin said. When he realized he was still grasping Yoshi's wrist, he let go quickly and muttered, "Sorry. Awkward much?" He turned to River and said, "I wasn't hitting on your boyfriend or anything, I swear. I just forgot I was holding on to him." The kid looked mortified. His hair was short in back and on the sides with a long section at the front, and that part fell forward like a curtain and gave him something to hide behind when he tilted his head down.

"Oh no, he's not my boyfriend," River said. "Ol' Yosh here is in love with a rock star, so all I can do is yearn for him." He flashed his friend a toothy smile.

Yoshi said, "I'm hardly in love with him."

River pretended to cough and slipped in the word, "Bullshit."

"A rock star? For real?" Darwin swung his hair out of his wide, multicolored eyes. "Is it someone I've heard of?"

"I occasionally go out with the lead singer of Mayday, but it's nothing serious," Yoshi admitted, frowning just a little. "He's on the road about fifty weeks a year. In fact, right now, he's in Amsterdam. We just get together when we can."

Darwin exclaimed, "Oh my God, you're talking about Gale Goodwin! He's so hot, and I love Mayday! Whenever I get depressed, I put their first album on repeat and it always makes me feel better. I'm surprised I didn't know he was gay."

"Bi, actually. That's not a secret, but he doesn't advertise it, either." Yoshi pulled a silver case from the pocket of his black jeans and handed Darwin a business card. "If you're serious about wanting a tattoo, come by sometime. I could use a hand around the studio, so maybe we can work out a trade."

"Thanks, I will!" Darwin looked delighted.

"Can I have one of those?" I asked. "There's something I need to get done, the sooner the better."

Yoshi handed me a card and said, "I had a cancellation a little while ago, so if you're in a hurry, there's a spot open on Tuesday at one. That's the only hole in my schedule for the next two weeks, although you're probably working then."

"Actually, that's perfect. Thanks. My construction job just ended, so I'll be there." I glanced at the sleek, black business card before slipping it in my pocket and decided its modern design suited Yoshi. He was effortlessly sophisticated, from his precise haircut, which accentuated his handsome features, to the fitted black T-shirt and jeans that somehow seemed upscale on him. Even his all-black, almost architectural tattoo matched his aesthetic. Yoshiro Miyazaki was a class act, no doubt about it, and I figured his tattoo studio would be the same.

"Great." Yoshi got up and said, "I'm going to refill my drink, you guys want anything?" When we declined, he headed to the kitchen.

Darwin watched him go, then murmured, "I said something wrong, didn't I? He seemed sad all of a sudden, even though he tried to hide it."

"You didn't do anything wrong," River told him. "He misses his rock star, even though my friend refuses to admit how much that guy means to him. It sucks too, because Yosh basically gets treated like a booty call, and he deserves so much better."

Darwin mulled that over, then asked River, "Do you really yearn for him?"

"Nah. Yosh is a great guy, but I'm not looking for a relationship."

"Why not?"

"My last one totally imploded, and I guess I'm still shell-shocked. The fact that I'm staring at my ex right now and it feels like a knife in my chest tells me I'm in no way ready for whatever comes next," River said. "Besides, even if I was interested in Yosh, he'll never get over that rock star. I can just see him ten years from now, still waiting around for Goodwin to call him."

Darwin and I both followed River's line of sight and spotted his ex-boyfriend chatting with the DJ across the room. Cole was a slender guy of about twenty-five with a beautiful skin tone and wild, tightly curled hair, thanks to his half-African-American, half-Jewish ancestry. I'd noticed Cole glancing at River several times during the last couple hours, so clearly there was some unfinished business between them.

The song ended, and the DJ announced he was taking a break. He and Cole disappeared into the crowd as Kai and Jessie joined us in front of the fireplace. Murphy and I slid over to make room for them on the couch, and I handed my best friend the beer I was holding, since Kai looked overheated. He thanked me and took a drink before passing it to his husband. When I glanced over my shoulder and saw that Alastair and his friend had disappeared, I felt a little disappointed.

"So, what are we talking about?" Kai asked, resting his ankle on his knee and draping an arm over Jessie's shoulders. The two were physical opposites and just beautiful together. Kai was a tall, muscular Native Hawaiian with dark hair and eyes, and Jessie was a blue-eyed blond with a slight build, who looked younger than his husband, even though they were both twenty-five. The adoration on their very different faces when they glanced at each other was identical, though.

"We were trying to get your buddy Sawyer to go talk to a cute guy he had his eye on," River said, "but as you can see, his fine ass is still glued to that couch."

Kai sat up a bit. "Sawyer's interested in someone? Who?"

"Alastair." Murphy asked, "Do you know him?"

"Jess and I both do. The three of us used to be in the same street racing club." Kai turned to me and said, "This is great news. I've been saying you need to get back out there after—"

I interrupted him with, "He who shall not be named."

"Exactly," Kai said. "Want me to introduce you to Alastair? You'll like him, he's a great guy."

"Why does everyone think I need help with my love life?"

"I don't think that," Kai told me. "I just know you're probably a little gun-shy after your last relationship. I mean, it ended months ago, and you still seem so shut down. I'm worried about you."

"Don't be. I'm fine."

Jessie gave me a sympathetic smile and said, "No pressure. If you don't want to approach him tonight, I can make sure you have another opportunity. Maybe you can both come to dinner at our place next week."

"Thanks, but I've got this. I just need another drink first. I'll talk to you guys later."

I got up and went to the kitchen, which was just as crowded as the living room, and paused to look around. It was beautiful, with a warm color scheme, stone countertops, and maple cabinets, and would have looked like something out of a magazine if it wasn't for the dozens of photos stuck to the refrigerator and dotted all around the room. They were my favorite part of the space and made the house feel like a home.

Yoshi was leaning against the kitchen island/booze station talking to Rollie, but Alastair was nowhere to be seen. They both turned to me when I walked in, and Rollie exclaimed, "About damn time!" He had a Louisiana drawl and a lopsided grin, and he was actually kind of cute under the messy hair and thick glasses. When I raised an eyebrow at him, he added, "Don't bother lookin' surprised. I saw the way you were glancin' at Alastair, and I kept thinkin' sooner or later, surely you'd come over and ask him to dance. But you never did! What the hell were you waitin' on?"

"He could have just as easily come over and talked to me," I said as I poured myself a shot of whiskey.

"Here's what you need to know about my friend," Rollie said. When he leaned in, he swayed a bit and had to steady himself with a hand on my shoulder. That told me he was drunk and probably about to venture into TMI territory. "Alastair comes across as supremely confident, but a lot of that's an act. He was intimidated by the idea of approachin' you, not only because you're a babe, but because you were sittin' with a group of your hot friends, and he didn't want to strike out in front of them. Also, Alastair's pretty inexperienced, so go easy on him. But you did *not* hear any of that from me!" He pointed at me around the highball glass in his hand and tried to look stern.

"So, where is he now?"

Yoshi said, "He was hoping you'd come looking for him, so he left a trail for you. Follow the breadcrumbs."

"Not literally," Rollie chimed in, "because Alastair thought it was poor form to throw food all over our hosts' lovely home. So, follow the next best thing to breadcrumbs." He tilted his head to the right.

In the corner, a tiny blueberry muffin was centered on the bottom rung of a circular staircase. I grinned and asked, "Follow the mini-muffins?"

"You got it."

I tossed back the drink, then put my glass in the sink and retrieved the inch-high muffin. Its bottom half was encased in a tiny, accordion-pleated paper liner, and I wondered where someone would find wrappers that small. As I started to climb the stairs, I spotted another muffin up ahead and murmured, "Bonus points for originality."

The muffin trail led me to the third floor. It had been divided roughly in half, and part of it was a cozy family room with bookcases, a TV, overstuffed couches, and stacks of board games. I followed the muffins past that room and through a heavy, glass-paneled door, then stopped in my tracks and took in my surroundings.

The room was striking. That wasn't because of the ornate skylight that took up a lot of the high ceiling, or even the row of tall windows showcasing a sweeping nighttime cityscape, but because it looked like someone was losing a game of Jumanji in a big way. Dozens and dozens of plants, primarily orchids, were clustered on every available surface. The not-quite-greenhouse was warm and slightly humid, and smelled like soil and moss and something else, something organic and living.

As I wound my way through the plants, I spotted one more muffin on the sill of the last window in the row, which was open. I'd been collecting them along the way, and I arranged my baked good bounty on a rattan chair before sticking my head out the window. I didn't see Alastair, but could hear someone singing along, badly and enthusiastically, to an Alicia Keys song. After a moment, I realized the one-man karaoke show could only be coming from the roof, and I murmured, "Interesting."

I stepped up onto the sill and looked around. There was a trellis to my left, but I doubted it would support my weight. Instead of climbing it, I grasped the edge of the roof and pulled myself up. Good thing I wasn't even remotely afraid of heights.

After getting to my feet and wiping my hands on my black jeans, I admired the excellent view for a few moments. Not the city's skyline, which was actually behind me. Instead, my attention was riveted on Alastair's butt, which he shook with abandon in his snug white pants.

He was near the front of the flat roof, dancing in a pool of light spilling from a neighboring building and singing in an adorably tone-deaf falsetto. Alastair spun around while belting out, "This girl is on fi—" He almost tripped over his own feet and cut himself off as he exclaimed, "Blimey, you actually followed me onto the roof!"

"I did. Way to make me work for it."

He smiled flirtatiously as he tapped the phone in his hand and turned off his musical accompaniment. "You bet your arse I made you work for it, after the way you've been teasing me with those smoldering looks all evening! Would it have killed you to ask me to dance when we were both downstairs?"

"Would it have killed you to do the same thing?"

"Oh no, that's not how this works. If you want me, you have to come and get me. I've learned over the course of my short, tragic dating history that it's far better to be chased than to be the one doing the chasing. The latter is bloody exhausting." His British accent was sexy, no doubt about it.

I stepped around the large skylight, and he held his ground as I slowly approached him. My voice was already low, but I dropped it even lower as I asked, "So, now that you've been chased down and cornered, what do you suggest I do with you?"

"Anything you'd like." He tried to sound confident, but he fidgeted a little, as if his own boldness made him uneasy.

I came to a stop maybe a foot from him. Alastair was tall, but I was taller, by a good three or four inches. When he looked up at me, his full lips parted and he leaned toward me ever-so-slightly. God, so sexy.

He was absolutely striking, with high cheekbones, a long, lean body, and thick, dark blond hair, which was swept back from his forehead in a perfect wave, as if a stylist had just dropped by and arranged it for a photoshoot. I was so taken with him that I forgot what we were talking about for a moment. Finally, I murmured, "Um, my name's Sawyer MacNeil."

"I know. I'm Alastair...Wilde." There was the slightest hesitation between his first and last name, and his gaze strayed from mine for a split-second. I knew with absolute certainty that he'd lied to me, but I didn't call him on it.

"Well, Alastair Wilde, can I have this dance?"

"There's no music."

"You're holding the solution to that in your hand."

"Oh, right. Forgot all about it." He fumbled with his phone and almost dropped it. I liked the fact that I rattled him. When 'Sabotage' by the Beastie Boys started to blast from the tiny speaker, he exclaimed, "Shite, I didn't mean to click that," and turned it off with a quick jab.

I took his hand in mine and turned it so we could both see the screen. He had a staggering number of songs in his phone, and as I scrolled through them, I said, "You know, a lot of people claim to have eclectic taste in music, but you've taken it to a whole new level."

"Last year, I had this idea that I wanted to expand my musical horizons," he said, watching me instead of the screen. "I bought dozens of songs from every decade, from the 1920s to the present. I found that, in addition to the modern stuff, I had an inexplicable affinity for music from the 1960s and the 1980s. I'm not sure what that says about me."

I found his 80s playlist and tapped my selection, then slid the phone into the pocket of his pink button-down shirt. As I drew him close and took his hand in mine, 'Time After Time' by Cyndi Lauper began to play. When we both tried to lead, he grinned and said, "Sorry, force of habit. Years of ballroom dancing classes with my cousin Abigail as my partner. Not my idea, I swear."

Both of us began to sway to the music, and he felt wonderful in my arms. After a minute, I said, "I probably should have let you lead. I just realized the last time I slow-danced was at an awkward eighth grade mixer."

I grinned at the memory, and Alastair smiled and said, "I bet the girls were falling all over you."

"Nah. I didn't hit my growth spurt until the end of high school, so I was one of the shortest kids in my class. I also had a mouthful of braces. That dance was a lot of fun though, which can't be said for most of the social functions I was forced to endure back then."

"What made that one different?"

"I asked Gretchen Reiner to dance because no one else would, probably because she was a foot taller than every boy in our class. After that, all her friends on the girls' basketball team took turns dancing with me, and then we all hung out in the parking lot telling dirty jokes for the remainder of the evening."

"Fantastic."

"It was. I think it's poetic justice that Gretchen's now a supermodel living in New York. All those dumb straight boys who shunned the tall girl back in middle school would probably kill for five minutes of her time now."

"I've seen her on TV, she's fabulous!"

"Yup. Nice as can be, too. We still keep in touch." I spun us around and smiled as I said, "Heads up, I'm about to get fancy."

"As long as you don't Mission Impossible me through the skylight, have at it."

"I'm saving that for the grand finale. But first, I'm planning to dip you in three, two…." He whooped with delight, and I swore vividly and burst out laughing when he kicked up both feet in the middle of the dip, turning it into a swing dancing move.

I managed to right us both somehow, and when the song ended, we leaned on each other as we chuckled and caught our breath. "Next time, you're leading," I said, "and I'm going totally off plan in the middle of it and leaping at you like we're starring in the gay remake of Dirty Dancing."

"Bring it!"

"Oh man, I'm picturing that. It'd be exactly like a scene from a Road Runner cartoon. You'd be standing there, and a huge shadow would fall across you, and then blammo! You'd disappear when I landed like a ton of bricks."

"If you didn't have about sixty pounds of solid muscle on me, I'd suggest we try it," he said, running his palm over his forehead. "Oh, and before I forget to mention it, I adore that Cyndi Lauper song. I was a bit surprised when you selected it."

I leaned against the brick chimney and said, "One of my dad's ex-wives, who actually still lives next door to us in our duplex, was a big influence on me. They were only married two years, but I think that's right when I was developing my taste in music, and she was permanently stuck in the 80s."

"One of his ex-wives? How many times has he been married?"

"Four, and yes, he's in the market for lucky number five. But let's not talk about him."

"Deal. Are you thirsty? I brought us refreshments, on the off chance you'd actually follow me up here." He retrieved a bottle of champagne that was stashed beside the chimney and peeled off the foil as he explained, "I brought a case of this to the reception. I only mention it because raiding our hosts' liquor supply must seem tacky."

"How'd you climb onto the roof while holding a bottle?"

"I possess the skill and grace of a ninja." When I raised an eyebrow at him, he admitted, "If you must know, I took off my shirt and fashioned it into a booze sling before climbing the trellis."

"Nice. I'm sorry I missed that." As he untwisted the metal cage over the cork, I asked, "Why the roof, exactly? We could have danced and gotten drunk indoors, too."

He flung his arms out and said, "Because it's fantastic up here! I think the Drifters said it best, hang on." He flipped through his playlist, then returned the phone to his pocket as 'Up on the Roof' began to play.

"A song for every occasion."

"Absolutely. Life should be more like the movies, especially the ever-present soundtrack." He launched the cork into space, and as he handed me the bottle, he said, "*Slàinte mhòr agus a h-uile beannachd duibh.*"

"Right back at you. Was that Klingon?" I took a sip and handed it back to him while he flashed me a smile.

"It's what a Scottish classmate taught me to say when we'd raid his parents' liquor cabinet. It's basically 'great health and all good blessings,' but that sounds far more interesting in Gaelic."

"And Klingon." He took a drink as I sat down on the roof with my back against the chimney, and I said, "So, Alastair Wilde, tell me about you. I only know a little through our mutual friends, including the fact that you go to college and are a street racer."

"About sums it up. I've heard you're in the Army. You on leave?"

I shook my head. "I finished my four-year commitment and got the hell out."

"So, what now? College?"

"I don't know. I got my A.A. before I enlisted, and I haven't made up my mind about going back for my bachelor's."

"You seem young to have done all that."

"I'm twenty-three. I took the high school equivalency exam at sixteen, spent two years getting my associate's degree, and enlisted when I turned eighteen."

He said, "Sounds like you had it all planned out."

"My dad was the one with a plan, not me. I was supposed to follow in his footsteps with a career in the military, starting as soon as I graduated. I wanted to continue my education, but all I could afford was two years at a junior college."

Alastair looked surprised. "I didn't expect us to have so much in common, based on what I knew about you from our friends."

"We have something in common?"

He nodded. "We both sped up our lives to go to college and do what we wanted before getting crushed under the weight of family obligation. Not unlike the coyote in those cartoons." He raised one hand over his head, bottle and all, and let it fall into the other, pantomiming the moment of impact.

"What does your family expect of you?"

"On my next birthday, I'm to return to London and begin being groomed to take over the family business. Say hello to a future captain of industry." He gave me a little salute, then took a long drink before handing the champagne back to me.

"Is that what you want?"

"What I want is irrelevant. That's what's happening."

"So, you must be a business major."

"God no, astrophysics. The deal I struck with my family was that I could go to the U.S. and study whatever I wanted, as long as I understood I'd be coming home and buckling down at twenty-one."

I asked, "Will you be able to finish your bachelor's degree by then?"

"I already did, and I've started on a PhD. I decided to begin the program anyway, even knowing I'll never complete it."

"And now I feel like a total slacker with my A.A."

"Don't. You found a way to work in two years of higher education before you turned eighteen. That's admirable."

He was shifting his weight from foot to foot, and I said, "Why don't you sit down?"

"Because I'm wearing white trousers, and when we eventually return to the party, I don't want to look like a chimney sweep."

My legs were stretched out and crossed at the ankles, and I indicated my thigh and said, "Sit here."

"But that'll be uncomfortable for you."

"It'll be fine."

Alastair straddled my legs and sat down facing me. We watched each other as we took turns with the champagne, and after a moment, he said, "You're extraordinarily handsome, Sawyer. I hope you don't mind me saying that."

I couldn't resist a bit of lighthearted teasing. "You didn't think so when we first met. In fact, you barely spoke to me. Do you remember when that was?"

"At Jessie and Kai's wedding. I thought you were gorgeous then too, but at that point it was a negative, because I incorrectly assumed we were both vying for Zachary's attention. I had a grand plan for making him my boyfriend back then. Since we watched him get married today, you can see how well that worked out."

"Do you wish things had turned out differently between you two?"

He shook his head. "Everything happened just as it should. Zachary and TJ are perfect for each other. I didn't think so at first, because I only saw their substantial age gap, but the love between them and the way they understand and support each other is exactly what each of them needs. Plus, they're both good friends of mine now. That's something I'll get to carry with me, even after I return to the UK."

"And the hunt for a boyfriend goes on?"

"No, that ship has sailed."

"What do you mean?"

"When I first met Zachary, I was just eighteen," he said. "By the time I got him to agree to go out with me, which was actually at Jessie's wedding, I'd already passed my nineteenth birthday. Still, I thought he and I could date for a while and keep it light, yeah? I liked the idea of someone to spoil, to take out to dinner and away for the weekend, that sort of thing. It was the one missing piece to my time in California, getting to be in an openly gay relationship with a cute boyfriend and just having fun together. But it would have been a mistake, I know that now. What if Zachary and I had gotten attached to one another? It might have hurt him when I had to go back home. And now, there's not enough time left to get involved with anyone else."

"So, what's the new plan? Random hookups until you're called back to jolly old England?"

"If only I could be that guy! But, as it turns out, I hate trying to be intimate with strangers I meet in bars or on the internet. It's far too impersonal." After he took another sip of champagne, he added, "Zachary says what I need is a fling, just a bit of fun with someone willing to keep it casual during my last few months here in the U.S."

"He's right."

Alastair smiled flirtatiously as he ventured, "Do you think you might want to come home with me tonight and figure out what a fling involves?" He tried to seem bold, confident, but there was no disguising the vulnerability in his eyes when he propositioned me. I was glad he couldn't hide it. That was the part of him I understood.

"I'd love to. I suppose we should probably go back to the party first though, so our friends don't think we're blowing them off. After that, I'm all yours."

*****

When we went back inside, Rollie and Alastair joined my friends and me in front of the fireplace. Alastair squeezed in beside me on the couch, and when I draped my arm over his shoulders, he snuggled close to me. It felt wonderful.

We spent a couple hours talking and laughing, until the party started to wind down sometime after midnight. Before we headed to the door, I hugged Zachary and his new husband and said, "Congratulations again to you both, and thanks for inviting me to your wedding."

"I'm so glad you were there, Sawyer," Zachary said, looking up at me with sincerity in his brown eyes. "I'm also happy to see you and Alastair are getting acquainted. I think you might have fun together."

"That's the plan."

A couple minutes later, River came up to me in the foyer as I pulled on my motorcycle jacket and said, "Great talking to you, Sawyer. Keep in touch, and have fun invading Britain tonight," he said with a big grin. "Hey, did you use one of my lines when you finally made your move?"

I grinned and said, "Uh, no. That's why he's actually going home with me."

After I said goodnight to Yoshi and Murphy and they took off with River, I stepped onto the front porch and leaned against the railing. One of Zachary's friends stood close by, peering through the open doorway, obviously waiting for someone. I'd kept noticing him throughout the party. He was beautifully androgynous with long, dark hair, and wore a sheer, black shirt over a fitted camisole, along with black skinny jeans, lots of makeup, and silver jewelry. "Is your name Gabriel?" I asked.

He glanced at me. "Yup. You're Sawyer, right?" When I nodded, he said, "Zachary's mentioned you."

"Yeah, he'd mentioned you, too." After a moment, I mumbled, "I, uh…I think you're brave. I just wanted to tell you that. I've always admired people who can just…be who they are." Okay, wow, that sounded stupid.

Gabriel turned toward me and appraised me carefully before asking, "And who are you, Sawyer?"

"I'm…." I hesitated, then pulled up the hem of my shirt a few inches, revealing a black silk corset. "I'm the same as you, but on the inside." I dropped the shirt and studied the welcome mat.

"I'm guessing most people don't know that about you, right?"

"Right."

He smiled at me and pulled out his phone. "What's your number?"

"Oh. Um, I wasn't trying to hit on you or anything. I just—"

"I know. You wanted someone to understand, and I do," he said. "I asked for your number because girls like us need to stick together. I truly believe that."

"Girls?"

"Too campy for your taste? I'm right about the sticking together part, though. It's always good to have at least one friend who gets it."

I recited my number, and he put it in his phone and shot me a quick text so I'd have his, too. After a moment, I confessed, "I'm about to go home with a guy I met at the party, and I'm worried about undressing in front of him. People aren't always receptive, you know? That, or they totally misinterpret it. I might just change in the bathroom and hide it from him."

"I hope he's cool with it if you decide to let him meet the real you." I was startled when he pulled me into a hug. "Please keep in touch with me, Sawyer. I'd love to have a friend who's gender fluid like me."

"I will," I said as he let go of me. "I'm not sure that's what I am, though. The couple people in my life who know are just like, 'oh, you're a cross-dresser.' But that label never felt right, either."

"Screw labels," Gabriel said. "Be who you are and call it whatever the hell you want."

"You're right."

His friend Scottie joined us, and after a quick introduction, Gabriel said, "Have fun tonight, Sawyer. I'm glad we talked."

"Me, too."

Alastair appeared on the porch about a minute after they left, waving his phone. "Found it! No idea how it ended up in the dining room. I don't even recall going in there."

"You did a lap of the ground floor when you were looking for Rollie earlier, maybe that's when you put it down. Speaking of your friend, where is he now? I don't think he should be driving home tonight."

"He won't. Our hosts tucked him into bed in their guestroom right before he passed out. I just checked on him, and he's sleeping it off."

"That's good."

As we headed down the stairs, he said, "I have a flat just a few blocks from here, at the corner of Green and Leavenworth. Feel like walking?"

"Sure."

We started down the sidewalk, and he slipped his hand in mine, then glanced at me and asked, "Is this alright?" When I told him it was fantastic, he looked happy.

Chapter Two

Alastair's building towered above the neighborhood. I looked up at the white, twenty-story art deco structure with its elaborate façade and murmured, "Well, damn."

"I bought the condo primarily for the views," he explained. "I want to drink in San Francisco while I'm here. The city's beautiful, I think, and so different than what I'm used to."

I turned to him and asked, "Did you grow up in London?"

"No. My family keeps a house there, but my childhood was spent in boarding schools and at our country estate. I'll live in London when I go back, though." It wasn't much of a surprise to find out he came from money. He looked the part.

We crossed the cavernous, vaguely Spanish-style lobby hand-in-hand. As we rode the elevator to the top floor, I put my arm around him and he leaned into me. Alastair was the perfect height. He fit into the space between my neck and shoulder like it was where he belonged.

When we reached his apartment, he led me straight to the bedroom, which was softly lit by a single lamp on his bedside table. We both tossed our jackets aside and I took a deep breath as we watched each other for a long moment. Anticipation crackled across my skin.

I approached Alastair slowly and stopped just inches from him. With a gentle touch, I tilted his face up with two fingertips under his chin. His breathing accelerated as he draped his arms around my shoulders.

Our lips met, tentatively. It felt like an unspoken question. I cupped his face between my palms and kissed him again, and his lips parted for me. Alastair reached up and caressed my short hair as the tip of my tongue met his, and we deepened the kiss just a little, savoring each other.

My heart was pounding as I lost myself in his sweet taste, his clean scent, the feel of his skin beneath my fingertips. I breathed in his little sigh of pleasure, made it mine. His lips were soft and wet and yielding, and I could have spent forever in that moment, reveling in that kiss, feeling it awaken every part of me, stirring needs and feelings and sensations long ignored, shut down, buried.

But when he reached for the buttons on my shirt, I was pulled out of my reverie. I caught his hands and said, "Just a little slower, okay? Come sit down with me." He looked up at me and nodded, confusion in his eyes as we both perched on the edge of the mattress.

"I didn't mean to rush. I'm sorry."

"You didn't. I just…need a minute." I wasn't ready to show him that other side of me just yet, the part so few understood, the part I didn't understand myself. But there was something else too that had made me slow it down, something in his eyes, his touch, his response to me, something a little uncertain that made me ask, "Alastair, are you a virgin?"

He chewed his lower lip for a moment before admitting, "Sort of."

I grinned a little. "How does that work, exactly?"

"I've messed around before, but when it came to, um, penetration, it never quite…worked out." He looked mortified.

"Where you bottoming?"

"That was my intent, but I just couldn't manage it. I want to, though. God, I want to. I'm hoping you're a bit more experienced than I am, so you'll be able to guide me through it tonight."

"Losing your virginity is a big deal. Don't you maybe want to wait until you're in a relationship?"

His voice rose a little as he looked up at me and said, "But I'm never going to be in a relationship. Don't you see? I only have a few months, and then I have to return to the UK. My family knows I'm gay, but they think it's just some rebellious phase I'm going through for shock value, and they expect me to be done with it by the time I come home. How the bloody hell am I supposed to just *be done* with who I am?"

Alastair took a deep breath before continuing, more quietly, "I came to California because I thought I could be open about who I was and explore my sexuality, but it hasn't gone like I thought it would. I had this idea that I'd be having loads of sex, a different bloke every week. I thought San Francisco would be the perfect place for that. But they don't tell you, do they? Nobody mentions the fact that it hurts like hell when you're inexperienced, and that it's terrifying to make yourself vulnerable with a stranger you've just met in a bar, or worse, through some sleazy dating app. So then I thought, alright, apparently I'm not a one-night stand kind of guy, so I'll just find myself a boyfriend. But that didn't work out either! I've been in the U.S. since I was sixteen, and alright, I didn't start looking for a boyfriend until I was eighteen, but still! Nothing turned out like I thought it would. And now here I am, twenty years old, and I can't go back a virgin. I just can't!"

I said, "You won't. We're going to make sure of that tonight."

He searched my eyes. "I'm surprised you're still willing, now that you know I don't have the first clue what I'm doing."

"Of course I am. I'm honored that you'd trust me with something this important, and I'm going to take good care of you, Alastair."

He picked up my hand and wove our fingers together. "If you don't mind my asking, what was your first time like?"

"It sucked. Neither of us had been with a man before, and we were so clueless. The good news is, it taught me what not to do, so your first time will be much better than mine."

"Who was the guy?" Alastair shook his head and amended, "Never mind, that's none of my business."

"It's fine. He was...I almost called him my boyfriend, but that's not accurate. All I can say is, he was a guy I was involved with when I was in the Army. He was also the officer in charge of my military unit, which is all kinds of messed up, but that's another story." I looked at our joined hands and added, "He's the only person I've ever been with, and he refused to bottom. So, tonight's going to be a first for me, too, one I've wanted for a long time."

"How long were you and he involved?"

"It dragged on for three years. When I left the Army, I left him, too. In fact, he's part of the reason I didn't re-enlist."

Although I'd tried to keep my expression neutral, the pain I felt must have slipped through somehow, because he asked, "You loved him, didn't you?" I hesitated before nodding. "Do you still?"

"No. It took a long time, but I finally got over him. I had to. He was never going to treat me as anything more than his dirty little secret."

"I see why you were alright with the idea of a fling," he said. "After all of that, a relationship must be the last thing you're looking for."

"Exactly."

"Thanks for being so open with me."

"Well, I think you should know who you're taking to bed." I hesitated before adding, "You don't have the whole picture yet, though. There's something I need to show you. It might be a deal breaker, but I don't want to hide it from you, like I do with almost everyone else."

He watched me curiously as I pulled off my shoes and socks, then got up and turned to him. I took a deep breath as I began to unbutton my shirt. "If you're not into this, that's fine," I said. "I know it's…different."

Alastair stared at me with rapt attention as I began to undress. I tossed my shirt on a nearby chair before unfastening my jeans, stepping out of them, and kicking them aside. My heart was pounding, and I swallowed hard and mumbled, "So, this is me," as I stood before him. I was wearing one of my favorite outfits, a corset, stockings with garters, and a thong, all black.

His eyes went wide as they ran down my body. I was sure I'd freaked him out. He didn't know what to make of me, he didn't even know what to say. I was mortified, and so sad that I'd fucked up what could have been a great night. I should have hidden it and changed in the bathroom. I never should have—

"You're the sexiest thing I've ever seen in my entire life." Alastair's voice was low and thick with desire, and he pulled me to him and kissed me with raw hunger.

It was like a fire had been lit in him. We fell back onto the mattress and he climbed on top of me as we kissed. I grabbed his ass, totally turned on by his reaction, and pushed up against him so I could grind my swelling cock against his. When I began kissing his neck, he murmured, "I never expected that. You seemed so butch! And maybe that's why it's so sexy, the juxtaposition of hard and soft, the lingerie against that big, muscular body."

I chuckled a little and rolled over so I was on top. "Let's maybe not analyze it right this moment."

He smiled at me and rolled us over yet again. "I tend to ramble, sorry. But I have a solution for that."

Alastair slid between my legs and pulled the thong below my cock and balls, and I moaned as his warm, wet mouth engulfed my hard-on. He fumbled with his clothes and pushed his shoes off as he sucked me. After a minute, he tossed his shirt aside, unfastened his belt and pants, and managed to free his erection.

He'd been planning to jerk himself off, but I flipped around and took him in a side-by-side sixty-nine instead. He was uncircumcised, which was new to me. I grasped his shaft and slid his foreskin back, exposing his pink, glistening cockhead before taking it between my lips. He cried out as I sucked and stroked him, and then he grasped my cock and began sucking me again, hard and fast. No way was I going to last long, not with all of that. In just a few minutes, I let his cock slip from my mouth and murmured, "You're going to make me cum." His cock twitched in my hand, and he sucked me even harder.

I wrapped my mouth around his cock again and moaned as my orgasm slammed into me. Moments later, he shot onto my tongue. I swallowed without hesitation and he did, too. As I thrust into his mouth, he grabbed my ass and tried to push me deeper down his throat. My yell was muffled by his cock as we rode out my orgasm and his.

Finally, both of us fell back, sweating and trying to catch our breath. After a few moments, Alastair turned around, crawled over to me, and curled up against my side. I put my arm around him, and he draped his leg over mine and whispered, "That was wonderful, thank you." When I chuckled, he looked up at me and said, "What?"

"You're so polite. It's cute."

"Don't most people say thank you after oral sex?"

"I have no idea. I haven't slept with most people."

That made him smile. "For a couple blokes who've only been with one and three-quarters men in our lives, I think we did quite well just then."

I smiled, too. "Three-quarters?"

"I had three false starts. Two managed to force their tip into me before I made them stop. The other didn't even get that far. I can't count them as sex partners, but I don't want to pretend they never existed, either."

"Got it."

He ran a fingertip down the little silver hooks along the front of my corset and was quiet for a while before saying, "I know what I like about these clothes, but I want to hear your take on it, if that's alright."

I thought about it before saying, "It just feels…right. That's the only way I can explain it. This isn't a fetish, I don't get off on dressing this way. It's just, well, me being me, I guess. I've been like this all my life, long as I can remember. This part of me isn't optional. It's who I am."

"I'm grateful that you shared it with me."

"I seriously considered changing in the bathroom before we had sex, so you wouldn't find out about this. It felt like a coin toss: maybe you'd be okay with it, maybe you'd think it was weird and a total turn-off. But…I guess I just wanted to be honest with you. I spend so much time hiding, and I didn't want to do that here, too."

He kissed my bare shoulder and said, "Thank you for trusting me with it." Then he looked up at me and grinned. "Manners again. They're deeply engrained. I'll be fighting the urge to send you a lovely, hand-written thank you note tomorrow."

I chuckled and said, "That'd be a first."

Alastair chewed his lower lip for a moment as he watched me. Finally, he said, "I'm an intensely curious person by nature. I think that's part of the reason why education's always been so important to me, because I just have this need to know things. This is absolutely none of my business, but I have to ask anyway." He gently ran his fingers across the six-inch-long tattoo above my left nipple, the one that said 'Tracy' in a simple script. "Who is she? Or was, I suppose."

"He. That's who I was telling you about. The tattoo is one of the stupidest things I've ever done, and it's going away next week. I have an appointment at Yoshi

Miyazaki's tattoo studio on Tuesday, and it's getting completely obliterated."

"It was quite serious then, the thing between you and Tracy," he said.

"For me it was. I had this idiotic idea that if I got that tattoo, he'd finally understand what he meant to me. Hearing me say I loved him never made a difference, but maybe if he saw it...." I shook my head. "Stupid. All it did was piss him off. He was so afraid someone would see it and figure out he and I were involved. He tried to make me go to a clinic and get it lasered off, but I refused, out of sheer stubbornness."

"God, I'm sorry. It must have hurt to have him react like that."

"I should have expected it. Our relationship was so fucked up. Not that it was even a relationship." After a moment, I forced myself to shake off the weight of those memories. I kissed Alastair's forehead and said, "I don't blame you for being curious. I would be, too. But let's stop talking about my ex, pretty much forever, okay?"

"Absolutely." He traced my bicep, and after a pause, he said, "I suppose I doomed myself to never losing my virginity with that blow job. Or, my technical virginity, I suppose. You know, I've always wondered how the term 'technical virgin' applies to gay men. If all you ever do is top and never get penetrated, or similarly, if you only ever bottom, at what point can you declare you're no longer a virgin? It always seemed a bit murky to me." When he noticed me grinning at him, he said, "Apologies. As I mentioned earlier, I do tend to ramble. I'm trying to learn not to verbalize every random thought that crosses my mind. Clearly it's a work-in-progress, but I'll try to keep it contained."

"Don't. I like listening to you."

"Give it time. It'll probably drive you round the bend after a while." He lightly ran a fingertip down one of my sideburns and changed the subject by asking, "Are you hungry? I could fix you a sandwich and some tea if you'd like."

I caught his hand and said, "Let's eat afterwards."

"Afterwards?" When I brought his hand to the growing bulge in my thong, a smile spread across his face. "Ah, I see."

He rubbed me through the thin fabric, then sat up and shucked the last of his clothes. When he tried to reach for my cock again, I guided his hand to the garter on my right thigh and said, "Undress me first, Alastair." He actually moaned at that, and his cock twitched.

He studied how the garter was fastened before unhooking it with shaking hands. I raised my leg to give him access to the second garter at the back of my thigh. When he got that unhooked too, I draped my leg over his lap and said, "Now the stocking."

His breathing sped up, and a flush rose beneath his fair skin. I liked the fact that he started at my ankle and ran both hands up my leg first, savoring the feel of the silk, until he finally reached the black lace band at the top. He made himself go slowly, rolling down the stocking inch by inch. When he'd revealed a bit of skin, he paused to run his fingertips over it and murmured, "You shave your legs." Before I could worry about how that revelation would go over, Alastair slid the stocking down to my knee and licked my inner thigh, moaning again before nuzzling my hard-on through the thong.

The lick sent a jolt of pleasure through my balls and up my spine. I drew in my breath, but then I reminded him, "The stockings first." I was determined to let the anticipation build.

It was a struggle to slow down, but he did as I asked. When both stockings were finally off, he ran his hands up my smooth legs as his swollen cock pressed against his belly, and he whispered, "You're so unexpected, in the best possible way."

He followed my instructions and removed the corset next, unfastening it hook by hook before finally spreading it open on either side of me. It always left marks on my body, because I cinched it tight. His hands went to those red spots automatically, massaging them and trying to sooth them away. The long, slow build-up had left him literally shaking with need, but he didn't rush, opting to take care of me instead of trying to get himself off.

I couldn't wait any longer and pushed Alastair onto his back before parting his thighs with my knee. When I straddled him, he rasped, "Fuck me, Sawyer."

He rocked his hips, thrusting against me. His pale blue eyes were so dilated that they looked black, and the flush that had begun in his chest had spread throughout his body. He looked so sexy, and I was dying to sink my cock into him, but there was absolutely no rushing it.

"We need lube and condoms," I told him as I shucked my thong and tossed it aside.

"Nightstand. I bought them for you this morning." He had to be kidding about the 'for me' part.

We both got comfortable, and I spent a long time working him open with plenty of lube while we kissed and jerked each other off. His hole was so tight, and the anticipation drove me wild. He kept begging me to fuck him, and when I murmured, "Soon," he looked at me with trust in his eyes.

When he seemed ready, I prepped myself with a condom and more lube, and wiped my hands with some tissues before kneeling between his legs. He was flat on his back, clutching the sheets, and I spread his legs and pushed them toward his chest with my hands on the backs of his knees. As my cock pressed against his opening, he looked worried, and I said softly, "You can do this, Alastair. Push out while I push in, it'll open you up for me." He followed my instructions, his eyes never leaving mine.

I sank into him inch by inch, making myself go slowly. When he whimpered a little, I froze, but then he whispered, "Keep going. Please, Sawyer. I need you in me." I did as he asked, stopping only when I bottomed out in him.

He propped himself up on his elbows and looked down at our joined bodies. When he realized he'd taken all of me, a glorious smile spread across his face. As I began thrusting, slowly and carefully, I asked him how he was doing, and he murmured, "So good."

He'd started to go soft when I first entered him, but as I thrust into him and stroked his cock, he stiffened in my hand. Before long, he arched off the mattress and cried out as he began to shoot across his body, once again gripping the bedding with both hands. His ass clamped down on my cock as he came, and that set me off, too. I bit back a yell, thrusting again and again as my head spun and my vision blurred. It was wild and intense, and I clutched him to me, trying to ground myself.

When that huge orgasm finally ended, a pair of gorgeous, pale blue eyes came into focus. They crinkled at the corners, and I smiled too before kissing him. I slid my cock from Alastair as I asked, "You alright?"

"Never better." He looked perfectly happy as he wrapped his arms around me and kissed me again.

Eventually, I sat up and peeled off the condom, and he said, "We both need to clean up. Want to take a quick shower with me?" I wasn't going to say no to that.

I hadn't gotten much of a look at his apartment on the way in, but if the bathroom was any indication, it had to be pretty grand. Rich earth tones and Carrara marble made it look like a picture in a magazine, the kind that made you wonder if anyone actually lived like that. Turned out, some people did.

He got the water running as I tossed the condom in a silver trash can. When he turned toward me, his eyes went wide. I glanced over my shoulder and smiled as he muttered, "Bloody hell." He'd left a bulb-shaped douching device beside the sink. "Just, God, ignore that. Or better yet, hang on." He grabbed it and ran from the room.

When he returned a few moments later, he looked mortified, and he murmured, "So, yes, I had every intention of making a move on you during the reception. I thought it was best to be prepared, just in case a miracle occurred and you were actually interested."

I followed him into the shower, and as I soaped up my hands and ran them down his arm, I said, "It's okay that you went to the reception hoping to get lucky, and you don't have to make me think you did that for me in particular. My ego can take it." He frowned for a moment, then dispensed some soap into his palm and began massaging it into a lather on my skin.

We took our time, washing each other tenderly. It was intimate in a way I'd never experienced. I relaxed under Alastair's touch, thoroughly enjoying the feeling of his hands on my body and the citrusy aroma of the body wash.

When we were both clean and dry, we returned to the bedroom with towels around our hips, and he hesitated before pulling open a drawer in his nightstand and removing a leather-bound journal. He flipped to the last page with writing on it and held it up to me, his fingertip indicating the last couple lines. They said: *Please, don't let me mess this up today. I want Sawyer so badly I can taste it.*

To say I was surprised was an understatement, and I mumbled, "You didn't have to show me that. It looks private."

He tossed the journal on top of the nightstand and said, "It must have sounded like utter bollocks, saying I'd been getting ready for you," he said. "But the truth is, I'd noticed you months ago and wanted you ever since, and I was hoping I'd have my chance today, since I knew you'd be at the reception."

"Months ago?"

Alastair nodded. "I remember it like it was yesterday. I was headed to the Castro Theater with my friend Rebecca. It was shortly before she moved to Florida and decided it was too much effort to keep in touch with me, but that's neither here nor there. Anyway, we'd run into Zachary and TJ and were chatting with them when you drove by on a motorcycle. You wore a gray kilt and black leather jacket, and you were the sexiest thing I'd ever seen. My jaw hit the pavement when you flashed your dimples at me."

"I remember that day, too. It was around Christmas, and you were dressed like you'd stepped out of a Dickens novel. All you needed was a top hat."

He grinned and said, "Was I?"

"More or less. You looked cute in your overcoat and wool scarf, though."

"You're just being nice. I must have looked like a complete git if you're describing my outfit as Dickensian."

"You always look great. I've thought so ever since the first time I saw you, back at Kai's wedding." I cleared my throat and changed the subject by asking, "Does that offer of a sandwich still stand? I'm starving."

"Absolutely."

As I followed him to the kitchen, I noticed that the entire apartment coordinated with the bedroom and bathroom. The earth tones were offset with white, while shots of orange in some of the artwork, throw pillows, and knickknacks added a dash of color. I thought the dark brown walls in the living room were a little odd at first, but then I got what the designer had been going for. The room, attractive as it was, paled in comparison to the stunning city views outside the big, arched windows, and maybe that was the whole idea. The financial district and its skyscrapers, including the iconic Transamerica Pyramid, glittered in the distance. There was no competing with that view, so the apartment fell away instead, directing the focus to San Francisco's glorious skyline.

I'd paused before one of the windows in the living room, and a light touch on my lower back drew my attention from the view. "I'm going to miss that," he said softly. "It's the entire reason I bought this condo, as I mentioned. I suppose I'll have to look for a flat in London at the top of the tallest building I can find. That way, if I squint, maybe I can pretend I'm looking at San Francisco. Not that anything's wrong with London, mind you. It's a fabulous city. But this one holds a special place in my heart."

"I can see why."

He asked, "Have you always lived here? Apart from your time in the military, obviously."

"Not always. I moved around a lot as a kid, because my dad was in the Army. When I was thirteen, he got transferred to the Bay Area. It was just supposed to be for two years, but soon after we moved here, he ran into some health problems and had to retire. I've always liked it here and was glad it was where we ended up."

When we got to the kitchen, he filled a kettle and put it on the stove, then began pulling sandwich ingredients from the huge refrigerator, which for some reason was paneled to look like the cabinets. Was it somehow uncouth to let people know you owned major appliances? A ten-thousand-dollar Sub-Zero fridge? Better hide that shit.

"How can I help?" I asked, dragging my attention away from the mysteries of a designer lifestyle.

"By making yourself comfortable and telling me what you'd like on your sandwich."

"Everything." I noticed a high-end Italian espresso machine on the counter and asked, "Mind if I make some coffee?"

He glanced at the chrome appliance and told me, "Good luck, that thing's a beast. The instruction manual, coffee beans, and whatnot are in the cabinet above it."

His coffee grinder was still in the box, and as I set it up, I said, "I guess coffee's not your thing. It doesn't look like you've used any of this stuff."

"On the contrary, I love coffee. But it's so much easier to just pop into the cafe on the corner every morning, rather than trying to coax that thing into producing a decent cuppa."

"Why don't you skip the tea and let me make you a cup?"

"Sounds lovely, thanks." When I opened the bag of beans, dumped a few into my palm, and examined them, he said, "Should I ask what you're looking for?"

"Since you don't make coffee very often, or ever apparently, I wanted to see if the beans were from the Mesozoic era."

"You can tell if they're fresh just by looking?"

"Usually. It has to do with their oily residue."

"Lovely."

"Well, you asked."

"I bought the beans last week at that shop on the corner, when I was getting my morning latte. I thought I should have some on hand for Rollie when he visits, since he's cultivating a world-class caffeine addiction."

"I knew I liked Rollie."

Alastair leaned against the counter and grinned at me. "You're one of those people, aren't you? A proper coffee snob."

"Nah. Give me a great, simple cup of diner coffee and I'm happy as can be. I hate all that pretentious, hipster 'drink this and be cool' bullshit."

"Well, that's a relief. I was ready to don a false beard and hang about one of those trendy places to get myself up to speed. Then I'd planned to impress you by lacing our conversations with phrases like single-origin, artisanal brew…micro-roasts? Is that a thing?"

I chuckled and said, "Sounds like you've already been hanging out in those places."

"My corner café might be a tad pretentious."

I collected a few supplies from around his kitchen, ground the beans and got the espresso machine going. As I began to steam some milk, he said, "And not a single glance at the inch-thick manual. Impressive."

"When I was in high school and college, I worked at a fantastic, family-owned coffee house in North Beach.

That's where I met my best friend Kai, incidentally. The shop owner liked me for some reason. He promoted me to assistant manager, even though I was just a kid, and encouraged me to participate in some local and regional barista competitions. It's been a while, but let's see if I still remember a few tricks."

As I dispensed the rich, dark espresso into a cup, Alastair said, "It sounds like a great place. Is it still there?"

I shook my head. "A Starbucks moved in right across the street and drove them out of business, after over thirty years in the same location. The shop owner moved to Tucson after that, to be closer to his grandkids. We still send Christmas cards." I concentrated on pouring steamed milk into the cup, then layering the lighter foam on the surface of the espresso. Next, I used the tip of a sharp knife to pick up tiny amounts of the dark liquid and draw a few details on the white design.

I grinned at what I'd made and handed it to him, and Alastair's face lit up. I'd drawn two carp on the drink's surface, swimming in opposite directions and curling around each other like a yin and yang symbol. He exclaimed, "Blimey! How did you do that?"

"I'm out of practice, that's why it's a little sloppy."

"Sloppy! It's absolutely beautiful. You're an artist!"

I was embarrassed by his enthusiasm and concentrated on wiping down the machine with a dish towel as I murmured, "Anybody can learn to do that. It just takes practice."

"I could try for a hundred years, and it'd never turn out like this." He looked around and said, "Where's my phone?" Alastair rushed from the room. While he was gone, I made myself a latte and took a sip, then sighed contentedly. There was nothing quite as perfect as a good cup of coffee.

Alastair returned a few moments later and snapped a picture of the carp. Then he spun around, leaned against me and held the phone up for a selfie. "Say cheese, mate," he said, and I grinned at the camera. He put the phone aside and asked, "Those competitions you entered back when you were a teen, how did you do in them?"

"I um…won."

"All of them?"

"I mean, I only entered five or six, but yeah."

"See? You're absolutely brilliant at this, and you have more than my opinion to prove it! Where do you work? I'm coming to your coffee house every morning!"

"Actually, I'd been working construction since I got back to the city, but the job was completed last week. Now I'm looking for pretty much anything."

He stared at me for a moment, then picked up the cup and gestured with it as he said, "You love this, don't you? You well and truly love it."

"Yeah, I do."

"So, why are you doing anything else? I obviously understand family obligation and that you felt you had to join the military, but you're out now, and you're free to follow your passion!"

"I need to earn a living, and construction pays more than being a barista," I said. "Besides, the latte art trend peaked ages ago. Nobody cares that I can do this."

"I care."

"Your coffee's getting cold, you should drink it."

"I don't want to destroy your creation."

"It's meant to be transitory. Here, I'll help you let go."

I picked up a teaspoon and reached for his cup, but he shielded it with his hand and exclaimed, "No! They're too pretty!"

"They won't last anyway, so you might as well enjoy your drink."

He frowned at that. But then he took one last look at the cup, covered his eyes, and held it out to me as he joked, "Be quick about it, make sure they don't suffer." I grinned and swirled the spoon in his latte. The koi disappeared instantly. When he finally took a sip, he said, "It was totally worth ganking those wee bastards. This is fantastic! Promise me you'll come over every morning and make me a cuppa."

"Or I could just show you how to use your machine."

He shook his head and smiled flirtatiously. "Not nearly as good as a big, sexy, mostly naked man in my kitchen, making it for me."

I smiled and pulled him to me by the front of his towel. Alastair drained his cup and put it on the counter, then slid his hands around my waist. He kissed me almost shyly, then said, "I promised to feed you. Some host I've turned out to be," before turning and picking up a loaf of bread.

The sandwich he made for me was enormous and delicious. We sat on the kitchen counter as we ate, and kept the conversation light. When we finished our meal, I put my plate in the sink and helped him clean up, and then I said, "Well, I guess I should go. It's late."

He studied the counter and murmured, "But your motorbike is back at Trevor's house, and it just seems like a hassle, trudging all that way in the dark and cold…."

I grinned and took his hand. "If you want me to stay, just ask."

He glanced up at me and said, "I'd love it if you spent the night."

"Then that's what I'll do."

We returned to the bedroom and discarded our towels before climbing under the covers. It was pure heaven, between Alastair's smooth, naked body in my arms, the ridiculously fluffy duvet, and the pillowy thing on top of his mattress. He brushed his lips to mine, and I pulled him on top of me and returned the kiss as I ran my hands down his back. God, he felt good.

Eventually, he fell asleep in my arms, and I shifted around so I could see Alastair's face. It occurred to me that I clearly didn't have a type, because he couldn't have been more different than big, loud, dead-serious Tracy. It was like comparing a sports car to a tank.

The entire night, every minute with Alastair, had been a revelation. It was tender and effortless and intimate, words I never could have applied to my...what exactly? Tracy never called himself my boyfriend, or referred to what we had as a relationship. But it was. It may have been one-sided, but I'd loved him, and that made it real, no matter what we called it.

It had been nearly a year since I'd left the Army and Tracy. It still hurt whenever I thought about my ex. I wondered if the pain had become a permanent part of me. But why the hell was I thinking about that now?

I focused on Alastair, and after a moment, I grinned. I remembered thinking he'd look great after I mussed him up a bit, and I'd been right. He was sexier than ever with his tousled hair and the color I'd brought to his cheeks.

In fact, he was absolutely beautiful. But he was so much more than that, too. He was kind, and smart, and fascinating. Someone could spend a lifetime discovering all that went on behind those captivating blue eyes.

But that someone wasn't me. This was just a fling, and Alastair was leaving in a few months. Maybe that was okay. Nothing could have come of it anyway, even if the circumstances had been different.

Someone like him just didn't need a guy like me. I was...well, just fine if all you wanted was a warm body and a stiff cock and maybe a bit of companionship. But I didn't have anything to offer him beyond that.

I'd gladly share his bed as long as he asked me to, but I'd have to avoid getting attached to him. So much of life was one big lesson in letting go. This would be, too.

Chapter Three

I awoke slowly. The bed was warm and comfortable, but something was definitely missing. I raised an eyelid and spotted that missing piece sitting in a chair by the window with his feet tucked under him.

Alastair was writing in his journal. He wore a pair of glasses with tortoiseshell frames and a long, unbuttoned, pale blue cardigan over a pair of skimpy white briefs. The morning light bathed him in a golden glow and made him look angelic. I murmured, "God, you're cute in the morning," and sat up and scratched my stubbly cheek. I always woke up looking like Sasquatch.

"I didn't know you were awake," he exclaimed as he pulled off the glasses and put them with his pen and journal on the windowsill.

"I'm not. I'm basically a reanimated corpse until I've had coffee." I tossed the covers aside and grinned as he fumbled for his glasses and quickly shoved them back into place, possibly because I was buck naked.

"Can you stay for breakfast? I baked you something," he called after me as I headed to the bathroom.

"Love to. I hope you didn't go through too much trouble, though."

"No trouble at all." After I used the facilities and some of his mouthwash, I returned to the bedroom and found him kneeling on the mattress with a white shopping bag on his lap. "I bought you a present," he said, and handed me the package with a hopeful expression.

"When did you have time to do that?"

"This morning. I always take a walk first thing and spotted this in the window of an import store. It took some convincing, but I got the shop owner to open early so I could buy it for you. I hope you like it."

He chewed his lower lip as I slid a silk kimono out of the bag. It was pale blue and printed with a white, graceful pattern of koi and water. I murmured, "Oh wow," as I ran my hand over the delicate fabric, and then I grinned at him. "It's the coffee koi, in a more permanent form." It was something else, too, a subtle nod to that other side of me, just a bit feminine without being frilly.

"Exactly! I thought about getting you a black robe, based on what you were wearing yesterday, but this one made me think of you. If you don't like it, I can take it back and exchange it."

"It's perfect, thank you. No one's ever given me anything like this."

He looked anxious. "Try it on. I hope it's big enough."

I pulled it on, and as I tied the sash, I said, "It fits like it was made for me. The fabric feels fantastic, too."

Alastair got up and ran his hand down my arm. "It does." He snuggled close to me for a few seconds and rubbed his cheek against my shoulder. But then he looked embarrassed and stepped back from me as he said, "Excuse me for a moment, I'm going to put in my contacts."

"Sure, but you look great in your glasses."

He called as he headed to the bathroom, "No I don't. They make me look like a twelve-year-old, and also a nerd. While the latter is entirely accurate, I choose not to advertise it."

I lingered in the bedroom at first, waiting for him to come back. But then I decided to do something constructive, so I popped my head through the open bathroom door and said, "I'm going to make us some coffee. And for the record, I think men in glasses are completely sexy." I flashed him a smile, and he knit his brows at me. One of his index fingers was pointed straight up, with a contact balanced on its tip.

"People always say that, but they never mean it."

"Where did you put your glasses?" He took them from the pocket of his cardigan and handed them to me, and I put them on and said, "Jesus, this is a strong prescription." Then I looked at him, or more specifically, the smear of color visible through the lenses, and said, "Try to be objective. How do they look?"

He popped in his contact (I was glad I couldn't watch that, because anything eye-related made me flinch), then murmured, "Blimey. Well, if I was a gorgeous, six-foot-four, muscular god like you, then the glasses would look amazing. But I'm me, so it's primary school science fair all the way."

I took the glasses off and put them on the vanity as I said, "They're sexy no matter what you say. So's your outfit. I love the fact that you came home from your walk and ended up in nothing but tiny briefs and a sweater."

He looked down at himself and smiled self-consciously. "I started to get dressed after I took a shower, but only got as far as the knickers before something distracted me. Later on, I added the cardigan when I got cold. I'm a bit absent-minded, you'll find."

"That's not a bad thing."

"Except for the part where I lose my phone about once a month and have to get a new one." He shook his head. "Pathetic."

"You're working on a PhD in astrophysics. In other words, you're literally a rocket scientist. So what if you can't keep track of your phone? It's probably just because you have much more important things on your mind."

He said, "Thanks for giving me the benefit of the doubt," before leading the way to the kitchen.

When we got there, I stopped short and exclaimed, "I never realized I was such a sound sleeper! I obviously missed a major earthquake." The room was completely trashed.

"Like I said, I tried to bake for you. Mistakes were made." He grinned embarrassedly as he held up a plate of blueberry-studded hockey pucks.

"Are those pancakes?"

"Muffins. I thought I didn't need a recipe, because they seemed simple enough. Bit of flour, an egg, some butter and sugar, and Bob's your uncle. Suppose it goes without saying that I don't bake a great deal."

I selected one and took a bite. It was on the solid side, but it tasted good, and I said, "I love it, thank you. It was nice of you to bake something."

"It was a complete cock-up."

"You tried. That's what counts." I finished the muffin in three bites, then turned my attention to the espresso maker. He pushed aside some of the stuff on the counter and brought me the milk, then watched closely as I made our drinks. I went a bit simpler than the night before, drizzling in the milk in a controlled stream, then drawing it across the top of the espresso. When I handed the cup to him, he beamed at me. The pattern looked like a heart-shaped flower with a stem and a couple leaves. In other words, it was pretty basic, but I'd learned early on that people didn't want to wait around while you got fancy with their first cup of the day.

"I could get used to this, a world-class barista in my kitchen." He blew on the surface, then took a sip and said, "It's outstanding. Thank you, Sawyer."

"You're welcome. It's nice to get to use such a great machine."

"What do you have at home?"

"My dad has a Mr. Coffee," I said with a grin. "If I'm feeling fancy, I have a little stovetop Bialetti I can use to make espresso."

"How is it, living at home?"

"Awkward."

"Does your father know you're gay?"

"Kind of."

He tilted his head and echoed, "Kind of?"

I leaned against the counter and took a sip from my cup before saying, "You don't actually want to hear this story, do you?"

"Oh, I do."

"Alright. Well, one day, when I was fifteen, I was sitting at the kitchen table, studying with this boy from school. We'd been flirting for weeks, and I finally got up the nerve and leaned over and kissed him. Right at that moment, my dad came into the kitchen. Just my luck. My first kiss, and in walks Dad."

After taking another drink, I continued, "I expected him to flip out, but Dad just went completely still. The kid grabbed his books and ran out the door like he'd been caught committing murder. There was this long pause, and then all my dad said was, in this low, menacing growl, 'I'm gonna pretend I didn't see that.' I know it doesn't sound like much, but the tone of his voice and the look in his eyes was frightening. It was compounded by the fact that my dad's this huge, intimidating guy, and like I said before, I was tiny until the end of high school. Usually, he loses his temper at the drop of a hat. If he'd flipped out and screamed and yelled like I'd expected, I think I would have pushed back. I might've flaunted the fact that I was gay, just to spite him. But that other thing, that calm, quiet threat, of what I could only imagine, just completely unnerved me." I shook my head and said, "It sounds stupid when I try to explain it, but I was so rattled that I actually apologized and swore I'd never do it again. That was the last time we spoke of it."

Alastair said softly, "I'm sorry he did that to you."

After a pause, I said, "I always wonder, does he believe I was literally scared straight that day? And I keep thinking, how ironic that my ex would have this completely unisex name, because my dad's seen me shirtless since I've been back, he's seen my tattoo. If it said 'Harold' or 'Steve' then my dad would have to say something, right? He'd probably feel like I was challenging him with a blatant display like that, and we'd finally have it out. But instead, it says 'Tracy', so the truth stays in the shadows. I mean, obviously I could talk to him about it, but I just...don't."

"It must be awful living with someone like that."

I drained my cup, then said, "Aside from the great, big, rainbow-colored elephant in the room, my dad and I get along okay, I guess. By that, I mean we don't fight or anything. Not that we pal around, either. We just kind of co-exist. He was completely pissed off when I didn't re-enlist at the end of my commitment, but he's calmed down about it over the last few months. That's probably because he's convinced I'll go back, whenever I get over this rebellious phase he thinks I'm going through." I sighed and reached for another muffin.

"You don't have to eat that," he said as I packed half of it in my mouth. "I know you're just being nice."

I ate the rest of it, then told him, "They're good, kind of like pound cake with blueberries."

When I ate a third, he actually hugged me and kissed my cheek. Then he started to clean up the mess he'd made. After a minute, he asked, "You won't, will you? Re-enlist, I mean."

"No chance. I did my time, including two tours in Afghanistan. My dad will just have to get used to the fact that I'm a huge fucking disappointment."

Alastair stopped what he was doing and said, "I didn't realize you'd been sent overseas. Were you an infantryman?"

I shook my head. "I worked in the motor pool. Not a bad job most days, except…."

"Except for what?"

I turned from him and rinsed my cup in the sink, then began wiping down the espresso machine as I said, "Except for that time when it was my job to clean the blood out of one of the vehicles. That day wasn't so good. Way worse for my buddy who took that stray bullet and bled out in the back of a Jeep, though." I took a deep breath and tried to force myself not to remember, focusing instead on making the machine shine.

"I'm so sorry. I shouldn't have asked," Alastair said in a whisper.

"I shouldn't have brought it up. I don't know why I did."

"Maybe because you needed to talk about it."

I changed the subject by saying, "Let me help you clean up, and then I'll get out of your way. I'm sure you have things to do today."

"I want to check on Rollie, he probably has one hell of a hangover. But don't help with the kitchen. It's my mess, I'll deal with it."

I began gathering cooking implements and piling them in the sink. "It'll go a lot faster with two of us."

I was right. After ten minutes spent loading the dishwasher, putting away ingredients and wiping down the counters, it was as if the Alastair earthquake had never happened. I hung up the dish towel, and then we headed to the bedroom to get dressed.

We were a little uncertain around each other. What was proper morning-after etiquette, anyway? Clearly, neither of us had any idea, so we didn't try to initiate anything, even though I would have loved to pull him back into that bed.

I pulled on my jeans and shirt, then rolled the corset tightly and stuck it in a deep pocket inside my leather jacket. The stockings, garters and thong were stashed in another pocket. It was time to get back to reality.

After I was fully dressed and the silk robe was packed in its bag and tucked under my arm, I turned to Alastair. He'd put on a white, button-down shirt and a sleek leather jacket, along with dark jeans that accentuated his perfect ass and a pair of expensive loafers. He looked effortlessly gorgeous, like he'd stepped out of a magazine. Meanwhile, there I was, in my rumpled clothes from the day before.

"I'll walk you out," he said, firing off a quick text before slipping the phone in his pocket. "I'm going to drag Rollie out of bed, so Trevor and his family can get on with their Sunday."

We were quiet on the short walk back to where our night had begun. When we reached my motorcycle, I said, "Thanks again for the present."

"I hope I didn't overstep. I just…wanted you to have it."

"It was nice of you."

He looked up at me as we both hesitated for a long moment. The city was waking up around us, and a few people passed by on the sidewalk. I cursed myself for not kissing him goodbye when we were back in the apartment, while we still had privacy. What a missed opportunity. I glanced longingly at his full, inviting lips, and thought—

Alastair pulled me to him and kissed me passionately. I was shocked at first that he'd be so open about it, but then I stopped thinking and sank into it. If any of the passersby had something to say about two guys making out on the sidewalk, it was totally lost on me, because all my attention was riveted on Alastair and that kiss.

After a while, I rested my forehead against his and we both caught our breath. He clutched the front of my jacket, while I ran my hand around the back of his neck. "I was going to play it cool," he said. "Just like, 'call me, or whatever.' But I'm about to blow that straight to hell by telling you last night was the best of my life, hands down. Not just because I finally lost my virginity, although halleluiah to that! You were so patient, and kind, and I felt wonderful with you. So, thank you, Sawyer. I'll never forget it."

"Thank you, too. Last night meant a lot to me." What an understatement! It had been amazing, a revelation, a night that realigned my world. I wasn't the type of guy who could say that to someone though, not without feeling like an idiot. So instead, I wrapped my arms around him and held on tight.

"I'm going to call you this week," he said. "I want to take you on a proper date, a nice dinner, followed by a bit of live music. I think that's well within the parameters of a fling, don't you?"

"For sure. As long as we both go into it knowing what to expect, we can keep seeing each other."

"Exactly. I still have several months in San Francisco, so why not enjoy ourselves? We know to keep it casual, no strings attached. Just a harmless bit of fun."

"Works for me." We exchanged numbers, and I kissed his forehead before getting on my motorcycle, then zipping the bag with the robe inside my jacket for safekeeping.

The bike was a gunmetal gray 1957 Harley, which I'd inherited from my grandfather. It roared to life when I used my heel to kick-start the pedal. As I put on my sunglasses, Alastair called over the engine, "No helmet? You must like living dangerously."

"They keep getting stolen, even though I chain them to the bike. Somewhere there's a secondhand store filled with my helmets."

"Be careful, please." That from the guy whose hobbies included illegal street racing and dancing on rooftops. The concern was sweet though, and I gave him a smile and a nod before pulling away from the curb. I couldn't resist a look back as I rolled down the block. He was right where I left him, watching me go. Alastair raised his hand in a little wave before he disappeared from sight.

*****

The blocky duplex in the Richmond District looked like it suffered from a severe split personality disorder. The right side sported a fresh coat of purple paint with crisp white trim. Cheerful pansies and violas filled a window box and the series of terra cotta pots lining the right side of the shared staircase. Meanwhile, the left side of the house had downgraded from white to dishwater beige over the years, and the only living things were the hearty weeds in the three-foot-square 'front yard' beneath the left-hand window.

Sherry, my dad's most recent ex-wife, was watering her flowers when I cut the engine and rolled the bike onto the little walkway to the left of the building, which I used as a parking space. She and my dad had both been too stubborn to sell their share of the duplex they'd bought together during their brief marriage, so they existed in a perpetual state of annoyance with one another. Sherry and I had always gotten along great, though.

When I walked up to the staircase, she greeted me with a big smile and a lilting, "Well, good morning there, sunshine!" She'd left Minnesota more than twenty years ago, but her regional accent was thick as ever. I suspected she played it up, because it was one of the things that made Sherry Sherry, along with her short, red curls and a penchant for pastel jogging suits that had never seen the inside of a gym.

I greeted her with a big hug and picked her up off her feet so I could kiss her cheek, since she was only five-foot-two. She was one of my favorite people, and my dad was an idiot for failing to hang on to her. "Oh good gravy, put me down!" She said that every time. "One of these days you'll throw your back out from hauling my fat self around."

"You're not fat."

"You lie like a rug. Keep doing that." Sherry beamed at me as I returned her sneaker-clad feet to the pavement, then asked, "Are you just getting in? Must've been a wild night."

"A friend of mine got married yesterday, and at the reception, well...."

"You got lucky! No need to explain, I was twenty-three once, too. Of course, back then I was crimping my hair and wearing enormous shoulder pads that made me look like I played for the Minnesota Vikings. It's amazing anybody got laid in 1985, given what passed for fashion!"

"I'll bet you were adorable."

"I was a train wreck! We all were." She looked up at me and asked, "So, are you going to see him again?"

"Him who?"

"The fellow from last night!"

"Wait…what?"

"You heard me."

I stammered, "But…I didn't think you knew…."

"That you're gay? Of course I do," she said as I sank onto the stairs and she sat down beside me. "I've always known."

"But how?"

"I noticed things. Like, I'd take you to the mall when you were fourteen or fifteen, and a group of cute girls would walk by, but you didn't give them a second glance. Then we'd go to the food court, and you'd get all flustered by that adorable emo boy working at Hotdog on a Stick."

I grinned a little. "That emo kid really was cute."

"You never talked about it growing up, and I thought as your stepmom, maybe it wasn't my place to bring it up, either. Your father's a grade-A jackass, and I guess you were worried about his reaction. But I should have said something sooner and let you know I've always accepted you for who you are."

I told her the story of my first kiss and my dad's reaction, and she thought about it before saying, "Could just be you caught him off guard, and he didn't know how to react. But he's had a lot of years to process the fact that you're gay, so maybe he's come to grips with it."

"Or maybe he'll flip the hell out if I bring it up."

"Maybe. Your father can be a real douche canoe, but sooner or later you need to talk to him about this." I chuckled at that, and she said, "What's funny?"

"Douche canoe," I repeated. "That's hilarious with your accent. Where'd you even learn that expression?"

She grinned at me. "From my girlfriend Rosalie. I thought of your father right away."

After a few moments, I said, "You're right that I need to talk to him. I've just been putting it off. We've been getting along pretty well lately, and I just know that's going to be a huge setback."

"If he kicks you out, you can come and live in my guestroom."

"Thanks, but I'm not worried about getting kicked out. I have plenty of savings and could get my own place if I wanted to."

"Oh! I figured you moved back home for financial reasons."

I shook my head. "I was in a bad relationship while I was in the Army, and...I guess I chose to come back here because I wanted the comfort of home after the breakup. I also wanted to build a friendship with my dad, now that we're both adults. He still treats me like a kid though, and none of it's gone like I'd hoped. I should just give up and find my own place."

Sherry patted my arm. "I'm sorry things haven't worked out with your dad, but that's no reflection on you, Sawyer. He has to be willing to meet you halfway, and let's face it, that's like asking for a gosh-darn miracle."

"True."

I tilted my face toward the almost-warm May sunlight as Sherry said, "Back to my original question. Are you going to see the guy from last night again?" I nodded, avoiding her gaze. It felt odd to talk candidly about a subject I'd always kept under wraps. "So, when do I get to meet him?"

"It's not like that. Last night wasn't the start of something, because he's going away in a few months. We've just agreed to have some fun in the meantime. It won't turn into a 'meet the parents' type of thing."

"I see." She crossed her short legs and got comfortable. "So, tell me about the fellow you were seeing when you were in the Army. How was it a bad relationship? He better not have hurt you, or so help me I'm going to find him and kick his butt!"

I grinned at the mental picture of five-two Sherry going after my enormous ex. Then, instead of going into detail, I just told her, "I was in love. He wasn't. It was more complicated than that, but ultimately that's what it boiled down to."

We started talking about relationships in general and what a minefield they were. It was a subject Sherry knew all too well. About half an hour into our conversation, we paused and turned our attention to a white van, which double-parked in the street. The name of a local delivery service was printed on the side, along with a cartoon of Hermes in winged sandals.

The middle-aged courier who got out of the van wore a baseball cap with puffy gold wings jutting out of each side. He must have loved that. After he retrieved a box from the back, the man headed toward the house and called, "Sawyer MacNeil?"

When I nodded, he produced a pen and slip of paper. "Sign at the bottom."

"I didn't order anything," I told him, while doing as he asked.

"Well, somebody did." He traded the box for the pen and paper, and tacked on a completely insincere, "Have a nice day," before returning to the van.

The box contained a top-of-the-line black motorcycle helmet, a lock to fasten it to my bike, a receipt, and an envelope with my name on it. I removed the single sheet of paper and immediately recognized the graceful, old-fashioned handwriting. The note said: *Stay safe. Love, Alastair.*

I handed Sherry the note and tried on the helmet. It was a perfect fit. "Now, how did he know what size to get? How'd he know my address, for that matter?"

"Alastair. Is that the fellow from last night?" When I nodded, she said, "I like him already. Look at him, taking care of you!"

"He's a great guy." I took off the helmet and turned it over in my hands, then pulled the receipt from the bottom of the box. Alastair had bought the helmet and lock twenty minutes earlier at a high-end shop in the city. A hand-written message on the receipt said: *Paid by phone with credit card, can exchange for different size/style.* No need, he'd totally nailed it.

"So I see."

I got up and said, "I'm going to call him to say thank you. Want to have lunch later?"

Sherry got up too and brushed off the seat of her yellow track suit. "I'll have to take a raincheck, sunshine. Rosalie and I are going shopping. I have a date next week, and she thinks I need a new dress for the occasion."

"A date, that's terrific!" As far as I knew, it had been about two years since the last one.

She brushed it off with a wave of her hand. "I don't want to make a big deal of it, but hey, any excuse to shop!"

The house was blissfully quiet when I went inside. My dad spent every Sunday morning at a diner with a couple of his Army buddies, so I got to enjoy a few hours' reprieve from the otherwise constant blare of the television. I carried the box upstairs, then took off my jacket and unpacked the silk robe. The fabric felt great in my hands, and on impulse, I stripped myself and put it on. It was an immediate comfort.

I climbed onto my bed, leaned against the wall and glanced at my surroundings. I'd left for the Army at eighteen and hadn't felt motivated to change a thing since I'd been back. The walls were dingy white and covered with posters that didn't reflect who I was, then or now. Three were versions of 'Go Army' and a couple more were for the San Francisco Forty-Niners. Never mind that I hadn't wanted to enlist in the first place, and that my interest in my dad's favorite team was lukewarm at best. My room wasn't a time capsule, it was a charade.

The only other decorative item in the otherwise stark space was a framed picture on the desk. It was the only photo I had of both my parents and me together, taken when I was about a year old. It hurt a little every time I looked at it, so I had to wonder why I kept it on display.

I sighed and turned my attention to my phone. Before I could text Alastair, it rang in my hand and Gabriel's number appeared on the screen. I answered with, "Hey!"

"Hey yourself! I'm checking to see how it went last night. Did the guy you went home with get to meet the real you?"

"He did."

"How did he react when he saw what you were wearing?"

"He was totally accepting. This morning, he even gave me a silk kimono. I figured that was his way of letting me know he truly is okay with it."

"Damn, that guy's a keeper. What does the kimono look like?"

"It's pale blue with a white pattern of koi and water, and it's mid-calf length with wide sleeves. He found that balance, not drag, not a costume, just…right." I smiled to myself and touched the lapel.

"You're wearing it right now, aren't you?"

"Yeah. I put it on as soon as I got home. I can't even tell you how much it meant to me."

"You don't have to tell me, because I already know. I'd feel the same way if someone understood me like that."

"It's nice that you get it."

Gabriel said, "So, besides checking in, I'm also calling to tell you there's something we have to do tonight. Tell me you don't have plans."

"I don't. What do we have to do?"

"Two things, actually. We have to go shopping, and then we have to head on over to Club Scandal."

"What's that?"

"It's a gay burlesque club, and tonight is amateur night. You and that hot bod are going to kill it when you take the stage!"

"You're kidding, right?"

"Hell no, I'm not kidding! It'll be glorious!"

"No way."

"First prize is two hundred bucks, and you'll also make a bundle in tips. Money aside, you need this!"

I said, "You met me yesterday, Gabriel. How do you know what I need?"

"Oh, I know. What could be more validating than revealing your true self to a couple hundred hot guys and having them worship you for it?"

"Well, last night with Alastair was pretty damn validating."

"So, take that momentum and run with it!"

"Why is this so important to you?"

"Two reasons," Gabriel said. "First, I like you and I think this'll be great for your confidence. Second, I don't want to do this shit by myself, and you're the only person I know who wouldn't just go up there and treat it like a joke."

"I didn't realize you'd be participating, too. That almost makes me feel better about it."

"I always wanted to do it when I lived here, but I kept chickening out. Tonight I'm finally going for it."

"You don't live in San Francisco?"

"I used to, and I will again. I'm temporarily in exile in my shitty, rural hometown a couple hours south of here, but I snuck back in for Zachary's wedding and intend to make a weekend of it."

"Why'd you have to sneak in?"

Gabriel sighed and said, "Long, horrible story, but in a nutshell, I'm hiding from my former Dom, who's royally pissed off at me and a straight-up thug, so he'll probably come close to killing me if he ever finds me."

"Shit!"

"Sums it up."

"So, maybe appearing onstage isn't the best idea, right?"

"That's why I'm using a fake name and wearing a mask. Plus, this club is totally off his radar. He'd have no interest in a place like that, and neither would any of his cronies."

"Still seems risky."

"I need the money, though. Not that I have a chance of winning, but I've heard the tips are phenomenal."

I asked, "Do you want me to go talk to this guy, get him to back off?"

"Thanks for offering, but no. He's not the sort of person you can reason with."

"He sounds awful. What were you doing with a guy like that?"

"Honestly? I was getting off on letting him hurt me, and I was too naïve to realize that BDSM had crossed the line into abuse."

"Jesus, Gabriel."

He said, "I know, but let's stop talking about this, it's depressing. Will you come with me tonight?"

"I guess so. I'm mostly agreeing to this because I don't like the idea of you doing it by yourself, especially with a sadistic Dom after you."

"I'm so glad you're coming!"

"This is going to be humiliating. I've never even been to a burlesque club, and I won't know what to do."

"It's amateur night, so it'll be a mixed bag. Some people will go old-school with a sexy strip-tease, others are just going to tear their clothes off and shake their ass. Find something between those two and just go for it."

"Am I supposed to have a routine? Because you know I don't. And what am I supposed to wear?"

"A suit and tie, with your favorite lingerie underneath. And no, you don't need a routine," he said. "They'll play some music and you'll dance around a bit while you strip down to something sexy. It's burlesque, not 'The Full Monty', so it doesn't even have to be all that revealing."

"You make it sound easy."

"It is! If you want, we can put our names at the very bottom of the sign-up sheet. That way, you'll be able to watch a lot of other men and women perform before it's your turn and see what the crowd responds to. Copy what works for you, or just dance and have a good time while you take your clothes off. Either way."

I'd never thought of myself as much of an exhibitionist, but I wasn't shy either, and the prospect of celebrating my other side like that was undeniably appealing. It had always been easier to show that part of myself to strangers, as opposed to friends and family, and the few times I'd revealed a little of it in public had been gratifying. Getting up on stage and completely owning it would probably feel great too, and I said, "Alright. We'll see what happens."

"You won't regret this, Sawyer."

"I already am."

"No you're not, you're looking forward to it. Admit it!"

I grinned and told him, "Maybe a little."

"Have you ever worn women's clothing in public? So it shows, I mean?"

"Just a handful of times. I have a couple friends who are drag queens, and I went out with them when they were dressed up, which made it easier, somehow. I didn't do anything too over-the-top, just a corset under my leather jacket, or stockings with combat boots, stuff like that. Tonight is going to be something else entirely."

"It'll be great! I'll text you the address of a fabulous secondhand store where we can meet ahead of time. If you don't know what to wear under your suit tonight, I can help you pick something out."

We chatted for a few more minutes, and when we disconnected, I muttered, "What the hell was I thinking?" Admittedly though, I was more excited than apprehensive.

Next, I texted Alastair and told him: *Thank you for the helmet. That was very thoughtful.*

He texted back a moment later. *You're quite welcome. Did it fit?*

Perfectly. Impressive, as was the fact that you knew my address.

My phone rang, and when I answered, he said, "That was creepy, wasn't it? Now you're thinking I have distinctly stalkeresque tendencies, and you want nothing more to do with me."

"It wasn't creepy."

"I should have gone through proper channels. But instead, I just asked my friend to look you up so I could send you the helmet as soon as possible. I didn't stop to consider how that would be perceived."

"Your friend?"

"Yes. He's also my bodyguard. I knew it would take him just a few moments to get me your address." He sighed and said, "You're going to think I'm a complete tosser after this conversation."

"Why do you have a bodyguard?"

"As you probably gathered from the condo, my family is wealthy. Actually, it's at a level that…well, let's just say, it draws attention. Because of that, they worry about me, especially since I'm on my own here in America. It's all a bit daft, since most people have no idea who I am. I've always been kept out of the public eye, and I don't even use my real surname. Nevertheless, the only way my family would let me venture out on my own at sixteen was if I agreed to bring along part of their security detail."

"I see."

"The more I try to explain, the more bizarre it sounds. I wish we were having this conversation face-to-face, because I have no idea how you're reacting to any of this."

"Maybe this'll help." I hit a button on my screen.

He answered the video call a moment later and grinned at me. "You're wearing the kimono."

"I put it on as soon as I got home. Where are you?" I glimpsed a pool and palm trees in the background.

"At my house in the South Bay. I drove Rollie home and got here right before you texted. It's about five minutes from the university, so I stay down here when I plan to spend a lot of time on campus."

Because he was frowning, I asked, "What's wrong?"

"I lied to you during our first conversation, and I apologize for doing that. As I said, I don't use my real name. I'm supposed to tell everyone I'm called Alastair Wilde. It's all part of this elaborate scheme to keep me safe, but it's utter bollocks. I hate going around deceiving everyone, on the off chance the wrong person might find out who I am. My real name is—"

"You don't have to tell me. Your security is more important than my idle curiosity. I already know you gave me a fake name, by the way, and I'm glad I know why now."

"How did you know?"

"You're a terrible liar."

He flashed me a big smile. "Am I?"

"Oh yeah. The worst."

"What did I do?"

"You hesitated and broke eye contact. Dead giveaway."

"You realize you're coaching me in how to be a better liar, don't you?" Alastair looked highly entertained.

"Somehow, I don't think you'll abuse your new superpower."

"I won't, I swear. No more lies. Cross my heart." He drew a huge 'X' on his chest with his index finger.

"And all the rest of your vital organs. That's quite a pledge."

"Indeed. Cross everything from my heart to my spleen." He shifted a bit, then said, "In all seriousness though, I promise to be truthful from here on out. I feel like a complete arse for having given you a false name."

"Don't. I get it."

"Let me start over. Hello, I'm Alastair Spencer-Penelegion."

"Wow, that's—"

"The same as the famous department store in London, yes. We are, in fact, those Penelegions."

I grinned at him. "I was going to say that's the most British name ever."

"Oh." He grinned, too. "I suppose it is quite British, although I went to school with a lad named Nigel Shufflebottom Popplewell, and I'm certain that's even more British than mine."

"It's dead even."

"It isn't!"

"Okay, maybe the Shufflebottom part puts him slightly ahead."

"Slightly!"

"I do have one question for you," I said, and a little frown line appeared between his eyebrows. I could only imagine the invasive questions he must have endured when people found out he belonged to that famously wealthy family. But what I asked was, "When you were a kid, did you ever get to run around the department store after hours? You know: jump on the beds in the furniture department, sneak desserts from the restaurant, that sort of thing?"

The slight frown was replaced with a genuine smile. "I never did! It's a shame, isn't it? The toy section alone, my God! I could have spent weeks there as a child!"

"I've seen the toy department on TV, it looks spectacular."

"It is. My grandfather would take my sister and me every Christmas and let us pick out anything we wanted. I love that place, and at the holidays, it's absolutely magical."

I stretched out on my side and propped my head up with my hand. "With all that selection, how could you even choose?"

"It was easy, actually. I always got the same thing. There was this line of toy cars, lovely things made by a craftsman in Surrey. The detail was just incredible. They had tiny, working steering wheels, and upholstered seats, and perfect little engines under their bonnets. Anyway, every Christmas I'd go straight to that display case, like a horse with blinders on, and pick out a car. My granddad would always ask, 'Don't you want something bigger, Sonny?' But I never did. All year, I looked forward to adding another car to my collection."

"Do you still have them?"

"God yes, I'll never part with them. They're in my bedroom at my family's country house. I regretted not bringing them along when I came to the U.S. But I was trying to convince my parents I was a grown man at sixteen, so I couldn't very well pack up my toys and take them with me. I'd also never admit this to any of them, but I was bitterly disappointed when I turned twelve and my grandfather declared me too old for the toy department."

"What did he give you instead?"

"Stocks."

"You're kidding."

He shook his head. "I know I should be grateful. He's very generous and is thinking about my future. But at twelve and thirteen, hell, even at twenty, all I wanted for Christmas was another Dunford Racer for my collection."

"You know you could just walk into Penelegion's next time you're in London and buy every car in that case, right?"

"I can't actually, because the company went out of business two years ago. It wouldn't have been the same, anyway. The anticipation was part of the fun. So was the fact that I was limited to just one, oddly enough. I suppose it's like eating cake three meals a day, versus only having it on your birthday. When you have all you want, it no longer seems like something special."

"Makes sense."

Alastair grinned and said, "Listen to me, rattling on about toy cars. I'm sure you have better things to do besides listening to my childish ramblings. What are you up to today?"

"I need to scrape up some enthusiasm and take a look at the online job listings. Later on, I'm going to get nearly naked for a roomful of strangers."

"Do tell!"

"A new friend somehow convinced me to don some lingerie and participate in amateur night at someplace called Club Scandal. Apparently, it's a gay burlesque club downtown."

"How bold!"

I sighed and said, "I'm going to make a fool of myself."

"No chance. You'll be sensational, I just know it! Will you wear what you had on last night?"

"I haven't decided yet. Speaking of last night though…I wanted to say thanks. I wasn't sure how you'd react to that side of me. But you were so supportive, and it boosted my confidence enough to say yes to this crazy idea."

"You're welcome, and you have every reason to feel confident. You're absolutely gorgeous, Sawyer. Both sides of you."

"Thank you."

He smiled at me as I ducked my head embarrassedly, and after a moment he asked, "Can I come to the show tonight? I'd love to watch you absolutely slay it."

"Oh. Um, next time, okay? I think I'd be too embarrassed if I knew you were in the audience."

"I hope there is a next time."

"If I don't trip on my heels, fall off the stage, or totally freeze up and humiliate myself, or even if I do, maybe I'll try it again. The first time's bound to be a bit awkward, but maybe it gets easier with practice."

"I love that you're willing to give it a go. And here I had you pegged as this serious, reserved bloke when I first laid eyes on you. The strong, silent type, and all that."

I shrugged. "Not so silent." Not so strong, either. I changed the subject by asking, "So, what are you doing today?"

"I'd intended to go to campus and work on my dissertation. To be honest though, I'm feeling discouraged, because I know I'll never complete the program. But that's stupid, because I'm here for an education, not a piece of paper printed with a degree. Enough of that, though. I have almost a year left to lose myself in academia, and I know how I must sound, whining about my so-called problems instead of being grateful for all I have."

"You're not whining, Alastair."

He pulled up a smile. "I'd better let you go, but we'll talk soon, yeah? I need to get off my arse, and you need to pick an outfit for tonight that'll bring grown men to their knees. Knock 'em dead, Sawyer."

"I'll settle for not knocking myself dead by falling off the stage in my five inch-heels."

"Promise me you'll let me see you in those shoes sometime."

I said I would, and after we disconnected, I swung out of bed and retrieved a duffle bag from the back of my closet, the one containing my secret wardrobe. As I sorted through the silk, lace, and leather, I regretted telling Alastair not to come to the show. A friendly face in the audience would have been nice. But then again, if (and when) I made a fool of myself, he was the last person I would have wanted witnessing that.

After picking out a few pieces of lingerie and stashing them in a backpack, I sat down at the desk and opened my laptop. The job listings were wholly uninspiring. After twenty depressing minutes, I switched over to an online auction site and typed 'Dunford Racers' into the search bar.

The tiny cars were spectacular and incredibly detailed. I could see why Alastair was so enthralled with them. They weren't cheap, either, but I wasn't going to let that stop me. After narrowing my search to models made in the final year the company was in business (knowing he wouldn't have anything that recent), I selected a flawless red convertible. I was so excited as I placed my bid and imagined the smile that little toy would bring to Alastair's face.

Chapter Four

I slammed back the whiskey and muttered, "What the hell was I thinking?"

"You got this, Sawyer." Gabriel rubbed my back while I took a couple deep breaths.

"It's amateur night. Why's there a full house? And why do none of the people who've gone already even sort of seem like amateurs? The woman in black lace was ready to go on tour with Beyoncé, and that bearded guy was channeling Marilyn Monroe and Channing Tatum, all at the same time. And Jesus, that ass! Did you see that ass?"

"Oh believe me, *no one* missed that ass. But so what? I got a good look at your Little Debbies while we were trying on clothes earlier tonight. Actually, there might have been some staring involved. I'm just saying. So, I know for a fact the audience is going to go off like two hundred Mentos dropped into a pool of Coke as soon as they catch a glimpse of what you've got going on. In fact, we need to find you a cumbrella, because it's going to be coming down thick out there!"

I laughed and said, "Thank you for that colorful mental picture. And dude, Little Debbies?"

"I was gonna call them honey buns, but eh, seemed uninspired." He squeezed my shoulder and said, "You're going to be great."

"I'm going to throw up."

"Pro tip: aim away from the audience."

"Good advice, and speaking of pros, you killed it out there. You know that, right?" He'd gone out in full drag with red lipstick, an elaborate scrollwork mask, stilettos, and a slinky stretch velvet gown. Then he'd stripped slowly and seductively, down to a garter belt, stockings, and bikini briefs while keeping his nipples covered, alternately with his hands or a scarf. When he bared his chest with a graceful sweep of his arm as the song ended, the audience (who'd clearly reached the wrong conclusion about his gender) responded with gasps, then wild applause. Gabriel definitely had a flair for the theatrical.

But he just shrugged. "I did okay. I had fun, that's the main thing. Remember that! If you have a good time, the audience will, too."

"The audience is doomed."

"Look, here's what you do. Pick out one friendly face in the crowd. Then just focus on that person and pretend you're in the bedroom, seducing your lover."

"And two hundred of his closest friends."

He grinned at that and straightened my tie. "Okay, so maybe it's more like an orgy."

The stage manager stuck her head into the dressing room and consulted her clipboard. She was about forty, and sported short, white-blonde hair with black roots and a double-pierced lower lip. Given the way the piercings were spaced, they looked a hell of a lot like fangs. I wondered if that had been intentional. She called, "Sawyer MacNeil?" When I nodded, she said, "You're up in two minutes, follow me." I and one other guy were the last 'performers' of the night. But since he was sweating profusely and drinking directly from a bottle of vodka, I doubted he'd make it onto the stage.

"Break a leg. On second thought, scratch that. Those heels are super high. Leg breaking is probably a very real possibility," Gabriel said as he followed me.

"Because that's helpful."

"Sorry. Have fun, though. Seriously!"

When we reached our destination, I sighed at the sight of the guy onstage high-kicking like a Rockette. "Not amateurish," I muttered.

I adjusted my trench coat and fedora, which I'd layered over my only suit to give me more to take off, then shook out my hands and bent to wipe a smudge from my black stilettos. The stage manager angled the clipboard toward me, pointed to the song I'd requested, and asked, "Is this what you're stripping to?"

"Yeah. It was going to be 'I Want your Sex' by George Michael, but we've already heard that six times tonight, so I figured I should change it up."

She thought about that for a beat, then said, "Good for you. It's always the same dozen songs, over and over and over, including that one. If I have to hear 'Diamonds are a Girl's Best Friend' even one more time, I swear I'll end up punching somebody in the face." I didn't doubt it.

The Rockette finished his routine to thunderous applause, then bounced down the steps at the front of the stage, dressed only in a pair of red briefs. The audience crowded the center aisle with bills and waiting high-fives. He harvested the money and slapped palms as he strutted through the theater, then exited out a side door that led back to the dressing room. Meanwhile, one of the stage hands rushed around and gathered up the performer's discarded clothes.

The woman with a clipboard told me I was up. I swallowed hard and took center stage, keeping my head dipped down so the hat shielded my face. My heart pounded in my ears, and the MC announced me as Sizzling Sawyer, which made me wince.

A moment later, the drumbeat at the start of the original, kick-ass version of 'Ballroom Blitz' blasted from the bank of speakers. I felt anything but confident, but so what? I was just going to go ahead and act like I was. Fake it 'til you make it. That philosophy could get me through the next four minutes. I tore the hat off and flung it to my right when the vocals kicked in.

As my heart raced, I remembered Gabriel telling me to find a friendly face in the audience. It was good advice. I scanned the crowd, and then I found a very friendly face in an aisle seat in the eighth row, just beyond the glow of the stage lights.

Alastair had slid down in his seat a bit, as if that would somehow hide him from view. Nope, not from my vantage point up on the stage. I grinned at him, then pulled off my overcoat and threw it aside. I ran the fingers of my right hand through my hair as he and I locked eyes, then stalked the stage as I pulled off my suit jacket, dragged it behind me, and finally threw it into the wings. Gabriel caught it and waved it over his head. He was dancing along and looked like he was having a great time.

There were a few props around me, including a metal folding chair, and I grabbed it and held it over my head, then leapt off the stage. I was careful to land on the balls of my feet in those very high heels and was relieved that I actually pulled it off without face-planting onto the carpet. When I reached Alastair, I took hold of him by the front of his waistband and he scrambled to his feet and followed me into the aisle. One glance told me he was completely turned on, from his flushed skin to his fully dilated pupils and the unmistakable bulge in his khakis. So hot.

I pushed him into the folding chair, then removed my tie and draped it around his neck. I was vaguely aware of a lot of yells and whistles from the audience as I grabbed his knees, then spread Alastair's thighs and began dancing between them in time to the music, shaking my ass while I unbuttoned my shirt. He was breathing hard as he gripped the edges of his seat. I dropped my shirt, revealing a black leather corset that was laced up the back. That got a huge response from the audience, probably because all the men who'd gone before me had just stripped down to briefs.

I ran the pointed toe of my shoe over the bulge in his pants, very lightly. He mouthed the words, "Oh God," and licked his lips, his expression one of pure lust. I licked his lower lip for him, then straightened up and held up each foot in turn, and he slid my shoes off. When I tapped my belt buckle, Alastair grinned wickedly. Once he got them unfastened, I let my pants fall to the floor, and stepped out of them and kicked them aside.

That left me in only the corset and garters, a leather jockstrap, and stockings, all black. I held up my left foot for him again, and he surprised me by running his tongue up my shin before slipping the shoe back on. When I held up my right foot, he grabbed my leg, swung it outward, and licked my inner thigh before slipping on the other shoe. The audience roared, while I fought the urge to fuck him right then and there.

I turned my back to him and gave Alastair a lap dance as the music pulsated. When I turned to face him again, I used the tie to pull him to his feet, then kept hold of it and danced with him. He moved with me, his hands on my hips, looking blissfully happy as he smiled up at me.

Just as the song ended, I tipped him back and kissed him. The kiss I got in return was wild, passionate, burning with need. When I swung him upright again, he pulled me down to his height with a hand on the back of my neck and whispered in my ear, "I need you in me. Now."

Two words: *Fuck. Yes.*

Alastair and I ran backstage hand-in-hand. Our extremely hasty retreat left little doubt where we were going and what we were going to do once we got there. I didn't even care that the audience was waving bills at me as we left the theater, or that they were on their feet and cheering. He was all that mattered.

The stage manager greeted us with knit brows and arms crossed over her chest. But then she grinned and tilted her head to the right, where there was a narrow staircase. I shot her a smile, and as we bounded up the stairs, she called, "Come see me after you get your rocks off. You were made for burlesque, Sawyer."

There was a small storeroom at the top of the stairs, and we tumbled inside, kissing and pawing at each other. Somehow, we managed to get him naked without just ripping his clothes off, despite the fact that we were frantic with need. I picked him up and sat him on a couple stacked boxes, then grabbed the backs of his thighs and pushed them up and out. I dove onto his clean, tight little opening, licking him, tonguing him, and he writhed and moaned, "Fuck me, Sawyer. I can't wait another minute." I couldn't either.

He directed me to his wallet, and I fumbled for some condoms and lube packets, pulled my jock strap below my balls, and prepped both of us. But then I asked, as I slid my lubed finger from his hole, "You sure you're ready?"

Alastair nodded, then pushed back as I sank into him, opening himself up for me. We fucked wildly, urgently, while I jerked him off. He bounced on my cock, biting his lip to hold back his moans, totally lost in the moment.

It was so intense that I didn't last long. I moaned as I came in him a few minutes later, and after I slid out of him, Alastair surprised me by jumping off the boxes, grabbing me, and spinning me around. I murmured, "Fuck yes," as I got on my knees on a low box, bent over, and arched my back for him.

He grabbed another condom and more lube, pushed a slick finger into me and quickly worked me open. When I told him I was ready, he claimed me with a long, hard thrust, filling me with his thick cock, stretching me. I moaned and rocked back onto him, taking him deep. Not surprisingly, given how aroused he was, Alastair didn't last long. In just a few minutes, he grasped my hips, impaled me with a hard thrust and came with a stifled yell.

He slid out of me, and when I straightened up and turned to him, we both burst out laughing. "So, that happened," I said.

"Yes! Came out of nowhere, so to speak."

"You okay? We didn't do much prep this time."

"I'm fine," he said as we both tossed the condoms in a big trash can in the corner. "Totally worth the slight ache. What about you? I didn't give you much advance notice before jumping you."

"I'm excellent. Any time you feel like jumping me, go right ahead." I ached a little too, but I didn't even sort of mind.

As we washed our hands in a big, industrial sink next to the mops and buckets, he said, "I hadn't planned that part, though I did hope we'd have sex this evening, hence the dozen condoms and lube packets stuffed in my wallet. I have to admit, I pleasured myself twice this afternoon thinking about you performing in a sexy outfit. It got to the point where I just couldn't stay away. Are you mad at me for showing up here when you told me not to?"

I grinned at him. "Do I seem mad?" He shook his head, and I told him, "I was wrong to ask you not to come. Good thing you don't listen."

"I'm so glad I didn't miss that. You were sensational, Sawyer! You're already unbelievably sexy, and then to see you up on stage, proud and confident, my God! You took my breath away."

"You didn't think it was tacky, stripping in front of strangers?"

"Well, it was far more than a strip tease, wasn't it? That was you boldly and bravely declaring, 'This is who I am.' I got a sense of how important my reaction was last night when you showed me what you had on under your clothes. So, to see you up there thrilled me, because I knew what it meant to you."

I pulled him into my arms. "You were pretty bold yourself. Thanks for letting me drag you into the act."

"It was my pleasure. You realize that for the rest of my life, whenever I hear that song, I'll think of you and instantly bone up. Bound to get embarrassing when I hear it out in public." I kissed his cute little grin, and then he asked, "When's the next time you absolutely have to be somewhere these next couple days? Appointments, I mean, that sort of thing."

"I'm going in for a Tracyectomy on Tuesday afternoon." When he raised an eyebrow at that, I tapped the name on my chest and said, "I have a tattoo appointment. I can hardly wait to obliterate my ex's name. Other than that, I'm planning to spend the week job hunting."

"I think you just found one. The woman with a clipboard sounded as though she intends to hire you."

"Think so? I suppose it could be fun in the short term, until I find a real job. You know, one that doesn't involve baring my ass in public."

Alastair grinned as his hand slid down and cupped my bare butt cheek. "The leather jock strap was quite shocking."

"You don't approve?"

"Oh now, I never said that, love." He gave me a flirty smile, then said, "Back to my original question, though the memory of you flaunting that perfect arse is quite a distraction. If you have nowhere you need to be these next couple days, will you go away with me?"

"Go where?"

"I have a list of places I intend to visit while living in the U.S. It's over two pages long, and I'm embarrassed to admit that even after four years, much of it remains. I'd love to pick a destination and enjoy it with you. San Diego, for example. I promise to bring you back in plenty of time for your Tracyectomy."

"Sounds fun. When do you want to leave?"

"Tonight, if that's alright with you."

"Sure. A little spontaneity is a good thing."

His face lit up. "Wonderful! I just need to send a text, and we can take off as soon as we've found your trousers. Mine too, apparently. I'll just need to swing by my flat to pack an overnight bag, which won't take long. I assume you'll want to do the same." He looked around the storeroom, then bent over and retrieved his briefs from behind a couple boxes while I admired his smooth, sexy ass.

He pulled on the briefs, then found his phone. After he sent a text, I asked, "Was that to your bodyguard?"

"It was. He'll make our travel arrangements. His name's Roger, by the way. I sometimes call him Roger the Shrubber, just to irk him. It's from—"

"Monty Python and the Holy Grail. One of the funniest movies ever."

"Indeed! I jokingly asked Roger to try and locate your trousers when I texted him. I'm quite sure he was mortified." Alastair looked very pleased with himself.

"You mean he's here? In the building?"

He nodded. "Roger always shadows me when I'm going to be in a crowd. Not that anything ever happens, but as he keeps reminding me, 'those are the rules.' Bloody daft ones if you ask me."

"So, your bodyguard watched me strip, shake my bare ass, and dry hump you. Awesome. I'm lucky he didn't jump up and taser me."

As Alastair pulled on his white, button-down shirt, he said, "Don't be embarrassed. Roger's quite open-minded, far more than you'd guess by his outward appearance. His family has looked after mine for decades, and I've known him all my life. In fact, I think of him as an older brother."

"It's so much more awkward now that you've put it that way." He looked concerned, but then I smiled at him and kissed his forehead, and the little crease between his brows went away.

After Alastair was fully dressed, we went downstairs and found the stage manager and Gabriel waiting for us in the dressing room. My clothes where draped over a chair, and my friend smiled at me and said, "You killed it, just like I knew you would! And guess what? Joan wants to put both of us on the payroll!"

I glanced at the stage manager, Joan presumably, and she held out a business card. "If you're looking for work, I need someone to do three performances a night, Thursdays through Saturdays. Just FYI, the club owner generally wants old-school burlesque as opposed to pissed-off Magic Mike, but she liked your look and your act. We both did."

I slipped her card in my backpack and said, "I'm actually between jobs right now, so this could be fun. I wouldn't be able to commit to anything long-term though, it'd just be until I found something full-time. Is that okay?"

Joan just shrugged. "This is a high-turnover gig. Shocker, I know. If you're still here three months from now, it'll be a goddamn miracle. Show up at seven-thirty on Thursday to fill out your paperwork if you want to do this."

"You're hiring me, just like that? Don't you want to check my references or anything?"

She stared at me and said, "This isn't the FBI, kid. Just show up on time, take off your clothes, and get paid."

Gabriel waved a fan of bills and said, "Speaking of which, I collected your tips after you two ran off for a quickie. You cleaned up! I'm sorry to say you didn't win the prize money, but Joan said you were a very close second."

"Did you win?" He grinned and nodded as he tucked the money in my backpack, and I said, "Good. You deserved it."

Joan pushed off the makeup table she'd been leaning against and said, "Alright, I've got work to do. Good job tonight, I hope to see you both on Thursday." She turned to Alastair and added, "Come back anytime, Blondie, especially when your boyfriend's working. The heat between you two almost burned the place down. Keep that shit up." She sauntered from the room.

As I started to pull on my shirt, I realized I'd skipped the introductions and said, "Gabriel, you know Alastair, right? I assume you do, since you're both friends with Zachary."

"A bit, yeah," Alastair said as he held out his hand and Gabriel shook it. "Nice to see you again, mate. You were sensational tonight."

The two of them chatted while I got dressed, and as we headed for the door, I asked Gabriel, "Are you staying with your friend Scottie while you're in town?"

119

He shook his head. "We used to be roommates, so it's the first place that guy I told you about would look for me. I slept at a motel last night, but I can't afford to keep doing that, not even after tonight's windfall. So, I guess I'll head home to Martinsville, then drive in again on Thursday for this job."

"Martinsville is over two hours from here," Alastair said. "Why don't you stay in my flat instead? If someone's harassing you, my building has excellent security, you'll have nothing to worry about. And Sawyer and I are heading out of town for a couple nights, so you'll have the place to yourself."

Gabriel looked stunned. "Are you serious?"

"Of course."

"You'd trust me enough to leave me unsupervised in your apartment?"

"Zachary speaks very highly of you, so trusting you is a given. And it sounds like you're having a rough time of it, so I'm glad to help out."

"This offer is just for tonight though, right?"

Alastair shook his head. "Stay as long as you'd like."

Gabriel looked emotional as he murmured, "This means so much to me. I can't even tell you."

A minute later, the three of us found Roger waiting in the lobby. He was in his late twenties, six-foot-two and solidly built, with a frown that seemed right at home on his square-jawed face. Between his expression, the gangsteresque black-on-black suit, shirt and tie, and the long scar running down his right cheek, which suggested a violent past, he looked like someone you didn't want to run into in a dark alley.

But Alastair bounded up to him, linked arms, and gave him a huge smile as he said, "What did you think of the show? I'll bet you enjoyed the bloke with the red bikini briefs, yeah? He was one high kick away from his meat and two veg flopping out!" Roger tried to hide an amused expression and knit his brows at Alastair.

Gabriel came damn close to batting his eyelashes at Roger when the two of them were introduced. The big bodyguard actually colored a bit and grinned as Gabriel flashed him a flirtatious smile. I thought that little spark of attraction was interesting.

When Alastair introduced me, we shook hands, and I told Roger, "Wow, this is exciting. I've never met someone in your line of work."

He raised a brow and asked, with a pronounced British accent, "You've never met a bodyguard?"

I kept my expression serious and said, "Oh no, I've met plenty of those. What I've never met is a shrubber.

Must be exciting work, arranging, designing and selling shrubberies."

Alastair doubled over laughing at my Monty Python reference, and the corner of Roger's mouth quirked up, just for a moment. Then he turned and headed for the exit as he announced, "I'm calling your family, Gromit. I'll be requesting hazard pay now that you and Bonny Barebottom have teamed up." I liked him immediately.

Gabriel asked, "Gromit?"

"As in the dog from the Wallace and Gromit cartoons," Alastair explained as we followed Roger. "When I was twelve, I tried to put together a ferocious Hound of the Baskervilles costume for a fancy dress party, but it didn't quite go as planned. Ro will never let me live it down." He and his bodyguard chuckled at the memory. Their shared history and easy rapport did make them seem like brothers.

I found myself wondering if Roger planned to tell Alastair's parents about me, and how the news of a cross-dressing gay stripper would go over. But then, I didn't need their approval. This was just a fling, after all, and whatever his family might have thought of me was never going to matter. I frowned a little and took Alastair's hand.

Chapter Five

The privately chartered jet to San Diego hadn't been what I was expecting, and neither was the lavish suite at the Hotel Del Coronado. Given the standards he was used to, I couldn't help but wonder what Alastair would think if he visited my shabby house. Then I felt like an asshole when I realized I'd denied him that opportunity just a few hours earlier, because I couldn't face introducing my father to the man I was dating.

Gabriel had followed Alastair and Roger back to the apartment in his car, while I'd gone home to pack an overnight bag. It turned out my dad had already gone to bed, so my attempt at stealthiness was pointless anyway. I left a note on the kitchen table telling him I'd be gone a couple days, and then I'd waited out on the street corner for Alastair and Roger to pick me up on the way to the airport. I'd arranged that rendezvous just in case my father might still be up, and I knew I was being ridiculous. I was a grown man, but I was sneaking around behind my father's back like a guilty teenager, just because I didn't have the balls to come out to him. That conversation was years past due.

Alastair pulled me from my thoughts when he stuck his arms out to the sides and dropped backwards onto the bed.

He murmured, "Ahhh, that's nice," as he sank into the fluffy, white bedspread.

I walked over to him and sat on the edge of the mattress. "I'm sorry about earlier. That was bullshit, telling you to pick me up on the corner. I just realized I treated you the same way my ex used to treat me, like a dirty little secret, and I'm ashamed of myself."

He pulled me onto the bed with him, and after we stretched out facing each other, he said, "Don't beat yourself up over it, Sawyer. I know why you did it. I can't talk to my parents about my sexuality, either."

"Have you tried?"

He nodded. "I came out to them when I was fourteen, but it didn't make a bit of difference. My grandfather actually had this cliché-riddled talk with me last time I was home, after I refused to take out the granddaughter of a friend of his. It was all about how vitally important it was to 'keep up appearances,' and how, if I had 'an itch I needed to scratch' I was expected to keep that private. I asked him what exactly he meant by that, and he told me flat-out, my family expects me to marry a girl and raise a family, and if I need to satisfy my 'urges' with men, I'll just have to sneak off and do that on the side, unbeknownst to anyone."

"Are you serious?"

"Unfortunately, I am. My grandfather actually told me that's how it's always been done in our family, and how it always will be done. So, apparently I come from a long line of secretly gay adulterers. Is that not the most cocked up thing you've ever heard in your life?"

"It's pretty high up there." He sighed and lowered his lids, and after a moment I asked, "Why do you let them dictate your life, Alastair? You're such an intelligent, capable person, and you could go off and have a brilliant career as an astrophysicist and do whatever you want. It might not be as lavish as the one you have now, but it'd still be a good life, and it'd be on your terms."

He opened his eyes and looked into mine. "I don't jump through their hoops for the money. It's nice to have the means to do whatever I want, like this impromptu excursion, but I'm not selling out just for material gain, Sawyer. The thing is, my family needs me. Generations of Penelegions have worked so hard to make a name for us and to build a significant legacy. I'm the last of the line. My sister Penelope and my two cousins flat-out refuse to have anything to do with the family business, so it all comes down to me.

"They need an heir, someone to carry everything they've built into the future. It's a huge responsibility, and it's not the path I would have chosen if it had been up to me, but it's what has to be done. My family has poured their life blood into making the company what it is today. We didn't start out wealthy. In fact, my great-great-great-grandfather was the son of a butler and a scullery maid. He opened a little shop when he was just fifteen to help support his parents and sisters. Eventually, it grew into that famous department store, and over the next few generations, the family diversified into manufacturing and other industries.

"All of that isn't just about lining our pockets. My family employs over sixteen thousand people in the UK alone, and more than fifty-five thousand worldwide. And my mother and grandmother work philanthropically and have given millions to charities that are making a real difference. It's about all of that, and it's also about pride, and family honor, and reputation, three things I care sod all about, but that mean everything to the people I love. I don't have the luxury of shirking all of that responsibility the way my sister and cousins did. I have to step up, because literally thousands of people are counting on me."

I took him in my arms and said, "I get it now. For the record, you and I both know your family shouldn't have the right to dictate your personal life. But since I haven't even managed to come out to my dad, I won't pretend it's easy to make our families understand."

"No, it's not." He ran his fingertips down my cheek. "Sorry that turned into a long-winded speech. We're here to have fun, yet I'm going on about family obligation and the almighty Penelegion empire. What must you think of me?"

"That you're an extraordinary human being with a hell of a lot on your shoulders."

He leaned in and kissed me before resting his forehead against mine. After a moment, he said, "While we're on the subject of families, mind if I ask how your mum fits into the picture?"

"She doesn't. In the fitting into the picture analogy, she exists outside the frame."

"Where is she?"

"Chicago. I hear from her every now and then, but basically, she and I exist in separate universes. Hers has deep-dish pizza, the Cubs, and a distinct lack of Sawyer."

Alastair knit his brows. "What kind of mother goes off and leaves her son behind?"

I just shrugged. "She was in over her head when she had me. She got married young, to a much older man, and when the marriage failed...I don't know. Sometimes I think I reminded her too much of my father. He got full custody, and she barely looked back. I've always said Dad and I were her practice family. A few years later, she married again and had two more kids. That one took, so I guess the trial and error paid off."

"You're making excuses for her. I'd think you'd be angry."

"Nah. It just is what it is. You can't make people love you. That's a lesson I've learned more than once." Okay, that sounded pathetic. I swung out of bed and clumsily changed the subject with, "Enough about that. I'm hungry, are you? That café downstairs may still be open. Well, then again, maybe not. I just realized how late it is."

He jumped out of bed and caught my hand. "If you want to talk about it, I'm a good listener."

"Thanks, but I don't."

He picked up a leather binder and grinned as he held it out to me. "Then let me help in another way." I took the room service menu and kissed his forehead.

When I told him some dessert sounded good, he called downstairs and ordered ice cream and every topping they had on hand, and also asked that a full bar be set up in our room. Before he hung up, he also sent a top-shelf bottle of Scotch and a slice of apple pie to Roger's suite down the hall. When I commented on that combination, he said, "Ro never treats himself, and I know for a fact he has a raging sweet tooth and loves pie. The whiskey, well, that's just a given."

Later on, we sat on a blanket on the floor, because Alastair felt we should have a picnic, and he spooned a dollop of ice cream into his mouth and groaned with pleasure. Then he told me, "This is amazing! Here, try it." He fed me a big spoonful, even though our sundaes were nearly identical, and I grinned at him and licked some chocolate sauce off my lip.

I said randomly, "As a kid, I thought it was going to be so great to be an adult, because I could eat all the ice cream I wanted. I imagined I'd own a huge freezer that was jam-packed with the stuff. Needless to say, the whole grown-up thing hasn't gone as planned."

"Isn't that the truth! I imagined I'd have so much more freedom when I grew up. I'd come and go as I pleased, and I'd call all the shots. Granted, this four-year reprieve in the States has been wonderful, but overall, adulthood is just not what it's cracked up to be."

When we finished our ice cream, I said, "I know it's late, but do you want to go for a walk? I'd like to stretch my legs." He readily agreed and shot a quick text to Roger before we left the suite hand-in-hand. I was glad the bodyguard didn't feel compelled to join us.

The Hotel Del Coronado had been built in the 1880s and was a thing of beauty with a warm color palette, and charming period details. A downstairs hallway was lined with photos of the many A-list celebrities who'd visited the Hotel Del during the golden age of Hollywood. It still felt every bit as glamorous.

At two a.m., the hotel's public spaces were deserted. I liked the feeling that we had the place to ourselves. We exited through a door at the back of the lobby and strolled around the grounds for a while, amid palm trees and lush tropical flowers.

We walked past the pool and tucked our shoes and socks under a lounge chair before stepping onto the beach. Moonlight glittered across the gentle surf. I'd changed into a T-shirt and jeans when I'd stopped off at home, and bent to roll up my cuffs before taking Alastair's hand again and leading us to the water's edge.

After walking through the foamy surf for a few minutes, my companion turned to me with a mischievous sparkle in his eyes and asked, "Up for doing something a bit daft?"

That made me smile. "I'm pretty sure flying to San Diego on a private jet in the middle of the night already qualifies."

"It does, but I want to dial it up a notch. How would you feel about some skinny dipping?"

"Sounds fun, except for the part where we get kicked out of the hotel for running around naked and using the pool after hours."

"Oh no. I wasn't talking about the pool."

When he tilted his head toward the vast, dark expanse of ocean, I exclaimed, "Seriously? You've seen the movie Jaws, right?"

"I have! But nothing's going to happen."

"What are you basing that on?"

"Statistical probability." The skeptical look on my face made him add, "Come on, Sawyer, live a little," as he began to unbutton his shirt.

"This is exactly how the movie started."

"It'll be fine."

"Or not."

Alastair tossed his shirt on the sand, followed by his pants and briefs. Then he put his hands on his hips, and I ran my gaze down his gorgeous, naked body as he said, "Come with me. Please?"

"Maybe...."

He took that as a yes and turned and ran into the gentle surf. When he was waist-deep, he dove beneath the waves and emerged a few moments later with a loud whoop. Cute, sexy, naked Alastair totally trumped my paranoia of big fish and dark water, and I quickly stripped myself and waded into the surf.

The water temperature was probably in the low seventies, about the same as the air, but a lot more bracing somehow. I dove under a wave like Alastair had, and emerged with a loud, colorful string of curse words. When I reached my companion, who was bobbing in chest-deep water, I lifted him up, swung him over my shoulder and gave his cute little butt a playful slap. "You're a bad influence," I told him as I deposited him back in the ocean. "And I'm dumb enough to succumb to peer pressure, especially when it comes from the most beautiful boy I've ever met."

He searched my face as he asked, "You think I'm beautiful?"

"Of course I do. I also think you're certifiable for wanting to swim in shark-infested waters. Obviously I am too, because I followed you out here."

"It's not infested. More like, lightly seasoned with sharks."

"Because that's reassuring. It's also fucking freezing."

When his lips met mine, they tasted salty and sweet, equal parts ocean and Alastair. Then he said, "Come on, race me. That'll get us warmed right up." He turned and began swimming parallel to the shore with sure, strong strokes. I let him get several yards ahead before following with a leisurely backstroke. No way was I going to trigger the competitive streak I was sure every street racer had to possess. Besides, it was immediately obvious that he was the far superior swimmer.

We swam for several minutes, rising and falling on the waves as they rolled past us. We were out past the break point, and the salt water kept us buoyant, so it was fairly effortless. It also succeeded in warming me up, and so did Alastair when he finally stopped swimming and let me catch up to him.

The water reached my neck, so it was a little too deep for him to stand. He wrapped his arms and legs around me and held on tight, and I ran my hands down his back and cupped his ass. We kissed each other again, and when my cock swelled, he rubbed himself against it. Alastair let go of me after a few minutes and dove beneath the surface of the water. I wondered why, until I felt his hands on my thighs. A moment later, he wrapped his warm mouth around my cock, and a deep moan rose from me.

He sucked me for a few moments before surfacing, and grinned at me as he pushed his dripping hair off his forehead. "The challenging part was keeping myself from bobbing to the surface," he said. "I know that was a tease, but I promise to finish what I started when we get back to the room."

Because he was shivering, I suggested we race again, and we both took off at a good clip, headed back toward the hotel. No contest. He ended up yards ahead of me by the time he stopped swimming, and when I finally caught up to him, I was exhausted. We waded to the shore, emerging where we'd entered the water, and I looked around and murmured, "Shit." I was sure we were on the right section of the beach, but our clothes were nowhere to be seen. Since the high tide was coming in, what had happened to them wasn't much of a mystery, but we searched the beach anyway, just to be sure.

Eventually, we gave up, and he said, "Damn, there goes another phone." His eyes went wide as he turned to me. "Tell me your phone and wallet weren't in your jeans."

"No, I left them in our room."

Alastair looked relieved. "No real harm, then."

He took my hand, and we started walking back toward the hotel. It was lit up in the distance, an idyllic postcard come to life. The sprawling, white Victorian was an architectural marvel, its red roofline an eclectic collection of spires and peaks, culminating in an enormous, round, main building. The whole thing was breathtakingly gorgeous. Too bad our naked asses were probably about to get kicked out of it.

When we started to get cold, we broke into a jog. Once we reached the hotel grounds, we slowed again, and I asked, "What's the plan here?"

"Two choices: walk up to the main desk and hope they issue us a new key despite our lack of ID and trousers, or go to Roger's suite and wake him. He has a spare key to our room. If we go with option B, he will never, ever let me live it down, but it still may be the better way to go. The hotel staff might not have a sense of humor, and getting locked up for public indecency would put a real damper on our getaway."

"One problem: we can't get to Roger's suite. All the doors are bound to be locked, and at this hour, there won't be anyone around to let us in."

When we reached our shoes, Alastair grinned and said, "I have an idea. Remember that Red Hot Chili Peppers video?" Before I could ask him what he meant, he picked up one of my white crew socks and pulled it over his cock and balls. I chuckled at that, but then I did the same thing with the other sock.

We also put on our shoes, and I said, "This is an awesome look," as I puffed out my chest and struck a pose.

"I wish I had my phone. This is a photo op if ever there was one." His sock fell off and he exclaimed, "Shite," before scooping it up and once again stuffing his junk inside it.

"Photographic evidence is probably a mistake. It could wind up as exhibit A after we're arrested for public indecency."

"Speaking of photographic evidence, the hotel is probably wired for surveillance, and I'd hate to wind up on the local news. Oopsy-daisy!" His sock fell off once more, and he pulled it back on with a cute little shimmy.

I grinned at him. "You did not just say that."

"Certainly not. You're clearly imagining things." Alastair flashed me a smile and jumped into the shadow of a nearby hedge, then exclaimed, "Operation Arrest Avoidance begins now!" He got down in a low crouch and began singing a tone-deaf approximation of the 'Mission Impossible' theme song, which came out, "Doodle ooo, doodle ooo, do do!" He then ran across the lawn, dropped into a quick barrel roll, and leapt to his feet in another shadow. I was smiling as I jogged after him and scooped up the sock he'd left in his wake.

When a security guard rounded a far corner of the building, Alastair grabbed my hand and dragged me into the landscaping, then whispered as he pulled the sock back on, "I'm guessing it's arrest first, ask questions later. We'd better not risk it."

We crouched down among the hibiscus bushes, and I glanced at Alastair, who was pressed against my side. He looked so happy and full of life, and he ran his hand around the back of my neck and kissed me passionately. We paused for a moment when the security guard walked past our hiding place, and then we went right back to kissing.

After a few moments, I felt him tremble and whispered, "You're cold. We need to get you inside."

"That's not why I shivered," he said as he ran a fingertip over my lips, "but you're right about needing to get inside."

As soon as the security guard was out of sight, we ran to the back of the building and tried one of the doors. Not surprisingly, it was locked, so we began to circle the hotel. After a few minutes, Alastair paused and said, "I think that's our suite. Roger's is two doors down, so that has to be his, right?" He pointed to a balcony on the fourth floor.

"I guess so."

"I'm going to climb up and knock on his patio door."

I said, "You wait here, I'll do it."

Alastair grinned at me. "No worries, I've got this. I'll toss a robe down to you, and then I'll put something on, come downstairs, and let you in."

"I'm doing this. I insist."

"Seriously, I do things like this all the time. I'll be fine."

I tilted his face up with a fingertip under his chin and kissed him gently before saying, "Please let me handle this. I don't want you to get hurt."

He searched my face for a moment, and then he said, "Alright, but please be careful. The dew will have made everything slippery, and I don't want you to get hurt, either." I promised him I'd watch my step and started to scale the building, climbing from balcony to balcony.

I'd almost made it to the third floor when a familiar voice at ground level said, in a loud stage whisper, "Let's set a goal, Bonny Barebottom. See if you can go an entire twenty-four hours without showin' me your arse." I glanced at Roger, who was standing beside Alastair and holding up his hand to block the view of my butt, and he added, "Incidentally, we're one building over. The folks you were about to traumatize with your sock puppet from hell don't know how lucky they are that I showed up when I did."

As I climbed back down, I asked him, "Out for a stroll?"

"Hardly. I'd dozed off and managed to sleep through Gromit's text saying he was going on a walkabout. Good thing I got up to take a piss."

"My phone, room key and our clothes washed out to sea," Alastair explained with a contrite expression.

"Fan-fucking-tastic," Roger muttered as he turned and headed to the next building. I fought to suppress a smile as we fell into step with him.

*****

Once we'd returned to our room (after thanking Roger profusely and promising we'd stay in for the rest of the night), Alastair and I headed straight to a very hot shower. He took the soap from my hands and washed me, his touch nurturing and gentle. When it was my turn, I lathered up my hands and ran them across his smooth chest. His breath caught when I grazed his nipple, and I could feel his heart racing beneath my palm.

I ended up jerking him off with his back pressed to my chest, holding him to me with one of my arms wrapped around his shoulders. A tremor went through him and he cried out as he came, bracing his hands against the tile wall. I kissed and nuzzled his ear while the hot water flowed over his skin, rinsing the cum from his chest and stomach.

Later, after we'd dried off and climbed into bed, he slid between my legs and finished the blow job he'd started in the ocean. I propped myself up and watched him as he sucked me. His hands grasped my thighs, and his gaze never left mine, not for a moment. There was so much longing in his blue eyes, and it spoke volumes.

After he brought me to orgasm, he put his head on my chest. I held Alastair securely as he whispered, "I wish I could give you so much more." It made my heart ache.

Chapter Six

"I want armor."

"In what sense?"

"I want a huge tattoo, not only to block out the name, but so I can never do this again," I told Yoshi, tapping the word on my chest. "I want it to cover my heart. Actually, I want it bigger than that. Extend it out, over my upper arm and shoulder, as if I strapped on a section of a suit of armor."

"Not a problem," he said.

"You sure?" Darwin asked. He'd been washing the plate glass window of the tattoo studio when I arrived and had been curious about what I was going to have done, so I'd invited him to sit in on my session. "Your original tattoo is so romantic. Even if that relationship didn't work out...I don't know. Maybe there were things about it that are worth remembering."

"There aren't, and getting that name inked on my chest was moronic. The fact that I was a lovesick nineteen-year-old is no excuse. You're eighteen, and you'd never be this stupid. Would you, Darwin?"

The kid grinned at me and tossed his head to swing the hair out of his eyes. "Well...I might. People in love aren't exactly known for their excellent decision-making."

My friend Kai stretched his legs out and crossed them at the ankles as he said, "This is true." He'd called me earlier in the day and invited himself along to my appointment. I suspected it was because he thought inking over Tracy's name might stir up some emotions in me, although he claimed he just wanted to hang out. Never mind that it was the middle of his work day.

Yoshi leaned back in his chair and said, "Show me exactly where you want its outer edges, and then let's figure out what you want it to look like." I traced my left pec with my index finger, then drew an invisible line up over my shoulder before encircling the top of my upper arm.

"I know that's a lot, and it's fine if you can't do it all in one session. We can just start with obliterating this." I put my hand over the name.

"I work fast, and I have four hours blocked off, since the person who'd originally had this appointment was going to get a massive tattoo. We might get it done in that time," Yoshi told me. "So, how literally do you want me to interpret the armor idea? I can make it completely photorealistic, as if you just strapped on a metal shoulder plate, or we can go abstract."

"Abstract, definitely. I don't want to look like I escaped from a Renaissance fair."

Yoshi thought for a moment, then grabbed a black three-ring binder from a shelf and flipped through the pages. While he did that, I glanced around the airy, high-ceilinged studio. As predicted, it matched Yoshi's aesthetic. The space was sleek and modern, with black leather chairs, chrome accents and minimalist décor...mostly. Each of the eight work stations had been personalized by the other tattoo artists, three of whom were working when I came in. The end result was a fairly eclectic representation of the many personalities coexisting in that workplace, from the blond rockabilly guy who collected clown figurines (talk about nightmarish) to the woman with cropped purple hair who'd lined her workstation with vintage rock and roll posters and memorabilia, mostly from The Fillmore, a local music venue that had been rocking it since the 1950s. I instantly liked her so much better than the clown guy.

"Tell me if any of these styles grab you." Yoshi flipped between photos of three large tattoos. Each was comprised of intricate, intersecting lines forming a bold pattern. One was distinctly Celtic, one Asian-influenced, and the last was more or less tribal.

"This one," I said, tapping the third. "I like that it's strong, dark, and symmetrical, with lots of black ink. I also like the way the lines end in sharp points. But I don't want to appropriate someone else's culture just because it looks cool."

Yoshi said, "This design is just one I came up with. It's not Maori or anything else, so no worries there."

"Sold."

As he pulled on a pair of black, latex gloves he said, "I'm planning to freehand it, are you going to be comfortable with that?"

"According to Darwin, you're the greatest tattoo artist in the city. I'm fine with you doing whatever the hell you want. In fact, feel free to totally improvise. Judging by the sleeve you inked on yourself, I'm in excellent hands."

The teen nodded at that. "You are."

While Yoshi unpacked several sterile implements, Kai glanced at me and asked, "Are you okay, Sawyer?"

"Sure. Why wouldn't I be?"

He shrugged. "When you said something about wanting to make sure you can never tattoo another name over your heart, you sounded upset."

I knit my brows at my far too observant best friend and said, "I'm fine," as Yoshi slid his chair close to me and prepped the area where the tattoo would go.

"That's what you always say, but I can tell something's up with you. Did your first foray back into the dating world go badly? I had high hopes for you and Alastair."

"It was spectacular, actually, and that's exactly the problem."

"Why, because you don't think he'll want to see you again after hooking up at the reception?"

"No, we already had a second date…of sorts. In fact, he dropped me off here on our way home from the airport, so I could make this appointment."

"The airport?"

"Long story," I said, then took a drink from the cup of coffee Kai had brought me.

"I can go back to cleaning if you want me to," Darwin said, pointing over his shoulder. "This conversation sounds personal."

"Stay." I told him, "I'm not going to start talking about my feelings, or any of that touchy-feely crap," and shot Kai a look.

Darwin's boyfriend Josh came into the shop just then and said, "Hi all." He kissed Darwin's forehead, and the teens exchanged the sweetest smiles before Josh turned to me, pushed his hair out of his eyes, and said, "Hey, Sawyer. I've never seen anyone get a tattoo before, mind if I watch?" Somewhere underneath the overgrown, dark brown mop and the Clark Kent specs was a cute guy who was in that transition phase from boy to man. He was fifteen, with a round face that was starting to thin out just a bit, intelligent eyes and a lopsided smile that usually held a hint of irony. At that moment though, he just looked intensely curious, and I invited him to pull up a chair.

"Sawyer was just telling us that his hook-up at TJ and Zachary's reception turned into a three-day fun fest," Darwin said with a little grin. I liked the fact that he was warming up to me enough to joke around, if not his choice of topics.

"That's not what I said."

"I might be paraphrasing slightly." His smile got bigger.

"So, what did happen," Yoshi asked as he picked up his tattoo gun, "and are you ready to do this?"

I frowned and bent my leg as I settled in, resting the sole of my motorcycle boot on the leather reclining chair. "Yes, I'm ready, but what's with this topic of conversation? It's like we're in the all-gay remake of Steel Magnolias, and I'm...who was Julia Roberts' character?"

Everyone within earshot said, "Shelby," all at once, and I chuckled.

"I just want to know what's going on with you, Sawyer," Kai said, as the tip of Yoshi's tattoo gun touched my chest and I flinched ever-so-slightly. "The guy whose name's being inked over as we speak did a number on you, and this is the first time in almost a year that you've shown any sign of moving past it."

I sighed, then gave him a pared down, all-ages version of the last few days (both because I wasn't a fan of TMI, and because I didn't want to say anything inappropriate in front of the fifteen-year-old). "That's so romantic," Darwin said when I finished, "running off to the Hotel Del on a whim. It's like something out of a movie."

"It was," I said, while trying my best to hold still. Yoshi was drawing an elaborate outline, his brows knit with concentration, and I didn't want to disrupt his work.

"So, why are you frowning?" Kai asked.

I hadn't realized I was doing that. When I glanced at him, he was leaning forward in his chair, his expression so concerned and sincere that I decided to be honest with him and admitted, "Alastair is...well, he's everything. He's fun and gorgeous and smart and kind...and he's going away in a few months, which is depressing. He's someone I could really care about, but I have to remind myself not to get attached, because this is just a short-term thing."

Darwin asked, "Where's he going?"

"Back to the UK."

Josh chimed in, "So, what's the problem? If you guys ended up getting serious, you could just go with him. I mean, it's Great Britain, not Jupiter."

"That's not what he wants. He told me right from the start that this is only going to be a short-term thing. When he goes back, he'll be taking over his family's business, and there's going to be a hell of a lot of pressure on him. I'd just be a complication, with both his job and his family."

"You can't just go, 'oh well, he's moving back to the UK.' Not if you truly like this guy," Kai said.

"Jesus," I muttered. "We've definitely drifted into full Steel Magnolias mode. Can we please talk about something else, like sports or some shit?"

"You only pretend to be interested in sports," Kai reminded me. "And this is important."

"Doesn't matter. Nothing can come of this." My best friend frowned at me, but finally let the conversation drop.

*****

Three hours and forty-five minutes later, I winced a little as I raised my arm over my head to pull on my T-shirt. Yoshi had done an amazing job on the tattoo, which he'd then covered in a large bandage. The area ached a little, as if I had a sunburn, more so when I moved my shoulder.

After I paid Yoshi and told him I'd keep in touch, I said goodbye to Darwin and Josh and stepped outside with Kai. "I'm starving," he said. "What about you?"

"I could definitely eat, but don't you have to get back to work?"

"Nah, it won't hurt anything to take the afternoon off. I'm caught up on my work, and Mel's holding down the fort in case we get any drop-ins."

"It's good to be the boss," I said.

"It is."

"What's your husband up to?" He and Jessie co-owned a garage in Bernal Heights and had hired our friend Zachary's dad when their business started to pick up. It seemed to be going well for them.

"He's out with Nana, she wanted to use the limo." Before going to work with his husband, Jessie had been employed by a firecracker of a little old lady named Mrs. Dombruso, as her chauffeur and assistant. They were more like family now, and he still gave her a hand when she needed it.

Kai drove us to Nolan's, an Irish pub and sports bar in the Richmond District. It was run by a gay couple who were friends of friends, and Jamie, the co-owner, greeted us warmly when we arrived. Since we were probably two hours ahead of the dinner rush, the place was pretty empty.

Two guys were packing up laptops and notebooks, and Jamie paused at their table and asked, "Hunter and Brian, do you know Sawyer and Kai?" The couple reminded me a bit of Alastair and me, since Hunter was a slim, blue-eyed blond and his partner was a huge, burly brunet with a distinctly ex-military look about him. It made me miss Alastair…even more than I already did.

It turned out Kai had met them at a few parties, and I shook their hands and said, "Sawyer MacNeil. What are you guys studying?"

"At the moment, econ, but not by choice. It's a general ed requirement," Hunter said as he tucked a long strand of hair behind his ear. "We're enrolled at S.F. State, and we're trying to figure out what we want to be when we grow up." He grinned when he said that, since they were both in their mid-twenties. "Here's what we know so far: not economics majors."

"I've been thinking about going back to school," I mentioned offhandedly.

Kai got way too excited at that, and said, "Awesome! I remember how important getting an education was to you before you enlisted."

"Army?" Brian guessed as he zipped his backpack.

I nodded. "You?"

"Marines. You get sent overseas?"

"Afghanistan."

"Same." He slid out of the booth and reached for a cane that had been leaning against the booth. That was when I noticed he was a double amputee.

Hunter slid out of the booth too and took Brian's free hand as he said, "If you end up enrolling at State, give us a call. We've been at this for over a year now and can pass on a few tips."

"Mostly, we can tell you which classes totally suck ass, so you can steer clear," Brian said. Kai promised to text me their number, and we exchanged 'nice to meet yous' before they headed for the door. Brian moved confidently and steadily on his prostheses, so I wondered why he felt he needed the cane. Then I decided it was none of my business.

When we settled into a booth and Jamie left us with a couple menus, Kai said, "Great news that you're thinking about going back to school."

"But just thinking about it. I haven't decided anything yet."

"I hope you give it a shot. Going to college was so important to you when we were teens."

"Yeah, but I'm not the same person now." Kai frowned a little, and I said, "What? Come on, you can say it."

"You've seemed kind of miserable since you've been back. It's like the Army, or your ex, or both sucked the life out of you. You always had so many big plans, and now...I don't know. You're just different."

"We're all different. Look at you! The guy who never thought he'd get married, madly in love with a wonderful husband! And your daughter's getting so big. I can't believe Isabella's in first grade already!"

"I'm worried about you, Sawyer. It's like you lost yourself somewhere along the road. You used to know exactly who you were and what you wanted. But since you've been back, it seems like you're just going through the motions. You took that job in construction, God knows why, and you let everything that used to matter to you fall by the wayside."

I told him, "I took that job in construction because I needed to earn a living."

"But that's not you! You were so passionate about wanting to get an education and opening a coffee house. I know those things still matter to you." He knit his brows and asked, "Why are you grinning like that?"

"If you think the construction job was unlike me, wait until you hear about the job I'm starting day after tomorrow."

"I'm almost afraid to ask."

"Say hello to Club Scandal's newest burlesque performer."

"You're shitting me." The look on Kai's face was priceless. "But…how?"

"I made a new friend at Zachary and TJ's wedding reception, and he convinced me to give it a shot on amateur night, which was this past Sunday. Turns out I'm kind of good at it, and they offered me a job. Well, I'm good at stripping anyway. I'm still not sure on how I'm supposed to burlesque it up, but I guess I'll figure it out. By the way, I need you to swear you won't come watch me. Seriously, Kai. I can't do this if you're in the audience."

"I won't, not if you don't want me to." He leaned back in the booth and said, "While that's pretty much the last thing I ever expected to hear from you, I like the fact that you're excited about it. When you took the construction job, it seemed as if you'd been issued a death sentence."

"Yeah, I wasn't too thrilled about it at first, but construction ended up being the right thing at the time. I was so tired at the end of each day that I was actually able to fall asleep easily. That was a challenge when I first got out of the Army." I grinned and added, "I assume stripping is going to wear me out, too. Or maybe not. Do you think I have to get undressed slowly if it's burlesque? On amateur night, I pretty much just ripped my clothes off, then grabbed Alastair and…well, let's just say we burned a hell of a lot of energy after my performance."

Kai grinned and said, "Well hey, as long as you're having fun, why the hell not?"

"You mean it about not coming to the club, right?"

"Dude, that'd be super weird, watching my best friend do some sort of sexy strip tease down to…what were you wearing, exactly?"

"A leather jockstrap." And stockings, heels, and a corset, but he didn't need to know that.

"You shook your bare ass in front of a bunch of strangers?"

"I did."

"Yeah, I definitely don't need to see that."

"Exactly."

"You were never shy, but I didn't quite have you pegged as an exhibitionist either," he said.

"I'm not, but this was actually liberating."

I felt like an asshole then, because my best friend knew nothing about my feminine side, and that meant he couldn't grasp what stripping had meant to me. Why the fuck did I feel the need to keep people I cared about at arm's length? I had no problem opening up to strangers. Hell, I'd revealed that side of myself to Gabriel within a minute of meeting him. But Kai, who I thought of as a brother, was kept in the dark.

I picked up the menu, but didn't look at it as I changed the subject with, "Enough about the bizarre trajectory my life has taken. Tell me about you. How's your business? And how's Isabella? What's she up to this afternoon?"

"Business has been steady, thank God. We've had this great momentum ever since Jessie started working at the garage, and we're to the point now where we have a lot of repeat customers. It's nice not to worry about money all the time. And Izzy's doing great. She's with my sister, mom and grandma this afternoon, and I think they were planning a princess movie marathon. Again."

"Aw, and you're missing it."

"Oh believe me, I can recite that shit backwards and forwards."

"Do you know all the words to the songs, too? Come on, let's hear the one from Frozen. You always had a great singing voice, I bet you could do Elsa proud."

Kai sneered at my teasing grin, just as the waiter appeared at our table and put down two glasses of water. It turned out to be Cole, and he pushed his curly hair back from his face and said, "Hey guys, sorry to keep you waiting. I had to go chase down my ex, because he left without his key lime pie."

"River was here?" I asked.

"No, my other ex. Hunter. He and Brian come in a couple times a week to eat lunch and study, and always order pie to go. I have to wonder how they manage to forget it half the time." His grin was affectionate. Then he got down to business and asked, "You guys ready to order?" We both ended up going with burgers and shakes.

When Cole left with the menus, Kai turned his attention back to me and asked, "So, what are you going to do about Alastair?"

"What, no lead-in or anything? We're just talking about my love life now?"

"Yup."

I sighed and fidgeted with my napkin before saying, "There's nothing to do. He's amazing, he's leaving, and that sucks. End of story."

"Do you know how sad you looked when you said that, Sawyer? I can tell you're totally into this guy."

"I'm an idiot. I know better than to get attached. He told me right from the start that he was just looking for a fling before he goes back home. I should just accept that and enjoy myself, instead of cursing the entire fucking universe for putting the perfect guy in my path and then giving us an expiration date. And that's the last I'm going to say about it." I was relieved when he actually let the subject drop.

After we ate our lunch, Kai read a text from his husband and said, "Jessie wants me to meet him at an old building just off Valencia. I don't know what that's about, but since Nana Dombruso is involved, it might get bizarre. Want to go on a field trip?"

"Why the hell not?" I signaled Cole for our check.

Chapter Seven

"Is Nana thinking about a new career busting ghosts?"

Kai chuckled at that as we stood on the sidewalk with his husband, looking up at a rundown, ninety-year-old firehouse, and said, "Apparently. It's cool though, don't you think?"

"It's amazing. I just don't get why it's in this condition. It's the kind of place that should have been snapped up the moment it went on the market, then turned into a pretentious microbrewery or some shit."

Jessie said, "Actually, it goes on the market tomorrow, and that's why Nana's trying to make up her mind about it this afternoon. The fire department moved to modern facilities in 2009, and that's when a couple bought it as an investment. They never got around to doing anything with it, obviously, and they're selling it now so they can divvy up the money as part of their divorce agreement."

The building's brown brick facade had been tagged by pretty much every graffiti artist in the city, and all the windows in the two stories above the huge, arched, bay door were smashed out and boarded over. But beneath that was an attractive structure with period details from the nineteen-twenties, especially along the flat roofline, which was accented by a series of decorative cornices. It did look a hell of a lot like the building in Ghostbusters, but in true San Francisco style, this one was sandwiched tightly between its neighbors on either side.

As we wandered through the open doorway, I asked, "What's Nana planning to do with this?"

A bunch of people were bustling around, and I recognized a lot of them from various parties and gatherings Kai and his husband had taken me to. Nana overheard us, and she came over and said, "Hi, boys! I'm thinking about buying this place and turning it into a shelter. I found out the other day that forty percent of the kids living on the street are gay homosexuals." I raised an eyebrow at her turn of phrase, although her statistics were right-on. "That's a crying shame! These poor kids come out to their families, then get kicked out and wind up living in dangerous conditions. I don't know a damn thing about running a shelter, but I got some friends who do, and we're all trying to decide if this space is right for what I have in mind." She turned to a slender guy with blond, curly hair, who was talking to a young-looking brunet with glasses, and asked, "Christopher Robin, what do you and Jeffrey think about this place?"

I knew Christopher a little. He was actually an up-and-coming artist, so I wondered why she was asking his opinion on a shelter. He said, "We think it'd be great. There are a lot of bedrooms upstairs, and the kitchen and dining area were made to feed a big group. Plus this ground floor open space would make an excellent living area. I can just imagine it with a bunch of couches, a big entertainment center, some foosball tables, stuff to make it fun and welcoming. And that, well, that's just epic," he said, gesturing at the three brass poles connecting the upper floors to the former garage. "Living in a place like this would have been a dream come true when I was homeless. Don't you think so, Jeffrey?" That answered my unasked question about why she was consulting him.

"God, could you imagine?" His friend looked around the drab, dirty space wistfully, clearly envisioning it the same way Christopher was. "A vintage firehouse would have seemed like heaven when I was living on the street."

"Jeffrey and I both work at the shelter where we used to stay when we were teens. I'm a volunteer, he's on staff," Christopher told us. "That doesn't make us experts, but in my personal opinion, this building is ideal." He turned to Nana and said, "You'd be able to house maybe sixteen to eighteen kids, I think. Of course, you know you'll need to bring in trained counselors and get state licensing to make this possible. But as far as the layout and size of this building, I think it's perfect."

"So do I," Jeffrey said. "I've learned a fair amount about administration over the years, and I'd be happy to help with all the paperwork and red tape."

"I'll help, too," I said. "I have experience working construction, and this place is going to take a lot of elbow grease to get it in shape for those kids."

"Count us in," Kai said. "We don't know shit about construction or running a shelter, but we can paint walls or do whatever you need." Jessie smiled at his husband, then stretched up to kiss his cheek.

Nana beamed at us and said, "Such good boys, every last one of you. Now I just need to know if this place is structurally sound. We can't put our kids somewhere unsafe!" She looked around, then yelled, "Vincent! Is your building inspector done yet? I need to make a decision ASAP, before that money-hungry real estate agent sells it out from under me!" She pronounced it Ay-sap.

"Not yet, Nana," her grandson Vincent called from across the room. "It's important for him to take his time and find all the hidden problems, so don't rush him. You and Alastair can't sink your funds into a money pit."

My heart skipped a beat at that name, and I looked around and asked, "Is he here?"

Jessie nodded, obviously pleased at my reaction. "He's shadowing the building inspector. He'd dropped by my garage to say hello and talk cars earlier this afternoon, just as I was leaving to take Nana to look at a few properties. When he heard what she had in mind, he was instantly on board."

"He sounds like a great guy," Christopher said.

"He is." I kept scanning the ground floor, wishing he'd appear.

"Last I saw, they were headed for the attic," Jessie told me. "Maybe you want to go up and say hello."

"Oh. Um, I shouldn't bother him. What he's doing is important." I tried to pull up a neutral expression, so Jessie and Kai would stop grinning at me.

"It wouldn't be a bother," Jessie said, "especially since he's mentioned you about a hundred times over the last few hours."

That was nice to hear, but I tried to play it cool by saying, "I'll just wait until he comes down," and followed Nana when she offered to give us a tour of the building.

I kept looking for him though, and finally spotted Alastair a few minutes later when we were taking a look at the spacious kitchen. Trevor, the guy who'd hosted the wedding reception on Saturday, and who was married to Nana's grandson Vincent, was trying out the appliances and telling Nana the six-burner stove was shot when

Alastair and a man with a clipboard appeared in the doorway.

He was wearing the same outfit he'd had on when he'd dropped me off at the tattoo studio, now with the addition of a yellow hardhat and a layer of grime. His face was smudged with dirt, and so were his white button-down shirt and indigo jeans. I thought he looked sexy as hell like that.

His expression and demeanor were all business. Alastair's brow was knit with concentration as he asked the building inspector a question, then listened intently to the answer. All of a sudden, it was easy to imagine him running his family's company. He just exuded confidence and came across as effortlessly in charge. It was good that he'd chosen to get involved with Nana's project, not only financially, but because he was clearly going to get things done.

Alastair gestured to the kitchen as he said something else to the inspector. When he spotted me, his game face instantly fell away. He stopped talking in mid-sentence, and his handsome features lit up with a glorious smile. I grinned at him, and he turned and said something to the man with a clipboard before heading in my direction.

I met him halfway across the kitchen, and he started to reach for me. But then he noticed his hands were dirty and held them up with an embarrassed smile. "I've been in every nook and cranny of this place this afternoon. I'm afraid I'm a bit of a mess."

I pulled him into a hug and said, "It looks good on you."

"I was going to text you when I finished here and find out how your appointment went. Does your new tattoo hurt?"

"Nah."

"Would you tell me even if it did?"

"Probably not," I admitted.

"Can I see it?"

"It's all bandaged up. I'm supposed to keep it that way for a couple hours, but I can send you a photo later."

"I look forward to it." He smiled up at me, and I caught the hardhat as it fell off his head.

I kissed a clean spot on his forehead and said, "I'll let you get back to what you were doing. I know everyone's trying to make a decision quickly here. I think it's wonderful that you offered to be a part of this, by the way."

"The thing that keeps the family business from feeling like an albatross around my neck is exactly this, being able to do some good with the resources available to me. As soon as Jessie mentioned what his former employer had in mind, I knew I wanted to help in any way I could."

I brushed my lips to his, then whispered in his ear, "I think you're an amazing man, Alastair. Not just because of this. I already knew you were something special."

He put his arms around me and kissed me tenderly. I forgot about everything, from the throbbing in my shoulder to all the people in that kitchen as I held him and returned the kiss, parting my lips for him, sighing with pleasure as the tip of his tongue found mine. A deep feeling of contentment settled in me as the heat of his body radiated through our clothes, and I breathed in his pleasant scent, not quite masked beneath the layers of deodorant, cologne, and shampoo, and even dust and wood from his forays into the deep recesses of the firehouse.

Eventually, a loud voice cut through the bubble of pleasure around us, as Nana exclaimed, "Isn't that just the sweetest thing! It must have been a long time since they saw each other."

"About five hours," Kai told her, the amusement unmistakable in his voice.

I stepped back from Alastair, and he colored a little and said, "I've gotten you dirty. Apologies."

He tried to brush a couple streaks of dust from the front of my shirt, but I grinned at him and said, "Totally worth it."

"I'd better go finish up that inspection," he murmured, his blue eyes focused on my lips. I nodded, handed him the hardhat and told him I'd talk to him later, and he smiled at me before leaving the kitchen.

"Jesus," Kai muttered. "There was enough heat between the two of you to burn down the firehouse. What exactly happened during your weekend in San Diego? I was imagining sightseeing and some nice dinners out, maybe a bit of polite getting-to-know-you conversation. But obviously I'm wrong, because that was not a 'I've known you four days' kind of kiss."

I glanced at the people around us, who'd all gone back to whatever they'd been doing before the Sawyer and Alastair show grabbed their attention, and lowered my voice as I said, "We barely left the bed. Well, except for the first night, when we went skinny dipping in the Pacific and our clothes washed out to sea. I don't just mean we had sex the whole time, though we certainly did plenty of that. We also talked, and hung out, and watched movies, and ordered room service, and just enjoyed each other's company. It's funny, we went because Alastair had never seen San Diego, but once we got there, he had no interest in anything other than—"

"You."

"Yeah."

Kai's brown eyes crinkled at the corners as he smiled and said, "Shit, Sawyer. I'm going to miss you."

"What are you talking about?"

"You're going to end up following him to London. It's so obvious."

"And do what, work at a UK Starbucks while he runs a multimillion-dollar empire? Someone like me doesn't fit with someone like that." Kai frowned at me, and I said, "That's not poor self-esteem talking, it's a simple statement of fact. Alastair and I exist in separate worlds. There might be a tiny bit of overlap while he's here and going to college, but this isn't his life. It's a temporary reprieve before he takes on a huge amount of responsibility and rejoins his homophobic family. I'm sure they'd love me, by the way."

"What does any of that matter in the face of a connection that intense? I've never seen anything like it, aside from…."

He grinned embarrassedly, and I filled in, "You and Jessie."

"Exactly. It was every bit as intense when we first got together. I literally couldn't stay away from him. Still can't. I miss him like crazy when we're apart, even if it's just for a few hours." Kai raised an eyebrow and asked, "Sound familiar?"

"No."

He chuckled at that and said, "You lie."

"And you're a sappy, lovesick dork."

"You know what else I am?"

"Happy. No need to point out the obvious, it's written all over you."

"I am, and I want that for you too, Sawyer, especially after watching that shitty relationship tear you apart for three fucking years."

"Speaking of which, I'm glad I got this done today," I said, lightly tapping the new ink on my chest. "It still doesn't feel like closure, but then, I figured that would take more than an appointment at a tattoo parlor."

"If you ever decide closure involves finding that asshole Tracy Garcia and kicking him in the nuts, I call shotgun on that little excursion."

"For all I know, he's still in Afghanistan. Be a bit of a commute."

My best friend grinned at me. "Totally worth it, though."

*****

Nana and Alastair decided to buy the firehouse. Based on the building inspector's verbal report, the place was in good shape, aside from the cosmetic issues. He was going to be busy with paperwork, so I told Alastair to call me when he was done, and Kai dropped me off at home.

I found my dad eating dinner in front of the TV, which he did every night. He looked a good ten years older than he actually was, thanks to an overall failure to give a shit about things like combing his hair, exercising, putting on clean clothes, or shaving. Sometimes when I looked at him, I saw my future, and it was enough to break me out in a cold sweat.

"Well, look what the cat dragged in," he muttered. "What're you doin' running off to San Diego with friends when you should be job hunting?"

"I already found a new job. I start Thursday," I told him, pausing in the doorway to the living room.

"Oh. Well, that's something at least. Is it another construction job?"

"No, it's something else."

My dad shot me a look and asked, "Am I supposed to guess?"

"I, uh, got a job in a nightclub. I'll be working nights, Thursdays through Saturdays. It's just until something better comes along."

He sighed and turned back to the TV. "Well, it's a goddamn good thing you left the Army for a lucrative career slinging drinks in some dive."

I felt like telling him the truth, just to see what would happen. I could imagine his face at the news that I was stripping and parading around in lingerie in front of a bunch of men, not tending bar. But of course, I didn't say anything.

Instead, I hoisted my backpack onto my shoulder, the one without the tattoo, and started to head for the stairs. But then I paused and asked, "What happened to bowling?" Every Tuesday night like clockwork, my dad could be found at the lanes with his group of Army buddies.

"Rubio's got some kind of stomach bug, sounds nasty. Since tonight's league night, we need four to compete, and none of our alternates could make it."

"I can take Rubio's place if you want. I know how much you hate to miss bowling night."

My dad flipped channels with a remote so worn out that the numbers weren't legible anymore. He didn't bother to glance at me as he said, "You suck at bowling. I'd rather sit home than go and lose."

"Suit yourself." I pushed down the hurt that sprang up in my chest and climbed the stairs, then closed and locked my bedroom door behind me.

Why the hell did I let him get to me like that? I should be glad he didn't want to take me bowling, because that would have been an epically shitty way to spend an evening. There was no reason for it to hurt. I was twenty-three, not seven! If he didn't want to spend time with me, then fuck him.

I tossed my backpack in the corner and took off my T-shirt before stepping into the bathroom and carefully peeling off my bandaging. I checked it out in the mirror above the sink, and the tattoo looked good. Strong. Stronger than I felt. Without resembling armor in any literal sense, it still felt like it, especially the way it covered my heart and anchored itself to my arm and shoulder. I found myself wishing every inch of my skin was covered in that same strong, black, interlocking grid. Then nothing could get to me.

"Of course it could," I muttered to myself. It was just ink. It couldn't protect me, no matter how much meaning I assigned to it.

I washed my hands, then cleaned the new tattoo with antibacterial soap and patted it dry. As I carefully applied a bit of lotion, I stared in the mirror, scrutinizing the pattern on my skin, looking for any sign of Tracy's name. There was nothing, not a single stray line peeking out from beneath the new ink, and no tell-tale shape as it wove over the word. Yoshi really was a genius. The sharp precision of his lines and the totally symmetrical pattern was another testament to that. He'd actually freehanded a flawless design. Go figure.

After pulling off my boots, I climbed onto the bed facing the wall and stretched out on my right side, the one without the new ink. It wasn't even eight p.m., so I didn't know why I was in bed, aside from the fact that I felt a little lost and was hoping it would be comforting. Instead, it felt lonely and pathetic.

Why had I thought obliterating a word from my skin would somehow end that chapter of my life? I was glad Tracy's name no longer marked my flesh, but he was still seared into me at the cellular level. I didn't love him, not anymore, but as long as memories of him had the power to make me miserable, I wasn't free of Tracy.

Against my will, a night from four years earlier started to play in my mind's eye. I'd been so nervous as I cut across the base, headed to the disused storeroom where Tracy and I usually met. I'd gotten the tattoo three days earlier, but that night would be the first time he saw it.

I got there before him, same as always. I let myself in with my key, then paced as much as I could in the nine-by-twelve space. It was hot and stuffy as usual, and empty except for a metal folding chair and a bare twin mattress on the cement floor. The mattress was stained with semen and sweat and blood, the latter from our earliest days together, when fucking would tear me open and I'd have to grind my teeth to keep from screaming.

I was supposed to take my clothes off, lube myself up, and wait on that mattress, so I'd be ready for Tracy when he arrived. We always only had minutes together, and then we left separately to make sure we didn't raise suspicion. Since Tracy was my commanding officer, he could have been dishonorably discharged for what we were doing. I was sure he feared the shame and humiliation of being outed even more than that, though.

He was annoyed when he arrived and found me clothed. Tracy was a huge guy, six-foot-six with a muscular build, and he filled that little room. "Please sit down for a minute, okay?" I said, taking his hand and leading him to the chair.

"We don't have time for this, Sawyer. I'm expected somewhere in less than twenty minutes."

"Please? I have something I need to show you. It'll only take a minute."

He sighed, but finally dropped onto the chair and said, "What is it?"

I knelt in front of him. I don't know why I did that. Then I dropped my dog tags inside my green T-shirt and pulled the shirt off. I said softly, "I love you, Tracy. It always seems like you don't believe me when I tell you that, so…well, this is my way of proving it to you." I didn't look at him as I said that. I was afraid to see his reaction.

He went perfectly still. It was a solid minute before he whispered, "What the fuck did you do?"

I looked up at him and my heart leapt at the rage in his dark eyes. "I went to that shop in the village, the one that's friendly to soldiers. I heard they did tattoos in the back. It took some convincing and a lot of cash, but they finally—"

He leapt to his feet, grabbed the chair and snapped it in two as a low growl rumbled in his massive chest. His head bumped the bare lightbulb, and as it swung, it cast bizarre shadows and gave the room a nightmarish quality.

I fell back to get out of his way and held up my hand to shield myself. He had never hit me, but his rage that day was a tangible thing, filling that small space, surrounding me, and I was scared of him. "You fucking idiot," he growled. "What part of *this is a secret* don't you understand? You shower in the barracks. Everyone's going to see that! Everyone will know!"

"They won't! Nobody knows your name is Tracy, you go by your middle name! Even your nametag says D. Garcia. If anybody asks, I'll say it's the name of my girl back home. No one will know."

"But my full name is all over my military records, Sawyer. Did you ever stop to think of that? My superiors know that's my name! I thought you understood what it could do to me if this ever got out!"

"I thought about that, but the higher ups won't see the tattoo. The only people who see me in the showers are grunts like me, and they don't have access to your records."

He was so mad that he was literally shaking, and he balled his huge hands into fists and turned his back to me. I got to my feet as I whispered, "Please don't be mad, Tracy. I wanted you to know I belong to you. This proves it. I'm yours, heart and soul. I love you so much, and I didn't know how else to make you see that."

Tracy turned and glared at me. "I'm taking you to the main hospital in Kabul tomorrow. I'll have to think of some excuse. They have a clinic that can remove tattoos. I had to take that fucking idiot Perkins there last year when he came back from leave with the words 'fuck you' and a racial slur tattooed on his forehead. I never imagined I'd have to take you there, too. Fuck Sawyer, how could you be so goddamn stupid?"

I squared my shoulders and stood at my full height. Tracy was one of the few men on the planet who could make me feel small. I scraped up all my stubbornness and told him, "The tattoo is there for life. No fucking way can you make me remove it."

"Are you insane? Didn't you hear me when I told you what that tattoo could do to me?"

"It's not going to come back to bite you! It's just not! Tracy is a common name, they'll believe me when I say it belongs to a girl back home. You and I have been together for months, and we're so careful! Nobody even suspects. I promise you this'll be okay. I love you so much, Tracy, and I'd never do anything to hurt you! You know that."

"Fuck, Sawyer, stop saying you love me! We're just two men blowing off steam, you know that as well as I do."

I shook my head. "That's bullshit. Deny it all you want, but I feel it, Tracy. I see it in your eyes sometimes, too. Not now, of course, because you're royally pissed off at me. But I know it's there. You love me just like I love you."

"You're lying to yourself, seeing what you want to see."

"I'm not," I insisted. "Look me in the eye, Tracy, right in the eye and tell me you don't love me. I bet you can't do it."

He took a step toward me. A muscle worked in his jaw as he locked eyes with me. His voice was low when he said, "I don't love you."

It felt like a knife in my chest. But I was so stubborn. I shook my head as my heart shattered and said, "You're lying. I know you're lying."

"Fuck, Sawyer, you refuse to listen!"

He left the storeroom, letting the door swing shut behind him. I sat on the concrete floor and put my hand over the name on my heart as I studied the blood stains on the filthy mattress. I'd lost my virginity in that little room, lost it to a man I loved with every part of me.

A man who swore over and over he didn't love me in return.

I had a weird thought as I sat there, sweating in that cramped storeroom. In a way, that horrible, stained mattress was Tracy's and my version of the Picture of Dorian Gray, ugly, dirty, and ruined. The truth of our entire relationship was spelled out in cum and blood and sweat, right there on the blue striped ticking. Meanwhile, there was the face we showed the world, indifferent, emotionless, near-strangers. It was such a lie.

*****

I sighed and rolled onto my back in my cramped bed in San Francisco, trying to chase away the memories that hovered in the air like spirits. It had taken Tracy weeks to forgive me for the tattoo. Eventually, we began having sex again. Maybe a year after that, we started to become friends. He kept saying he didn't love me, though.

"He was lying," I whispered.

Not that it mattered.

But some part of me would have loved to hear him say it, just once. Even though Tracy was firmly in the past and all the feelings I'd ever had for him had been laid to rest, the words still would have meant a lot. They would have been validating somehow, casting a different light on those three years we spent together. Maybe they would have made me feel like something other than a stupid, lovesick kid who let himself get hurt and used by someone who didn't give a shit.

Or maybe I really had been stupid, and maybe the words wouldn't have made a damn bit of difference.

*****

I was staring at my dingy wall and trying like hell to stop thinking about the past when my phone beeped sometime later. When I saw Alastair had messaged me, I grinned like an idiot. The text said: *Hey. What are you up to? Seems I've bought a firehouse. Am I daft for undertaking this project with Nana Dombruso? She's a dear woman, but possibly also a bit of a loose cannon.*

I sat up and wrote: *Fortunately, she has you as the voice of reason. It's a good thing you swooped in and offered to be a part of that project. P.S. You looked ridiculously sexy in that hardhat with dirt all over you.*

He replied with: *Oh dear, seems autocorrect got the better of you. Surely you meant to type 'you looked ridiculous' and it added in the rest.*

I dialed his number, and when he answered I said, "I mean it. As gorgeous as you are when you're all proper and buttoned-down, somehow you become utterly irresistible when you're a bit tousled."

He chuckled and said, "Interesting perspective."

"So, what are you doing to celebrate your new philanthropic venture?"

"Wandering around my house in the South Bay and cursing myself for not bringing some groceries with me. I can have a meal delivered, but I have an overwhelming urge for a bowl of cereal. Somehow though, I just can't find the motivation to run out to the market. Pathetic, isn't it?"

"Nah, I've been there. Why did you go back to the house, instead of your apartment here in the city?"

"I have to be on campus for much of tomorrow. I'm a teaching assistant, and the quarter is ending in just a couple weeks. Lots of nervous freshman to talk off the ledge."

"I can imagine."

He asked, "What were you doing when I messaged you?"

"Nothing. Literally. I'm in my room, staring at a blank wall. And you thought being too unmotivated to run to the market was bad."

"What were you thinking about?"

"Who says I was thinking about anything? Maybe I was in a total vegetative state."

"Was it Tracy? I'd imagine getting his named covered over stirred up a few memories today."

I sighed and admitted, "It did, none of them good."

"I know what you need," he said.

"What's that?"

"A ride on your motorcycle. I suggest pointing it south and continuing on for about an hour, give or take, depending on traffic."

I grinned and asked, "Is this an elaborate scheme to get me to bring you some cereal?"

"It's an elaborate scheme to get you to bring me Sawyer. If you happened to stop off for a box of something very American, hoop-shaped and sugary on the way here, I wouldn't complain."

"I can do that." I was already out of bed and stuffing my feet into my boots.

"Terrific! I look forward to seeing you, and also your tattoo. Are you pleased with the way it came out?"

"I love it. It'll be interesting to hear your take on it, since you don't strike me as the tattoo type."

"While I have no desire to get one of my own, I can certainly admire a tattoo on a gorgeous, sexy body. I have no doubt yours is a thing of beauty."

As I opened my closet door to look for a loose-fitting shirt, I asked, "Should I bring anything besides cereal?"

"You don't actually have to do that. I was joking."

"But you do want some, right?"

"Yes, but still."

"Text me the address, and I'll see you in about an hour, sugary cereal loops in hand."

"You're fantastic."

I grinned and said, "It's nice that you think so."

Chapter Eight

"Holy shit, how many people live here?"

I stood back a few feet and gawked at the Mediterranean mini-villa Alastair had bought solely for its proximity to Saithmore University. It looked like a small hotel. That was reinforced by the palm trees and lush, tropical landscaping that framed the white house with its terra cotta tile roof.

"That number fluctuates between zero and two. Roger prefers to stay in his townhouse next door most of the time. He says there's such a thing as too much togetherness. And my friend Elijah stays with me on occasion. He was new to dorm life at Saithmore this year, and his roommate was a git. I told him he should just move in here, especially since the place stands empty half the time, but he feels he's imposing. I need to get him over that." Alastair stepped back a little and opened the huge, carved wood door as far as it would go. "Do you suppose you'll be coming inside at some point?"

I handed him a canvas shopping bag as I crossed the threshold, and he said, "Thank you for the cereal. Three different kinds, each more sugary than the next, fantastic! You're a prince among men."

"Welcome." The inside of the house was just as breathtaking as the exterior, with high ceilings, lots of potted plants, and a hand-painted tile floor. I carefully slid off my leather jacket, which hadn't felt all that great against my tattoo, and said as I wandered into the foyer, "I feel like I'm on vacation in the tropics. This is spectacular."

"I'm glad you like it." He looked around and asked, "Where's your backpack? I hope you brought your stuff so you can spend the night."

"I didn't want to be presumptuous. You could have just been inviting me to hang out for a while."

When we reached a massive terra cotta-colored kitchen, Alastair put the shopping bag on the counter and slid his arms around my waist. "If 'for a while' means all night, followed by tomorrow morning before I have to go to Saithmore, then yes. In fact, if you'd like, you can come with me and amuse yourself on campus while I'm doing my T.A. gig. Afterwards, I'd like to take you to dinner, then show you one of my very favorite places in all the world. That is, if you don't already have plans tomorrow."

"The next thing on my almost nonexistent schedule is Club Scandal Thursday night, where I'll be figuring out what the hell burlesque looks like in front of a live audience. Don't forget, you promised you'd be there as my moral support."

"I wouldn't miss it for the world. You still need to practice your routine, by the way." He gave me a wicked little smile.

"I tried three times while we were in San Diego. Each time, I only made it about ninety seconds into my routine before you jumped me." I grinned at him.

"I couldn't help myself. You're already the sexiest man I've ever seen. Combine that with taking your clothes off seductively and my libido preempts all rational thought."

"You should probably wait until after I get off the stage to fuck me on Thursday. Just saying."

"Well, if you insist." When I rolled my left shoulder, Alastair asked, "Everything alright?"

"Yeah. The leather jacket was just a little heavy on my new tattoo."

He immediately started unbuttoning my black shirt and said, "I'm so sorry, Sawyer. I should have sent a car for you, or come up to the city and gotten you myself. I didn't think about what your motorcycle jacket would feel like resting against your skin." He opened the front of my shirt and murmured, "Oh my God."

"You hate it, don't you? I knew it wouldn't even sort of be your taste. I—" I drew in my breath and forgot what I was saying when Alastair caressed my left nipple with the pad of his thumb.

"You're so unbelievably sexy." He was staring at the pattern on my chest. I hadn't thought about the way it framed my nipple, but clearly that riveted his attention. "My God, look at you." He let the shirt drop from my shoulder, and his lips parted as he took in the rest of the ink.

"Do you like it?"

"I adore it," he said. "It's strong and beautiful, so it suits you to a T." I grinned embarrassedly, and he asked, "Does it require special care while it's healing?"

When I told him what I needed to do for the next few days, he took off my shirt and draped it over the back of a chair, then picked up my hand and said, "I want to help if you'll let me."

"You don't have to."

"I know. Let me do it anyway."

He led me to the master bathroom and had me sit on the edge of the tub as he carefully washed my tattoo and patted it dry. Next, he took his time lightly massaging lotion into my skin, and I relaxed under his touch. When I looked up at him, he kissed me tenderly, then said, "Come on, love. Let's get comfortable, and then I want you to tell me what you were thinking about when I called you. I know it was something troubling, and I want you to get it off your chest."

The master bedroom matched the rest of the house with its high ceilings, textured white walls, and distinctly Mediterranean feel. The centerpiece was a huge bed with a rustic, wrought-iron frame and a stack of fluffy, white pillows and blankets. Aside from the bedding, the house was completely different in tone and style from his apartment in San Francisco. I had no idea what Alastair's personal tastes were, since his surroundings obviously reflected interior designers' aesthetics, not his.

I hesitated and told him, "I shouldn't get in bed. The ink could seep through and ruin your sheets."

But he said, "Your comfort is far more important that the bedding. That's just stuff, and it can be replaced if need be."

We both stripped down to just our briefs and crawled under the puffy comforter. He held me close, and after a while, I started talking, despite myself. I'd had no intention of telling him about the memories the tattoo stirred up, but the words just tumbled out of me. Once I started, I couldn't have stopped them even if I wanted to.

We ended up talking well into the night. I told him things I'd never told anyone, not only about Tracy, but about how lost and alone I'd felt in Afghanistan. "All I wanted was just to come home," I said at one point. "I didn't know what I was doing there in the first place. I was just a kid, eighteen when I enlisted. I joined to try to please my father, but I should have known that would always be a losing proposition.

"When I finally got my wish, when my commitment was up and I got to come home to San Francisco, I crawled into the same bed I'd slept in as a kid, under my father's roof, and then I realized that place wasn't home either. There was no love there, no comfort. There were no happy memories or cherished belongings, or people who were glad to see me and who welcomed me home with open arms.

"There were just four dingy walls, and my dad, who was pissed off at me for failing to re-enlist, and…hell, I actually found myself missing Afghanistan. At least there, I knew what to do. As I soldier, I followed orders. There was no guesswork involved. As Tracy's lover, I got on my knees and took his cock. I understood what was expected of me.

"Here, nothing I do is good enough, and it never will be. I don't even know why I care. So what if I'm a disappointment to the people around me?"

"I need you to do something for me." Alastair's voice was gentle.

I pulled back a couple inches and met his gaze. "Anything."

"Move into my condo in San Francisco, as my roommate."

"Are you serious?"

He nodded. "You need to get away from your father and that toxic relationship and start fresh. It also gives us a chance to spend time together before I have to leave. And after I go, I hope you'll stay on for as long as you'd like."

"You're not going to sell it when you return to the UK?"

"Never. It means too much to me, and I'll still get to use it once or twice a year on holiday. That seems like a waste though, letting it sit empty most of the time. But if you continue to live there, I'll be happy knowing it's being put to good use."

"I...don't know what to say."

"Say you'll move in tomorrow. Gabriel seems a little lonely, and I'm sure he'll love the company. I stopped by to check on him today, before I drove down here."

I kissed him and said, "I need to think about it, okay?"

"Take all the time you need." He sat up and smiled at me. "You know what we need to do now, though?"

"Midnight cereal party?"

"Exactly." I slid out of bed and followed Alastair to the kitchen.

*****

The next day, I got to live out a fantasy by getting to pretend I was a student at one of the top universities in the country. I accompanied Alastair to Saithmore, and while he was off at his teaching assistant job, I sat in on a class in a huge lecture hall. Since it was the end of the semester, the other students had to know I was a party crasher, but they didn't seem to care. And with over two hundred people in the class, the professor either had no idea or didn't give a shit that there was one extra student seated in the back row that day.

I listened intently as the teacher reviewed the material covered that quarter, in preparation for final exams. The subject was Psychology 101, and it was fascinating. When the two-hour lecture ended, I wandered into the main quad and grinned as I texted Alastair: *One psychology class, and suddenly I know what's wrong with, like, half a dozen of my friends and family.*

After a minute, he messaged back with: *Well done, Dr. Freud. So tell me, what's my diagnosis?*

Extreme hotness, coupled with an animal magnetism totally irresistible to people named Sawyer MacNeil. I sent the text, then headed toward a brick building that appeared to be a café.

He wrote: *Ha, thank you for that. What are you up to now?*

I replied: *I've found a place that looks like it might sell coffee. This is the ultimate test. If they can't get the java right, then I can no longer be impressed with your fancy university.*

Well, fingers crossed, since clearly my school's honor is at stake! Are you at the Book and Bean? I glanced up at the name above the elaborately lettered chalkboard behind the counter as I got in line and told him I was, and then he wrote: *Do you know Elijah Everett? Chance and Finn are his guardians, and they're good friends of Zachary's so maybe you've met them.*

I replied: *Yeah, we've met briefly.*

Terrific. I'm going to send Elijah your way. Could you make sure he gets some lunch? He's stressed out about finals, and I'm pretty sure he hasn't eaten today. I'm stuck in the office for another couple hours, otherwise I'd do it myself.

I told him I was happy to help. When I reached the counter, I ordered a ton of food, including three sandwiches, a latte and an Americano, some baked goods, a smoothie and a salad. All of that was my awkward attempt at taking care of Elijah as best I could.

My order came up a few minutes later, and I picked up the tray just as a tiny blond appeared in the doorway, clutching the strap of a huge backpack. I went up to him and said, "Hey, Elijah, I'm Sawyer. I don't know if you remember me. I've seen you at a couple weddings, and we were both a part of a group camping trip a few months back. I guess we have a lot of friends in common."

"I remember you," he said softly.

I gestured at the tray with my chin and told him, "I'm under orders to feed you. Want to sit outside? It's nice out." He held the door for me, so apparently that was a yes. Then he followed me to a table under a big oak at the edge of the brick patio.

I glanced at him as we sat down. Elijah was eighteen, but he looked a lot younger. In part, that was because he was short and very thin, but there was something else too, a vulnerability about him that made him seem almost childlike. The fact that he was almost disappearing in a gray hoodie three sizes too big for him just added to it. I could see why Alastair had taken him under his wing. Elijah's big blue eyes flickered to me before returning to the tabletop. They were partially hidden behind blond hair that curled a little, almost reached his shoulders, and looked like it hadn't seen a brush in a day or so.

"I didn't know how long you'd be, so I just ordered a bunch of stuff to save time," I told him. "Help yourself to whatever you want, my treat." He hesitated for a moment, then picked up the smoothie and put it in front of him. When he made no move to take anything else, I said, "Dude, you can't leave me with three sandwiches. I know I'm a big guy, but come on. Do you want tuna, a Mediterranean sub, whatever that means, or this healthy thing with hummus and stuff they dug out of the landscaping?"

He grinned, just a little, and put the tuna sandwich next to the smoothie. He had a pronounced southern accent, evident even when all he said was, "Thank you."

"You're welcome. Do you think Alastair is hungry? I can save the lawn clipping sandwich for him. I'm not being mean, I actually think it's less weird than the Mediterranean sub. That one features something called an olive mélange. I don't even know what that word means, but it kind of sounds dirty."

His grin got a little wider and he said, "Maybe you're thinkin' of ménage, like in *ménage a trois*."

"You know what? I am. Now when you report back to Alastair, you're going to have to tell him how creepy I was, because I kept making inappropriate comments about sandwich fixings."

I was being goofy on purpose, and Elijah totally picked up on it. "Thanks for tryin' to put me at ease," he said, studying the wrought iron tabletop. His voice was always so soft, and I had to lean in a little to hear him. "I know my conversational skills are kinda…nonexistent. But please don't feel you have to entertain me over lunch. That's just too much work."

"Sorry if I was trying too hard," I said as I pried the plastic lid off my latte. After I took a cautious sip, I murmured, "Damn it."

He glanced up at me. "Somethin' wrong?"

"This is one of the best lattes I've ever had. I was kind of hoping it would suck."

"Why?"

"Because Saithmore is already way too perfect. Just look at this place!" I swung my arm to indicate the rolling lawn, heritage oaks, and neoclassical red brick buildings with white columns. "It's straight out of the pages of the totally unrealistic dream college brochures I collected when I was in high school."

He studied me for a moment, then said, "If you wanted to enroll here, maybe you could look into some scholarships. That's the only way I afford it."

"But I've heard about you, Elijah. You're a math genius, so it's no wonder they're willing to give you scholarships. Me, I'm just an average guy with an A.A. from a junior college. I do have access to a little money through the G.I. bill, but that wouldn't even cover a semester here."

"Does the place matter all that much, though? Don't get me wrong, I'm grateful that I get to go to Saithmore. But ultimately, learning can happen anywhere. It's about makin' the most of wherever you end up."

"You're right. This place just looks so much like the picture in my mind's eye, you know? The quintessential college experience."

He took a sip of the smoothie, then asked, "What did you want to study at that dream school?"

"I don't know. Everything? I know that's not an answer, but I loved studying a broad range of subjects when I was getting my associate's degree. Every class was eye-opening." I took a sip of coffee, then asked, "How'd you pick math as your major?"

His voice was softer than ever when he said, "I didn't. It picked me. Ever since I was little, it just made sense to me. I didn't know that was unusual at first, but soon enough, I realized none of my classmates were like me, and I tried to hide it. I didn't want to be different. When we had math tests, I'd miss one on purpose, just so I didn't stand out. When I was eight, a teacher finally figured out I had this 'gift'. That was the end of havin' any chance to fit in. I mean, not that I would've anyway. It seemed like everyone in that small town in Mississippi figured out I was gay before I even knew what that word meant. And then that math thing on top of it…sometimes, it felt like a curse."

"I'm sorry you had to grow up feeling like an outsider."

He shrugged beneath that giant hoodie. "That's what I am, though, and what I'll always be. Not just 'cause I'm gay, or this total freak when it comes to math, but because that's who I am. And maybe it's not such a bad thing, know what I mean? Mainstream society is, well, pardon my language, but it's pretty fucked up in a lot of ways. There's so much pressure to fit in, to be like everyone else. The older I get, the more I think existin' on the fringes is the way to go."

"You've figured out more at eighteen than most people do at eighty." He looked a little embarrassed, and after a moment I said, "I know Alastair probably twisted your arm to have lunch with me, but I want to say thank you for the company. It's good to talk to you, Elijah."

He grinned a little. "Alastair was hopin' you and I would hit it off." When I looked confused, he added, "Not in, like, a romantic sense, of course. He worries about me, so he keeps tryin' to build up my social circle. Jessie's brother Jed goes here, and we joke that Alastair keeps arrangin' playdates for us. That's what it feels like, a concerned parent tryin' to help his awkward kid make friends. I get it, though. He wants to make sure I have a safety net in place before he goes back to the UK."

"He's such a great guy," I said softly, "and a total caretaker, in the best sense of the word. He keeps trying to look after me too, and we haven't even been going out a week."

"He likes you so much, Sawyer. I've seen him smitten before, but this is another thing entirely. I was hangin' out in his office this morning before drop-in tutoring began, and he kept gettin' this far-away look in his eyes and a goofy grin on his face. When I'd ask what he was thinkin' about, he'd tell me some random Sawyer fact. For example, I know without lookin' that your eyes are a 'gorgeous shade of cornflower blue rimmed in dark sapphire'. His words, not mine."

I grinned at that, then told Elijah, "You're wrong, you know."

He glanced up at me and said, "No, that really is your eye color. A bit overstated maybe, but otherwise, it's dead-on."

"Not about that. You were wrong when you said your conversational skills are nonexistent."

"You're easy to talk to," he said as he went back to studying the tabletop. "You're nice too, but I already knew that. You were so kind to me on one of the worst days of my life. I don't know if you remember. We were on that campin' trip with a bunch of people, and I was falling apart, because I'd just broken up with my boyfriend. You gave me your trailer so I could have someplace safe and comfortable to get myself together. I don't even know where you slept that night." I hadn't expected him to recall any of that, because he'd been deeply upset at the time.

"Breaking up with Colt must have been doubly tough, since you were living with his family, and his brother's husband is your legal guardian. Did things work out after that?"

"Colt and I are friends now, but I'm kinda dreading goin' home for the summer. He and his family are so nice to me, and they're making this big show of welcoming me back with open arms, but they're tryin' too hard, you know? It's just awkward. I'd rather stay here and take summer classes, but the dorms will be closed, so I have to go back."

"Why haven't you taken Alastair up on his offer? He really wants you to move into his house that's right off campus. It sounds like there are plenty of reasons to say yes to that."

"I just hate that I'm so dependent on people. After I ran away from home, I depended on Colt, and later on his family, to survive. Since I've been at Saithmore, Alastair has taken on a big brother role. You saw that for yourself when he sent me over here to make sure I ate something. I love him for it, and I don't think I would have made it through this school year without him, but I have to grow up sometime. I'll be nineteen soon, I'm not a kid anymore. And I kinda feel like acceptin' Alastair's offer is a step back on that whole road to adulthood, you know?"

"But needing and accepting a helping hand doesn't make you a kid. It just makes you human. And life is so much easier when we don't try to go it alone."

"But how would I ever pay him back? My part-time job on campus only provides pocket money. I couldn't pay my fair share of the utilities or anything else. I'd just be taking from him, with nothing to give in return."

"Alastair doesn't need or want your money, Elijah. What he wants is to know you're safe and happy. Just be his friend, and let Alastair be Alastair. He's a caretaker, like I said. He wants to know you'll be okay after he leaves. He wants to know we'll both be okay." Those last few words stirred up a lot of emotions, and I cleared my throat and frowned at my empty coffee cup.

Elijah sounded sympathetic as he said, "He told me he asked you to move into his apartment in San Francisco, and that you're considerin' it. I think you should say yes."

"I don't know about that. But you should take him up on his offer and stay at his house down here, at least during the summer when the dorms are closed."

"Why me and not you?"

"It's a lot more complicated in my case. He and I are romantically involved. Usually, moving in together is this major moment in a relationship, but of course he's not talking about that at all. We'd just be…well, roommates who sleep together, I guess. How's that supposed to work?"

"Exactly like that, a variation of friends with benefits. As for all the other things you're probably worryin' about, take the advice you just gave me and let Alastair be Alastair. I know you're not gonna take advantage of his generosity, and he knows that, too. If he's talking about opening up his home to you, it means he trusts and cares about you."

"Or maybe he just cares about everybody. I don't say that to downplay his generous offer, it's just an observation. He invited this guy named Gabriel, who's a friend of a friend, to stay in his apartment without hesitation when Alastair found out he was in a bad situation."

"It's one of the beautiful things about him," Elijah said. "Alastair truly cares about and wants to help everyone around him. I'm sure people must try to take advantage of him sometimes. But somehow, he's managed to hold on to the belief that people are good and worthy of his trust. I hope to God nothin' ever crushes that optimism."

There was something in his eyes as he said that, something dark and haunted. I knew in that instant that something awful had happened to Elijah in his past, and I knew it had shaken his trust and optimism to the core. Even without knowing what it was, my heart ached for him.

As if he knew he'd let something slip, he quickly steered our conversation toward lighter topics. When we finished our lunch, I said, "Can I give you my phone number? It's been great talking to you, Elijah, and I'd like to stay in touch."

"Sure." He grinned a little and said, "Score one for Alastair. This is exactly what he'd hoped would happen when he sent me to find you."

"Let's reward him with a lawn clipping sandwich and a fresh cup of coffee," I said cheerfully as I got up and began to gather our wrappers. "Although maybe you should take them to him. I'm trying not to be a distraction."

"Oh no, you need to deliver them in person," Elijah said. "A little distraction is just what Alastair needs."

*****

Alastair ended up working three hours longer than the designated drop-in tutoring session, to make sure everyone who needed help got it. After we delivered lunch, Elijah pulled a thick textbook from his backpack, and I picked out a dusty tome from the cluttered shelves of the student advisors' shared office. Then we tucked ourselves into a corner and tried not to be intrusive. Eventually, Elijah had to leave for his part-time job, but I stuck around.

I kept peeking at Alastair over the top of my book. He was tutoring freshmen in an intro to astronomy class, and he would explain the same thing over and over to an endless string of students, who ranged from overwhelmed, indifferent, and hopelessly confused to borderline hostile. I was beginning to think he was an absolute saint with an ungodly amount of patience. But then he pantomimed stabbing a particularly surly student in the back repeatedly, as if reenacting the shower scene from Psycho. I fought back a laugh and bit my lower lip when the student glared at me on his way out the door.

Finally, when it appeared no more desperate freshman were going to filter in, Alastair got up from the wooden swivel chair and stretched his arms over his head. "You must be bored out of your mind," he said. "I didn't expect it to take that long, and I apologize."

"I couldn't possibly be bored," I told him. "I not only had the freshman doofus parade to entertain me, I also got to watch you explain stuff so many times that even I understand it now. Ask me anything about the electromagnetic spectrum. Here's what I need to know, though. Have those students actually attended any classes all semester? Because I'm pretty sure you taught the entire course beginning to end for at least half of them."

"Freshmen sometimes assume an introductory astronomy course will be the easiest way to fulfill their science requirement, as if all they'll have to do is learn to identify the Big Dipper or some such nonsense. When they realize what's actually involved, it sends a lot of them into a tailspin."

"Do you have to do the student teaching thing as part of your PhD program? Because it seems like a pain in the ass."

"It's not required, but let's just say it's highly encouraged. Many people in my program will go on to teach at the university level, so this is a bit of practical experience."

"That's not you, though," I said, "so why go through this?"

"Because every once in a while, it rewards you profoundly." He pulled a royal blue V-neck sweater over his head, then adjusted the collar of his button-down shirt as he said, "On a handful of occasions, I've ignited a passion for astronomy in a student. It's the most wonderful feeling, knowing you helped shape and influence someone's future in a positive way." I thought that explanation was pure Alastair.

*****

We ate dinner at a little café just off-campus, and then we got in his fire engine red Acura, because he had something he was dying to show me. It was the same car he used for street racing, and its engine growled with pent-up power. He drove into the wooded foothills above the campus, while he shuffled his eclectic music collection and sang along badly and enthusiastically. After about twenty minutes, we reached the summit, and as we entered a clearing, I murmured, "Oh, wow."

The domed observatory before us looked like something from a Jules Verne novel, art deco futuristic, yet timelessly elegant. Alastair turned down the music and said, "This is the reason I chose to attend Saithmore."

There was one other car in the parking lot, and we parked beside the vintage Range Rover. "Rollie practically lives here," Alastair said as we walked up to the building. He had his own key, and as he unlocked the door, he said, "I'll see if I can convince him to give us a bit of privacy."

His friend was in the main part of the observatory, the huge room under the dome, which housed an enormous telescope. He was blasting Metallica while reading a comic book. When he saw us, he let his feet drop from the edge of the desk and yelled over the music, "Hey, y'all! I didn't know you were comin' by tonight!" He jumped up and wiped his hand on the front of his Han Solo T-shirt before sticking it out to me and saying, "Good to see ya again, Sawyer."

As we shook hands, I yelled, "You, too."

Alastair headed for the giant boom box on the desk and hit the off button, and Rollie opened his mouth wide, as if he was trying to pop his ears. Then he beamed at us and said, in his thick Louisiana drawl, "I suppose y'all are plannin' to get romantic up in here. Am I right? Well, the good news is, I just stocked the mini-fridge with wine coolers, you just go ahead and help yourselves. There's some leftovers in there, too. I don't know why I always order the macho nachos at Senor Steve's. Eight pounds of chips and cheese sauce is not an attainable goal! I'm just not macho enough for them, that's the bottom line. Anyway, y'all can help yourselves to those too, after you work up an appetite. And I know you will. Nudge nudge, wink wink! Hey, that reminds me. Do y'all need condoms? Because I have this big box of 'em from one of those discount warehouse places, and they're about to expire. I just gotta remember where I stashed 'em...."

"Thanks, mate, but we've got it covered," Alastair said with a smile. "Also, your discretion and subtlety are a lost art, truly."

"Got it covered," Rollie snorted. "Literally. Because you brought condoms, and they—"

Alastair interrupted with, "Wasn't there something you were supposed to do in San Jose tonight? A film festival or something?"

Rollie's eyes went wide behind his thick glasses. "Aw hell, how could I forget about the X-Men marathon? I even left my Wolverine claws at home."

"But your Beast slippers are right under the desk," Alastair said, "and they'll do in a pinch, won't they?"

"Oh yeah, you're right." He looked at his Boba Fett wristwatch, then dove under the desk and pulled out what looked like a pair of huge, hairy, blue feet. "I can just make it if I leave now. Have fun, you two! Don't do anythin' I wouldn't do!"

He ran out the door, and Alastair said, "I adore Rollie, but if he doesn't lose the cheese-stained nerd shirts, I'm afraid he's going to die a virgin."

"He's cute, under the weed-whacker haircut and ThinkGeek wardrobe. I bet he could find someone if he wanted to."

"He could, definitely. He just doesn't know that. When he turned thirty last month, it was a blow to his already shaky ego. I worry, because he's stopped trying to put himself out there and meet people." Alastair was tossing food wrappers into a plastic trash can as he said that. When he unearthed a partly eaten burrito on the desk, he murmured, "Crickey, that's foul."

"I wouldn't have guessed he's thirty," I said. "Is he close to graduating?"

"No. By that I mean, Rollie has two master's degrees and is working on a PhD. Once he finishes, he'll just start another. This is what he does, he hides out in academia. Ten years from now, he'll probably still be right here. With whatever this is." Alastair used a tissue to pick up a crushed, half-eaten something or other and sighed as he threw it in the can.

"Expensive habit. Who's footing the bill for the never-ending private university education?"

"His trust fund covers it. His family owns a restaurant empire in New Orleans."

"And they don't care that there's no end in sight to his studies?"

"I met them when I went back to Louisiana with Rollie for a family function, and I got the impression they don't particularly care what he does. They're just glad he's out from under foot."

"Now I see why he's hiding out here."

Once he got the shared workspace cleaned up, Alastair turned to me with a grin. "Alright, let's pretend we've just arrived. Sawyer, welcome to my sanctuary. Please ignore the fact that it smells like nacho cheese, and let me introduce you to Priscilla, queen of the foothills." He indicated the huge telescope with a sweep of his arm, then said, "Hang on, this needs a soundtrack." He pulled out his (latest) phone and started playing some dramatic classical music that I couldn't name.

When he turned a key on a vintage-looking control panel, a low rumbling sound echoed through the building, and the massive dome parted down the middle. The two halves stopped when they were about ten feet apart. Alastair stepped over to a computer terminal that had been retrofitted onto the archaic system with a jumble of cords and wires, and he quickly typed something. Then he raised his arm with a flourish, smiled at me, and jabbed the enter button.

My hands shot out and I crouched slightly when the entire room engaged with a jolt, then began to rotate slowly. A bark of laughter slipped from me, just because it was so unexpected. When the room came to a stop, Alastair typed another command, and the end of the telescope rose upward until it jutted through the gap in the dome. As he peered through the telescope's eyepiece and made a series of adjustments, he reminded me of a mad scientist, especially with that classical music playing in the background.

When he finished his preparations, he turned to me with a hopeful expression and asked, "Would you like to take a look?"

I joined him beside the brass telescope and peered through the eyepiece. Saturn and its rings looked luminous and dreamlike, and I murmured, "Holy shit."

He talked animatedly about the gas giant for a few minutes, and then he said, "May I show you more?"

"Yes! God yes. Please!"

For the next forty-five minutes, Alastair gave me a tour of the galaxy. He was passionate and excited as he talked about what I was seeing, and his enthusiasm was infectious. It felt a little like he was introducing me to his oldest friends.

He brought over a stool for me so I wouldn't have to stoop to look in the eyepiece and swung the computer terminal closer so he could keep realigning the dome and telescope. I put an arm around his waist and pulled him to me, and he sat on my lap as the words tumbled from him. He was so alive, his eyes sparkling with joy.

When the music stopped, Alastair blinked and looked around, as if coming back to earth. Then he colored a little and said, "I just rambled on for the duration of Dvorak's Symphony Number Nine. I apologize, I hadn't intended to go on that long."

He started to get up, but I pulled him back onto my lap and kissed him before saying, "I loved every minute of that. Thank you for sharing it with me."

His look of surprise gave way to a delighted smile. "You didn't find it tedious?"

I shook my head. "Your passion is a beautiful thing, and the subject matter was fascinating."

He draped his arms around my shoulders and kissed me again. Slow and tender soon gave way to hot and heavy. I ran my hands down his body and clutched him to me.

We ended up having sex beside the big telescope, on a pile of our clothes. Afterwards, Alastair curled up in my arms, and I covered him with my leather jacket. It was kind of chilly in the observatory, but we didn't want to get dressed. Instead, we just snuggled closer and watched the night sky through the open dome.

After a while, I whispered, "Okay." When he looked up at me, I said, "I'll be your roommate for the next few months. I want to spend as much time as possible with you before you have to go. I'm not sure about staying in the apartment after you return to the UK, though."

"I'm so glad you're moving in! What you do long-term is your call, of course. I just need to know you're going to be alright, Sawyer, and it breaks my heart to think about you moving back to your father's house when I'm gone."

"I won't. I'll find my own place, after…."

He looked in my eyes, and I pulled up a smile. I tried to pretend I could keep it casual and say goodbye to him in a few months, and that I'd be okay after he left.

Yeah, right.

Chapter Nine

It didn't take long to pack. All my clothes, including my secret wardrobe, fit in one suitcase and a duffle bag. I studied my childhood belongings, trying to decide what, if anything, had sentimental value. I'd never been someone who assigned much value to stuff though, so in the end, all I packed were a stack of books I'd loved as a kid.

I had mixed feelings about taking the only photo I had of me and both my parents. Since it depressed me a little every time I looked at it, a case could certainly be made for leaving it behind. But, for reasons I couldn't explain, that made me feel guilty. As a compromise, I removed the four-by-six snapshot from its frame and slid it between the yellowed pages of one of my books. Even if it seemed like something I should hold on to, I didn't need to see it all the time.

I slung my backpack over my shoulder and looked around the drab little room. I'd missed it when I was overseas, but since then, I'd realized what I'd been missing was the idea of home, not the actual place. And now, I was putting it behind me. I'd visit my dad of course, maybe spend an occasional awkward afternoon sitting in front of the TV watching a game with him, but this wasn't home anymore. Maybe it never really had been.

The staircase creaked as I carried my suitcase and duffle bag to the ground floor. My dad was in his usual spot, parked in the recliner in front of the TV. He'd been on the phone with one of his Army buddies when I'd come home that morning, so I hadn't told him I was moving out.

He glanced at me as I paused in the doorway, and when he saw my luggage, he said, "Tell me you've re-enlisted."

"No, Dad. I'm never going back. I've told you that a hundred times."

"I know what you told me, but I was hoping you'd come to your senses."

I put down my bags and said, "I was miserable in the Army. I don't expect you to care or understand, but it was the worst experience of my life."

"You're soft, that's the problem." There was no malice in his voice. To him, he was simply stating a fact. "All they had you doin' was fixing cars. What was so hard about that?"

"I just didn't belong there. Don't you see? Your experience in the Army and mine were very, very different. For one thing, you actually wanted to be there. I only enlisted out of a sense of obligation."

"You could've fit in if you wanted to," he said, knitting his thick brows. "You barely gave it a chance."

"I gave it four years of my life! I put aside everything that mattered to me, including school, and I tried, Dad. I know you don't see that. To you, it all just comes down to the fact that I walked away after my commitment was up. But there were things that happened while I was there, things you don't know about, and I had to get away from a bad situation. Although even without that, I wouldn't have re-enlisted anyway, because it wasn't where I belonged."

Why was I bothering? He never heard me, no matter what I said. I picked up my luggage and told him, "Anyway, I'm going to get out of your hair. I'm moving to a place here in the city. I wrote the address on that notepad on the refrigerator. I wrote down my cell number, too. I mean, you already have it, and it's not changing. But I just wanted to put it there so you can call me if you need anything."

As I started to head to the door, my father asked, "Did Tracy Garcia hurt you?"

At first, I was sure I'd misunderstood, and I turned back to him and stammered, "What?"

"Did he force himself on you?"

"How…how could you possibly know about Tracy?" The conversation felt surreal all of a sudden.

"You came home with his name tattooed over your heart. What, you think I didn't notice?"

"But how did you know that was his name, and not some girl's?"

"Well, for one thing, I know that because you're gay, Sawyer."

A cold feeling trickled down my spine as I waited for the other shoe to drop, but nothing happened. I just stood there dumbly, holding my heavy luggage, and stared at my father. When he didn't say anything else, I asked him, "Okay, so why'd you think the name was Tracy Garcia's, and not some other guy's?"

"When you came home on leave, you mentioned Garcia a couple times. You tried to act like there was nothing between you, but I knew right away something was up. I figured you had a crush on him. Since he was your commanding officer, I assumed nothing would come of it. I knew Tracy's father, we served together. He was an honorable man, so I assumed Tracy would be, too. I never thought he'd cross that line with you. But then, when you moved back here with that tattoo, I got the picture."

"Why didn't you say something?"

"What was there to say?"

"Anything!"

He shrugged and said, "We would have just ended up fighting if I brought it up, because I was pissed off about the whole thing. It was wrong that Tracy got involved with someone under his command, not to mention a direct violation of Army regulations. You should have known better, too. But it obviously had ended, since you moved back home and never mentioned him again. I didn't see the point in stirring things up after the fact."

"So, why are you bringing it up now?"

"Well, when you said you didn't re-enlist because you had to get away from a bad situation, my first thought was Tracy. It made me wonder if maybe he coerced you, or took advantage of you in some way. If he did, I'm calling his commanding officer, because that's unacceptable."

"Please don't make trouble for him. Tracy never did anything like that," I said. "By bad situation, I meant that I was in love with him, but it wasn't mutual. I wasn't forced into anything. He made a mistake by getting involved with me. We both made a mistake. But he's still an excellent officer and a good man." Why was I defending him?

"An excellent officer wouldn't have gotten involved with someone under his command."

Apparently my dad was done with the conversation, because he turned back to the TV. After an awkward pause, I said, "You were so angry when you caught me kissing a boy at fifteen. Now you're talking about the fact that I'm gay like it's no big deal."

"I know I didn't handle that right," he said, staring at the screen. "It caught me by surprise. But I've had a lot of years to think about it, and…I dunno. I guess I've gotten used to the idea."

"You know, you probably could have told me that at some point."

"I just did." He flipped through the channels with his worn-out remote while I frowned at his profile.

The throaty rumble of Kai's Impala announced my friend's arrival, and I said, "I have to go, but I'll talk to you soon, okay?"

He didn't look at me. All he said was, "Take care of yourself, Sawyer." I hesitated for a moment, then headed for the door.

Kai was unlocking the trunk when I joined him, and he said, "Happy 'moving in with a guy you've known a week' day."

"Thanks for helping me out," I said as I heaved my suitcase into the trunk. "Although, as I explained, Alastair and I aren't moving in together, not in the way you're suggesting. I've just agreed to be his roommate for the next few months."

"Roommates with a guy you happen to be sleeping with."

"Yup, roommates with benefits. Is that so weird?"

"A little bit." After I loaded my backpack and duffle bag, Kai slammed the trunk shut, then turned to look at me and asked, "You okay, Sawyer?"

"Yeah. I just had a totally unexpected conversation with my dad. I'll tell you about it when we get to the apartment." He got behind the wheel, and I told him, "Just a sec. There's one more thing I need to do before we take off."

I'd already texted Sherry that morning to tell her I was moving out, and when she answered my knock, I gave her a hug and said, "I don't have to tell you I'll keep in touch."

"Of course you don't! We're family, Sawyer, so it's a given. And moving out is a good thing," she said as she squeezed me tightly and rubbed my back. "Maybe your dad won't take you for granted once he realizes how much he misses you." I doubted he'd miss me much at all, but whatever.

"Keep an eye on him, okay? Let me know if he needs anything."

"Believe it or not, I already do that. You don't have to worry about him." I kissed her forehead before jogging down the stairs.

I followed the Impala across town on my motorcycle, and then we both pulled into the underground garage beneath the tall, white apartment building, using the passcode Alastair had given me. Kai insisted on carrying my duffle bag as we headed for the elevator, even though I told him he didn't have to. "Kai's Moving Company is full-service, there when you need us with a big trunk and a helping hand."

"Well, thank you. I'm sorry to bother you with this. I just couldn't get my stuff here on my Harley."

"It's no problem at all. Usually, when people ask for help moving, it involves a whole day of schlepping heavy furniture and reconsidering the friendship. This is a piece of cake in comparison."

"Yeah, lucky for you, my whole life fits in three bags."

Gabriel let us in with an enthusiastic welcome after we rode the elevator to the top floor. He was barefoot and wore a pair of black leggings with a long, chunky sweater that dipped off one shoulder. I once again admired how stylishly and effortlessly he expressed himself.

Kai looked around the apartment and muttered, "Holy shit. You're movin' on up, Mr. Jefferson."

Alastair burst from the kitchen. He was wearing a navy blue apron that looked like it had taken a direct hit from an exploding bag of flour, and he exclaimed, "I'm so glad you're here! I was trying to bake you something, but my first go had issues. This time, I'm actually using a recipe."

He went to hug me, then looked down at himself and said, "Oops, don't want to get you messy."

But I dropped the suitcase, pulled him to me and kissed him, then said, "Never let that stop you."

He put his arms around me and gave me a big smile before directing it at my best friend. "Hello, Kai. Can you stay for coffee and attempted baked goods?"

"Sure. Where do you want this?" Kai indicated the duffle bag.

Alastair's eyes searched mine, and he said, "We never talked about this part, but are you okay with sharing the master bedroom with me? Gabriel's in the spare room."

"Shit, I'm in the way, aren't I?" Gabriel said. "I'm sorry. I'll move back home to Martinsville and commute to my job at the club. You probably never intended for me to stay this long anyway."

"You're not in the way as far as I'm concerned," I told him. "Actually, the sleeping arrangements sound perfect."

"Like I said before, you can stay as long as you'd like, Gabriel," Alastair said. "It's much too far to drive back and forth for work. Plus, I like having you here, and I'm glad you're someplace safe with no risk of your ex discovering you."

"You sure?" When Alastair assured him he was welcome, Gabriel looked relieved. He then glanced at Kai, who looked perplexed, and said, "Long story short, never cross a sadistic Dom, especially if he's also a criminal. My life is a little…complicated right now, and Alastair offered me a safe haven."

Kai said. "Is there anything I can do to help?"

"I don't think there's anything anyone can do." Gabriel pulled up a smile and said, "It's nice of you to offer, though."

The four of us moved to the kitchen, and while Alastair pulled a loaf of something out of the oven, I went to work with the espresso machine. Even though it had been years since I'd worked at that coffee house, I fell right back into the old rhythm and quickly and efficiently produced four lattes (per everyone's request), then took an extra minute to line up the drinks and draw a picture across their surfaces with foamed milk, adding a few details by using the tip of a knife to draw with a bit of the dark espresso. Kai grinned at my rendering of San Francisco's skyline and snapped a picture with his phone as he said, "You haven't lost your touch. I still remember what you taught me, by the way. I even get to practice a bit, since Nana and her husband gave Jessie and me a fancy espresso machine as a wedding present."

"It's nice to know some good came out of my totally useless skill," I said as Alastair leaned around me to get a look at the coffees and flashed me a big smile.

The four of us settled in at the small, round table in the breakfast nook. As I polished off a few slices of the cranberry-orange loaf Alastair had made (which he kept apologizing for, even though I liked the fact that it was on the tart side), I told my friends about the conversation I'd had with my father. "I agonized for years about how to talk to my dad about the fact that I'm gay," I said. "Then finally, he brings it up and is just like, 'yeah, I got used to it.' He couldn't have said something sooner? And why did we have the longest, most significant conversation of our lives as I'm moving out, literally headed to the door? Not like we didn't have a million opportunities to talk over the last year."

"Maybe that was intentional on his part," Kai said. "Timing it like that meant it couldn't turn into a huge discussion or an argument."

I thought about that, then said, "Makes sense, actually. Like, 'let's talk about this, but only for ninety seconds and then I'm just done.' I mean, it's kind of nuts, but I could see my dad using that logic."

"At least he seemed concerned and wanted to make sure your ex didn't hurt you," Gabriel said, pushing his long, dark hair behind his shoulder.

"Well, kind of. He didn't think to check and see how I was when he realized I'd gotten involved with my C.O., tattooed his name on my body, and later broke up with him. There were plenty of clues that I was having a hard time those first six months I was back." I sighed and added, "But, whatever."

"Commanding Officer," Gabriel muttered. When I glanced at him, he grinned and said, "Just figured out what C.O. stands for."

I smiled at him, then reached for another slice of the cranberry loaf and said, "Anyway, enough about my dad."

Gabriel nodded in agreement. "Exactly, no need to dwell on the negative. This is the start of a whole new chapter of your life: new home, new job, new boyfriend. You have so many positive things to focus on!"

"I do."

As I took a big bite of the cranberry loaf, Gabriel added, "Speaking of work, can we take some time today to practice our routines? Also, we could figure out what to wear if you haven't already."

At that last sentence, I felt a pang of anxiety and glanced at Kai, who was obliviously sipping his latte. And then I got mad at myself. Why the hell was I keeping a secret from him? Right then and there, I made a decision.

Since my mouth was full, I held up a finger in a 'just a minute' gesture, then went and retrieved my duffle bag from the living room. When I sat back down, I took a deep breath, unzipped the bag and told my best friend, "Like Gabriel said, today's a fresh start for me in a lot of ways. In that spirit…well, there's something I want you to know about me."

I pulled out a corset and some stockings and tossed them on top of the bag, and Kai guessed, "You're a drag queen?"

"No, although a couple drag queens were the ones who initially encouraged me to stop hiding this side of myself. Gabriel has been helping, too. He suggested participating in amateur night at the burlesque club because he thought it'd be empowering. I stripped down to this."

"Do you have a lingerie fetish?" Kai looked like he was trying to understand.

"Not at all. I just tend to use lingerie as an outlet for this side of me because I can wear it under my clothes and hide it easily."

"I get it. But what I don't get is why you'd keep it a secret from me," Kai said. "You had to know I'd never judge you."

"I did know that. At first, I hid it from everyone, not just you. And when I started to let others see this side of me...I don't know. I guess I figured you'd ask why I do this. I've never been able to answer that question for myself, so I knew I wouldn't be able to answer it for you, either." I stuffed the clothes back into the bag and zipped it shut.

"I don't need an explanation, Sawyer. It's obviously something that's important to you, and that's all I need to know."

I said, "It's a relief to have it out in the open. I mean, I'm not going to start dressing like that on a regular basis, but it feels good knowing it's not this big secret anymore."

"Why not?" That question came from Alastair, who'd been following the conversation intently.

"Well...because people don't understand. Plus, on a guy with my build, it's just awkward."

Gabriel asked, "What does your build have to do with it?"

"Well, look at you, and look at me. Whenever I see pictures of androgynous models, they're all small and thin, just like you are, and the clothes work as part of their overall look. But I'm this huge guy, six-four with big arms and shoulders. How would it look if I put on a skirt?"

"Like you're a total badass who doesn't give a shit what anyone thinks," Kai said.

Gabriel told me, "I get weird looks and rude comments from people every day of my life. It makes no difference that I'm small and slender. I get what you're saying though, about the media only celebrating a certain body type when it comes to androgyny. I see the photos too, of the slender waifs with long hair who look like they weigh eighty pounds soaking wet. But it's the same as any other beauty ideal perpetuated by the media. It's narrow, and biased, and it holds all of us to impossible standards. It's also wrong. Beauty doesn't come in one size or shape or body type. And I'm here to tell you you're absolutely gorgeous, Sawyer, no matter what you choose to wear."

I mumbled an embarrassed thank you, and Kai said, "If certain clothes feel right to you, screw other people's opinions."

"I wish I could adopt that attitude, but I'm just not there yet," I admitted.

"One step at a time, love," Alastair said. "For the first time in your life, you're in a safe, supportive home environment, and you can be yourself here. Maybe it'll help you explore and become more comfortable with that other side of you."

That hadn't occurred to me until he said it. I'd found a place where I didn't have to hide. Just the thought of it was exhilarating. I leaned over and kissed him, then rested my forehead against Alastair's as I whispered, "Thank you."

Chapter Ten

Three Weeks Later

How was he just twenty? I watched Alastair as he led a team of people on a tour of the firehouse. He was wearing a dark blue suit that fit like it was made for him (and, okay, it probably had been), and carried himself with poise, confidence and an unmistakable air of authority. Alastair was in charge. Period. The architects and structural engineers who trailed after him clearly knew that. Everyone did.

I thought it was sexy as hell. He glanced over at me, and I gave him a smile that I hoped let him know exactly what I intended to do to him later, when I got him home and out of that suit. Apparently, my message was received, because that perfect composure faltered for just a moment. A bit of color rose in his cheeks, and he grinned flirtatiously before pulling his game face back up and resuming the tour.

"So that's what that expression means."

I turned to Darwin, who stood between me and a large table saw, and asked, "What expression?"

He slid his yellow hardhat back a couple inches and said, "Eye fucking. I now have a visual to go with that term, after that thing you and Alastair just did."

"That obvious, huh?"

"Uh, yeah. Not that there's anything wrong with it. You two are great together."

"Today, we're pretty much the prince and the pauper," I said, gesturing at the dusty, faded T-shirt, ripped jeans and work boots that had become my uniform while volunteering at the firehouse.

Because Alastair and Nana had paid cash for the property, the sale had gone through quickly, and we'd gotten to work right away. Even before the sale was finalized, Alastair and his lawyers had begun hiring experts, drafting plans, and initiating the licensing process that would eventually allow the firehouse to be used as a shelter for homeless LGBT kids. Then, once the building was officially Nana's and Alastair's, a team of us had gone to work on renovations. It would probably be months before the paperwork went through and the shelter could open its doors, but we'd all been eager to start making the place both safe and welcoming for the kids it would house one day. Since my job at the burlesque club was very part time, it felt good to do something productive with my days.

Darwin, on the other hand, had very little free time, but he still showed up at the firehouse daily, even if all he could manage was an hour or two. He worked four part-time jobs and told me he was saving up so he could afford top surgery. I'd been pretty sure I knew what that meant, but I'd looked it up anyway and confirmed he was talking about a mastectomy, which was part of his female-to-male transition. It occurred to me later on that I probably could have just asked him, but then, I figured he already got a lot of dumb questions from people and I didn't want to add to it.

Despite working constantly, saving money was challenging for him, because a lot of his income went to testosterone treatments, which his bare-bones insurance refused to cover. He was living with Nana, who was his boyfriend's great-grandmother, and she'd offered to pay for the surgery, but he was determined to do it on his own, fulfilling a promise he'd made to himself as a child. I admired the hell out of him, for a lot of reasons.

I'd been teaching him how to do some basic construction and was continually astonished at how quickly and easily he picked up everything I showed him. It wasn't news to me that he was a bright kid, but I soon realized he was flat-out brilliant. Besides being able to learn effortlessly, he also had a love of science in all its forms, and he'd entertain me with random, off-beat stories while we worked, on topics ranging from entomology to physics to marine biology.

When I asked him about his plans for college (because that was clearly where he belonged), he'd told me it had to be put on the back burner. His priority was working and saving money for his surgery, and he was driven to achieve that goal. When I told him I'd recently enrolled in an online college program, he'd thrown his arms around me and said he was proud of me. I'd been so touched by that.

A big guy named Guillermo, who was part of the construction team Nana had hired, called, "Hey Sawyer and Mini Sawyer, the fellas and me are gonna grab a late dinner. You wanna join us?"

We both thanked him and declined the offer, and after he took off, Darwin glanced at me and said, "If I was bothering you, you'd tell me, right?"

"Where did that come from?"

"That Mini Sawyer comment. I guess it's pretty obvious to everyone that I've latched on to you. I just hope it isn't annoying."

"It's not at all. We're friends, Darwin, and I'm glad you're spending time with me."

"I am, too. You make me feel safe in this environment," he said quietly, looking down at his slender hands as he picked at the end of a two-by-four. "And you're a patient teacher. It doesn't seem to bother you that I don't know how to do, well, pretty much anything. Plus, it's been nice to have a male role model. I've always wanted that."

I grinned a little and said, "I'm no role model. But hey, if you want to learn to make a good cup of coffee or how to build something, then I might be of some use."

"Why would you think you aren't a role model?"

"Because I've got absolutely nothing figured out. I'm working part-time at a burlesque club, I only went back to school a couple weeks ago with no real plan other than 'get an education', and I have no idea what my future holds. My life is one big question mark."

"But I admire you, Sawyer. I spend a lot of time trying to figure out what it means to be a man, for obvious reasons. I'm also trying to find a balance between who I was and who I'll become," he said, glancing at me from beneath his hair. "You're strong and tough, but you're also not afraid to let a bit of vulnerability show through. I think that's a beautiful thing about you, and it's something I aspire to."

"I admire you, too. Not only are you focused, scary-smart and a hell of a nice guy, you're also one of the strongest people I've ever met."

"You think I'm strong?"

"I know you are." He smiled shyly before turning to the table saw and cutting a floor board exactly like I'd shown him.

Alastair joined us a few minutes later. He leaned over a stack of lumber and kissed me, and I asked, "How'd the walk-through go?"

He loosened his pale blue tie as he said, "Quite well. The seismic retrofitting had all been done to code, confirming our initial inspection. My lead structural engineer still thinks the additional reinforcements I've requested are overkill, but I'm proceeding anyway. This isn't the time to cheap out, as they say. We need this to be a safe place for our kids, in every sense of the word."

I touched his cheek and told him, "You're a wonderful man, Alastair."

"I'm just a bloke trying to do the right thing."

"You're so much more than that." I kissed him again, and when I straightened up, I said, "Sorry, I got you dirty," as I indicated a smudge on his cheek. "You know, you and I look like we're from different planets right now. Yours is way more posh and populated primarily by tailors and dry cleaners."

"But you know when we come back here tomorrow, I'll be wearing jeans and rolling up my sleeves just like everyone else. The suit's just for those times when I need to come across as something other than a college student."

"You totally pull it off. When I put on a suit, I just look like a high school football player on his way to the winter formal."

"Oh no, that's most definitely not what you look like in a suit," he said with a wide grin, as his gaze strayed down my body.

I chuckled at that. "The only time you ever see me in one is when I'm about to strip down to lingerie in front of a couple hundred people, so granted, your perspective might be slightly skewed."

"Entirely possible."

He'd circled the pile of wood and started to reach for me, but I said, "Hold that thought while I go and change. You might not care what hugging me would do to your outfit, but I do."

I started to turn from him, but he grabbed my arm, pulled me back to him, and kissed me deeply as he ran his hand down my back. When we broke apart, he looked up at me with amusement in his eyes and said, "My dry cleaner is a bloody alchemist. There's nothing we can do to this suit that he can't remedy. I once wore it to the observatory after a meeting with the president of the university and accidentally sat on a forgotten plate of Rollie's macho nachos. If the dry cleaner could remedy that, he can certainly handle a bit of construction dust."

"Well, in that case." I pulled him against me and kissed him passionately.

"Now that's what I like to see!" We glanced around at the sound of Nana's voice, and after a moment I realized she was poking her head out of the hole in the ceiling beside one of the brass poles. "Don't stop on my account, boys!"

My mouth fell open as the tiny octogenarian hoisted up her slim-fitting wool skirt, wound her legs around the pole and slid down. The skirt rode up and got turned inside-out on the way down, so she arrived on the ground level with her pantyhose and a racy pair of red bikini underwear on full display. The skirt engulfed her head and torso like a condom, and she held her arms straight up and spun around as she exclaimed, "What the hell happened? Is this one of them wardrobe malfunctions? I feel like I'm in one of those things we put on Tom Selleck to keep him from licking his nuts!"

I fought back a laugh as Alastair and I exchanged baffled looks. Meanwhile, Darwin rushed to Nana's aid and told us, "Tom Selleck is the name of Nana's dog. He had to be put in a plastic cone recently when he humped something he shouldn't have and needed stitches. He's fixed, by the way, so technically, he doesn't have nuts. But that doesn't seem to have curbed his sex drive in the slightest."

"Morbid curiosity is forcing me to ask this question," Alastair said. "With what exactly did he try to procreate?"

"A big crab. We have a few as pets in the backyard, and one got out of its enclosure. I don't know what Tommy was thinking. He didn't even have it by the right end!"

"Pet crabs?" I asked.

"Long story." Darwin hesitated before gingerly grabbing the skirt's hem and yanking it down, so it once again reached Nana's calves.

"Thanks sweet pea," she told him, smoothing her white hair, which was up in a bun. "You're a peach. Want to go out and do some politics with me tonight? You too, Sawyer and Alastair. I could use some backup and a fast car, just in case my plans go awry and I need to make a break for it."

"Um...define *do some politics*, Nana," Darwin said.

"Well see, my neighbor, that red-faced blowhard Humpington across the street, has decided to run for mayor. He's a homophobic yahoo with a giant ego and a tiny brain, and no way should he be trusted with any decision beyond whether to buy his condoms in extra-small, elfin, or petite. My grandson Dante tells me it's illegal to tamper with Humpington's campaign posters and made me promise I'd leave them alone. There's no rule that says I can't put up my own signs, though."

Darwin asked, "But isn't it kind of early for a covert operation? It's barely eight p.m."

"When you skulk around doing shit in the middle of the night, that's when people get suspicious," Nana told him. "Here's what you do when you want to get away with something: act like what you're doing is perfectly normal and you have every right to be there. We're just out putting up some campaign posters. Nothing to see here. I obviously don't want to attract the attention of Humpington's minions, but we don't have to go deep cover, either."

"Good point. And I'm in, of course," Darwin said.

Alastair's eyes lit up. "Count me in as well! A bit of civil disobedience sounds like a fantastic way to spend an evening."

From somewhere nearby, Roger asked, "What are you up to, Gromit?" A moment later, he slid down one of the fire poles, put his hands on his hips, and shot his friend a look. He'd volunteered to help with painting, and even though he'd been working all day, the white coveralls he wore were pristine.

"You'll see, since I know you'll never agree to sit this one out," Alastair told him.

"Speaking of sitting it out, my hubby's gonna be sad he missed this," Nana said. "He's in New York helping his friend Ignacio, who's having an art show. I'm sure I'll think of some more fun for us when he gets back, though."

Nana retrieved her purse while I quickly swapped out my T-shirt for a clean one. As we followed her to the back door, Darwin said, "We have to swing by and pick up my boyfriend. Josh can't miss this! He's studying for finals tonight, but I'm sure he could use a break."

"Miss what, exactly?" Roger wanted to know.

"We're just putting up a few campaign posters for the upcoming election," Alastair said, trying and failing to suppress a grin.

Roger frowned at him. "Why don't I believe you, Gromit?"

Nana told Darwin, "Be sure Josh doesn't say anything to his dads. You know I love my grandson Vincent and his sweet husband Trevor, but I don't think they'd be onboard with this plan of mine. Plus, they might go blabbing to my grandson Dante, and he's definitely a buzzkill."

We stopped by the back door, and I picked up a cardboard carton for Nana that was maybe eight inches thick and three feet square. Alastair grabbed a bag containing wooden pickets, tape, and various other supplies, and said, "If I'm driving the getaway car, I hope that box fits in the boot. Between all of us and Josh, it's going to be a bit cramped."

"I could call Jessie and ask him to bring the limo," Nana said, "but since it's painted with a big rainbow, Humpington will know it's me if any of his minions spot it. Not that I care about pissing him off, I can take the heat! But I'd rather remain in stealth mode for as long as possible, just to rattle his cage."

Alastair told her, "We'll make it work. May I ask what he did to anger you, Nana?"

"The jackass lives across the street from me, like I said, and we got a long history. First, he stole a gay pride flag from the front of my house. Later on, he removed some dick balloons from my porch, because the man is cockphobic. But the thing I absolutely cannot forgive him for is the hateful comments he made to my face a few days ago, about someone I love." She glanced at Darwin, then quickly looked away. He was texting and didn't notice. Nana added, "I already knew Humpington was a hateful person, and that just confirmed it. I'm not going to stand by and let a bigot run our city!"

"Let's do this," I said, and we headed for Alastsair's Acura.

Roger insisted on driving, and Nana rode shotgun. That meant Alastair and I were stuffed in the less-than-spacious backseat with Darwin (who for some reason had decided to keep wearing his yellow hardhat). I wasn't complaining. When I put my arm around Alastair's shoulders, he snuggled even closer to me and gave me the sweetest smile.

We drove across town to Trevor and Vincent's place, and their son Josh met us out front. I glanced up at the house and grinned, remembering that night a month ago when Alastair came into my life. My whole world had transformed completely since then. The biggest change was that I was truly happy, which had never really been the case before. I nuzzled his shoulder, and when Alastair climbed onto my lap to make room for our newcomer, I wrapped my arms around him.

"I told my dads I had to help Nana with a project," Josh said as he squeezed into the backseat. "They assumed I meant the firehouse. It should be noted that I didn't actually lie to them." Josh looked around at all of us and grinned. "Interesting choice of outfits on pretty much everyone's part. You're basically a cop away from forming a Village People tribute band. And hey, one might be added to the mix before this night is through."

As we pulled away from the curb, Alastair ran his fingers through my short hair and kissed me before curling up in my arms. "We need another getaway," he told me.

"How about Seattle? It's near the top of my list. We could fly up on Saturday night, after you finish your shift at the club."

I said, "Sounds fun. My friends I told you about, the ones who moonlight as drag queens, have been up there working for the last month. We could have dinner with them, and in the process, we might actually end up seeing one of the places we visit." After San Diego, we'd spent a couple days in New York City, then two more in Chicago. For the most part, we'd spent those trips in our hotel rooms, alternately having sex and talking for hours. In other words, they were absolutely perfect vacations.

"We see all the places we visit," Alastair said. "We had lovely views of New York's and Chicago's skylines from our beds."

"Can't argue with that." I held him to me and my lips met his. Kissing Alastair was one of life's most perfect experiences. I let myself get swept up in the warmth, the pleasure, his sweet taste, as everything else fell away.

"Nobody would fault me if I turned a garden hose on you two. Clearly, I've been left with no other alternatives." Roger's voice startled us, and we both sat up a bit and looked around.

We'd failed to notice that the car had been parked on a busy street. Our companions stood on the sidewalk, peering at us through the open door. "We should've just let them go at it," Nana said. "I think they're adorable."

"They can take a break from the tonsil hockey, right now we've got a job to do." Roger headed around to the back of the car, and we tumbled out and followed him.

The big box jutted from the open trunk. I was surprised it was still there, since all that held it in place was a flimsy bungee cord. While Roger took out a pocketknife and slit the cardboard, I looked around us. No fewer than half a dozen signs for Nana's arch enemy dotted the intersection. It turned out his name was actually Richard Huntington, despite what Nana called him.

His slick, obviously expensive signs were red, white and blue, and they featured a picture of a bald eagle and a tacky portrait of the candidate. His photo was so retouched that he looked like he was made of plastic, but there wasn't enough photoshopping in all the world to make his smarmy grin look sincere. My dislike for him instantly multiplied. There were a few other campaign signs around the intersection as well, even though it was early in the election season, and they were modest by comparison. It was clear Huntington's strategy was to win by plastering the city and outspending every other candidate.

Alastair beamed at me as he held up a sign, and I had to chuckle. Nana had printed up a totally unretouched and not at all flattering picture of a yelling and red-faced Huntington with his toupee flapping in the breeze, under the slogan 'Let's All Lick Dick'. I liked her style.

After we put up a poster beside each of his, Nana stepped back and admired her handiwork. "I know his minions are just gonna tear 'em right down, but I have a feeling they'll live on anyway." Across the intersection, a group of pedestrians were laughing and taking pictures of our signs with their phones.

We worked our way around town for the next couple hours. Sure enough, by the time we backtracked to that original intersection, all our posters were gone. "They're showing up on the internet," Josh said with a grin as he scrolled on his phone. He paused to read something, then said, "Turns out, Huntington is hosting a big fundraiser downtown tonight. It's in the George Washington Ballroom of the Hotel Liberty. I can only assume he stuffed it with bald eagles to bring the 'Merica theme home. Hey, we should put up some posters out front."

Nana clapped her hands. "That's exactly what we need to do! We'll line the street! Everywhere you look, nothing but Dick, Dick, Dick! Humpington's going to bust a nut!"

I fought back a laugh and said, "Um, do you know what that expression means, Nana?"

"Sure! It's like, flip your lid. It means he'll be really upset," she said. I couldn't quite make myself explain its actual definition to her. Alastair just chuckled, pulled out his phone and started searching for something. By the glint in his eye, I knew he was up to something, but I decided to be surprised instead of asking about it.

When we arrived at the hotel, Nana decided she needed to sneak in and take a look at the fundraiser, and Alastair muttered, "Knew it."

Roger frowned as Nana leapt from the car, and he turned to us and said, "You lot go after her, make sure she doesn't do anything that'll wind 'er up in the slammer. I can't park in this red zone, so I'll move the car, then start on the posters." Darwin and Josh were right behind Nana, and Alastair and I followed them.

The fundraiser was being held on the top floor of the lavish hotel. Nana had made a beeline for the elevators and was immediately intercepted by security. By the time we caught up with her, the three guards where just about to haul her out of the building, and she was kicking up a fuss.

Alastair stepped in and handed one of the men his ID and a business card as he said, "Apologies, lads. Gran forgot to stop off at the front desk for our keys. Be a dear and fetch them for her, would you?" Despite being rumpled and covered in dust, Alastair exuded confidence, and after a moment, the scowling guard walked over to the desk and gave the clerk the card and identification.

Less than a minute later, the desk clerk literally ran over to us. She began ass-kissing and apologizing like nobody's business as she handed Alastair a pair of keys and his ID. He thanked her and said, "My colleague Roger Foster will be joining us in a few minutes. You'll recognize him because he's wearing a pair of white coveralls. Bit eccentric, that one. Do make sure he's allowed through without incident, will you?" The clerk assured him they would.

We stepped onto the elevator and the doors slid shut. As Alastair used the key to access the top floor, Josh asked, "Okay, so how did you manage that?"

"I reserved the presidential suite online on the way over here. I've been to functions at this hotel before, so I knew they don't let you on the lift without either a room key or an invitation to an event."

While he fastened the top button of his white shirt, straightened his tie and dusted off his suit jacket, I said, "Fuck it, I'm not even going to tuck in my shirt. Not like I stand a chance in hell of blending in anyway." I did turn to check my reflection in the mirrored wall and grinned when I realized I was wearing a T-shirt from the Indian Motorcycle Company. That made Josh's earlier Village

People comment even funnier, and when I chuckled belatedly, Alastair glanced at me and grinned.

"So, you just spent hundreds of dollars on a suite, just so we could access the elevator?" Darwin asked. "I mean, way to think on your feet. But isn't that a bit wasteful?"

"It would be if we didn't use the suite, but I have every intention of enjoying it. After Nana gets a chance to spy on her foe, you're all invited to a hearty supper, provided by room service. We've earned it, after a long day at the firehouse and a full evening of freedom fighting. And you should all plan to spend the night, if you can. We'll turn it into a slumber party."

Nana exclaimed, "Hot damn, count me in!"

When we reached the top floor, we encountered another obstacle. Two grim security guards were stationed at the door to the ballroom, checking invitations, even though the staff downstairs would have already done that. Alastair muttered, "Dick has some serious trust issues. A mayoral candidate does not need this level of security for a fundraiser."

"It's to keep out the riffraff," Darwin said, knitting his brows as he crossed his arms over his chest. "You know, everyone who's not like them. I know that type all too well. In fact, I was raised by a couple of 'em. But I know how to get us in there, so come with me."

I assumed he'd lead us to the kitchen, where we'd all don cater-waiter uniforms, like they did in pretty much every movie involving someone trying to sneak into an event. Instead, he led us through an unmarked door into a no-frills corridor used by the hotel staff. It was a huge contrast to the posh, gold-toned public spaces the guests enjoyed.

"The nice thing about working a crapload of miscellaneous part-time jobs," he said, "is that you get to peek behind the scenes at a lot of different places. For four months last year, I worked maintenance at this hotel's sister property. I thought it was interesting that every ballroom came equipped with one of these." We stepped into a small room that was basically an electrical closet. "This is the nerve center for the ballroom. Lighting, heating and air conditioning, and music are all controlled from here. Then there's this, which seemed odd to me at first." He activated a little black and white screen, which showed the ballroom, and spun a dial, which piped in the ambient noise from the fundraiser.

"Weird. I mean, I know every hotel has security cameras," Josh said, "but why would you have this redundant security system?"

"It's actually not for security, it's for the staff." Darwin pulled out a stool from beneath a narrow counter and sat down as he said, "They can use this screen during an event to check and see how everything's going without being obtrusive."

We watched as one of Huntington's lackeys took the podium at the front of the room and began introducing Dick with a ridiculously glowing monologue. "Wow, that's awesome," Darwin muttered. "Huntington is a prince among men, truly. Just ask his hand puppet." He glanced at Nana over his shoulder and said, "Do you just want to watch and listen, or do you want to ruffle some feathers?"

She said, "Honey, if you've got a way to be a fox in that hen house, let 'er rip! I'll pay your bail if we get busted."

Darwin said, "Okay then, everybody try to stay quiet. They'll be able to hear us as soon as I flip a switch on this control panel. Josh, will you please film this?" His boyfriend readily agreed, and Darwin smiled at him before accessing something on his phone.

The man at the podium said, "Ladies and gentlemen, I give you the next mayor of our great city, Richard Huntington!" The crowd cheered, and Darwin turned on a small microphone, then held his phone next to it. As Huntington strode toward the stage, the Imperial March from Star Wars began to blast over the ballroom's P.A. system. Huntington looked furious as he took the stage. When he tried to speak into the microphone, Darwin tapped his phone's screen, and Darth Vader's deep, commanding voice invited the crowd to join the dark side. I had to bite my lip to keep from howling with laughter.

But then, Darwin swung the mic up, leaned into it, and said, "Hi folks. Sorry to disrupt your party. It looks real nice, and I'll let you get back to it in just a minute. But first, I want to share something with you that Mr. Huntington said to me earlier this week. If what you're about to hear doesn't bother you, then hey, go ahead and write that man a big, fat check, because clearly, he's the right candidate for you. But if you think it's wrong for anyone to speak to another human being like this, well, maybe think twice about giving him your hard-earned money."

He tapped another sound file on his phone, and for the next forty seconds, we all listened as Richard Huntington swore at and belittled Darwin. It ended with, "Why don't you just kill yourself, you little freak?" It made my flesh crawl.

Darwin turned off his phone, then said into the mic, "For the record, I'm an eighteen-year-old kid who happens to be transgender. I know that doesn't sit well with some of you. But I'm hoping for one or two of you out there, that kind of hatred and bigotry doesn't sit well, either. That's all I wanted to say. Enjoy the party." He flipped the switch, pushed the microphone aside, and got up from the chair with a sigh. "That probably won't help at all, but the truth about who they're voting for still needed to be put out there."

Josh put down his phone and wiped a tear from his cheek, then grabbed Darwin in an embrace and said, "You didn't tell me you recorded it."

"I guess I wanted to document the type of stuff I deal with on a regular basis," Darwin said, resting his cheek against Josh's hair. "I wasn't going to let you listen to that, because I knew it'd hurt to hear it. But then, I thought maybe some good could come of it if I showed people the real Huntington."

I muttered, "I'm gonna fucking kill him," and took a step toward the door.

"Not if I kill him first," Nana growled.

But Darwin stepped in front of both of us and said, "There are better ways to hit Huntington where it hurts. And right now, we just need to get out of here before security shows up."

I made myself shake out my clenched fists, and then I nodded, even though I was still seething with anger. Nana muttered, "You're right. We need to get you boys to the suite before the fuzz rolls up on us and hauls us all to the pokey. But this shit ain't over! Humpington's ass is grass and I'm the fucking lawn mower!"

When we reached the suite, we found Roger waiting for us, and Nana filled him in on what had happened. Meanwhile, Alastair grabbed Darwin in a hug and said, "I'm so sorry, mate. What that man said to you is inexcusable. I want you to know I'm going to research the other mayoral candidates and contribute heavily to the best one, to help ensure Huntington never reaches office. He's a brute and a bigot, and no way should he be in any position of power."

When Alastair let go of him, Darwin looked at the floor and murmured, "Thanks, all of you, for, you know. Caring about what happened to me."

"Of course we care." Nana's dark eyes were misty. "You're family! And I tell you what, I could not be prouder of you, Darwin, not only because you're one of the smartest, handsomest, kindest young men I've ever known, but because what you just did back there was gutsy as hell."

"Plus, I almost pissed myself laughing at the Imperial March," I said, in a clumsy attempt at lightening the mood.

Surprisingly, it worked. We all had a good laugh and started talking about the perfection of that song choice and

Huntington's dumbfounded reaction. A smile spread across Darwin's face, and pretty soon, he was chuckling with the rest of us.

*****

Alastair ordered us a huge feast from room service. He even included cake and ice cream, because he said we had reason to celebrate after 'striking a blow against tyranny'. We all made ourselves comfortable in the suite's beautiful red and gold living room and ate ourselves silly while we talked and laughed and enjoyed one another's company.

Roger's phone jingled at one point, and he grinned when he looked at the screen. We learned he'd outsourced the poster job when we left him downstairs. A police officer had sent him packing when he tried to put up a sign across the street, so Roger paid a man with a delivery truck a hundred bucks to tape a couple posters on the side of his vehicle and drive up and down in front of the hotel. Apparently the driver and Ro had bonded quickly and exchanged business cards. The man texted him photos not only of the big truck, which he'd absolutely plastered in the 'lick Dick' posters, but also of the 'gob-smacked' faces of the well-to-do patrons who filtered out of the hotel. When I asked what gob-smacked meant, Roger let his mouth fall open and slapped his hand to his cheek. I chuckled and swore I'd try to work it into daily conversation.

Later on, Nana called Josh's dads and told them her great-grandson would be spending the night with her. Once that was done, she took a big bite of cake, put her stockinged feet up on the coffee table, and said, "This is fun! I haven't been to a slumber party since…well, never, now that I think about it. We should do this more often!" She fell asleep five minutes later, snoring loudly with her head back and her mouth open. I carried her to one of the bedrooms and tucked her in under a fluffy comforter, then rejoined my friends. Alastair pulled a throw blanket over both of us, and I held him close as he snuggled against my side.

"Today was wonderful," he said softly. "We did so much good, between the work on the firehouse and taking a stand against a bigot. And I get to cap it off among friends, in the arms of the most handsome man in all the world. Every day should be just like this."

"Plus, there was cake," Josh said, raising a dessert plate to us as if he was toasting. He grinned and rested his head on his boyfriend's shoulder.

Moments later, Roger's phone rang. He glanced at the screen, sat up and answered with a formal, "Yes, ma'am?" His expression grew grave as he listened to whoever was on the line. After a minute, he said, "Yes, ma'am," again before holding the phone out to Alastair and saying, "You may want to take this in another room, mate."

Alastair looked perplexed as he put the phone to his ear and said, "Hello?" A few seconds later, he got up and wandered into the master bedroom.

Roger was on his feet and looked like he was trying to think through a lot of things at once. When I asked who'd called, he muttered, "Alastair's mum. She tried his phone first, but it kept going to voicemail."

"I think he left it in the car. Is something wrong?"

"Alastair's dad had a heart attack, and we need to fly home tonight. May I borrow your phone? I need to arrange our flight."

"Yeah, of course," I mumbled as I handed it over. Roger paced beside the windows as he placed the call.

When Alastair came back into the room a few minutes later, he looked so lost and pale, and my heart ached for him. I crossed the room and grabbed him in an embrace, and he murmured, "I have to go," as he clung to me.

"I know. Roger's arranging the flight right now."

"I need my passport, it's in the flat." He sounded dazed.

I said. "Mine is, too. I'll pack a bag for both of us when we stop off there, it'll just take a minute."

He looked up at me and whispered, with heartbreak in his eyes, "My father's in grave condition. If I brought my boyfriend home, it would upset him and the rest of the family, and I just can't do that. Not at a time like this, when it might actually have an impact on his health. I'm so sorry, Sawyer."

I totally understood what he was saying, so it shouldn't have hurt. But it took some effort to sound positive as I said, "You're right. Please just call me as soon as you can and let me know what's going on." Tears streamed down his cheeks as he stepped back from me and nodded.

Roger ended his call and handed me the phone as he said, "You'll take care of everything here, right Sawyer? Make sure Nana and the boys get home safe?" I told him I would.

My heart broke into a million pieces at the raw agony in Alastair's eyes. He took my face between his hands and kissed me. Seconds later, he and Roger were gone. I stared at the heavy, gilded door as it swung shut slowly in their wake.

I'd never felt so helpless in my entire life.

Chapter Eleven

"You need to eat something, Sawyer."

"Not hungry."

"You need to eat anyway," Gabriel insisted. "Otherwise, you're going to get run down and feel terrible."

"That whole feeling terrible thing is a done deal."

"All the more reason to eat. I made my mom's tortilla soup, guaranteed to cure whatever ails you."

He grinned at me when I glanced at him. Gabriel was in full makeup, since it was Friday night and he was scheduled to work. He wore black jeans and a slim-fitting black sweater, and the garment bag with his burlesque costume was draped over the back of the couch.

After a pause, I muttered, "Yeah, okay," and followed him to the little table in the breakfast nook.

While we ate, he tried to distract me with stories about his mother and her relatives. They were migrant workers from Mexico, and devout Catholics who never quite knew what to make of Gabriel. When I asked about his dad, he said, "I barely know him. He and his family are a bunch of stuck-up, rich white people who've never wanted a damn thing to do with me. As far as they're concerned, I'm just some mistake my dad made in his reckless youth. I hate the fact that my mom gave me their last name."

"I'm sorry they treat you like that."

"It sucks, but fuck 'em. I don't need or want anything from those people. They think I'm not good enough for them, but in truth, they're not good enough for me." He grinned a little and said, "When I was a kid, I used to tell people my last name's Moriarty because I was named after the villain in the Sherlock Holmes books. I like that better than the truth."

"You're better off without those assholes, and it's totally their loss," I said before eating a spoonful of soup, which was both delicious and rejuvenating. Ever since Alastair had taken off for the UK three days earlier, I'd been worried and distracted, and things like sleeping and eating properly had fallen by the wayside. Gabriel had been right about how much I needed a good meal.

"For real." Gabriel tossed a few jalapenos into his bowl and added a squeeze of lime as he changed the subject with, "So, are you skipping work again tonight?"

"Yeah. I called Joan yesterday and told her I wouldn't be in this weekend. Surprisingly, she didn't fire me on the spot."

"Are you sure you don't want to change your mind and come to work with me? It might be good to keep busy."

"I just…can't. Every single time I stripped, Alastair was in the audience. I always focused on him and pulled him into my act, and I just don't want to do it without him. Besides the fact that I'm worried and distracted, the last thing I feel like doing right now is shaking my ass for a bunch of strangers."

"I'm worried about Alastair, too. He must have been so stressed out during his dad's quadruple bypass. But…I guess I don't understand why you're still so concerned, Sawyer. I mean, you're barely eating, and I hear you pacing around the apartment half the night, even though his dad made it through surgery and is going to be alright. Alastair's probably relieved, but with each day that passes, you seem more worried, not less."

I put my spoon down and said, "That's because I don't think he's coming back, Gabriel. His dad won't be able to work for quite a while, and Alastair was supposed to return home in less than a year anyway. I bet they'll expect him to stay and begin training to take over the company."

"Shit, I didn't think about that."

"I hope to God I'm wrong. I'm not ready to say goodbye to him."

"You know what, Sawyer? You'd never be ready to say goodbye to him. Even if he'd left months from now as planned, you were going to end up devastated, no two ways about it. You can try calling it a fling all you want, and you can claim you just moved in here to be his roommate, but come on. You and Alastair are crazy about each other! When he walks into the room, you come to life! I can only dream about finding what you two have."

"I knew it was going to kill me when he went back home," I said quietly. "I've always known that. But I thought I could just focus on making the most of every minute we had while trying like hell not to think about the future."

We talked for a few more minutes, and then Gabriel sighed and said, "I have to get going or I'm going to be late for work. Are you sure you don't want to come with me and just hang out? I hate to leave you like this."

I told him, "Don't worry about me. I'll be alright." If only that was true.

*****

I paced around the apartment for the next hour or so, wishing Alastair would call. That was pretty unlikely though, since it was three a.m. in the UK. Plus, he was always at the hospital with his family and rarely had a moment to himself. He'd managed to contact me three or four times a day since he'd been gone, but they were always just quick texts or calls lasting only a minute or two.

When my phone buzzed in my hand, my heart leapt. But the message was from Kai, and it said: *Hey. What are you up to? I assume you didn't go to work tonight, since you seemed out of sorts when I talked to you a few hours ago.*

I wrote back, confirming my hermit status, and not twenty minutes later, the apartment's intercom beeped. It turned out to be Kai and his family, and when I buzzed them in, little Isabella yelled, "Surprise!" She and her dads were all dressed in pajamas, and Izzy was clutching a big, white teddy bear, which matched the polar bears on her pink PJs. "We're here for a pajama party," she announced. "You need to put your 'jamas on!"

I stepped back and held the door open for them as Kai explained, "It's an ambush pajama party. I know you've been feeling blue, so we're forcing ourselves on you with junk food and a stack of Disney movies to try to cheer you up."

"Make yourselves at home while I change. Now, is this pajama level acceptable," I indicated Kai, who wore a white T-shirt under a leather jacket, along with plaid pajama bottoms, "or do I need to go full Jessie?" His husband's matched set of flannel pajamas were bright yellow and covered in a repeating pattern of cartoon dogs dancing with cartoon cats.

"Hey, you do you," Jessie said cheerfully.

Since I normally slept naked, the best I could do was a pair of black cotton sweat pants. I paired them with some red wool socks and a red sweatshirt, hoping it would seem like I was making an effort at least, and joined my friends in the living room. Kai's brows were knit as he pressed buttons on Alastair's ridiculously advanced remote and kept alternating between the wrong menu and a black screen. Meanwhile, Jessie unpacked some snacks while Izzy tiled the coffee table with the movies they'd brought. She had the teddy bear in a headlock under her arm, and her expression matched her father's, though in her case it reflected concentration, not frustration.

"Is it okay if we eat in here?" Jessie asked. "Alastair's apartment is gorgeous, and we don't want to mess anything up."

I murmured, "It's fine," as I thought back to all the meals Alastair and I had shared on that cream-colored leather sofa. I remembered a moment in particular from the week before, when Alastair had been laughing about something as he fed me a huge spoonful of rocky road ice cream. His eyes had been full of light, and he'd looked so beautiful that I'd taken the spoon from his hand and kissed him, tasting the chocolate on his lips. That memory made me miss him so damn bad that my chest literally ached.

*****

About an hour later, I was staring unseeingly at the Lion King, and Izzy was curled up on my lap. The little girl had said, "You look like you need a hug, Uncle Sawyer," and climbed on me about five minutes into the movie, and then she'd stayed there. It was nice, actually. She was warm and smelled like shampoo and the popcorn she was snacking on.

She was also far more attuned to what was happening that evening than I'd realized. When my phone rang, Izzy immediately rolled off me and exclaimed, "I hope that's your boyfriend so you don't have to be sad anymore!"

When I saw Alastair's name on the screen, I jumped up and mumbled, "I'll be right back."

I answered as I rushed to the bedroom, and Alastair whispered, "It's so good to hear your voice, Sawyer."

He was obviously upset, and I asked, "Is your dad okay?"

"He's doing well, all things considered. They moved him out of the ICU. The doctor even had him get up and walk already, just for a minute, but still. I couldn't believe they did that so quickly after open heart surgery."

"Are *you* okay?"

"No," he admitted, so quietly I almost didn't hear him.

"Let's switch to video chat. I need to see your face."

He did as I asked. Alastair was so pale, and there were dark circles under his eyes. He touched the screen on his phone, and a tear tumbled down his cheek as he whispered, "Oh God, look at you. My sweet, beautiful Sawyer."

There was so much heartbreak in his words that I said, "You're not coming back, are you?" I was pretty sure I already knew the answer, but it still hurt like hell when he shook his head.

"I wanted to. God I wanted to. I needed so much more time with you! I didn't even get to say goodbye, not to you, or my friends, or the city." He took a shaky breath and said, "My father has to retire. Even though the surgeon told him he could go back to work in a couple months, my mother and grandmother won't let him. His stress level is always through the roof, and it's going to kill him, either through his heart disease or some other way. Our family doctor said he didn't expect my father to live another five years if he didn't make immediate, major changes. You see why I have to stay, don't you, Sawyer?" All I could do was nod, because I didn't trust my voice, not with all the emotions flooding me.

After a moment, Alastair said, "I'm supposed to begin on Monday. My father's plan was always to start me at an intern level and train me in every aspect of the business over the next ten years. He was going to retire at sixty-five and hand over control of Penelegion Enterprises. I would have been thirty-one at that point. No one's dumb enough to think I can just be thrown in the deep end and run the company, of course. But forget about that nice, slow, easing in process. I'm going to have my work cut out for me, and there's so much riding on this!" He paused before saying, "And yet, all I can think about is you, Sawyer. I miss you so much. God, I miss you. I feel like I left a huge part of me back in California."

"Just say the word, and I'll be on the next plane to London. I know you can't tell your family about me because it'd upset your father, and that's the last thing he needs right now. But they don't have to know! I'll get a little apartment somewhere close by, and we can be together whenever you can sneak away. I know you'll be busy, but even if it's just a few minutes here and there, at least it'll be something!"

"But that's exactly what Tracy did, he treated you like his dirty little secret! How can I do that to you, especially knowing how much it hurt you in the past?"

"I don't care! I'll do whatever it takes to be with you."

"But I do," he said softly. "You deserve so much better. You deserve the world, Sawyer."

"I can't say goodbye to you. I won't!"

"I won't do that either. We'll figure something out. At the very least, I can come to San Francisco a few times a year to see you. I'm not going to prison, even if that's what it feels like. I'll get time off now and then." He tried to sound hopeful, but he looked devastated.

I took a deep breath and struggled to keep my expression neutral. The thought of only seeing Alastair a handful of times a year was heart-wrenching. But the last thing he needed was me putting pressure on him and making demands on his time, not when it must already feel like the weight of the world was on his shoulders. After a moment, I nodded. I even attempted a smile and hoped it at least sort of looked convincing.

Then I asked, "Have you gotten any sleep? It's around four a.m. there."

"I tried, but my mind keeps racing."

"Please try again."

"I will. I'll call you in a few hours, alright?" When I nodded, he said, "Please take care of yourself, Sawyer. And take care of Gabriel and Elijah, too. They're both so vulnerable, and I worry about them."

"Count on it."

"Speaking of Elijah, I asked Jessie's brother Jed to move into my house in the South Bay as his roommate. Elijah's been settling in, but I hate the thought of him rattling around all alone down there. Will you follow up with Jessie? Maybe he can encourage his brother to take me up on my offer."

"I will. Jessie's here right now actually, along with Kai and Izzy."

"Oh, I didn't realize you had company. I'm sorry I've kept you."

"Don't apologize. You're always more important than anything, Allie."

He smiled at the nickname, then said, "I just realized it's Friday night there, I'd lost track of the days. Why aren't you at work? You're not ill, are you?"

"No. I'm just…thinking that isn't the job for me after all."

"I can put you on the payroll with the firehouse renovation. You've been putting in so much time there, and you don't have to do all that hard work for free."

"I'm fine. You don't have to worry about me, financially or otherwise."

He smiled, despite the sadness in his eyes. "I'll always worry, Sawyer. That's just what I do with the people I care about."

"Me too, and my biggest worry right now is that you're going to collapse from exhaustion. Please go to bed, Alastair."

"Okay. I'll talk to you soon." He kissed his fingertips and pressed them to the screen.

After we disconnected, I sat there for a few minutes, looking around at that generic designer bedroom and realizing how little of Alastair was reflected in it. Maybe he'd never bothered to personalize it because he always knew it was temporary. His real home had always been in the UK.

Then I thought of something and opened the nightstand drawer. His leather-bound journal had been forgotten in his rush to the airport. I took it out and turned it over in my hands. No way would I read it and violate his privacy. But I hugged it to my chest for a few moments before putting it on the bedside table. I'd have to send it to him, but not just yet. Even though plenty of clothes and other everyday items had been left behind, they didn't hold the same meaning as that journal. It had been a part of him, and it was one of the few truly personal things I had left.

I curled up on the bed, put my head on Alastair's pillow, and breathed in his clean scent. That was another thing I had to hold on to. The housekeeper had shown up earlier that day, and I'd probably scared the poor woman when I saw her reaching for the sheets and yelled at her to stop. I told her I'd be washing the linens myself from that point forward, and asked her to please leave them alone. She smiled and nodded, but clearly thought she was dealing with a crazy person.

And maybe she was. My grief had left me a desperate shell of a man, one who'd panicked at the prospect of a washed pillowcase. But I couldn't stand the thought of losing even one more piece of him.

Eventually though, his scent would fade from that pillowcase. Before too long, I'd have to mail him his journal, since he wrote in it every day and must be missing it. I'd always thought I was a person who didn't assign much value to material objects, but I found myself desperate for something tangible, some part of him to take comfort in and to let me keep reliving the best month of my life with the most wonderful man I'd ever known.

It just hadn't been enough time! I needed more. So much more, not just vague promises of a few visits a year.

How would I get through all those days and weeks and months in between? Before I'd met him, I'd barely been living. I couldn't go back to that. *I needed Alastair.* He was absolutely everything, and life without him felt pointless.

Chapter Twelve

The next week passed slowly. I spent my time working out like a man possessed, followed by twelve-hour shifts on the firehouse project. My remaining time was filled with my two online classes. It had been tempting to drop them after Alastair left because it was tough to concentrate, but my need to keep busy ultimately won out. Whenever I was idle, missing Alastair swallowed me whole.

One good thing that week was getting to see Alastair's vision for the youth shelter coming together. The building had been in pretty good shape overall, and before long, renovations would be complete. Then it was just a question of waiting on paperwork that had to be approved by various government agencies before it could open its doors.

Alastair called me every day, and I told him all about the progress being made on the building and what was going on with our friends. I tried to keep it positive, so I left out the fact that I was unraveling without him. He was already under enough stress without worrying about me. His first week on the job had been spent getting a crash course in the company's finances from his uncle, who was chief financial officer. Alastair had summed up the week as, "Overwhelming."

When he called me on Saturday, he was in the office, even though it was eight p.m. his time. Despite sounding discouraged and more exhausted than ever, he said he planned to work all weekend. We chatted for a few minutes, and after we disconnected, I sighed and scrubbed my hands over my face. It was depressing to know he was miserable, and that I was helpless to do anything about it.

Sometime later, as I sat in the living room with my laptop, staring unseeingly at a lesson for my online Psychology class, the intercom buzzer sounded. I headed to the panel beside the door, pushed a button and called, "Hello?"

A deep voice said, "I, uh, I'm looking for Sawyer MacNeil. This is his father. I'm not sure if I got the right place."

"Hey Dad, I'll buzz you in. Take the elevator to the top floor."

I hit another button on the panel and turned to Gabriel. He was sitting by the window with a book on his lap and his hair in hot rollers, and he asked, "What do you think he wants?"

"No clue."

My friend raised an eyebrow, then got up and said, "I'll be in my room so you two can have some privacy. Good luck with whatever that's about."

I pulled on a sweatshirt to cover the camisole I'd been wearing with my jeans, then opened the door and stuck my head into the hallway. A few moments later, the elevator doors slid open, and my father wandered out, holding a small box and looking all around. He walked right past me without saying hello, and once he took in the apartment, he turned to me and asked, "Is there something you need to tell me?"

"Like what?"

"How are you paying for an apartment this nice? The rent must be thousands of dollars a month. I can't think of many jobs that pay that well and are moral or legal."

I resisted the urge to sigh and said, "The apartment belongs to my boyfriend."

"What does he do to afford a place like this?"

"Nothing illegal or immoral."

He waited for an explanation, and when none was forthcoming, he knit his brows. After a moment, he held out the box to me and said, "This came for you. I thought maybe it was important."

I turned the box over and looked at an unfamiliar return address in Germany. As I peeled back the packing tape, I told my dad, "Thanks for bringing it to me. Next time, just call and I'll come by."

He watched curiously as I opened the package and said, "I wanted to check on you anyway."

"Why? Were you worried about me?" He just shrugged. God forbid he'd actually admit that. I got the box open and unfurled a cocoon of bubble wrap, then murmured, "Shit, I forgot all about this. I ordered it weeks ago."

I held up a little red convertible that I'd bought on an online auction site and sighed, and my dad asked, "Why the hell did you buy a toy car?"

"It was a gift for my boyfriend. He used to collect them when he was a kid, and I thought he might like it."

"Did they send the wrong one or something?"

"No. It's absolutely perfect."

"So, why are you upset?"

"Because I would have loved seeing Alastair's face when he opened this present. I'll send it to him, and I hope it makes him happy, but it would have been great to do this in person."

My father looked perplexed. "You're living in his apartment. What am I missing?"

"He moved to London last week. His dad had a heart attack and can't go back to work, so my boyfriend had to take over the family business a lot sooner than planned."

"So, what the hell are you doing here?"

"What do you mean?"

"You obviously care about this guy. Why'd you stay behind when he moved back to England?"

"It's complicated."

My dad thought about that for a minute, then said, "If this guy means something to you, and it seems like he does, then you need to go after him. Long distance relationships usually don't stand a chance."

I glanced at my father as I wrapped the little convertible in bubble wrap and returned it to the box. "It's weird, you giving me relationship advice. Until recently, I was afraid to even bring up the fact that I'm gay. Now you're trying to encourage me to follow a guy to the UK."

"Like I told you, I've had a long time to come to terms with the fact that you're gay. Eventually, I realized a relationship's a relationship. At their core, they're all about two people trying to work it out. So, my advice is the same, regardless of whether it's a girl or guy you're pining for: if you think you two have a future together, go after them. I let a fantastic woman slip through my fingers by not showing her how much she meant to me. Don't make the same mistake I did."

"Sherry really is terrific. I hope that's who you're talking about."

"It is, but she thinks I'm a pain in the ass."

I grinned a little and said, "She's not wrong, Dad. But she also cares about you. I asked her to look out for you when I was moving last week, and she told me she always does that anyway."

"She actually said that?"

"Yup. That means there's still something there. Let her know how you feel before it's too late! She's been going on dates, and sooner or later she'll meet someone else. Once that happens, it's all over. But for now, you still have a chance to make things right."

"I don't know...."

"You're telling me to fly to the UK and take a chance. Take one, too. All you have to do is knock on the door that's right beside yours."

"And then what?"

"Talk to her, and listen to what she has to say. And try like hell not to argue. Your problem is that you always have to be right. That's got to be a pretty hollow victory, if it means ending up alone."

My father thought about that before saying, "I guess I could give it a shot. Hell, I probably can't mess it up more than it already is. Plus, no matter what comes of it, it'd be good to bury the hatchet with Sherry. Even if she wants nothing to do with me, at least we could coexist a little more peacefully."

"Good. So, do you want to sit down? I could make us some coffee."

It was a little disappointing but not particularly surprising when he said, "Nah, I'd better go. Good luck, Sawyer."

"Good luck too, Dad."

When Gabriel ventured out of his room a few minutes later, I was sitting on the couch, deep in thought. He asked, "What did your dad want?"

"To bring me a package that had been delivered to the house, and to check on me. I think it was out of curiosity more than concern."

"He didn't stay long."

"No. He's never been one for drawn-out conversations. That was pretty good for him, though, because we actually talked about stuff that mattered, instead of, like, sports or the weather."

"What'd you talk about?"

"He thinks I should go after Alastair. What do you think?"

Gabriel sat beside me, and as he began unwinding the curlers and lining them up on the coffee table, he said, "As someone who's had a front-row seat to your relationship, I don't know how you two can stand to be apart. But then, Alastair asked you to stay here. So the question is, do you respect his wishes, or do you go anyway, because you think it's what you both need? I don't know him well enough to be able to predict how that would go over. He's totally stressed out right now, so maybe the question is, would you going to London add to his stress level, or help alleviate it?"

"I wish I knew." I got up and said, "I'm going to go out for a while and think this through. Good luck at work tonight."

"Thanks." He got up too and shook out his cascading, dark curls. "Did you call in sick again?"

"Yeah. I can't see returning to that job, so I need to talk to Joan and make it official, instead of just dodging it."

I grabbed my leather jacket and the motorcycle helmet Alastair had given me after our first night together, then headed down to the parking garage. It was hard to believe only a few weeks had passed since then, because he'd completely transformed my world in that time. I could recall how lost, aimless, and alone I'd been when he came along, but it felt like a distant memory.

I wound through town on my motorcycle for a while, trying to make a decision. Stay like Alastair told me to, or go anyway? Eventually, I realized I was close to my friend Zachary's shop and made a quick U-turn.

After finding a parking spot, I tucked the helmet under my arm and headed down the narrow side street where Zachary and his new husband TJ lived and worked. The ground floor of their building was part showroom, part workshop. They made clever, intricately detailed wind-up toys that were equal parts whimsy and fine art.

The two men were seated side-by-side at their workbench when I came in. Their heads were close together, and they were deep in conversation, the little figures in their hands momentarily forgotten. My arrival was announced with a bell jingling on the door, and both men smiled when they looked up at me.

"Hey," I said, "is this a bad time?"

"Not at all," Zachary told me. "Come on in."

He pushed his brown hair back from his dark eyes and his smile widened. My friend looked good, healthy and happy, in marked contrast to how he'd seemed when we'd first met about a year ago. He'd been battling a heroin addiction back then, not that I knew it at the time because he was good at keeping it a secret. I would have called him a former addict since he'd been clean for months, but he'd told me 'once an addict, always an addict.' He didn't use anymore, but I got what he meant. Recovery was a lifelong process.

His husband asked me, "How've you been, Sawyer?"

"Not so great." I perched on a stool across from them and put my helmet on the floor, then took a look at the hundred tiny gears and metal parts spread out on the workbench.

Zachary said, "You must be missing Alastair like crazy."

"Every minute of every day."

TJ got up, and when he kissed his husband's forehead and smiled at him, love shone in his eyes. He said, "I'm going to go upstairs and make us some coffee. Be right back," and left the room. It was pretty obvious he was doing that to give us some privacy.

Zachary said, "So, what are you going to do? I know Alastair hadn't planned on going away so soon, and when I messaged him a couple days ago, he told me his job is going to keep him in the UK."

"I have no idea, and that's what I wanted to talk to you about. You've known Alastair longer than I have, and I wanted to get your perspective on this. When he left, he asked me to stay behind. At the time, he didn't want to upset his father right after the man had had a heart attack, or the rest of his homophobic family, for that matter. Since then, he's said he doesn't want to hide me from them and treat me like his dirty little secret, since that's pretty much exactly what my ex-boyfriend did, and Alastair knows how much it hurt me. But I'm miserable without him. I know he's miserable, too, with all the pressure he's under. If I was in London, I think I'd be able to provide some support, even if it was just a friendly face and a shoulder to cry on. Or maybe I'd just stress him out more, because he'd have the added pressure of keeping a secret from his family."

"Have you talked to Alastair about this?"

"No, because he's already overwhelmed with his new responsibilities. I feel like asking him to rethink the decision to have me stay behind would just put more pressure on him."

"So, you're thinking about going to London without telling him ahead of time."

I nodded. "I wanted to ask you though, as one of his best friends, how do you think this'll go over? The goal here is to make Alastair's life better, not worse."

Zachary reached across the table and squeezed my hand. "Here's what I know, Sawyer. Alastair is crazy about you, and leaving you behind tore him apart. So, I think you should go, even though he asked you not to. Initially, it made sense to tell you to hang back. He was worried about upsetting his dad when the man was gravely ill, and understandably so. But now, Alastair's trying to do what's best for you. He doesn't want to hurt you like your ex did by keeping you a secret, but you should be able to make that decision for yourself. If you two feel you have to hide your relationship from his family, and if you're fine with that, then it shouldn't be a problem. You and Alastair need each other, and neither of you will be happy as long as you're apart. I'm sure of that."

"You're right, and you just helped me make up my mind. I'm going."

"Terrific!"

"Now that I've decided, I can't even get there fast enough."

Zachary pulled out his phone and said, "So let's make the arrangements. I'll help."

I opened my phone's browser and typed in the name of a discount travel site. After entering a bit of information, I said, "There are actually a couple flights tonight. The last-minute thing isn't cheap, but I don't want to wait any longer. I've already let too much time go by."

"Will you be staying with Alastair once you get there?"

I shook my head. "He hasn't had time to find his own place, so he's living with his family in their home in London. Needless to say, I won't be going within a mile of them."

He said, "In that case, I'll help you find something."

"Thank you. Cheaper the better."

"You're not just going for a week or two, right? You intend to stay awhile."

"I want to stay as long as I can, but that's up to Alastair." I thought about that and said, "I wonder what the rules are for visitors to the UK."

"I believe you can remain in the country up to six months as a tourist. I don't know what you'd have to do to get permission to stay longer. There are all kinds of rules about getting a job there, too. I guess they don't want visitors taking jobs from UK citizens."

"So, I won't have any income while I'm there, and after half a year, I'll have to leave. That sucks. Like I said though, it's up to Alastair. If he doesn't want me there, this is going to be a very short trip." I selected one of the cheaper flights, though none was exactly a bargain, and murmured, "I hope I'm doing the right thing."

"You are. He'll be so happy to see you." Zachary turned his phone to face me. A no-frills bedroom was on the screen, and he asked, "What do you think about something like this? It's a week-to-week rental, right in the heart of London."

"I'm not picky. I just need to be in the same city as Alastair. Nothing else matters." I booked a one-way flight, since I had no idea when I'd be returning, and as my confirmation number popped up on the screen, I said, "Thanks for helping, Zachary. I appreciate it."

"No need to thank me. You and Alastair belong together. I'm glad to be a part of making that happen."

*****

My next stop, after visiting with Zachary and TJ for another half-hour, was Club Scandal. Joan wasn't the least bit surprised when I told her I wouldn't be returning to work. She'd seen Alastair and me together every time I stripped and told me she'd fully expected me to follow him to the UK. She even gave me the phone number of an acquaintance of hers who ran a gay strip club in London and told me to look him up, because he'd probably let me work under the table for tips only. It was hardly my ideal job, but I was glad to at least have one option for earning an income while I was in the UK.

I found Gabriel backstage, and when I told him what I was doing, he gave me a big hug and said, "You're making the right call. I'll miss you, but I'm so glad you and Alastair will be together."

When he let go of me, I held him by his shoulders and said, "Are you going to be okay, Gabriel? I've been worried about you with this hiding in plain sight thing you've been doing. What if your ex Dom catches up to you?"

"Then he does. I'm not going to go out of my way to let him find me, but I won't let fear keep dictating how I run my life, either. I belong in San Francisco, and I love this job. If that comes at a price, so be it."

"I wish I could do something to help."

He smiled at me and said, "You're a good friend, Sawyer, and I appreciate the fact that you're concerned. But make no mistake: I'm a survivor. I've lived through shit you couldn't imagine, and I'm sure as hell going to live through this, too." I believed that.

*****

Around nine p.m., I knocked on Kai's door, and when he answered, I told him, "So, guess who's boarding a redeye to London tonight?"

"I'm not even sort of surprised," he said as he stepped back to let me in.

He and Jessie had built a beautiful apartment on top of their garage. It had high ceilings and an open floor plan with a spacious blue-and-white living room/dining room/kitchen area, plus two bedrooms. Izzy's was a pink, totally girly dream room with a built-in castle playhouse, made by her dads, and she came running out of her room when she heard me. The little girl was wearing a princess costume over pajamas, and she exclaimed, "Hi Uncle Sawyer," as I picked her up and gave her a hug.

"Hi, beautiful girl." I kissed the top of her head and said, "I came by to tell you and your dads that I'm going to London for a while. I'll miss you."

She leaned back and studied me with her big, brown eyes. "Is that where your boyfriend is?" When I nodded, she said, "I'll miss you too, but I'm happy you're going to be with your one true love. That's important."

Izzy obviously watched a lot of Disney movies. I grinned at her and said, "It is."

Jessie came out of Izzy's room with an armload of pink laundry and asked, "How long are you going to be gone, Sawyer?"

"I have no idea."

I sat on their light blue chambray couch with Izzy on my lap, and she put her head on my shoulder. I was going to miss that kid. She'd warmed up to me quickly when I returned from the Army, and I hoped she wouldn't forget me, no matter how long I stayed in London.

We chatted for a few minutes, until Jessie told Izzy it was bedtime. I carried her to her room, then kissed her cheek after her dads tucked her in. She asked, "Will you mail me a surprise, like when you were gone to the Army?" I was surprised she even remembered the little trinkets I sent her whenever I had the chance.

"Of course I will, Iz." She seemed excited at the prospect.

When Kai, Jessie and I returned to the living room, my best friend said, "I'll get my coat." I turned to him and asked why, and he explained, "So I can drive you and your luggage to the airport. And we should get going, because they want you to check in ridiculously early for international flights."

I thought about that, then said, "Do I assume I'm only visiting him for a week or two and just take a backpack? Or do I bring all my stuff, because I'll be staying in London long-term? I know I want to be wherever Alastair is, and if it was up to me, this would be a move, not a vacation. But I don't know how he feels about any of this. We never talked about our relationship turning into something long-term. In fact, right from the start, he told me about his family obligations and how he'd have to return to the UK, and never once did he say, 'hey, why don't you come, too?' I know I'm going to go see him. That's something I absolutely have to do. But I have no idea what it's going to mean for us." I looked at my friends and said, "So, what do

I do here, bring a backpack, or everything I own? Is this a visit or a move?"

I must have looked as lost as I felt, because Kai's expression turned sympathetic, and he squeezed my shoulder as he said, "If you believe Alastair really cares about you, then you already have your answer."

Chapter Thirteen

The hour it took to go through customs was uncomfortable to say the least, especially the part where I had to explain why my luggage was half-full of corsets, stockings and high heels. But I made myself hold my head high, look the judgmental customs agent in the eye, and tell him the truth: all the apparel was mine, and last I checked, there was no law in bringing clothing designed for the opposite gender into the UK. He'd started off smirking, but I squared my shoulders and kept staring him down, until finally he broke eye contact and told me to proceed. I was sure he'd have a good laugh with his coworkers later on about the guy with all the lingerie, but fuck him.

I adjusted the strap of my backpack and looked around, trying to get my bearings. Then I picked up my duffle bag and suitcase and wandered through Heathrow airport. I followed the signs for ground transportation, pausing to exchange my currency along the way. There were a lot of people around, and they all seemed to be in a hurry. I, on the other hand, felt like I was moving in slow motion. My neck and back ached from the long flight in a cramped coach seat clearly not meant for someone with my build (or anyone with legs), and I was exhausted. With one layover along the way, it had taken me about fourteen hours to reach London.

After consulting a crumpled piece of paper with my scribbled directions and stuffing it back in my pocket, I boarded the Heathrow Express bound for Central London. I tried my damnedest to stay awake and avoid missing my stop during the brief train ride. That was followed by a bus and a walk. Eventually, I reached the attic apartment I was renting week-to-week. I trudged up the steps at the back of the four-story building and found the key that had been left under the welcome mat for me. As soon as I got inside, I dropped my luggage, fell onto the bed fully clothed, and passed the hell out.

*****

For some reason, I awoke only an hour or so later, and I turned on the small lamp on the bedside table and took in my surroundings. The narrow apartment had white walls and worn wood flooring, and in addition to the bed and nightstand, it also contained a dresser, a small bathroom, and absolutely nothing else. When I got up and used the facilities, I glanced at the tiny shower stall and wondered if I'd actually fit in it.

According to my phone, it was midnight, but my body was still on California time and thought it was four p.m. No wonder I'd only been able to nap. Since I knew it would be almost impossible to get back to sleep at that point, I decided to stretch my legs and pocketed the key to the apartment before heading down the back stairs.

It had been raining. My boots splashed on the wet pavement as I navigated the narrow street where the apartment was located, then turned and headed toward the river. After a few minutes, it began drizzling lightly. I zipped up my leather jacket, stuffed my hands in my pockets, and kept going.

Eventually, I passed a huge former factory turned art gallery, called the Tate Modern, and ventured onto a pedestrian bridge spanning the river. I had it to myself at that late hour. When I was halfway across, I paused and contemplated the wide, dark Thames, which reflected the blue lights of the bridge. A small vessel passed beneath me, something squared off and built for work. I resumed my walk, taking in the sharp contrast between the breathtaking, classical dome of St. Paul's Cathedral directly ahead of me and the sleek, steel Millennium Bridge beneath my feet.

That contrast was echoed over and over in London. Historic buildings coexisted with modern architecture, the past and present coming together in a tapestry that should have seemed disjointed, but instead struck me as beautiful. I felt an immediate affinity for the city. Even though I'd never been there before, it felt like coming home in some inexplicable way.

During my layover, I'd memorized the route between my apartment and the building that housed Alastair's company. It ended up taking about half an hour to reach it, as expected. I was torn between wanting him to be in his office and hoping he'd gone home at a decent hour and was getting some much-needed sleep.

I'd been imagining a skyscraper, but instead, the executive offices for Penelegion Enterprises were in an elegant, white, four-story building that took up most of a block. It reminded me of a high-end hotel. Square columns framed the historic building's ornate entrance, and perfectly maintained square planters with small trees and colorful flowers dotted the sidewalk. Most of the building was dark, except for the lobby and three windows in the top, left corner of the building. I wondered if that was Alastair's office.

The rain picked up a bit, so I ducked under an awning and pulled out my phone, but then I hesitated. What if he was home in bed? The last thing I wanted was to wake him, knowing how sleep-deprived he'd been all week.

For the next few minutes, I watched the lit windows, feeling a bit like a stalker while I debated sending him a text. But then, my phone buzzed in my hand. The message from Alastair said: *I miss you.*

I replied: *I miss you, too. Are you in your office?*

He wrote: *Sadly, yes. I've actually started sleeping here. It's just so late every night by the time I finish work that there's little point in going home. I just have to be right back bright and early.*

I dialed his number, and when he answered, I asked, "Will you do something for me?"

"Anything."

"Look out your window." My heart leapt when a figure appeared in that corner office, backlit but unmistakably Alastair. "See the black and white striped awning across the street?"

"I do. But what—" When I stepped out from beneath it and waved, Alastair yelled, "Oh my God!" It sounded like he dropped the phone, and the line went dead.

I chuckled at that and returned the phone to my pocket. After a black taxi slowly rolled past me, I started toward the entrance to his building. Moments later, Alastair burst out the front door and ran toward me at top speed. I ran for him, too, and when we reached each other in the middle of

the street, I grabbed him in an embrace and lifted him off
his feet.

He sobbed against my lips. His kiss tasted like mint
and rain. I returned the kiss frantically. How had I gone
days without this? I needed him like I needed air.

Alastair wrapped his legs around me and touched my
hair, my face, my neck as the rain ran down both of us.
After a few moments, he whispered in my ear, "Are you
really here? I'm so afraid I've fallen asleep at my desk and
this is just a dream."

"I am, Allie. I just had to see you."

He clung to me as his body trembled in my arms.
"Thank God you followed me. I've been lost without you,
Sawyer."

"I've been lost without you, too. Utterly, completely
lost. Please don't send me away."

"I would never do that."

"Your family never has to find out," I said as I held
him and buried my face in his wet hair. "Whenever you can
get away, I'll be here for you. I know you were worried
about treating me the same way Tracy did, but this isn't the
same thing. Not at all. This is my choice. I need to be close
to you. I know you won't have much time, but even if it's
just a stolen moment here and there, at least it'll be
something."

He whispered. "I wish I could give you more."

"I know, but it'll get better. Eventually, you won't be working such long hours, and we'll have a little more time. I know that'll probably be months from now, but you're absolutely worth waiting for."

He leaned back and studied my face in the glow of a streetlamp. The rain ran down his cheeks and dripped from his hair and from the ends of his long lashes. "We'll figure this out," he said as he ran his fingertips along my jaw.

When I felt him tremble again, I put him down, then took off my jacket and draped it over his shoulders. The rain immediately soaked into my black T-shirt. When he took my hand and began to lead me to the main entrance of his office building, I said, "I know it's late, but what if this gets back to your family?"

"It won't. It's just me and the guard at the front desk, and Kenneth won't say anything."

"How can you be sure?"

"Because he's a good man." He glanced and me and said, somewhat embarrassedly, "I also sign his paychecks now, so he's going to do as I ask."

He didn't hold my hand as we crossed the ornate, marble lobby. Alastair paused at the dark wood front desk and told the security guard, "Kenneth, this is my friend Sawyer. He'll be visiting me occasionally when I'm working late. This should go without saying, but my friends are none of my family's business."

Kenneth was a man of about sixty, with a shaved head and a stern demeanor. It was a pleasant surprise when he smiled and said, with a thick cockney accent, "Mum's the word, Mr. Penelegion."

"Thank you, Kenneth, though I know I've asked you to call me Alastair on more than one occasion."

"You've asked me four times, Mr. Penelegion. As I've explained each time, a man in your position deserves respect, and that's what I'm gonna give ya."

"It's not disrespectful to call me Alastair."

"That's not how I was brought up, Mr. Penelegion."

Alastair grinned and said, "Be prepared to have this discussion again."

"I look forward to it, sir. Oh, and thanks again for supper tonight. That place does a right proper curry."

"You're welcome. I think I'm going to order from there tomorrow night, too. Will you be working?"

The man shook his head. "Mondays and Tuesdays are me nights off. If you're of a mind to order curry on Wednesday, I'd be inclined to tell the missus to skip the sack lunch. She's the only woman alive who can cock up a cheese sarnie, bless 'er 'art."

Alastair smiled at him and said, "It's a date," before heading to the elevator and punching the call button. The door slid open immediately, and as we rode to the top floor, he took my hand and told me, "I'm going to get him to call me Alastair if it kills me."

"It's nice that you bought him dinner."

"It's usually around midnight by the time I realize I haven't eaten, and he and I are the only ones here. It's only right to order something for him as well. He was a bit thrown off when I did it the first time, especially because I then proceeded to sit behind the desk with him while we ate, but I figured we could both use the company. I think he's gradually learning to accept the fact that I intend to run this company very differently than my father. Step one: getting to know all my employees on a first-name basis, beginning with the ones in this building. After that, I'll start learning the names of everyone at the department store and go from there."

"I'm surprised you have time for that."

"Oh, I don't, but I'm doing it anyway. Penelegion Enterprises is more than just columns of numbers, despite what my uncle's been trying to drill into my head all week. It's about people, many of whom have dedicated their lives to this company. Take Kenneth, for example. He's been working here forty-two years. I asked why he was still on the night shift after all that time, and he says he prefers it, because it's quiet. He admitted to me yesterday that he uses the downtime to write. Isn't that fabulous? He's been working on this epic, Tolkienian tome for more than a decade. He even let me read a bit of it."

"How was it?"

Alastair smiled at me as we arrived on the fourth floor and said, "Completely filthy! Imagine The Hobbit, but with everyone shagging for maybe seventy percent of it. To his credit though, it's fairly well-written."

I chuckled at that as we entered his office and said, "I'm sorry to say I am, in fact, imagining that." He closed and locked the door behind us, and I asked, "Are you sure I should be in here? What if your uncle or another of your relatives decides to come in late?"

"No chance. My father was the only one who ever burned the midnight oil."

"Was this his office?" The large room was decorated with dark wood paneling, stiff-looking leather-upholstered furniture, and a lot of framed photos of people and buildings that seemed to span the last century.

"It was. I think my mother gave it to me to further discourage my father from trying to return to work."

"They're all so concerned about his well-being," I said as he led me through to a large bathroom, "but at the same time, they don't seem to have any qualms about piling the same crushing workload on your shoulders." I looked around as he handed me a towel and said, "I assume this bathroom has a shower because whoever has this office is expected to spend most of his life here."

He handed me a towel and said, "I'm not going to let this job wreck my health the way my father did. Right now, I have a steep learning curve to get up to speed. That means long hours, but I won't keep working twenty-hour days forever. They've already delegated most of my father's workload to other executives. Not like they're dumb enough to trust me with anything important at this point. It's just a question of learning the ropes."

"I don't think anyone can handle twenty-hour days! It's not like people your age are immune to the effects of long-term sleep deprivation."

"I don't have a choice. Not right now. It was stupid and selfish of me to go away to university. I should have begun interning here right after secondary school, so I'd have a better handle on the way this business operates. Since I chose to run off and do as I pleased, I'm now paying the price. As I said though, it's just for a few months, while I learn the business."

My voice rose, despite myself. "And then what? You'll drop back to nice, relaxing eighteen-hour days?"

"I don't know. If that's what it takes, then—"

"Shit!"

He crossed his arms over his chest and asked, "Why are you angry?"

"Why? Because I care about you, Alastair!"

"I know, but—"

"But nothing! How did you feel all those years, watching your dad work himself to death? Because that's how I feel, watching you do the same thing. And I can see the writing on the wall! After you finish this training period, you're not going to drop back to a normal workweek. Your father never did, so why would you? I know what this company means to you. I remember you telling me what it represents to your entire family and to the tens of thousands of people who rely on it for their income. But this job almost killed your dad. Are you going to let it do the same to you?"

"What would you have me do? Say, 'sorry everyone, but I'm more important than the lot of you,' and walk away? That is not an option, Sawyer!"

"You don't have to walk away, but you do have to figure this shit out! There has to be a way to do this job without letting it destroy you!"

"Don't you think I'd love to figure out how to do this job differently? My goal isn't to be a martyr and sacrifice my life for this company, or even for my family! That said, it's hardly destroying me!"

"You look like you're down at least ten pounds, Alastair, ten pounds in a matter of *days*, and you didn't have it to lose in the first place. On top of that, you're physically and mentally exhausted! Am I supposed to just sit back and watch while you try to find your breaking point?"

He stared at me for a long moment, and then he asked, "Did you come all this way just to lecture me?"

"Of course not!" I forced myself to lower my voice, and said, "I'm here because I care about you, Alastair, and I didn't mean to lecture. It's a terrible time to try to have this conversation, because we're both exhausted. But I'm worried about you, and I hate feeling useless and unable to do anything to help. This is just making it worse though, and putting even more pressure on you, and I'm so damn sorry."

He closed the distance between us and took my hand as he looked into my eyes. "You help me so much more than you realize. Being able to call and hear your voice is what got me through this last week. And now you're here! I'm so grateful that you came all this way for me."

"One of the first things you ever said to me was, 'If you want me, you have to come and get me.' I want you,

Alastair. More than anything." I drew him into my arms and kissed his hair. He was cool to the touch, and shaking a little. "Shit, you're freezing. Do you have something you can change into?" He nodded and I said, "Get in the shower, and I'll bring you some dry clothes."

"Join me."

We got undressed and held each other as we stood under the steady stream of hot water. When he relaxed in my arms, it felt like a personal accomplishment. After the shower, Alastair turned up the heater, and instead of getting dressed, we curled up together in a nest of blankets on the couch in his office. I pulled a thick duvet up to his ears and kissed his forehead as he snuggled against me. "I'm so glad you're here," he said. "This is the best I've felt all week."

I held him close and whispered, "Me, too."

Chapter Fourteen

"Ello, Bonny."

I started a little, then put aside my newspaper and squinted at Roger over the top of my sunglasses. He dropped into the seat across from mine and scanned the headlines of the sports section as I said, "Hey. How'd you know I'd be here?"

"Simple matter of deduction. Gromit told me your address, and also that you'd left his office at about five this morning. I figured you'd sleep for a few hours, then immediately gravitate to the nearest pretentious coffee shop for a fancy cappuccino."

"You're almost right. I ran an errand first, and it's actually a latte," I said, raising my cup. "You should have called me. I would have met you wherever you wanted and saved you a trip to Southwark." When he chuckled, I asked, "What?"

He mimicked my American accent and repeated, "South-*wark*. That's hilarious."

"Isn't that how you say it?" He shook his head, still looking highly amused. "How else would you pronounce that?" Roger slurred something so quickly that I muttered, "Huh?" He repeated himself more slowly, exaggerating the pronunciation. It sounded a bit like 'Suv-urk', but even more fucked up. I exclaimed, "Oh, come on! How could you possibly get that out of South w-a-r-k?"

Roger shrugged and said, "That's just the way it is."

"I wonder what else I've been mispronouncing."

"Pretty much every word that comes out of your mouth."

Roger grinned at me, and I asked, "So, are you here as my cultural liaison? Because that's going to be a full-time job. And speaking of jobs, what are you doing with yourself now that Alastair has stopped doing things like going outside, or ever actually leaving his desk?"

"For starters, Gromit made me the head of security for Penelegion Enterprises' executive offices, so I'm auditing the existing alarm system and doing background checks on all personnel."

"Out of curiosity, did you do a background check on me when he and I started going out?"

"Of course."

I raised an eyebrow at that. "Seriously?"

"It's my job to look out for Alastair. Do you think I'd let someone get close to him without thoroughly investigating them?"

"How thoroughly?"

"Well, let's see. Your middle name is Eugene, you're allergic to penicillin, and you had a dog when you were seven, but you were told he ran away after six months, and you never saw him again."

"Jesus, that's creepy. Wait, what do you mean, 'I was told?' Are you saying my dog didn't run away?"

"Your step-mum at the time didn't like the mutt, so she took him to the pound and told you he ran off."

"And you know that how?"

"Public records."

"Why would animal shelter records be public?"

"They're not, but news stories are."

"My dog was in the news?"

"He was adopted by another family and went on to save a child from drowning. Your step-mum tried to get him back after that, possibly because the dog's owners were given a sizeable reward. That's what made it into the local paper. She was a piece of work, that one. Incidentally, her real name was Martha, not May like she told you and your dad."

"Oh, come on." I stared at Roger for a few moments, trying to decide if he was pulling my leg. "What else are you going to tell me, that there's no Easter Bunny? Because Willie Garmin beat you to that one in the second grade."

"There's no tooth fairy, either."

"There's no way that story about the dog is true. He was an idiot who used to bark at his own tail."

"Turns out, he also barked at drowning kids, so loud that it drew a neighbor's attention. She hopped the fence and saved the unbuoyant moppet, right in the nick of time."

"Did you track me down just to tell me some tall tales about a moronic dog I owned when I was seven?"

"Nah. That was just a bonus." Roger leaned back in his chair and grinned at me. A moment later, a barista came out of the shop, looked around the patio, and brought Roger a coffee and a scone in a white paper bag. My companion smiled at him and said, "Cheers mate, thanks a lot."

The guy called, "No worries, Roger," as he went back inside .

"Wait, they know you here? You just called this place pretentious."

"I was having you on. Me mum lives just down the road, and I pop in here whenever I visit her. She's a love, but her idea of a decent cuppa is four heaping spoonfuls of Sanka and a splash from the kettle. You practically have to chew it, and you don't even get a jolt of caffeine for your trouble."

"Is it my imagination, or has your accent actually gotten thicker since you've been back in the UK?"

"Has it?"

"Pretty much. So, back to what we were saying. Why'd you track me down? Is it to warn me to be discreet around Alastair's family? Because I actually know that. It's why I snuck out of the office this morning at the ass-crack of dawn. And no, I'm not going to make a habit of playing dodge-the-relatives at Penelegion central. Until Alastair gets his own apartment, he's going to visit me whenever he can here in…Suffolk? It's way off his family's radar."

"Suvurk."

"How is what I'm saying different from what you're saying?"

"You're going to do fantastic here in London, mate."

I swung my hand in a rotating motion and said, "So, the actual reason you're here, besides dog tales, discretion warnings and mocking my accent, is…."

"Two reasons. First, I'm checking to make sure all's well with you. Gromit has enough to worry about these days without also needing to look after you."

"I'm actually perfectly capable of looking after myself, but thanks for making me sound like a—"

"Lost puppy?"

He grinned again before taking a sip of coffee, and I asked, "What's the second reason?"

Roger returned his cup to the tabletop and studied me for a few moments before saying, "I debated whether or not to tell you this. Finally, I decided I should just make the information available, and you can do with it as you see fit."

"Um, okay. What is it?"

"While researching you, I also dug up information on your ex-boyfriend."

I knit my brows and asked, "Why would you bother?"

"I needed to know if there was unfinished business between the two of you, which could affect Alastair."

"You're very thorough."

"Alastair's more than just a job," he said. "I care about him."

"I know, and I'm glad he has you to look out for him."

He took another sip of coffee before saying, "In that case, maybe you won't mind telling me if there's any hostility between you and Garcia. Any grudges? Did you leave it on bad terms? Might he be jealous if he got wind of your relationship with Alastair?"

"No, none of that. Why are you asking?"

"Because he's stationed less than four miles from here."

"He's…wait, what?"

"He got promoted to a liaison position here in London. At least, I think it's a promotion. His job basically involves arse-kissing and playing nice with the higher-ups. Sounds a bit crap if you ask me."

As I tried to absorb that, I muttered, "Where exactly is he stationed?"

"At the U.S. Embassy. He's working for the Defense Attache."

"Oh."

"If Garcia learns you're in London, you sure he won't try to cause trouble for you and Alastair?"

"Positive. I meant nothing to him."

Roger watched me for another moment before saying, "Now that you know he's here, will you go see him?"

"Maybe. I'd like to find out how he's doing. We were friends once, and I don't think we'll ever be that again, but I guess I still care what happens to him."

"Honestly, I expected a flat-out 'hell no' there. From what I've heard about your relationship, I assumed you'd want nothing more to do with him. I hope I didn't throw a spanner in the works for you and Gromit."

"God no! Tracy's in the past, where he belongs, and I'd never start something up with him, not in a million years. You have to know I'm crazy about Alastair. If you need proof, just look at Exhibit A: the fact that I dropped everything to follow him to the UK."

Roger said, "Took you long enough. Another couple days and I was going to fly back to the U.S. and chuck you on the next transatlantic flight."

"But I thought you were on board with the whole keeping me away from the Penelegion clan idea."

"Now, clearly this isn't the time to go ruffling feathers, what with Gromit's dad being on the mend following major surgery. But his family's opinions on homosexuality are utter bollocks! Telling their own grandson to marry someone he doesn't love, then sneak around with men on the side? Who gives advice like that, especially in this day and age? Granted, the family's mentality is stuck in the 1800s in many ways, but that's just beyond the pale."

"So, you don't think we should hide our relationship? I mean, once Mr. Penelegion is well?"

"That's not my call, it's Gromit's. But my two cents is this: what you and Alastair have is the real deal. You don't hide something like that, you celebrate it. With all he's doing for the family, they ought to be grateful, not trying to shove him into a mold and make him more 'acceptable'. It's all about keeping up appearances with that lot, at any cost." Roger looked annoyed.

"I know you practically grew up with the Penelegion family, so I'm surprised to hear you say negative things about them."

"My loyalty to Alastair comes first, and he doesn't deserve the shite his family puts him through. I hope someday he stands up to them, and I also hope I'm there to see it, because I suspect it'll be glorious."

Roger finished his coffee, then stood and picked up the scone. "Not hungry after all?" I asked.

"It's for me mum. She's got a bit of a sweet tooth, that one. Figured I'd pop in and see her, since I'm in the neighborhood."

I smiled at him and said, "You're a nice guy, Ro. But don't worry, I won't tell anyone and ruin your straight-up gangster rep."

"You have my cell number, Bonny. Don't hesitate to call if you find yourself in need of anything, translation services, English lessons...."

"Will do. Hey, have you heard of a place called Mad Jack's?"

"Aye, it's a strip club. Why do you ask?"

"I applied for a job there today. My former boss put in a good word for me."

Roger rolled his eyes and said, "Not even in the UK twenty-four hours, and already Bonny Barebottom is looking for ways to expose his arse to a whole new group of unsuspecting onlookers."

"Hey, a guy's got to make a living."

"You know Alastair would put you on the payroll at Penelegion Enterprises, no questions asked. There are ways to circumvent the rules against employing U.S. citizens."

"It isn't Alastair's responsibility to support me. Stripping may not be my dream job or anything, but it'll do until I figure out something better."

He thought about that for a beat, then said, "You could do worse than Mad Jack's. It's a fairly classy establishment. At least, that's what I hear."

"Not that you've been there or anything."

"Nice boy like me? Perish the thought!" Roger was smiling as he headed down the sidewalk.

After I finished my coffee, morbid curiosity more than anything propelled me toward the metro, which would take me to the U.S. Embassy. I texted Alastair as I walked to the station, because he had a right to know I was going to check out the place where my ex-boyfriend worked. He called me when he received my message and said, "If you run into Tracy and decide to throat-punch him, please get it on film. That would make my day."

I smiled and said, "Throat punching isn't the plan. I'm not angry about what happened between us. If I happen to run into him, I'd just like to see how he's doing. I wonder sometimes whatever became of him."

"Well, I for one am not nearly as forgiving and would happily inflict body harm on him for the way he treated you."

"Tracy and I both made a lot of mistakes, and I let myself get hurt. I should have just believed him when he told me he didn't love me and accepted it for what it was: meaningless sex, with a side of friendship."

"He's a complete git who toyed with your emotions. But if you want to give him the benefit of the doubt, be my guest."

"Are you really okay with me going to see him? If not, just say the word and I won't go."

"If you're asking whether I'm jealous, no worries there. I am a little concerned that seeing him will tear open a wound you've spent a long time healing, but I also know you need this."

"I do?"

"Sure. You'd hoped tattooing over his name would provide closure, and I know you were a bit disappointed when it didn't make a difference. So, maybe seeing him will do the job," he said. "As for jealousy though, there's no need. You're mine, and I'm yours. Nothing could possibly change that, least of all a wanker from your past."

"Say that again."

"Wanker?"

I grinned and said, "No, the other part. The one about us belonging to each other, because that was awfully nice to hear."

"You know it's true."

"I'm smiling ear-to-ear right now. The people in the Underground probably think I'm deranged." A loud noise let me know a train was coming into the station a few moments before it appeared, and I said, "I think my ride's here, I'd better go."

"Good luck, Sawyer. If you happen to run into Tracy, say hi for me. Just remember, in my family, that's traditionally done with a throat punch."

*****

The U.S. Embassy was a boxy, off-white building with a huge eagle on the edge of the roof, centered above the front entrance. I stood in the park across the street and stared at it while trying to decide if I should go over there and ask for Tracy. Even if he was available and actually agreed to see me, we'd probably end up having an awkward two-minute conversation, and then I'd leave, and closure would remain ever-elusive. It was pretty pointless.

Just as I decided to skip the exercise in futility and head back to my apartment, a deep voice to my right exclaimed, "Oh my God, Sawyer!"

Tracy Garcia stood about ten feet away, dressed in uniform and holding a shopping bag. He was tall, muscular, and nearly thirty, with close-cropped dark hair and a face that, although handsome, seemed to naturally default to a scowl. Right then though, his expression was pure astonishment. There was something different about him, aside from that stunned look, and I tried to figure out what it was.

In the next instant, Tracy dropped the bag, closed the distance between us, and crushed me in an embrace. I was so stunned that I went completely rigid and kept my arms pressed to my sides. He was really tall, with huge arms and shoulders, and I felt completely engulfed by him. I found myself musing that getting crushed by a giant anaconda would probably be exactly like this.

After a moment, the shock of what was happening wore off enough to mumble, "Um…what are you doing?"

He let go of me, but then he took my face between his big hands and searched my eyes. "I can't believe you're here. I'd given up hope. All this time, all those emails, and you never wrote back. Not once. I was sure you'd forgotten all about me. But now, here you are!"

When he went in for a kiss, I jumped back and exclaimed, "Whoa! Can we just take a moment here? I don't understand what's going on right now."

Suddenly, I realized what was different about Tracy: there was raw emotion in his dark eyes. He was one of the most stoic people I'd ever met, and about the only emotion he tended to display was anger. And what the hell was he doing, trying to kiss me in public? His fear of revealing his sexual orientation was almost pathological.

Tracy looked confused too, but then he said, "I'm about to be late for a meeting. I would just blow it off, but I'm already on probation and can't afford another screw-up. Will you meet me for dinner tonight? There's a little restaurant in Covent Garden called Café Valerie. It's right at the entrance to the market. I can be there at seven."

"I…guess?"

He pulled me into another hug and whispered, "I'm so glad you came to London, Sawyer. I'll see you in a few hours." The fact that I remained as responsive as a corpse with rigor mortis seemed lost on him. Tracy kissed my forehead before retrieving the shopping bag and jogging across the street and into the embassy.

I wandered back to the Bond Street tube station in a daze, wondering what the hell was going on with my ex.

The man I'd known never would have acted like that. He seemed like a completely different man. A stranger.

And apparently, I'd just accepted a date with him.

*****

When I got back to my apartment, I paced for a while, then pulled my laptop from my backpack, consulted the laminated instruction sheet I'd found in the dresser, and typed in the Wi-Fi password. Tracy had said something about emails, and I was reminded of an old, free account I'd opened when I was in the military, specifically for him so we could contact each other privately, far away from the prying eyes of the United States Army. It hadn't even occurred to me to access that account after we broke up.

It took five tries to remember my password. I tried every variation of the passwords I used for pretty much everything, then sat there staring at the blinking cursor for a solid minute. Finally, a vague memory stirred, and I frowned as I typed 'S_loves_T' into the password box. Ugh, what a stupid, lovesick sap I'd been.

After a moment, my in-box appeared on screen. I had four hundred and thirty-seven messages. But how? Exactly one person had that address. I scrolled through the emails and muttered, "Holy shit."

They were all from Tracy, every last one of them. I navigated to the very end of the list, where the oldest messages were, and clicked on the first one. He'd sent it the day after I broke up with him and left Afghanistan, and all it said was: *We need to talk.*

The first couple dozen messages were just like that, simple, emotionless requests for me to get in contact with him. But as time went on, the messages started to get more in-depth. He began talking about his feelings, which for Tracy was a major break-through. I clicked and scanned message after message in a daze. He admitted he was wrong, and that he'd screwed up.

And then, a month after we broke up, in the thirty-third message he sent me, Tracy told me he loved me. He said he always had and always would, and that he'd been afraid to admit his feelings to anyone, especially to himself. It made my heart ache.

A month after that message, there was a period of seven weeks where he didn't send a single email. I wondered what happened during that time. But then they started back up again. He wrote every day, sometimes even twice daily. He seemed to use the emails almost like a journal. I could practically chart Tracy's evolution, his gradual opening up to me and to himself as the weeks went on.

At the same time though, something else was happening, which he alluded to in vague terms. Tracy had been in complete control of every aspect of his life when I knew him. He was an excellent soldier in part because he was highly disciplined. It seemed as though, the more he started being honest with himself about who he was and what he wanted, the more he started unraveling in other aspects of his life. He began getting in arguments with senior officers, something I couldn't even imagine him doing, and expressing feelings of discontent about life in the military.

Eventually, his father intervened. He had enough pull to get Tracy reassigned to that desk job in the UK, when it became clear he was too emotionally compromised to remain in Afghanistan. Tracy hated every minute of the new job, and he'd put in a request to be transferred to a position near San Francisco...so he could be closer to me.

I opened one of the more recent emails, which said: *I love you, Sawyer. I know you're still angry, and that's why you're not writing back. But I refuse to give up on us. My transfer to the Bay Area was approved and will take place at the end of August. Once we're living near each other, we'll have a chance to work this out. I've changed. You'll see that for yourself when I finally get to California. I wish you'd taken me up on my offer and visited me in London, but I get why you didn't. I was such an asshole, and I know you have no reason to trust me. I'm so sorry I hurt you, and that I could never admit how much I loved you. It wasn't just you I was lying to. I was also lying to myself. The end of summer can't get here soon enough. I'm going to make this right and show you I'm worthy of you now.*

A new message popped up as I sat on the bed with my computer balanced on my knees. It said: *You made me the happiest man in the world today, Sawyer. I know I came on too strong, and that you were thrown off by it, but I was just so overwhelmed to see you standing there. It was a dream come true. I promise I'll dial it back over dinner tonight. We have so much we need to talk about, and I won't try to rush anything. I'm so excited to see you, though.*

I muttered, "Fuck," and closed the laptop.

How often had I wished Tracy would admit his feelings? Later on, how many times had I wished he'd apologize? I'd thought hearing those words would give me closure, but they didn't. Not at all. It was just a great, big mess, and I had no idea what I was supposed to do about any of it.

*****

"It's odd that he'd keep sending dozens upon dozens of emails while getting absolutely nothing in return. The fact that you weren't writing back didn't dissuade him in the slightest," Alastair said.

He was in his office, and we were video chatting. I noticed he looked more rested than he had in a week. It felt great knowing he'd been able to get a few hours' sleep in my arms the night before.

As soon as I'd closed my computer, I'd texted him and told him everything that had happened. A couple hours later, when he had some time to himself, we'd decided to video conference so we could talk about it. I felt bad for disrupting his workday with this shit, but he said he was glad to take a break and focus on something other than numbers and spreadsheets.

I said, "I don't think I should meet him for dinner. It feels too much like a date, and he's bound to get the wrong idea."

"You clearly need to talk to him, though."

I leaned against the headboard and said, "This must be weird for you, and I'm so sorry. You already have way too much to deal with, and the last thing you needed was a front-row seat to this drama with my ex."

His voice was gentle as he said, "Don't apologize, love. I'm glad you're finally going to be able to reach some sort of resolution with Tracy. That's been a long time coming, and I know how much you need it. I've known ever since you went to get that tattoo over his name, right after you and I got together."

"Thank you for being so understanding."

"Of course."

We talked for a few more minutes, and then I scrubbed my hands over my face and muttered, "Shit, I suppose I should get ready."

"What will you wear?"

"The least sexy thing I own. Maybe some sort of sack, with a hole cut out for my head. I have a very clear, concise message for Tracy tonight: nope." Alastair chuckled at that, and I said, "I feel bad for him though, and I'm going to try my best to let him down easy. He's come so far in terms of accepting his sexuality and opening himself up to a relationship, and I don't want this to push him back to square one, you know?"

"I have every confidence in you."

"Thanks. I'll just be glad when this is over."

*****

When I left my apartment a few minutes later, I was surprised to find Roger waiting for me. He'd been leaning against the building across the street, and when he saw me, he stood up straight and adjusted the cuffs of his black suit jacket. I called, "Hey Ro. Did you remember a few more bombshells from my past? Let me guess: my grandpa was actually Elvis, but he'd had a shitload of botched plastic surgery that made him look a hell of a lot like Dumbledore."

"What're you going on about, Bonny?"

"Just wondering what you're doing here."

"Gromit told me about the emails from your ex. Seems a bit unhinged, if you ask me. Who sends hundreds of messages to an ex-boyfriend, especially while getting nothing in return? Given that, I decided to accompany you on your date, just in case you need a hand."

"You get that I was in the Army, right? I can actually handle myself."

"But so's he, and by all accounts, Tracy Garcia is built like the bleedin' Rock of Gibraltar. What if he goes Fatal Attraction on you?"

"In a restaurant in Covent Garden? What's he going to do, order the boiled rabbit stew for dinner?" I grimaced a bit and added, "Since we're in the UK, that might actually be on the menu."

"Funny."

"It probably is, though."

He considered that, then said, "Possibly."

Roger fell into step with me as we headed down the street. After a moment, I asked, "Aren't you in violation of your mission statement right now? The one where it's your job to keep an eye on Alastair?"

"He's not going to leave his desk, let alone the building. And if he somehow deviates from his routine and decides to go for a stroll, a member of my security team will go with him."

"Alastair's life is weird. Do all rich people go everywhere with security details?"

"Those who've attained a certain level of wealth, certainly. It paints a target on your back."

"And you think someone might come along and, what exactly? Kidnap Alastair? He's a grown man, not a child."

"Doesn't matter how old he is. Did you know most truly wealthy people take out kidnapping insurance? That should show you the risk isn't as unheard of as you seem to think."

"It still seems far-fetched. Alastair told me once that his parents have always kept him and his sister out of the public eye, so no one even knows who he is. At what point does the fear of kidnapping become downright paranoid?"

"That's not the only reason why the Penelegions have tried to keep their children's identity a secret." We exited the side street, and he opened the back door of a black town car for me.

After I slid inside and Roger joined me, the driver merged smoothly into the early evening traffic, and I asked, "Why else would they do that?"

"Here's the thing, Bonny. When you're obscenely wealthy, everyone wants a piece of you. Aside from the risk of kidnapping, extortion, and a host of other ills that come with attracting the criminal element, there's another risk, too. It's less dangerous, but also far more common and quite insidious."

We stopped at a light, and Roger gestured at a bodega on the corner. At least a dozen gossip rags were prominently displayed out front, each vying for attention with lurid headlines. I said, "Ah. Yeah, I could see why you'd want to avoid the paparazzi at all costs."

"They're vermin. Best thing his parents ever did for him was to keep Alastair's identity hidden. It's the only way he can lead a semblance of a normal life, aside from certain concessions, such as yours truly."

"Well, I'm grateful for all you do, not only as Alastair's bodyguard, but as his friend. That said, I don't need a chaperone to have dinner with my ex, because he's not a risk to me." A thought occurred to me, and I raised an eyebrow. "Unless this is something else entirely. Are you here because you don't trust me, Roger? Do you think I might cheat on Alastair? Because just so you know, I'd never do that, not in a million years!"

Roger held up his hands and said, "Don't get your knickers in a bunch, Bonny. Assuming you're wearing any. You, I trust. It's Garcia I 'ave issues with. He's a loose cannon, that one. Over the last year, he's been spiraling out of control, from the looks of it. I did a little more digging after I spoke to you. A friend of a friend works at the U.S. Embassy, and he characterized Garcia as volatile. Not good, you must admit. But don't worry, as long as the situation stays under control, Garcia won't even know I'm there." It still seemed pointless, but so did arguing, so I decided to let it drop.

The driver dropped me off in front of the famous Covent Garden market. Roger was going to give me a couple minutes before getting himself a table at the restaurant. I thought as I crossed the cobblestone plaza that 'market' wasn't quite the right word for it, not anymore. It seemed more like a glass-roofed, open-ended mall, far removed from what it must have been like in the days of My Fair Lady.

To my left were a few storefronts on the ground floor of a row of stately buildings. Café Valerie was among them. The little French bistro looked cozy and unassuming through its plate-glass windows, which were underscored with bright flower boxes. It also looked closed. This was confirmed when I reached the front door and read the sign that said: closed Mondays and Tuesdays.

I'd just turned away from the café when the door swung open. A dark-haired guy dressed in a white chef's jacket asked, with a faint French accent, "Sawyer MacNeil?" When I nodded he held the door open for me and said, "We've been expecting you. Please come in."

"But the sign says you're closed."

"Tracy is a personal friend. For him, I'm doing this favor," he explained. I tried not to frown as I stepped past him and into the restaurant.

The lights were low, calling my attention to one table at the back of the café. It was surrounded by candlelight. Tracy jumped to his feet when he saw me and picked up a bouquet of red roses. He was wearing a dark suit and tie, and his expression was so hopeful. I muttered, "Shit," under my breath.

"Thanks for coming," he said, pulling out my chair when I approached the table. "You look great."

I was dressed in the same black T-shirt, jeans and motorcycle jacket I'd been wearing when he saw me earlier. I'd decided changing any part of my outfit would make it seem like I was treating this as a date. "Tracy," I said, "we have to talk." His friend slipped into the kitchen, so we had the place to ourselves.

"I know. That's why we're here." He was still holding the chair and the roses, and still looking at me with that expression that just broke my heart.

I was feeling so uncomfortable that I said, "Can we go for a walk or something? I know you and your friend went to a lot of trouble here, but this isn't what I had in mind when I agreed to meet you."

"It's too much, isn't it? The flowers, the candlelight. I wanted to make a gesture, show you I've changed. No more sneaking around or denying what you mean to me."

"I appreciate that, but you've misread the situation."

"I know you're probably still pissed off at me," he said. "I don't expect you to just forgive and forget. I'm willing to do the work, whatever it takes to earn your trust."

"Tracy—"

"Don't say no. Please? I need this. I need *you*, Sawyer. You're what I've always needed."

There was so much grief in his eyes that I stepped forward and gently touched his arm as I asked, "What happened? None of this is you, not even a little. Neither are the things I've been hearing about you lashing out at your superiors and having trouble on the job. I know it's not because we broke up, either. There's something else going on here. Did someone hurt you, Tracy?"

Anger flashed in his dark eyes, and he took a step back as he crossed his arms over his chest, instantly on the defensive. "Of course not! Who could possibly hurt me?" The denial was so vehement that I knew without a doubt he was lying.

"You don't have to tell me what happened. It's none of my business. But you really should talk to someone. A counselor, maybe. It could help."

He stared at me for a long moment, and finally he muttered, "There are some things you don't talk about. Not with anyone."

I said, "I hope someday, you find someone who you can open up to. I know you need that, Tracy, because it's what we all need. I also hope you find someone you trust enough to give your heart to, but that person's not me. Maybe it could have been at one time, but not anymore. I wish you all the best, but I don't know what else to say, so I'm going to go now."

His arms dropped to his sides, and he said, "That's it? You came all the way to the UK just to tell me thanks but no thanks?"

I decided I needed to be totally honest with him, and I admitted quietly, "Until today, I didn't even know you were in London. It's a coincidence that we're both in the city at the same time. When I found out you were here, I did come to see you. That's why I was in front of the embassy. But I was looking for closure, not reconciliation. I didn't know you still had feelings for me, because I hadn't read any of your emails until this afternoon. I'm sorry, Tracy. I know this isn't how you expected tonight to go, and you're probably pretty pissed off at me right now. But if you decide at some point that you want to talk or need a friend, send me an email, okay? I'll start checking that account again, just in case."

He dropped the roses on the floor and muttered, "I don't need your pity."

"That's not what I'm offering you! I miss our friendship, Tracy, and I'd like to get it back. Maybe that's impossible, given the million ways we've fucked this up. But I'd like to try, because I'll always care about you, as a friend. That's just the way it is. Maybe it seems like a poor substitute for what you wanted to happen here, but it's all I can offer."

"Is there someone else? Is that why you're not even considering this?"

"I do have a boyfriend, and he means the world to me, but he's not the reason I won't get back together with you. Long before I ever met him, I moved on from this relationship. It took a long time, but I finally did it. If I can do that, you can, too, and the first step is letting go of the past."

Tracy studied a spot on the floor. I didn't know what else to say, so I headed for the exit. After a moment, he called, "That guy you're seeing now. Does he treat you right?"

I paused and said, "Yeah, he does."

"That's good. Don't ever let anyone treat you like I did, Sawyer. You deserve so much better than that."

I whispered, "Please take care of yourself, Tracy," and turned and left the restaurant. My heart ached.

Roger was waiting outside, and he fell into step with me. "That was quick," he said. I just nodded. "Doing a bit of anger-walking now, are we?"

"Not anger." When I reached the street and the black town car, I hung a right and strode past it. Roger followed me.

"What exactly happened back there?"

"Closure, I guess," I muttered. "That thing I always wanted. Turns out, it fucking sucks."

"Why?"

"Because it's not this nice, tidy, tie-everything-up-with-a-bow kind of thing. I had to hurt Tracy back there, and I hate that."

"How did you hurt him?"

"By telling him the truth, that I'd moved on. He needed to hear it, because otherwise, he'll never be able to do the same. But it felt like I was taking a paring knife to his heart."

Roger said, "Gruesome mental imagery there, Bonny."

"It should be. What I just did back there was brutal, no two ways about it. I mean, here's this guy who must have had something horrible happen to him over this last year. What I don't know, because he wouldn't tell me. Part of it might have been our breakup, but something else happened too, and it changed him, profoundly. After that, he started pouring his heart out in literally hundreds of emails, and what did he get in exchange for opening up to me? A knife in his chest. Fuck. He'll probably never trust anyone ever again."

"You don't know that."

"I hope I'm wrong."

Roger said, "It had to happen. Like you said, he needed to know the truth if he was ever to move on."

We walked in silence for a couple minutes. The sidewalks were fairly crowded, but I didn't pay much attention to my surroundings. After a while, Roger ventured, "Is the plan to walk all the way back to your flat? It's a couple miles, just so you know. Not that I'm complaining, mind you. I'll simply mention that these are new shoes. Not exactly broken in yet."

I stopped walking and turned to Roger. "Since the nonexistent threat of violence from my ex-boyfriend has passed, and since it's early evening and I'm probably not in imminent danger of getting jumped by a gang of British street thugs who'd probably be armed with umbrellas instead of guns, you don't have to walk with me."

"Maybe I just like your company."

"I'm pretty sure you think I'm a pain in the ass."

Roger grinned at me and said, "Aye, you are that. But I've grown accustomed to you, Bonny. And it doesn't hurt a fellow to feel useful, now does it?"

I finally got why he was hanging around. "You miss Alastair, don't you?" Roger just shrugged and tried to play it off. I noticed we were standing in front of a bakery, and I said, "Come on, let's go inside and pick up some biscuits. I'm starving. Ridiculous name for cookies, by the way. Maybe your mom might like some, too. What do you suppose she's doing tonight?"

"Same as every other night. I'm sure she's got her arse parked in front of the telly."

"Well, you and I probably have three or four hours to kill before Alastair calls it quits for the night. What do you say to loading up on baked goods and parking our asses in front of that TV with your mom?"

"You're in London, Bonny. Without a doubt, this is one of the greatest, most fascinating cities in all the world. Is that all you can think to do with your free time, spending it with me and a pensioner while watching repeats of Are You Being Served?"

"Tomorrow night, I have an interview at that strip club I mentioned. When I went in earlier today, they took a couple pictures of me with my shirt off and had me pole dance, which made me feel slutty and awkward at the same time. I guess it went well though, because they told me to come back and meet the owner. Anyway, if I get the job, and if they ask me to start right away, this will be my last opportunity to enjoy a wholesome evening for a while. Besides, I can't wait to meet your mom. If she brings out old photos of you in short pants and a beanie hat, then my life will be complete." I flashed Roger a big smile, and he rolled his eyes as he pushed open the door to the bakery.

*****

Alastair met us at Roger's mom's house when he left the office at ten (an early night for him). He brought his driver in with him, and we all enjoyed tea and cookies while Mrs. Foster beamed delightedly, pinched Alastair's cheeks, and regaled us with stories from his and Roger's childhoods.

I finally had a moment alone with my boyfriend when we told Mrs. Foster we'd refill the kettle and retreated to the kitchen together. I pulled him into my arms and kissed him, then said, "Hi, Allie."

"Hello, love. How was your dinner with Tracy?"

"It wasn't dinner, just five awkward minutes of painful conversation. I'll tell you about it later, okay?"

"Sure, long as I know you're alright."

"I will be." I kissed his forehead and he nuzzled my cheek.

"Good. I was worried about you."

"So was Ro. He's a bit aimless since you've been spending so much time at work, and tonight he made me his project. I'm not complaining. He's a good friend, and I know he means well."

"That he does."

I looked around us and said, "His mom is a trip. She looks like a floating head with that perfect camouflage she's got going on. It's kind of freaking me out." Mrs. Foster's couch, wallpaper, and dress were all variations on a very similar pink floral print, so one blended right into the other.

Alastair laughed and said, "I hadn't thought about it."

"She's nice though, and she obviously adores you."

"She's a dear. I've known her all my life. Her sons, her late husband, and his father all worked for the Penelegion family."

"I don't say this to be rude, but she seems more like Roger's grandmother than his mom."

Alastair said, "He was a surprise baby, born when his parents were in their fifties. Ro's brothers are decades older than he is."

"Must have been a lonely childhood."

"Well, I came along when he was nine and tried my best to make sure it wasn't," he said. I was reminded once again that Roger wasn't an employee, not by a long shot. He was family.

When the kettle was hot, we replenished everyone's teacups, and Alastair carried the tray back into the living room. I watched him as he distributed the cups and joked and laughed with Mrs. Foster and his driver, a short, stocky man named Herbert. In his expensive suit, and with his two hundred dollar haircut and handmade Italian shoes, Alastair shouldn't have fit in at all in that middle-class parlor with its floral everything and collection of ceramic cats. He did, though, just by being himself, the warmest, most genuine, kindest man I'd ever known. I thought, not for the first or last time, how incredibly lucky I was to get to be a part of his life.

*****

I told him that, hours later when we were curled up naked under a couple blankets in my attic apartment, and he flashed me a lazy smile and said, "I'm the lucky one, Sawyer. My life is infinitely better because you're a part of it."

He stretched up and kissed me, and I ran my fingertips down the curve of his back. We'd spent the last couple hours fucking. It had been passionate and wild, as if it had been years instead of days since the last time we'd been together.

After a moment, he asked, "If you end up getting the job at the strip club, how late do you suppose you'll be working each night?"

"I don't know. Probably about as late as you do."

"You don't sound very enthusiastic about it."

"I'm not, but a job's a job. I can't just be idle while I'm here."

He watched me for a moment, then said, "Next Friday, I want to take you on a date. It'll be in the middle of the night, so it won't matter if you have to work late."

I grinned at him and asked, "What kind of date do you have planned at that hour?"

"You'll see."

He grinned at me, and I tilted his chin up and kissed him again. Then I said, "Hey, I just remembered something. Can you reach my suitcase?"

He leaned off the edge of the bed and said, "It's right here. We pulled it over so we could get to the lube and condoms."

"Look in the pocket inside the lid. I have something for you."

He pulled his leather-bound journal from the pocket and exclaimed, "Thank you, Sawyer! I've missed this. I'd taken to writing my thoughts on a yellow legal pad in its absence, but it's just not the same."

"You're welcome, but that's not actually what I wanted you to find."

He put the journal on the end table and fished in the pocket again. When he produced a cardboard box, he sat up, straddled my hips, and asked, "Is this it?"

I nodded. "Sorry about the shoddy presentation. I should have taken the time to wrap it."

"You got me a present? You didn't need to do that. You certainly didn't need to wrap it, either." Alastair opened the end of the cardboard box and extracted a cylinder of bubble wrap. He pulled on one end of it, raising his arm up over his head as it unfurled in a long strip. The little red convertible dropped into his other hand.

His mouth fell open and his eyes went wide. He stared at the four-inch car, and then at me, and then at the car again. Alastair dropped the bubble wrap and held the toy gingerly with both hands, as if it was the most precious thing in all the world. "I only mentioned these once, when we first started dating," he whispered.

"I found one right away, the night you told me about your collection of Dunford Racers," I said. "It took weeks to arrive."

"But these cost hundreds of dollars, and you barely knew me back then!"

"I already knew you were someone I needed and wanted in my life. I also knew it would make you happy, so buying it was a no-brainer."

He laughed delightedly and kissed me, then jumped off the bed. I sat up and watched him. Alastair crouched down, held the car to the floor, and drew it back, revving its wheels. When he let it go, it shot across the attic and he whooped with delight. "It's just fantastic," he exclaimed as he got up and ran after it. He brought the convertible back to bed, climbed on top of me, and kissed me again. "Thank you so much, Sawyer. I can't tell you what this means to me."

"It means everything to me too, to get to see you this happy."

He put the toy on top of his journal, very carefully, and used a fingertip to fold down the cloth roof. "It's the best gift anyone's ever given me," he said softly, before kissing me again.

After a few minutes, he leaned off the bed and pulled something else from the suitcase. As he draped the sheer, white, lace-trimmed chemise on my chest, he asked, "Will you do something else for me and put that on?"

It still had the tags on it, and I contemplated the silken garment for a moment. I'd bought it on a whim years ago, because I'd thought it was pretty. It was by far the most feminine thing I owned, years away from my hard-edged black leather corsets. And it was the purest, most undiluted expression of that other side of me, going so deep that I'd never actually had the courage to wear it, not even when I was alone.

I sat up, so I was face to face with Alastair, who was straddling my thighs, and tore off the tags, being careful not to rip the delicate fabric. When I pulled it over my head and looked down at myself, I smiled a little. I'd worried that it was a step too far, but it felt good.

"You're so incredibly beautiful, Sawyer." Alastair's voice was husky as he ran his hands down my sides, clearly enjoying the feel of that wonderful fabric. We laid back down, and he curled up in my arms. After a moment he said, "I was stupid to come home without you. Since you've been here, it all just seems manageable somehow, the job, my family, all of it. You're essential to my well-being."

"I feel the same way about you."

He glanced up at me, his fingers idly tracing the lace neckline between my pecs, and said, "What if I asked you not to go to the interview at that strip club?"

"Then I'll cancel it. I'm not going to do anything you're uncomfortable with, Allie. I don't want to do anything to embarrass you, either."

"It's not that. I just know that job isn't what you want. If you give me a few days, I can come up with something so much better for you, something I think you'll love."

"You don't have to put me on the payroll," I told him. "Seriously. I'd feel like a bum if you were paying me for no reason. And that's what it'd have to be, since I'm hardly qualified for any of the jobs at your company. Well, aside from late-night security guard, but that position's filled until Kenneth retires."

"Just trust me, alright? Cancel or postpone that interview, and by Friday, I should have something to show you."

I kissed him and said, "I'll cancel first thing in the morning. Thank you for thinking of me. I feel bad though, because you already have so much on your plate without also trying to help me."

"I'm realizing the only way I'm going to survive this job is by learning to delegate, *a lot*. My father never wanted to do that, because he was a complete control freak. I handed off a couple minor projects today, and already, I feel loads better. I also hired a brilliant personal assistant, and she's helping me pull together the surprise for you. Not that I'm handing it all off. This is important, and I'm making sure it's exactly right."

"Well, thank you again. Any hints about what you have up your sleeve?"

He kissed the tip of my nose and grinned at me as he said, "Absolutely not." Whatever it was, I knew I'd love it, because of the way it made his eyes light up. But then his expression grew serious, and he said, "We've managed to keep you distracted all evening, but I know you're upset about what happened with Tracy earlier tonight, so let's talk about it."

"But it's late, and I don't want to keep you up and make you listen to my problems."

"This is important. *You're* important. And if something is bothering you, I want to help."

I studied his face for a moment. His expression was one of perfect sincerity. We both settled in, and then I started talking quietly about everything that had happened with my ex, and how bad I'd felt.

Alastair didn't try to offer advice or opinions. All he did was hold me and listen. It was exactly what I needed.

Chapter Fifteen

I ran a comb through my just-washed hair before crossing my apartment and sitting on the bed. It was my only option. The place could have benefitted from a table and chairs, no doubt about it.

It was Friday night, and Alastair was due to pick me up in less than an hour, at the stroke of midnight. I still had no idea what he was planning, but I appreciated his flair for the dramatic. I retrieved my laptop from under the bed and leaned against the headboard. The blue kimono he'd given me after our first night together fell open when I bent my knees to rest the laptop on them, revealing my freshly shaved legs, some new white lingerie, and a pair of sheer, white, thigh-high stockings, selected as much for Alastair as for me. I'd done a little shopping that week, and had been delighted when I'd found a shop that catered to cross-dressers and drag queens, which meant understanding salespeople and plenty of things in my size.

I waited for the laptop to power up, then checked my email. Every day, in addition to checking my main account, I took a look at the mailbox I'd gotten just for Tracy. The messages had stopped after Monday night and the dinner date that never was. I'd emailed him once since then, reminding him I was there if he needed to talk, or if he wanted a friend. He hadn't responded. I was going to keep trying, though.

There were a few emails from friends, and I was happy to see one from Elijah. When I read that he wanted to talk, I fired up my video chat program to see if he was online, then clicked the icon next to his name. A few moments later, he appeared on screen and exclaimed, "Hey! I just emailed you."

"I saw. How's everything, Elijah?"

"Fantastic! The house is great, and Jed's a fun roommate. His brother Jessie came to dinner last night with his husband and their daughter. It made me feel all grown up, co-hostin' a dinner party. That probably sounds dorky, right?" He grinned a little and pushed his blond hair behind his ear.

"Not at all."

"Yeah, it does. I'm almost nineteen and all excited about learnin' to make a lasagna and gettin' to serve it on nice dishes instead of paper plates. Meanwhile, Alastair's only a little bit older than me, and he's runnin' a huge company. It makes me think I'm like, stunted or somethin'."

"Actually, you're amazing and totally gifted. Never compare yourself to Alastair, because you both have your own unique set of skills. Hell, if I compared myself to him, I'd be completely depressed."

"You're doin' great, though. And what you said about my own unique skill set? Right back at ya."

"Except you're a math genius, and I can draw a bunny on top of a latte and walk in five-inch heels."

"Totally kick-ass skills." I chuckled at that, and he asked, "Speakin' of math, are you still likin' your online classes?"

"Yeah, I am. Next semester, I may take more than two at a time. Unless I'm busy with work, in which case I'll stick with just a couple."

"Did you find a job?"

"Possibly. Alastair has something up his sleeve, and he's planning to spring it on me tonight. I had applied for a job in a strip club, but I was happy when he talked me out of it."

"So, how long are you and he gonna be stayin' in London?"

"Hard to say. For now, he has to be here for his job. Maybe down the road, he'll have more flexibility. This is all I know for sure: I plan to be wherever he is."

Elijah smiled and said, "You two make me happy, both because it's awesome when nice things happen to good people, but also because you're makin' me believe in love."

"You didn't already?"

"I want to," he said. "I hate to be a total pessimist, you know? But…I don't know. For someone like me, it's pretty hard to believe I'll ever get it together enough to have a real relationship. What I had before, with Colt…it wasn't love, but sometimes I think that might be the closest I'll ever come. I just don't know if I have it in me to open up my heart and let another person in."

"You have all the time in the world, Elijah. And you know what? When the right person comes along, it'll just happen, and you'll wonder what you were ever worried about."

"I hope so."

The doorbell sounded, and he glanced to the right as Jed yelled, "I got it," in the background.

I told him, "I should let you go, since you have company."

"That's probably Colt, Chance, and Finn. We're gonna barbeque some corn and salmon and use the pool. I swear, this place is like a resort! The pool guy's cute, too," he said with a shy smile.

"Have fun. It sounds like you have a great summer day planned."

"I'm glad we got to catch up a bit. Tell Alastair hey for me, alright? I message him a lot, but I know he's real busy."

"He is, but he loves hearing from you. Never hesitate to get in touch with either of us, okay?"

"Alright. Talk to you soon, Sawyer. You look nice, by the way. I like the red lipstick on you."

I grinned and said, "I actually forgot I was wearing it."

"You should wear it more often. It suits you." I thanked him for the compliment before we said our goodbyes and disconnected.

I spent the next few minutes trying to decide what to wear. It would have helped if I'd had any idea where we were going. I just knew it was a big deal, based on the way Alastair had been acting all week. Eventually, I decided on black dress pants, paired with a royal blue button-down shirt. Then I thought maybe I should have gone with my suit, but I decided to stick with the original outfit, mostly because I liked the way I looked in that shade of blue. I had to laugh at myself when I realized I was acting like a schoolgirl, but that feeling of excited anticipation was fun.

At twelve sharp, Alastair knocked on the door (despite the fact that I'd given him a copy of my key). When I opened it, he murmured, "My God, you're absolutely gorgeous, Sawyer."

As he handed me a big bouquet of stargazer lilies, I asked, "Is the lipstick too campy? I was just playing around with it earlier. And if this outfit isn't right for whatever you have planned, I can change."

He was wearing a suit, of course, since he'd just come from the office. It was pearl gray and flawless, and he'd paired it with a crisp, white shirt that was open at the collar. I still marveled at his ability to look so pulled together at all times, even after a very long day at the office.

"You're perfection," he told me. "Don't change a thing."

"Thank you for the flowers," I said as he came into the apartment. "I don't think I have a vase, but I can figure something out." When he pulled a vase from behind his back, I kissed his cheek and said, "You always think of everything. I just left a mark on your face, by the way, and now I see the drawback of wearing lipstick. I'm going to go take it off, so I can kiss you properly."

When the lipstick was removed and the flowers were arranged in the vase and centered on the dresser, I drew him into my arms and gave him a long, slow kiss. "That was the very best part of my day," he murmured as he slid his arms around my shoulders.

"Well, the day's only five minutes old, so we'll have to see if we can top it. Do I get to know where we're going yet?"

He shook his head and kissed me again, then said, "Still a surprise. And we should probably get going, since I'm parked illegally."

I grabbed my leather jacket, and we headed downstairs. When we emerged onto the main thoroughfare from the narrow side street, I exclaimed, "Your Acura! I didn't know you had it shipped from the U.S."

He ran his hand over the gleaming red paint and said, "It was indulgent of me, and now I'll have to get something else to drive whenever I'm in San Francisco, but I missed the old girl. We had a lot of good times together."

"I'm surprised you had time to make the arrangements."

"I didn't. My fantastic personal assistant handled it. Her name's Lorelei, by the way, and she's looking forward to meeting you."

"She knows about me? That I'm your boyfriend, I mean?"

"She does. Lorelei also knows she's never to discuss it with anyone else in the company. I trust her to be discreet."

"Out of curiosity, what happened to the assistant you inherited along with your dad's office?"

348

"I reassigned her to another department. All I ever heard was 'that's not how the senior Mr. Penelegion did it.' Last thing I needed."

He held the passenger door of the Acura for me, and once we were both seated in the cream-colored leather interior, he turned the key and grinned at the roar of the engine. That made me smile, too. It felt great to see him happy. After a minute, he said, "If you decide you want your Harley here, I can have it shipped over as well. I almost did it as a surprise, but I didn't want to overstep."

"That'd be great, actually."

"Then consider it done."

As we drove across town, I peppered him with intentionally dopey random guesses about our destination, including, "You decided I need to continue my education, so you're dropping me off at clown college."

"Clearly."

"You're taking me to McDonald's for a Happy Meal, because you figure I must be missing the U.S."

He smirked and said, "Yes, that's it. You've utterly ruined the surprise now. I hope you're happy."

"I'm not, but the Happy Meal will take care of that. It's right in the title. Are you taking me to—"

"Stop guessing! What if you accidentally stumble across it?"

"If I was even sort of in the ballpark with clown college and fast food, I'm going to need you to slow down just a bit so I can jump out of this moving vehicle."

"Don't forget to tuck and roll. Safety first."

"Good tip, thank you."

"I'm here to help."

After a few minutes, we rounded a corner and the world-famous Penelegion's department store loomed before us. The nearly two-hundred-year-old, six-story building took up an entire city block. Its golden-yellow brick façade glowed in the darkness, lit by dozens of concealed floodlights, and a series of domes and turrets along the roofline made it look like a castle. I was awestruck, and I murmured, "My God, it's beautiful."

It was odd to see my boyfriend's last name spelled out in big, lit letters on the marquee, and when I mentioned that to him, he said, "It's always struck me as a bit surreal, to be honest."

We pulled into a VIP parking spot beside the store's main entrance. As we got out of the car, the double doors swung open and Roger stepped outside with a security guard and a young, black woman in an impeccable suit. As we approached the trio, Alastair said, "You didn't have to see to this in person, Lorelei, it's late! But since you're here, meet Sawyer."

She gripped my hand firmly and said, "I've heard a great deal about you. It's a pleasure." Lorelei had a quick smile, a refined British accent, and enviable hair, which grazed her shoulders in perfect ringlets. She turned to my boyfriend and said, "I don't mind late hours, Alastair. You know that."

He told her, "Well, thank you. I want you to know I appreciate it, and all you did to help pull together tonight's surprise."

"Instead of thanking me, text me later tonight and tell me what happened. Never mind the hour." They had an easy rapport, more like old friends than employer and employee.

"And where's my thanks for burning the midnight oil?" That came from Roger, who'd crossed his arms over his chest and was trying to look stern.

Alastair kissed his cheek, which made Roger color slightly, and said, "Thank you, Ro. Didn't mean to make you feel under-appreciated. You too, Harry."

The security guard grinned and said, "I'll take a pass on my kiss if it's all the same to you, Mr. Penelegion."

"Alastair."

"Alastair," the man echoed. "We all set then?" When Roger told him we were, the security guard nodded to us and took off down the sidewalk, whistling as he went.

Roger told us, "I shut off the security cameras, and the building is empty of all personnel. Harry and his team will be patrolling out here, instead of their usual routes. That means you'll have plenty of privacy. Good thing, since I can only assume you two have tawdry plans involving the mattress department."

Alastair chuckled and thanked him, and as he ushered me into the building, I heard Lorelei tell Roger, "Come on, mate, I'll buy you a drink. There's a grand lesbian bar just a couple blocks from here."

He muttered, "Oh, fantastic," but then he linked arms with her and they headed down the street.

As my boyfriend locked the door behind us, I wandered into the department store and whispered, "Holy shit." The ground floor was ringed with gilded pillars, and it had high ceilings and an open center section, revealing five stories of balconies topped by a stained glass dome. Soft lighting gave the whole place an ethereal quality. And of course, everywhere I looked, bountiful displays of beautiful things beckoned.

We were in the cosmetics section, and as we strolled down the main aisle, I ran my fingertips over a collection of lavish perfumes. Alastair caressed my lower back and said, "I have three things planned. There's a picnic dinner, ample time to shop and play around in any departments you wish, and the surprise I've been alluding to all week. What would you like to do first, love?"

"The surprise, please, although this is already amazing."

"I hope it's about to get even better." His expression was one of nervous anticipation as he took my hand and led me across the ground floor.

The building was so large that it took us a few minutes to reach the northwest corner. That part of Penelegion's housed several dining venues. It had been designed to resemble a miniature, eighteenth century English country village, including individual storefronts and a central seating area ringed with potted plants, which I would have called a courtyard if we were outside. Velvet ropes, a sign saying 'Under Construction', and a wide set of royal blue curtains blocked off whatever was located directly in the corner of the building, nestled between a bakery and an upscale deli.

Alastair turned to me and said, "You can absolutely say no to this. I won't be hurt or offended, I promise. It was just an idea I had, and I probably should have discussed it with you before I took it this far, but I thought it would help to see it partly set up. Just remember, it can go away if it's not what you want. Zero pressure."

"Got it."

"Wait right here and close your eyes."

I lowered my lids and put my hand over my eyes for good measure, and he took hold of my shoulders and rotated me about five inches to the right before hurrying in the direction of that curtain. He muttered, "Shite! Don't you dare stick on me, ya bastard," then grunted with effort at whatever he was doing. After a moment, Alastair exclaimed, "Finally! There we go." Then he called, "You can open your eyes, Sawyer."

My jaw dropped right along with my hand, and I murmured, "Oh my God." A glass-fronted café filled the corner of the building diagonally, framed by the now-open curtains. Above the door, an elegant sign in wood and brass read: *Sawyer MacNeil*. Smaller letters below my name proclaimed: *Purveyor of Fine Coffees*.

He said, "I had the store's display department make up the sign, just to give you an idea. You don't have to stick with it if it's not to your liking."

I wandered into the café in a daze. Rich wood tones made the space feel warm and welcoming. To my left, a polished counter fronted a workspace displaying a life-size photo of a professional-grade espresso machine. Alastair explained, "Lorelei had the poster made up to help you visualize this as a coffee house. She also printed up fact sheets with the specifications for several different models of espresso machines for you. She's very thorough."

"So, this space…."

"Is yours if you want it," he said. "Just so you know, I'd be your landlord, not your employer. You'd be leasing the space from me at the rate of one pound per month, and you'd hire your own staff and make all the decisions. All the shop owners in this part of the building are on a lease. Their rent is somewhat higher, however, so mum's the word, ay?"

"I could pay more than a pound a month."

"I know, but I don't like the idea of making a profit off you." I turned slowly, imagining a busy coffee house all around me, and Alastair added, "While this would be yours to run as you see fit, I do have one favor to ask."

I turned to him and said, "Anything."

"Please let me buy you the espresso machine and the rest of the equipment you'll need. It would mean so much to me to get to do that for you."

"But those machines cost as much as a car."

"All the more reason. Even without having to worry about the equipment, you'll still have plenty of start-up costs, and I don't want you to completely obliterate your savings and put yourself in debt right out of the gate."

"I appreciate the offer, and I am going to need some help at first, because my savings aren't nearly enough to cover all my startup costs. But as soon as I begin turning a profit, I'm going to pay you back. This is a prime location, and that intersection out there is probably busy during the day," I said, gesturing at the view out the plate glass windows at the back of the café. "I think I'd have more customers than I knew what to do with."

"You will. For forty years, and up until three weeks ago, this was a tea parlor. The purveyor made a fortune with it and retired to a villa in Spain. Incidentally, her tastes ran along the same lines as Mrs. Foster's, so I've had workers in here all week, taking down frilly curtains, refinishing the formerly pink wood floors, and stripping off layers of floral wallpaper."

"They've done a great job. It's beautiful."

"I'm glad you think so."

I asked, "I just thought of something. What about the rule against Americans getting jobs in the UK and taking them away from residents?"

"You'd actually be providing jobs, so no worries there. My lawyers could handle the business license and all the necessary paperwork for you. But that's assuming you actually want this."

I took his hand and said, "Of course I do! It's a dream come true, Alastair. I'm already envisioning what this place could be."

He lowered his gaze and said, "If you hired the right people and found a competent manager, you wouldn't have to remain on-site, you know. Not if you didn't want to."

"Why wouldn't I?"

"Well…what if you decided to return to the U.S.? As much as I want you to remain here with me, we've never talked about this. It would mean leaving your family and friends and your entire life back in the States. Offering you this business opportunity must seem like I'm trying to get you to put down roots, and that I've been making a lot of assumptions about us, but it's your life, and a huge decision, and…." He looked up at me and asked, so softly, "Am I really what you want, Sawyer?"

"More than anything! I came here because I *need* to be with you, Alastair, and wherever you go, I fully intend to follow."

"But you're giving up everything for me."

"No, I'm not. I'm gaining everything."

He pulled me into an embrace, and as I wrapped my arms around him and held him close, he said, "I can't begin to tell you what it means to me to have you here. I was barely holding it together before you arrived. But it all feels much more bearable now, because I know that no matter how bad my day is, I have this to look forward to at the end of it."

I kissed his forehead and said, "It's nice to be needed."

"You are, and soon you'll also be needed by scores of Londoners who'll come to depend on your delicious coffee. Oh, and I hope you incorporate your wonderful latte art, because the world needs more whimsy. I wholeheartedly believe that."

"I will." I kissed him and asked, "How soon can I start getting this place up and running?"

"Begin tomorrow if you'd like. The paperwork can happen while you're setting up the business."

I looked around and said, "I always wanted a place just like this, but it seemed like it'd always be out of my reach. Thank you, Alastair, for making this happen."

"You're the one who'll make it happen, love. All I'm doing is providing the venue and some equipment."

"Like I said, I'll pay you back for the espresso machine and the rest of it. I also want you to increase my rent to a realistic amount, although it may take me a little before I can afford to do that."

He smiled at me and said, "No."

I chuckled at that. "What do you mean, no?"

"If you want this space, the rent is one pound a month in perpetuity, nonnegotiable. And the espresso machine and equipment are a gift. You don't pay people back when they give you presents, Sawyer. You just say thank you."

"You drive a hard bargain."

"I know."

I hugged him and said, "Thank you, Allie. I appreciate this so much."

"You're welcome. So, just to be clear, this is a definite yes?"

"Absolutely."

"Fantastic!" Alastair looked delighted, and he pulled out his phone and sent a quick text. "Lorelei will be thrilled, too. She got quite emotionally invested in this place over the last week."

"I need to thank her for her help."

His phone beeped, and he read the text and told me, "She says she's jumping for joy, and also that she'll be in here daily for her coffee fix." He returned the phone to his pocket and looked up at me with a gleam in his eye. "Now, would you like to run amok in a major department store?"

"Yes please!" I grabbed his hand, and we raced out of the café.

*****

For the next two hours, we crisscrossed Penelegion's, bouncing from department to department. Whenever we found something we wanted to buy, Alastair tore off the tag and left it and his business card on one of the registers, so the sales associates could charge him for it in the morning. Even though his name was on the building, he was conscientious about paying his way (and, on a practical note, he didn't want to throw off inventory counts by shorting departments of their merchandise).

We spent a lot of time in the toy department, and when he showed me the counter that once housed his beloved Dunford Racers, I said, "Aw, I wish I'd known we were going to be here. It would have been the perfect time to give you that red convertible."

"I'm glad you gave it to me when you did. I have it on my desk in the office, and whenever I look at it, I think of you and smile. It's been a welcome bright spot." That was nice to hear.

As I ran my hand over a stuffed giraffe that was almost as tall as I was, something caught my eye, and I exclaimed, "I have to get that sparkly, pink princess dress for Kai's daughter Izzy, she'll love it!"

We found the right size, and Alastair had me write her address on the back of one of his business cards. We left the dress, card, and a request to mail it behind the counter, and he said, "You can count on the staff to wrap nicely and ship it for you. They're top-notch."

Our last stop was the lingerie department. Fortunately, it had an ample plus-size section, because that was the only way I could fit into anything. I stripped for Alastair while he sat in an upholstered chair in front of a trio of mirrors, and when he saw what I was already wearing under my clothes, he drew in his breath.

I proceeded to model several outfits for him, and he kept getting more and more worked up. A short, see-through red nightie finally put him over the edge, and he all but tackled me. We tumbled to the floor in a passionate embrace as I burst out laughing.

We ended up fucking right there in the lingerie department, both of us reflected over and over in the mirrors around us. Afterwards, when we were curled up in the upholstered chair, I asked, "So, which outfit should I buy?"

"I'm buying you everything you tried on."

"No you're not. It's too much, especially after all you're already doing for me with the café! I can't let you spend hundreds more on top of all that."

Alastair grinned and ran a fingertip down the thin strap of the red negligee as he said, "Buying you these sexy things is a gift for both of us. You get to wear them, and I get to see you in them. The epitome of a win-win situation." He kissed the frown line between my brows before climbing off my lap and holding out his hand to me. "Come on, let's pack up all your new treasures and get to that picnic. I'm bloody well starving after the way we just worked up an appetite."

"There's no point in arguing, is there?"

"Absolutely none."

I let him pull me to my feet, and then I kissed him gently and said, "Thank you, Allie. You're the most generous man I've ever met, and I want you to know I'm so grateful for all of this."

He caressed my cheek and said, "You deserve to be cherished, Sawyer." We kissed for another minute, and then he said, "Come on, love. I'll collect our purchases while you get dressed."

The third and final phase of our date took place on the roof. We left all our purchases beside the elevators so we could collect them at the end of the evening, and then Alastair led me through a staging area, up a small staircase, and out a creaky, disused door. I was unprepared for the hidden treasure awaiting us.

The graceful, rusted metal and glass pavilion resembled a round, Victorian greenhouse. Alastair said his great-great-great-grandfather had built it on a whim. "He envisioned opening a bistro up here, but didn't bother to check with anyone before he had it built. It was immediately deemed too dangerous by the rest of the family, what with the risk of guests tumbling off the edge of the roof and all, so it was never opened for business. The family calls it Bernard's Folly. I've always found it magical."

The turrets and spires around the edges of the building and the huge, stained glass dome in its center conjured a fantastical and otherworldly landscape, like something out of a dream. Beyond it, London's skyline sparkled against the night sky. I murmured, "This is astonishing," as I took it all in.

"You know what being up here reminds me of?"

I turned to him and smiled. "Our first night together."

"Exactly."

He played 'Time After Time' on his phone, and we slow-danced around the roof. When the song ended, he kissed me, then took my hand and led me into the pavilion. It was lit by a dozen tall, Moroccan lanterns, and in the center of the space, a red blanket was set with fine china and piled with a dozen jewel-toned pillows. We got comfortable, and Alastair served us champagne, which had been chilling in a silver bucket. Then he said, as he folded back the lid on a big, wicker picnic basket, "One of the shops downstairs, the one immediately to the left of your coffee house, makes these up. I've always loved them. On weekends in summer, my father would drive up from London to our country house, which is where my sister and I lived when we weren't away at school. He'd often bring along one of these hampers, so they make me think of my childhood." Alastair found a white box of cookies sandwiched with strawberry jam, and fed me one as he said, "These were always what I most looked forward to."

As we ate, he told me about each of the local delicacies and the memories they stirred in him, from the pastel meringues which were served at every birthday party to the cheddar-laced crackers that were taken on trips to the shore. He said, "These hampers have remained reassuringly consistent throughout the years. How many things in life can you say that about? If that shop ever closes its doors, it'll feel like losing a piece of my childhood."

"Then we're going to make damn sure it never closes," I told him. "Even if the shop owner tries to retire, we'll do something about it. We'll buy out his lease and all his recipes and hire someone to run it in his place." That made him happy.

After eating our fill, we curled up in the nest of pillows, and I took his hand. We ended up talking all night.

It felt wonderful, just being able to let my guard down and be myself. So much of my life had been spent pretending to be someone I wasn't and trying to please people who were never going to give a shit. It was so nice to know I'd never have to do that with Alastair.

Near dawn, I whispered, "Tonight was perfect. I just feel bad, because you've given me so much, and I have nothing to give you in return."

Alastair held my gaze as he said, "You've given me *you*, Sawyer. You left behind friends, family, and country just to be with me. The stuff I gave you tonight was trivial in comparison."

"It wasn't trivial. In fact, it was so much more than I ever dreamed of. And so are you. You're absolutely everything, Allie, and I'm grateful beyond words that you're in my life." As the sky turned pink all around the pavilion, he kissed me tenderly. I never even knew it was possible to feel that perfectly happy.

Chapter Sixteen

Eight Weeks Later

"You just smeared your eyeliner."

"Oh hell." I carefully ran the side of my index finger beneath my lower lashes and asked, "Is that better?"

Kai scrutinized me for a moment, then said, "Yup, you got it."

We were video chatting, so I took a peek at the little image of myself in the bottom corner of my screen to make sure. Then I grinned at my best friend and said, "Did you ever imagine you'd be giving me makeup tips?"

"That wasn't exactly a makeup tip, so much as a general heads-up."

"True."

"If I was going to give you a makeup tip, I'd tell you that lipstick's a shade too dark on you. Makes you look washed out."

"Oh see, I knew it." I pulled a tissue from the box on my desk and wiped my lips, then said, "I let Liza and Lisa in the cosmetics department talk me into trying that one when I went for a stroll earlier. They said it looked dramatic, but I was on the fence. Now I'm glad I didn't buy it."

I pulled a tube of red lipstick from the desk drawer and applied it with the mirror in my compact as Kai asked, "So tell me, my glamorous friend, how do you like running your own business? Is it all you'd hoped for?"

As I returned the cosmetics to the drawer, I said, "I love it. We've had our challenges in the four weeks we've been open, but it's getting easier. Thank God for Horton, the manager I hired. With his decade of experience, he's seen it all and has a solution for every problem that crops up. I'm pretty sure I would have run screaming from the building at least half a dozen times by now if it wasn't for him."

"Have you somehow resisted asking him if he hears a who?"

"Just barely. It was touch and go for a while there, but I think I've managed to get a handle on it."

"Well done."

"Thank you," I said. "I'm proud of that accomplishment."

"So, how are you adapting to life in London?"

"It's been a remarkably easy transition. I'm basically in the fine-tuning phase now, which includes looking for a slightly bigger sublet in my neighborhood with a few more amenities, like a kitchen. I have to stop eating out every meal, because I'm developing a raging fish and chips addiction. I joined a gym too, and I'm working on getting back into a routine."

"I'm surprised you're looking for a place, since you told me Alastair bought an apartment a couple weeks ago. You two have already done the roommate thing, so I assumed you'd just move in there."

"He actually spends every night at my place. He bought an apartment so he could move out of his parents' house without stirring up questions about where he was going. And we don't stay at the new place because one of his relatives could drop by unannounced."

Kai said, "So, he's sticking with the whole hiding you from his family thing. How do you feel about that?"

"I don't love it, but I understand. Besides, who am I to judge? I hid who I was from my dad for years, or so I thought, because I dreaded the fallout. And this is what I signed on for when I came to London. I told him I didn't mind us sneaking around, if that's what it took to be with him."

"It still must wear on you."

"It's a small price to pay. In exchange, I get to be with the most amazing, kind, generous, and gorgeous man I've ever met. I'd do anything for Alastair, including keeping us a secret from his family as long as he asks me to."

Kai grinned and asked, "Have you told him yet that you're madly in love with him?"

I grinned, too. "That obvious, huh?"

"Well, yeah, and not just because you dropped everything to follow him to the UK."

"I haven't told him yet. I want the timing to be right."

I could hear Isabella bounding into the room a few moments before she appeared beside her dad. She waved at the screen and called, "Hi, Uncle Sawyer!" She was wearing the sparkly princess dress Alastair and I had sent her from Penelegion's. According to Kai, she wore it every single day, and he had to bargain with her when he wanted to wash it.

"Hi Izzy! How are you?"

"Good! Are you having fun in London?"

"For sure."

She smiled at that, then turned to Kai and said, "Dad wanted me to tell you breakfast is ready, Daddy." I thought it was sweet that she'd started calling Jessie Dad.

Kai thanked her for delivering the news and kissed her forehead, then told me, "I'd better go, but I'll talk to you soon, Sawyer. Are you working all weekend?"

"Nope. I'm taking my first full day off since the coffee house opened. It's a little nerve-wracking, but I know my employees have it all under control."

"Are you doing anything fun?"

I grinned and said, "Alastair's leaving work a bit early this afternoon, and we're driving to his family's house in the country. He's been wanting to show me where he grew up. What about you, what are you guys up to?"

"We're camping at the coast with a bunch of Jessie's adopted family, including Nana. We wanted to do a little getaway before Izzy starts school in a week. I can't believe it's the end of August already." No kidding. Summer had passed in a blur, between getting the shop ready for its grand opening, then figuring out the day-to-day logistics of running a business.

After we promised to chat in a couple days and disconnected, I stretched my arms over my head and looked around my office. *My office.* That still blew me away, as much as seeing my name above the door of the coffee house. The office was actually a work-in-progress, with blank walls and a few boxes that had overflowed from the tiny storeroom, but I felt a sense of pride as I took it all in.

Horton stuck his head through the door and interrupted my reverie a minute later. Beneath the shaved head and tough-looking, tatted exterior was a capable, intelligent man who was becoming one of my best friends. He called, "Oi boss man, there's a bloke 'ere to see you. Right enormous bastard too, I tell you what."

"Did he say what he wanted?"

"He didn't say much of anything, aside from nearly ordering me to go fetch you."

As I got up, I asked, "Is he wearing a uniform?"

"No, but he's clearly military. He just has that air about him. Who is he?"

"I'm guessing that's my ex-boyfriend, Tracy." I stepped out from behind my desk and looked down at myself. I was wearing a basic T-shirt, but I'd paired it with a slim-fitting miniskirt, tights, and combat boots, all black. "He's never seen this side of me. It's kind of pathetic that I'm tempted to change before I go out there."

London had been a fresh start for me in many ways, a chance to both figure out and express who I was. I'd opted to keep my hair short, and at the same time, I started playing with lipstick and eye makeup. I also began combining traditionally masculine and feminine clothes, because expressing both sides of myself harmoniously instead of favoring one over the other felt right. My employees and regulars at the coffee house had only ever known that version of me, to them it was just Sawyer being Sawyer. But then there was Tracy.

Horton asked, "Why? Are you worried he'll judge you for it?"

"I know he will. Tracy just doesn't have it in him to think outside the box."

"Don't let a ghost from your past throw you for a loop, mate. Be proud of who you are. I think it takes balls to dress how you do and not give a damn what others have to say about it."

"The thing is, I do give a damn. I hate the stares and rude comments, but I'm slowly learning not to let other people's opinions matter that much to me." I sighed, and after a moment, I blurted, "Fuck it. Who cares what Tracy thinks? I don't need his permission or his approval."

"Too right!"

I squared my shoulders, trying to project more confidence than I felt, and left the office. The coffee house was crowded, same as always, but I spotted Tracy right away. At his height, he couldn't help but stand out. He was dressed in a grey T-shirt and jeans, but he might as well have been wearing his uniform, because just like Horton had observed, everything about him screamed 'military'. People used to say that about me, too, and I wondered if I'd ever managed to shake it.

When he saw me, his expression became perplexed. I held my head high as I crossed the shop. This was my turf, my world. He didn't get to make me feel bad about myself.

I held his gaze unwaveringly as I said, "Hi Tracy."

"What the hell are you doing?"

"Running a successful business. What are you doing?"

"I mean with the skirt and the makeup."

"You have a problem with it?"

He seemed to consider the question before saying, "I guess not. I just don't understand it. You were never like this before."

"Actually, I was. I just kept it hidden."

"Oh." He knit his brows as he tried to process that, and finally said, "I'm sorry you didn't feel you could tell me."

"Well, no. You had enough problems with me as it was. I can just imagine how this would have gone over."

"I never had a problem with you, Sawyer," he said quietly. "I had a problem with me."

"Why don't you come into my office?" I said, relaxing my posture a bit. "It's a better place to talk."

"It's okay, I don't want to take up your time. I just came to say goodbye."

He was scheduled to ship out to California the next day, and I said, "You never told me where you're going to be stationed. I thought all the Army bases around San Francisco were decommissioned."

A frown line appeared between his brows. "I'll be at Travis Air Force Base as an interdepartmental liaison. Me and a bunch of flyboys. That's going to suck."

"Doing what, exactly?"

"A useless, bullshit desk job."

"Sounds miserable."

"I know. I only applied for it because…."

"You thought I'd be nearby."

"Yeah." After an awkward pause, he blurted, "I'm thinking about leaving the Army when my commitment is up next year, but then what?"

"Well, then you'll figure out the next thing."

"But this is all I've ever known, and the fact that it doesn't feel right anymore is totally throwing me off, and…Jesus, why am I telling you all this?" He looked mortified.

"Because you need a friend, Tracy. You've never had anyone you could talk to, and with all those emails you wrote, maybe you got in the habit of opening up to me."

"I'm so embarrassed I did that."

"There's no reason to be."

He glanced at me before directing his gaze off to the side. "I hate acting weak in front of you."

"You should cut yourself some slack. Despite what you've been taught your whole life, showing emotion isn't a sign of weakness. It's a sign of being human."

That was a little more touchy-feely than Tracy could handle, and he said, "I should go. I just came by to congratulate you on your new business and say goodbye. Oh, and thanks for the emails these past couple months. Sorry I don't write back very often."

While that was the first time I'd seen him since that failed dinner in Covent Garden, I'd gotten in the habit of sending him an upbeat email once a week. At first he hadn't responded, but in the last couple weeks he'd started to write back. We both kept it light, just 'hey, how's it going?' and a bit of news. But it was a positive step toward building a friendship.

"My boyfriend and I will be visiting San Francisco this December," I told him. "Let's get together. I also want to introduce you to some of my friends. I know a lot of good people in the Bay Area."

"Why would you do that?"

"So you're not all alone in an unfamiliar place."

"I'm sure your friends will love me, given what you must have told them about our relationship."

"I didn't say much, and you should give them a chance. They'll give you one, too."

"Maybe. We'll see." He started to turn away, then paused and glanced at me. "I'm proud of you, not that you need to hear that. This place is fantastic, and it looks like a big hit with all these customers. But I'm even prouder of you for the way you're dressed. It takes guts to let people see the real you, more than I'll ever have."

I pulled him into a hug, which he returned quickly before letting go of me, and I said, "Good luck, Tracy. I hope California ends up being a positive thing for you. Keep those emails coming, okay?"

"I will, and I'll see you in December."

After he took off, I returned to my office and sat on the corner of my desk, and then I grinned a little. That had been progress. I was glad to be building a friendship with Tracy, and I thought it was great that he was questioning who he was and what he wanted. Change was never easy, and it certainly seemed like he was still experiencing some growing pains. But he seemed like someone come to life after spending way too long on autopilot, and that had to be a good thing.

*****

Maybe ten minutes later, Roger found me in my office, and after we exchanged greetings, I said, "Tracy Garcia was just here. He came to say goodbye, because he's leaving for the States tomorrow."

"So, you two are friends now, ay?"

"We're working on it." When Roger frowned, I asked, "Do you think it's a mistake to try to remain friends with an ex?"

"I guess I fail to see why anyone would want to, but no, I don't think it's a mistake."

"Are you friends with any of your exes?"

"In order to do that, I'd have to have some."

"You don't?" When Roger shook his head, I asked, "What do you have, then?"

"A job that keeps me too busy for a social life."

"Sounds like an excuse to me."

"Oh, look at the time!" He glanced at his wrist, even though he wasn't wearing a watch. "Do what you need to do, so we can get out of here. Gromit's excited for your night and day in the country, so let's not keep him waiting."

After I said goodbye to Sal and Lee, the two baristas on duty, Horton walked me to the door and promised to call if any questions or problems arose. "It'll be grand, you'll see," he said. "When you get back and find I haven't managed to run your business into the ground over the course of twenty-four hours, maybe you'll realize you can begin taking entire weekends off, like a normal person."

I paused for a moment and looked around to make sure I hadn't forgotten anything. When Horton sighed dramatically, I said, "Okay, I'm going! See you Sunday."

I'd ordered a huge picnic basket from the deli next door. Roger went with me to get it, and then he helped me carry it to his car. When I asked why he was grinning, he said, "It's nice, you 'aving a hamper made up for Gromit and taking care of him like that. He must have told you how he loved them as a kid."

"He did mention it."

"The housekeeper knows you're coming though, and she will have laid in some supplies. You probably didn't need the hamper that's meant to feed a dozen people."

"I didn't want to leave out anything that Allie might look forward to." I glanced at Roger as we exited the department store and asked, "Are you sure the staff at the country house won't say anything to the Penelegions about him bringing his boyfriend home?"

"Since the house is rarely used these days, the staff consists only of my brother, who handles security at the estate, his wife, who's the cook and housekeeper, and their son, who's the groundskeeper. I had a long talk with them and explained the situation, and they promised not to say a word. Even though they're loyal to the Penelegions, they hate the way the family has always tried to dictate

Alastair's private life." Roger looked amused as he added, "It's an outright rebellion among the Foster clan, I tell you. They'd never cross the family otherwise, but they love Alastair like he's one of their own, and they want what's best for him. I explained what's best for him is you."

"Aw, thank you, Ro. I'd hug you if my hands weren't full."

He muttered, "Thank God for small favors," then grinned at me when I shot him a look.

We loaded the hamper into the back seat of Roger's black Land Rover, and then he drove me to my apartment. The red Acura pulled up right behind us as I got out of the car, and when Alastair joined me on the sidewalk, I scooped him into my arms and kissed him, then said, "I missed you."

He grinned and kissed me again before saying, "I missed you, too."

Roger chimed in, "You saw each other this morning."

To which Allie replied, "Exactly. It's been hours!"

When I kissed Alastair again, Roger sighed and said, "You're making me damn glad I'm driving up on my own. A couple hours trapped in a vehicle with the two of you and I'd have gone round the bend."

"You know you can sit this one out, Ro," Alastair said. "We'll be in good hands with your family once we reach the manor, and all that's between here and there is a hell of a lot of traffic leaving London on a Friday afternoon."

"Yes, fantastic timing on your part," Roger said as he leaned against his fender. "Perhaps you and Bonny could snog on the pavement for another half hour or so, to make sure we hit the absolute worst of the commute."

I turned and headed toward the stairs. "It'll just take me a minute to pack a bag, I didn't get to it before work this morning."

Alastair and I exchanged grins, and Roger rolled his eyes. "One last shag before you had to run out the door, no doubt." He held up his hand. "Don't tell me if I'm right."

I called, "You are," just to irk him and chuckled as I bounded up the stairs.

Alastair followed me into the apartment and said, "I'll grab your toiletries while you find some clothes." By the time he returned from the bathroom with my shaving kit, I'd exchanged the skirt and tights for jeans and sneakers, and he said, "Aw. Why'd you do that?"

I'd done it automatically, and I had to think about the why behind it before answering. Finally I said, "My coffee house is a safe place. I'm comfortable being myself there. Actually, that's true for most of Penelegion's. But now we're venturing out into the English countryside and parts unknown, and I just feel better in camouflage. No point in attracting extra attention to us."

"Most of Penelegion's? Are there some staff members who treat you less than respectfully?" His hackles rose instantly, and I could just picture him reaching for a stack of pinkslips.

As I stuffed a change of clothes in my backpack, I said, "They're all perfectly polite to my face, but when someone's even the least bit different, you know how it goes: the stares when they think you're not looking, the whispered remarks behind your back, that little glint of disapproval in their eyes even when they're smiling at you."

He whipped out his phone and fired off a text as he exclaimed, "That's unacceptable! Penelegion's is supposed to be a safe and welcoming environment for everybody! I realize some of the staff have been around since the Mesozoic era, but that's no excuse."

"You're turning Lorelei loose on them, aren't you?"

"Absolutely. If they're doing this to you, then surely they're making others feel uncomfortable or unwelcome as well. I won't stand for that anywhere, but certainly not in a business which bears my name!"

"I almost want to make excuses for them and tell you it's not that bad, because ninety-five percent of the employees have treated me with nothing but kindness. You're right, though. I'm imagining a vulnerable, self-conscious kid like Darwin coming into the department store. A little sensitivity training could go a long way."

Alastair read his screen and said, "Lorelei promised she'd handle it, and that means it'll get done immediately and properly."

"She's a gem."

"You're right. I don't know what I'm going to do without her."

I looked up from my backpack and asked, "Is she going somewhere?"

"I'm promoting her. She's completely underemployed as my personal assistant. The woman has an MBA from the Imperial College Business School, for God's sake."

"In that case, I'm surprised she took a P.A. position."

"She was having trouble finding something fresh out of graduate school, since she had little on-the-job experience. But she's more than proven herself capable, and it's to the company's benefit to put her in a leadership position."

"When you hire someone at an executive level, do you need your board of directors to sign off on it, and if so, are they going to hassle you for promoting someone right out of school?"

"We have no board of directors. Penelegion Enterprises is privately owned, with just the family as shareholders. That's why no one kicked up a fuss when the family stuck me at the top of the food chain. Not that there was much to worry about. They're still channeling all the important projects and decisions away from me. I feel like a figurehead more than anything, or, at best, a manager. Obviously, that's the right call, since I'm still learning the ropes. But it's also a bit frustrating."

"I can imagine."

"I made sure my family knew Lorelei's promotion was nonnegotiable. They need to start trusting me with actual decision-making, beginning with that." He closed the distance between us and stretched up to kiss me. Then he said, "That's the very last thing I'm going to say about my job for the next twenty-four hours, I promise."

"It's good for you to vent, though."

"It is, and I just did. Now I'm done." He kissed me again and said, "This weekend is about you and me, nothing else."

*****

The Penelegion family's estate was located less than sixty miles from London, but the drive took a solid two hours. Once we got away from the city with its Friday traffic, it became a lot of fun, though. The last part was spent meandering through open pastureland on narrow country roads. When we turned onto a long straightaway with a sign that read 'private road, no trespassing', Alastair grinned and said, "Roger hates it when I do this, but he also knows I simply can't help myself."

Laughter burst from me when he threw the car into gear and slammed on the accelerator. The Acura shot forward, and as the speedometer sailed past a hundred, he let out a whoop of delight. It was so rare to see him acting his age and cutting loose, and it made me happy. All too soon, he downshifted, and before we reached a curve in the road that took us into a woodland, we were traveling at normal speed again. But his mood remained upbeat, and there was a beautiful sparkle in his eye.

Eventually, we came to a towering set of ornate, wrought iron gates. They looked like they were a hundred years old, but they opened with a code typed into a modern key pad. That was followed by another ten-minute drive through the forest.

When the trees parted and our destination was revealed, I exclaimed, "Holy shit!" Alastair parked in the circular drive, and I got out of the car and failed to keep my mouth from falling open. Roger pulled in behind us and parked his SUV as I murmured, "You grew up in Hogwarts."

Alastair had told me on our drive that Wordsworth Manor was begun in the early 1700s, with a major expansion in the mid-1800s when his family bought it. The green-roofed manor was built from some kind of yellow stone, and the setting sun turned it to gold. While it really did resemble the mythical school with its turrets and spires, the layout was different. It consisted of a huge, central building, with wings curving around to bracket a lavish front garden, which in turn framed a massive fountain.

Alastair looked up at the house and said, "You can tell my great-great-great-grandfather had a chip on his shoulder. We don't have so much as a drop of royal blood, and I think that must have made him feel less-than in high society. His solution was to build himself a castle. That made him a bit of a laughing stock, but his response to the ridicule was to just keep building and making the place grander and grander, and to keep buying up all the land around us, as far as the eye can see. It never earned him the respect he wanted, though. The press just called him a shopkeeper with delusions of grandeur."

Roger muttered, "Bastards," as he glanced at the beautiful estate.

"Sadly, things haven't changed much," Alastair said. "Even now, after almost two hundred years as one of the richest families in the country, we're still dismissed as nouveau riche. My family is actually embarrassed by this place, they call it flashy and ostentatious. Not me, though. I think the old girl is glorious."

"If they hate it so much, I'm surprised they haven't sold it," I said.

"Ah, but that would be like admitting the critics were right, that it is too big, too showy, too over-the-top. So instead, they cling to it stubbornly, and when people criticize it, they pretend to laugh it off and say, 'Ah, Bernard Penelegion, what an eccentric old fool he was!' Never mind that he was the one who built our financial empire from nothing, and we're all hugely indebted to him."

Ralph and Bertie, Roger's brother and sister-in-law, came out to meet us just then. They were easily twenty years older than he was, and Ralph looked and acted more like his dad than a sibling. After warm greetings and hugs all around, Roger and I fetched the huge picnic basket from his backseat and carried it into the house.

The inside was just as showy as the outside, possibly even more so. Everywhere you looked, there were rich tapestries, fussy antique furnishings, and priceless vases, paintings and statuary. I couldn't begin to imagine what it must have been like to grow up in a house where everything looked like it belonged behind a velvet rope.

We went all the way through the house, passing lavish parlors, a huge library, and other grand spaces. When we arrived in the kitchen, I didn't understand it at first. It was warm, comfortable, and a bit worn around the edges. In other words, it was a stark contrast to the rest of the house. For a minute, I didn't understand why people as wealthy as the Penelegions wouldn't have upgraded to a high-end kitchen. But then, I got it. The family didn't cook. They had people for that. And since the kitchen was the domain of their domestic employees, there was no reason to make it fancy. No guest would ever set foot in it. I doubted many of the Penelegions ever did either, aside from Alastair, who was perfectly at home there.

The five of us gathered around the long, well-worn farm table at the back of the kitchen. Bertie opened bottles of local wine while Alastair and I spread out the hamper's bounty for all to enjoy. A bouquet of wildflowers had been arranged in a glass milk bottle, and they delicately perfumed the air. We were at the side of the house, and a set of open double doors let in a gentle breeze and offered a view of a charming herb and vegetable garden. The open doors also let in a little black-and-white cat, who stretched out right in the doorway and began grooming itself.

A couple minutes later, Bertie and Ralph's son Mark, the groundskeeper, joined us. He had blond hair like his mother and a deep tan from countless hours making the gardens a thing of beauty. Mark shook my hand and offered me a warm smile before grabbing first Roger and then Alastair in bear hugs.

We all spent the next couple hours feasting, talking and laughing. The Fosters had a million stories about Alastair's childhood, but he had plenty about each of them as well. I loved watching him in that environment. He was so relaxed and happy, and perfectly at ease. He held my hand and curled up right beside me on the wooden bench, with absolutely no concern about what anyone might think about the fact that we were a couple. They, in turn, were perfectly accepting.

Sometime later, while Alastair was at the sink rinsing glasses, Bertie surprised me by pulling me down to her height, kissing my cheek, and saying, "Welcome to the family, love. It does me heart good to see Alastair so happy." That was one of the best things anyone had ever said to me. I smiled shyly and thanked her for making me feel so welcome.

Alastair dried his hands on a dishtowel, then came over to me and linked his arm with mine as he said, "Fancy a stroll about the grounds? I could do with a bit of exercise." I told him that sounded wonderful, and we left Roger to visit with his family as we headed out the side doors.

The herb and vegetable garden was lit by a trio of old-fashioned, decorative lampposts that had been converted from gas to electric somewhere along the line, but still looked like something from centuries past. That was true for much of the house and grounds. I could barely get my head around the fact that parts of the property actually predated the U.S.

We strolled down a worn cobblestone path hand-in-hand, and I marveled at the perfect stillness all around us. Alastair plucked a fat, ripe strawberry from a leafy bush and fed it to me, and after I did the same for him, I kissed him tenderly. "I'm so glad I get to share this with you," he said as I took him in my arms. "This place and the Fosters are very important to me."

"Did you hear Bertie welcome me to the family? No one's ever said that to me before."

"I missed it, but that's lovely. They truly are my family, every bit as much as the Penelegions. More so in a lot of ways. I always thought it was oddly appropriate that their last name is Foster, since they practically raised me.

When I look back on my childhood, what I remember most fondly are summer nights at that kitchen table with the Fosters and my sister, while my parents were in London attending galas or dinner parties or other all-important social events."

"You don't mention your sister very often. Why is that?"

"I guess it's because there's nothing to say. I almost never see her and have no idea what's going on in her life. She made it clear from the start that she wasn't going to get roped in to the family business and left for Spain right after she finished school. She barely keeps in touch with me, or any of the family. But she's young, maybe eventually she'll come around."

We continued our walk, circling around the back of the enormous structure. The gardens behind the house were fussy and regimented, everything tidy and squared off, in contrast to the casual beauty of the garden off the kitchen. When I pointed out how different it was, Alastair said, "The grand ballroom overlooks this, so it's all for show, while Bertie's kitchen garden is for real life."

The precise, geometric garden gave way to sprawling lawn, and it in turn eventually ended at the edge of a woodland. Alastair held my hand and guided me as we moved from manicured lawn to the natural environment.

The path was a bit overgrown, and the moonlight was partially blocked by the trees, but he knew where he was going and pushed ahead with confidence.

After a few minutes, a clearing appeared before us, and I murmured, "Oh wow." An ornate wooden bench sat among wildflowers at the edge of a creek. On the other side of the small stream, a ramshackle thatched-roof cottage was gradually being reclaimed by the forest and overtaken by vines. It looked like something out of a fairytale, and I asked, "What is this place?"

"It was a hunter's cottage once, long ago. I used to play in it as a child, but the floor's fallen away now. Eventually, nothing will remain but the stone walls, but those will outlast all of us." We sat on the bench and leaned against each other as we contemplated the cottage. After a few moments he said, his voice hushed and reverent, "There's a beauty to it I think, especially the way it's becoming part of the natural environment. Mark wanted to restore it, but I thought we should give it back to the forest. It's home to a family of rabbits now. They're welcome to it and are certainly making far better use of the cottage than I would have."

I turned Alastair's face toward me with a gentle touch and kissed him, and he climbed onto my lap and whispered,

"I've missed you," as he slipped his arms around my shoulders.

"I've missed you, too. I'm so glad we're going to be making a habit of taking Saturdays off and devoting them to us." We spent every night together and had made love at dawn that morning before we both rushed off to work, but it felt like we were just stealing moments here and there.

"I'm sorry it took me so long to get to the point of regular days off," he said. "I feel awful for neglecting you."

"That's not what you've been doing! The last couple months were insanely busy for me, too. And even if they weren't, it's still okay, Allie. Even if we're not able to spend tons of time together, the time we do have is perfection."

"It's the very best part of my life."

I kissed him again, and then I said, "Thank you for bringing me here, both to Wordsworth and to the cottage."

"It's my pleasure. There are a couple more things I want to show you tonight, so let's keep going."

We followed the stream as it wound through the trees, and in a few minutes we reached a swimming hole that had been created with a partial dam. Alastair turned to me and asked, "Are you up for a skinny dip?"

"Absolutely. It'll be like San Diego all over again, with slightly less chance of re-enacting Jaws."

He chuckled and repeated, "Slightly."

I pulled my T-shirt over my head and tossed it aside, then started unbuttoning his shirt while he unfastened my belt. When we were both naked, we waded into the water hand-in-hand. It was definitely brisk, but still a lot of fun. After maybe twenty minutes of alternately swimming, making out, and splashing and playing around, we emerged onto the grassy bank, dripping and shivering a bit. Alastair surprised me by retrieving a zippered duffle bag from behind a large rock and pulling out two thick beach towels. As he handed me one, he said, "I asked Mark to do me a favor this morning and leave these here for us."

"So premeditated," I teased.

"Oh, it was! I've been looking forward to bringing you to Wordsworth for ages," he said as he scrubbed his hair with a towel, "and I wanted it to be perfect. Fortunately, the Fosters are very kind about indulging my whims."

I ran my gaze down his smooth, sexy body as I dried myself off. He was too tantalizing to resist. I dropped my towel on the ground, knelt on it, and kissed my way down his blond happy trail before taking his cock in my mouth. He moaned and dropped his towel before running his fingers into my damp hair. After a few minutes of sucking him, he came in my mouth with a soft cry and I drank him down.

He was a bit shaky after that, so I spread out my towel and we curled up on it. I used the second towel as a blanket, and as I held him in my arms, Alastair whispered, "Thank you."

I grinned at his good manners and said, "You're welcome."

"I'll return the favor in just a moment."

"Later, Allie. For now, just rest."

He looked in my eyes as he said softly, "My sweet, beautiful Sawyer."

"I love it when you call me yours."

We spent a long time kissing, and it was tender and unhurried. Eventually, we got up and dressed, then headed to the house hand-in-hand. When it came into view, I was astonished all over again. "It's magnificent," I said softly. "I'll never get used to the sight of it."

Alastair frowned a little as he looked up at the house. "It's magical to me too, but knowing my family finds it an embarrassment always makes it bittersweet."

"Who cares what they think? I feel sorry for them if they can't see the joy in something so whimsical and spectacular, and you shouldn't let it color your perception."

"You know what? You're absolutely right. Wordsworth is beautiful, and I love the fact that my great-great-great granddad went so over-the-top with it. If only I

could have met him, he must have been delightful. I also
think he's my only kindred spirit in a very long line of
Penelegions."

When we reached the house, we cut through the
kitchen to reach a laundry room, and Alastair stuffed the
towels in the washer and turned on the machine. Then he
hung the duffle bag on a hook, picked up my hand again
and asked, "Fancy a tour?" Of course I agreed.

As he led me throughout the house, I said, "Games of
hide-and-seek must have been epic when you were a kid."

That made him smile. "Oh, they were. Roger, Mark
and I would play for hours when I was home from boarding
school. I'd usually win, since I was a lot smaller than them
and could fit into some pretty unusual spaces. I don't
advise hiding in a chimney flue, by the way. It takes ages to
wash soot from your hair."

"You actually did that?"

He grinned and said, "I took my hide-and-seek
seriously."

As we wandered through a long hall of family
portraits, I said, "I just realized Mark and Roger are the
same age, but Ro is actually Mark's uncle."

"It's odd, I know. They might as well be brothers,
though."

Eventually, the tour led us upstairs, to Alastair's blue, gold and white childhood bedroom, which was shaped like a piece of pie because it occupied a quarter of the largest of the round turrets. I was fascinated by the glimpse into his past, and asked him about several of his books, toys and mementos. The Dunford Racers were in a special glass display case, and I said, "Did you bring the convertible so it can join its friends?"

"Oh no," he said, squatting down so he could look inside the case. "That stays with me, always. Actually, I was thinking I should take these back to London when we leave tomorrow. May I keep them on your dresser?"

"Of course, but you don't want to put them in your new apartment?"

He said, "Then I'd never see them," as he crossed the room, hopped up on a bench seat, and opened a pair of tall windows.

When he stuck his head out, I asked, "Are you looking for Peter Pan?"

"No, but I used to. I desperately wanted him to be real when I was a child."

It made me a little nervous when he stepped onto the ledge of the dormer window, but it wasn't unexpected. He turned back to me and said, "There's one more thing I want to show you. There are foot- and handholds, but the roof is pitched at a fairly steep angle, so please watch your step and take it slowly, alright?"

"I will. Be careful too, please."

The roof of the turret was shaped like an inverted, pointy ice cream cone, and he wasn't kidding about it being steep. But two rows of metal spikes, an antique-looking version of something you'd find in mountain climbing, provided a sturdy path around to the back of the turret, and from there, it was an easy step down to a flat section of roof on the main building.

A little closet was nestled among the eaves and spires, hidden from the world below. Alastair pulled out an old wool blanket and set it aside, then carefully picked up an antique brass telescope on a tripod and flashed me a delighted smile. "This is where I began," he said. "Right here, on this roof, with this telescope. My love of astronomy, and in fact, so much of who I am, can be traced right back to this. As a bonus, the telescope belonged to Bernard Penelegion. Imagine my delight as a seven-year-old when I climbed out my bedroom window and found first the path around the turret, and then Bernard's secret closet and telescope."

I leaned over to peer into the closet and found it was lined with drawings of fantastical things like knights, castles and dragons, and yellowed newspaper clippings from the mid-nineteenth century with fanciful headlines, like a story about a lion who escaped from the zoo and was never found. I murmured, "This is amazing."

"Isn't it? As a child, it felt like my great-to-the-third-power granddad had left me a present through the centuries. It also gave me a wonderful glimpse into who he was. This part of the house wasn't built until he was in his fifties. That means he was a grown man when he installed those spikes, built this closet, and lined it with things that amused him."

"I love that." As he set up the telescope, I asked, "Do your parents know you come up here?"

He shook his head. "The only people who even know any of this exists are Roger and Mark, and they're sworn to secrecy. If my parents found out, they'd call it ridiculous and unsafe and would have the hand- and footholds removed immediately. Thank goodness the spikes blend in among the roof tiles. Even knowing they're there and looking for them specifically, I've never been able to spot them from ground level, and neither has my family."

Alastair made a couple adjustments as he peered through the telescope's eyepiece, and then he straightened up and said, "Take a look."

When I did as he asked, I murmured, "That's amazing." The surface of the full moon was in perfect focus, every crater well-defined.

We spent quite a while with the telescope, then stretched out on the blanket side-by-side, holding hands. I tucked my hand under my head and listened closely as Alastair continued his tour of the galaxy. He talked about what we were seeing with enthusiasm and passion, and after a while I said, "You have to make time for this. I know the company is important to you, but so is astronomy. I hate the fact that you had to walk away from your PhD program."

"This will always be a part of me," he said as his eyes searched the heavens. "It's in my blood. My time in school was wonderful, but I don't need it to feed my love of astronomy. All I need is a rooftop, a telescope, and you by my side." That made me smile. After a moment, he said, "When I'd come up here as a child, I'd dream about building a rocket and flying off to colonize a distant planet. That's how desperate I was to find a place worlds away from my disapproving family, where I could be happy and be myself. When I got older, I got my wish in many ways when I moved to California."

"And now? What's your wish?"

"Now, I just want to be wherever you are. It's unabashedly corny to tell you you're my happy place, but it's also absolutely true."

We rolled over so we were facing each other, and I kissed him before saying, "I feel exactly the same way about you. And if you decide to run away again, whether it's to California or the moon or Mars, I'll go with you."

"Too right you will! But there's no need for us to run away. Not today, anyway." Alastair smiled contentedly and said, "I feel wonderful right now. I don't think anything could ruin this weekend."

If only that was true.

Chapter Seventeen

I awoke before Alastair and shifted slightly so I could see his face, being careful not to disturb him. We'd left the windows and curtains open, so the bed was bathed in sunlight and a gentle breeze stirred our hair. I'd been kidding around when I brought one of his childhood stuffed animals to bed with us, but during the night, one of Allie's arms had wrapped around the toy, the other around my waist, seeking comfort in both of us. He always looked young and vulnerable when he was asleep, and the teddy bear just added to it and made me feel even more protective of him than usual.

My heart tripped over itself as I watched him. It was a sensation I was used to. Somewhere along the line, I'd fallen madly, completely in love with Alastair Spencer-Penelegion. Even though that had been my truth for quite a while, I had yet to tell him.

I'd said it too soon with Tracy, and then I was left hanging for the next three years. Even though I knew what Alastair and I shared was completely different, I still waited. I needed it to be the right time, the right place. I wanted it to be special.

And if I was being honest…maybe I wanted him to say it first. There was no real reason why it had to happen that way. But some insecure little part of myself needed it, somehow. But that was silly, and arbitrary, and part of me wanted to wake him and tell him I loved him right then.

Instead though, I let him sleep and ran my gaze over his handsome face. The sunlight turned the tips of his lashes and his short razor stubble gold. When his lips parted and he gasped softly in his sleep, as if in the throes of an erotic dream, it made me smile.

A moment later though, I swore under my breath when someone knocked on the door. Alastair spent his entire week functioning on not nearly enough sleep. So why the hell was someone disturbing him on a Saturday morning?

He stirred a bit, and I slipped out of bed and quickly pulled on my jeans, then hurried to the door before whoever it was knocked again and woke him. When I cracked the door and saw Roger standing there, I whispered, "What are you doing? You know as well as I do that he needs to sleep."

Roger kept his voice down too as he told me, "I wouldn't be here if it wasn't important."

I opened the door a little farther and asked, "Did something happen? Is it his dad? Did he have another heart attack?"

"It's not that. Come downstairs with me so we can stop whispering."

I stepped into the hall and had just begun to pull the door shut when Alastair called, "Did I hear Ro? What's going on?"

I opened the door again and Roger said, "Sorry to wake you, mate. Why don't you get dressed, and then you and Sawyer come talk to me in the kitchen, alright?" I was pretty sure that was the first time Roger had ever used my real name, instead of the nickname that amused him to no end.

"It's not your dad," I said as I went back into the bedroom.

"Well, thank God for that." He was sitting up in bed and pushed his dark blond hair back from his forehead, then looked around for his glasses. I found them in his overnight bag and handed them to him, and he murmured a thank you as he swung his bare legs out of bed.

It only took us a minute to get dressed, and then we descended the spiral staircase wordlessly. A muscle worked in his jaw as he ground his teeth. I took his hand when we reached the ground floor, and when he turned to look at me, I kissed the worry line between his brows and said, "Whatever it is, I'm here, Allie, and I'll help you get through it." He nodded and hugged me before we continued on to the back of the house.

As soon as we stepped into the kitchen and Alastair saw the grave faces of Mark, Roger, and Mr. and Mrs. Foster, he exclaimed, "Oh God, who died? Don't try to cushion the blow, just tell me."

"It's not that, love. Come and sit down, the both of you. Would you like some tea?" Bertie bustled over to us and tried to guide us to the table.

"No, thank you," Alastair said. "I'd just like to know what's going on."

Mark looked at his dad, who gestured at him as if trying to get him to say something. Finally, Roger stepped forward and said, "Mark went into town this morning, bright and early. Bertie wanted him to pick up some of those pasties, you like, Alastair. Anyway, he walked past a news agent on the way to the bakery, and...."

Alastair asked, "And what?"

Roger sighed and went over to a stack of newspapers on the counter. He pulled two from the top, and as he handed them to Alastair and me, he said, "We'll figure out a way to fix this."

The huge headline read: 'The Prince of Penelegion's and the Poofter.' Below that were four photos: one of Alastair exiting his office building, one of him and me stealing a kiss at a restaurant, a photo of me walking into my coffee house dressed in heels and a short skirt, and finally, a photo of me wearing only jeans and looking at the camera. While the first three had clearly been taken without our knowledge, it took me a moment to place the last one. Finally, I muttered, "Shit, that's from when I applied for a job at that strip club, right after I arrived in London. How the hell did they get their hands on that?"

"I don't know how they can even print that derogatory word," Mark said. "It's hate speech, that's what it is. I cleared out all the copies they had at the news agent's to make sure the locals don't get their hands on it. I suppose it's all over London, though."

My mouth had gone dry and it was hard to swallow. I unfolded the paper and scanned the article, which began: 'After years of speculation as to the identity and whereabouts of the heir to the vast Penelegion fortune, we here at The Spy bring you this exclusive! He's been identified as Alastair Spencer-Penelegion, age twenty, seen above exiting the offices of Penelegion Enterprises, where he recently seized control of the company. Long kept a secret by his family, possibly for his bizarre sexual proclivities, Spencer-Penelegion recently came home to roost, and he brought company in the form of American transvestite and stripper Sawyer McNeil.' "Could have at least spelled my name right," I muttered. "It's right above the door of my fucking coffee house."

"They've been following us," Alastair said. His voice was low and full of menace. "Those bastards have been sneaking around snapping photos without our permission. How did I miss the fact that this was happening?"

"I'm so fucking sorry, Alastair," Roger said. "I failed you, mate. I had no idea anyone was sniffing around."

Bertie clicked her tongue and said, "Ach, there's nothing you could have done, Ro. These paparazzo types are slippery as eels, and those first few shots were obviously taken with a telephoto lens. They could have been miles away."

"Not miles. They were right there in the restaurant when they took that second shot, and I fucking missed it. I want to go to that rag's offices, find the people responsible, and tear them apart!" Roger's eyes flashed with anger.

"Let my lawyers tear them apart," Alastair said as he patted his pockets. "Where's my phone?"

"It's upstairs with mine, I'll get it," I said as I threw the paper on the table.

I jogged up to the bedroom and found both phones. We'd turned our ringers off the night before so we could get some sleep, and when I glanced at the screens, I saw we had dozens of messages each. On my way back to the kitchen, I played my first voicemail. It was from Horton, who said, "You need to call me, mate, soon as you get this.

You're on the front of a sleazy tabloid, along with your boyfriend. The shop's only been open ten minutes, and already it's filling up with paparazzi and so-called reporters. I know I promised to handle whatever came up while you were away, but I gotta admit, this one's throwing me for a loop."

The next six messages were also from him. They spanned forty minutes and got more and more frantic. He sounded a lot calmer in his last message though, which was: "I've cleared the shop and locked the fucking doors. I wanted to get the okay from you before I did that, but it was turning into a bleedin' media circus. If I hadn't done something, the fire marshal would've shut us down for overcrowding. I'm holed up in your office, I sent the baristas home with pay, and I'd suggest you stay the fuck away from here for a few days until this blows over, because it'll be a feeding frenzy when the paparazzi catches up to you. Anyway, call me."

The rest of the messages were from reporters, and I muttered, "How the fuck did they get my number?" I stopped listening after the third message requesting an interview, and shot Horton a quick text telling him he'd done the right thing by closing early.

I'd reached the kitchen by that point, and when I handed Alastair his phone and he scrolled through his texts, he murmured, "Shite." He started on his voicemails next, but shut the phone off and put it on the table after a minute. "My parents and grandparents are on the way here," he said. "They left London an hour ago, so they'll be arriving any minute."

Mark asked, "How did they know you were at Wordsworth?"

"I told my uncle I was coming here for the weekend when I left work yesterday afternoon. I figured there was no harm in being truthful about my whereabouts. Of course, I also let him think I was going by myself." When Alastair turned to look at me, his expression was unreadable.

"Tell me what you need me to do, Allie," I said. "I can get the hell out of here before your family arrives if that's what you want. Maybe you can deny the whole thing and say that picture of us together was photoshopped. God, I'm so fucking sorry. I thought we were being careful, but obviously I was wrong. The last thing I wanted was to cause trouble between you and your family."

He took my hand and said, "You're not going anywhere, Sawyer. You belong right here, at my side."

"But, your family—"

"I was going to tell them eventually. The tabloid just beat me to it. I was waiting for two things: I wanted to be sure my Dad was out of the woods before upsetting him, and this may sound crass, but I also wanted time to get my financial affairs in order. I assume my family will try to coerce me into breaking up with you by threatening to disown me or cut me off from the family fortune. But I've been taking steps over this past month to make sure they don't have that power over me."

"They shouldn't have found out like this though, with the two of you all over the bloody papers," Bertie said. She was wringing her hands and looked like she wanted to cry. "And then there's the issue of your safety, Alastair. Your parents always tried to keep you out of the spotlight, and now you've been thrust smack-dab into it. I hate to think what's going to crawl out of the woodwork now that everyone in the UK knows who you are."

Ralph's phone beeped, and he glanced at the screen and said, "A car just entered the front gate. Your family's here, Alastair. What would you like us to do?"

Allie thought about that for a moment, then said, "Somebody put the kettle on. Poor Bertie looks like she could use some tea. I could too, as far as that goes." Mark looked surprised, but did as he asked.

My boyfriend was oddly calm as we waited for his parents and grandparents to arrive. He took several teacups from the cupboard, then turned to Mark and asked, "Did you ever get those pastries, mate? The ones you went to town for?"

Mark shook his head. "Sorry, I never made it that far. I saw the papers and came right back here with them."

"That's alright, I bet Bertie has something good to eat around here." Alastair turned to her and said, "By the way, I want you to teach me some of your recipes. I tried to bake for Sawyer when we first met, and it was a disaster. Sadly, I've been too busy lately to try again, but I fully intend to make time for that soon."

"Allie, are you alright?" I asked.

He turned to me and said, "Don't I seem alright?"

"Honestly? You seem like you've entered a level of denial rarely achieved by humankind. Your family is going to flip the hell out when they get here, and you're talking about muffin recipes."

"Scones, actually. Bertie makes them with fresh blueberries and serves them with a bit of clotted cream. They're lovely."

"Okay, now you're scaring me. Your family's approval means everything to you, and you're acting like what's about to happen doesn't matter."

"That's because it *doesn't*," he said. "My family is going to walk through that door any minute now, and they're going to be horrid. They'll yell at me, and tell me what a disappointment I am, and forbid me to see you again. But it's not going to change a thing, Sawyer. I love you. I'll always love you, until the day I die, and if there's a hereafter, then even death won't put an end to it. And here's the thing: there's not a bloody thing my family can do about it." From the other side of the huge house, we could hear a door being thrown open and someone yelling Alastair's name.

He smiled at me and continued, "They know I disobeyed them, and snuck around behind their back, and that I'm seeing you. Now that they're here, they'll also find out I intend to marry you one day. Incidentally, I sincerely hope you wear something sexy, outrageous, and totally you to our wedding. And yes, I know that's jumping the gun because we've only been going out a few months, but it's going to happen. If my family doesn't like it, then they don't bloody well get to come to the wedding."

I stared at him for a long moment, and then I closed the gap between us, took him in my arms, and dipped him back as I planted a huge, deep, passionate kiss on his lips. His family burst into the kitchen as that was happening. There were gasps and cries of outrage. We went right on kissing.

When we finally came up for air, I returned Alastair to an upright position and said, "I love you, too. You know what, though? I don't think I look very good in white.

Would it be weird to wear a black wedding dress when we get married?"

"It'll be sensational! We'll hire a designer and have something made that's one hundred percent you, a bit of leather, a little lace, and black of course, like you said. Pure Sawyer. I'm already picturing it, and I have to say, I'm also picturing tearing it off you on our honeymoon." Alastair flashed me a wicked smile before turning to his family, who were lined up on the other side of the kitchen table with their jaws hanging open. He said lightly, "Mum, do shut your mouth before you catch a fly. You too, Gran, it's rather unbecoming."

That reanimated his grandfather, who turned red and shouted, "How dare you speak to your mother and grandmother that way?"

Alastair just shrugged. "I didn't say anything rude to them. I just pointed out that it's not flattering to stand about with your mouth agape."

His grandfather stepped forward and said, "What's become of you, boy? You've never behaved like this!"

To which he replied, "Well, it's about damn time I did, then."

The elder Mr. Penelegion turned to me and hissed, "I can only assume he learned this rude behavior from you. I knew we shouldn't have allowed him to run off to

America! I told his parents he'd fall in with the wrong crowd, but I never thought he'd sink this low, cavorting with a stripper, a homosexual, and a transvestite!"

I said, "Calling me those things isn't an insult, so much as a simple statement of fact." He stared at me as if he had no idea what he was looking at, and I stared right back.

Alastair's mother spoke up. She was a petite but formidable woman with a helmet of blonde hair and an icy glare, and she turned to the Fosters and said, "What's gotten into the lot of you? You were loyal to my family for generations, but I have to find out from a tabloid what's going on under my own roof! I'm astounded that none of you had the decency to call and tell me my son has been associating with an individual who takes off his clothes for money and does God knows what else! And I won't stand for it. You're all fired! I want you out of my house within the hour. That goes for you too, Roger. I trusted you to look after Alastair, and yet you allowed him to associate with this lowlife!" She waved her hand in my direction.

Poor Bertie's expression was stricken. Alastair went up to her, put his arm around her shoulders, and said, "Don't fret, Bertie. You're all rehired at double your previous salary. Roger, I'm tripling yours. The amount of overtime you put in is truly staggering, and I should have taken over your contract from my family and done that years ago."

"Does this mean we'll be looking after your apartment in London?" Bertie asked, glancing around her beloved kitchen with big, sad eyes.

"No, dear, you'll be staying right here, under my roof," Alastair told her before turning a level gaze on the Penelegions. "And it is, in fact, *my* roof. Did you forget the codicil to Bernard Penelegion's will? It says Wordsworth Manor passes automatically to each new president of Penelegion Enterprises, so long as that person is a blood relative. He wanted to make sure the estate and the company always went hand-in-hand, since to him, this place was the ultimate bonus for whoever held that all-important position. I signed a stack of papers just last month naming me company president and taking ownership of this place. I'd intended to treat the change of ownership as a formality, but if you insist on treating the man I love and members of my family with rudeness, then I'm afraid I'm going to have to ask you to get out of my house."

His grandmother huffed, "Members of your family? Those people are *the help*, Alastair!"

At the same time, his grandfather exclaimed, "You can't be serious!"

"If you care to apologize and remain civil, you're more than welcome to stay. But only then," Alastair said. He poured Bertie a cup of tea and added some sugar, and she accepted it from him with a thank you before lowering herself onto the bench in a daze.

"You're an ungrateful brat," his grandfather snapped. "I'm taking back the company and this house right along with it, and then you're breaking up with that freak and remembering your place, boy."

"No, sorry, that's not actually happening," Alastair said, leaning casually against the kitchen counter. "I read all those contracts before I signed them, and they're iron-clad. That should go without saying. We employ the best lawyers in the country to make sure of that."

His grandfather glared at him while Alastair's mother exclaimed, "I don't even know you anymore!"

"You never did, Mum," Alastair said quietly. "You never bothered to. The fact is, I've always been this person. I've also always been gay, and that was never going to change. The advice Granddad gave me to marry a woman, then sneak around and sow my wild oats with men on the side is appalling! You should be ashamed of yourselves, the whole lot of you, for advocating infidelity."

"You're an embarrassment to this family," his grandfather said. "Don't try to turn this around on us!"

"I'm just me, and if who I am isn't good enough for you, well, that can't be helped."

"You knew what you were doing was wrong! Why else would you sneak around?" It seemed like his grandfather was grasping at straws.

Throughout it all, Alastair had remained perfectly calm and in control, and his voice was level when he said, "My father is just a couple months this side of a major heart attack, and upsetting him was never my goal. I was going to tell all of you about my boyfriend when the time was right, but the tabloids beat me to it. Now that's it's out in the open, here's all you need to know where Sawyer is concerned: he's completely nonnegotiable. Did you hear that? Under no circumstances will I give up the man I love. If you decide to disown me as a result, so be it. I'll miss all of you a great deal, even though you probably don't believe that right now. But my trust fund has already fully vested, and this house and the company will still belong to me. It's in my contract that I can't be fired, and the largest share of Penelegion Enterprises has already been transferred to me. Given all of that, disowning me would be a pretty hollow gesture overall, but if it'll make you feel better, then by all means, proceed."

His grandfather growled, "You ungrateful little shite," and started to rush around the table toward Alastair. I had no idea what he was going to do when he reached him, but

416

I wasn't going to wait around and find out. I squared my shoulders and stepped in his path. So did Alastair's dad.

His father had remained silent during the confrontation, but he said, in a voice that rang with authority, "That's enough. Go home, father, and take my wife and yours with you. You're all behaving like barbarians and embarrassing me in front of my future son-in-law."

The elder Penelegion looked stunned, and he exclaimed, "You can't possibly side with Alastair, after the way he's behaved!"

Alastair's dad said, "Of course I'm siding with my son. That's what fathers are supposed to do, not that you'd know that. Now please, all of you, just go back to London. If Alastair has to call the police to evict you forcibly from his home, you'll be a laughing stock. You know how the locals love to gossip, and it'll surely get back to our circle in London as well. Everyone will be talking about it for years to come."

That was enough to take the wind out of their sails. After a bit more blustering and complaining, his mom and grandparents headed for the door. On the way out, his grandfather huffed, "This isn't over. I'm calling my lawyers. There must be some loophole...."

And his wife said, "You'll do no such thing! How will it look if the family turns against one another? The press will have a field day! They've been waiting for us to fall apart for decades!"

We watched them leave, and then I exhaled slowly and turned to look at Alastair. He seemed as surprised by all of that as the rest of us. Our group remained rooted in place for a minute, until we heard the front door slam behind the departing Penelegions. Then a cheer went up around the kitchen, and everyone descended on Alastair and hugged him and patted his back.

"You were amazing," I told him as I pulled him into an embrace.

"I'd been dreading that for so long," he murmured, "but then it just…happened."

When I let go of Alastair, Bertie hugged him, and his dad turned to me and stuck out a hand. "Hugh Penelegion."

I shook his hand with a firm grip and said, "Nice to meet you, sir. I'm Sawyer MacNeil. Thank you for stepping in."

Alastair looked a bit dazed as he walked up to his dad. The two men stared at each other for a long moment, and then Alastair grabbed his father in an embrace. "Thank you, Dad. I didn't mean to upset you, are you alright?"

"I'm fine, son, just fine."

Alastair led him to the bench beside the farm table and said, "Sit down Dad, and let me fix you some tea. Do you still take it with milk?"

"Aye, and two lumps of sugar. Your mum never lets me have the sweet stuff, but she's not here to complain." He settled in on the bench, and when Alastair handed him the tea, Hugh clinked his teacup against Bertie's and said, "Cheers, old friend. I apologize for my wife, and I want you to know that even if Alastair hadn't stepped in, I never would have let her fire you."

I studied him as he took a drink. Hugh had a ruddy complexion, a spare tire around the middle, and his dark blond hair was shot through with gray. He also had a genuine smile and blue eyes like Alastair's, and looked younger than his fifty-four years.

We sat across the table from Hugh as Roger poured tea for everyone. Alastair took off his glasses, rubbed his hands over his face, and let out a ragged breath as Roger told him, "You were magnificent, Gromit. I always knew you had it in you to stand up to that lot. Er, no offense, Mr. Penelegion."

"Hugh, and none taken."

"I never wanted to ruffle anyone's feathers," Alastair said. "I let them boss me around my whole life, but when they turned on Sawyer, and Bertie, and all of you, I knew I had to take a stand."

"You did the right thing," his father said. "I'm so bloody sick of this family's obsession with keeping up appearances! I didn't know my father had given you the same speech he gave me about marrying a proper wife and sowing my wild oats on the side. It was appalling thirty years ago, and it's appalling now."

Alastair asked, "Dad, are you gay?"

"No. But when I was just a little older than you, I fell for a lovely girl from the wrong side of the tracks, and that got me the same lecture. She and I ended up breaking up anyway, and then I met and fell in love with your mother, who just happened to pass muster, as far as my parents were concerned. I don't believe in infidelity, and if I'd known my father was going to give you that speech, I'd have put a stop to it."

Alastair slipped his glasses in place and looked at his father closely as he said, "You seem different. I don't think we've ever had a discussion quite this candid."

"Well, it's high time we did. I've done a lot of re-evaluating these past couple months. Nothing like suffering a massive heart attack at this age, followed by a quadruple bypass to make you put things in perspective."

"I can only imagine," Alastair said.

"I've been meaning to say thank you, son, for stepping in and keeping the company together after I became ill."

"You're welcome. Honestly though, I'm not doing much. I'm a figurehead more than anything."

"Well, you're still learning. As far as being a figurehead though, don't discount it. That's an important part of the job. Our employees and customers feel good knowing there's a strong, competent leader at the helm. It instills confidence."

Alastair frowned and said, "But I'm not that, not by a long shot. I'm an inexperienced twenty-year-old who's in way over his head."

"You've always been the very best of us, Alastair," his father said. "For starters, you're absolutely brilliant. We've all known that since you were a child. You're something else too, something I always aspired to, but I fell woefully short."

"What's that?"

"You're kind, and you're loved by everyone who meets you. That instills loyalty and garners respect. I was in the offices last week, and I overheard a group of secretaries raving about you to another employee. One of them told the story of how you popped down to the shop for some cold medicine for her when she was feeling poorly."

Alastair shrugged. "I was already running out for some takeaway, and it was easy enough to drop by the chemist's and pick something up. The poor thing felt awful, but she refused to go home because she had too much work to do."

"Don't discount your actions. It's what makes you special, Alastair, the way you care about people. That and your intelligence will make you the greatest leader Penelegion Enterprises has ever known."

"I appreciate the vote of confidence. Meanwhile though, the department heads are going out of their way to funnel any real decisions away from me. The staff might like me, but management has no confidence in me whatsoever."

"Those old coots all work for you, Alastair. If you don't like the way they're doing something, you can change it with a single memo or phone call. I will say though, for now, let them reassign the majority of that stuff, because you're already busy learning the ins and outs of the company."

"That's very true," Alastair said. "I definitely have my hands full."

"I feel terrible about the long hours you've had to put in, but it's about to get a bit easier, son."

"How so?"

"I recently decided I'm coming back to work on Monday, just for two hours a day, five days a week. Your mother and grandmother will go ballistic when I tell them, but they'll just have to get used to it. I'm too young to be put out to pasture, and you're too young to devote every minute of your life to the company. You have far more important things to be thinking about at your age." Hugh flashed me a friendly smile.

"Are you sure you'll be alright though, Dad?"

"I'll be fine. I'm going from sixty-five hours a week to ten, and I'm not made of glass, for goodness sake!"

"Well, that's fantastic then. Between you and Lorelei, who I'll introduce you to next week, I think my life is about to get a whole lot easier," Alastair said.

"Aside from the fact that the tabloids just found their new favorite subject and are going to hound you and Sawyer every minute of every day," Mark said. When we glanced at him, he said, "Not to be a negative Nancy, but you seem to have forgotten that is actually happening, and you two are going to have to come up with some solutions."

"Not just those two," Roger said as he pulled out his phone. "The first thing I'll do is arrange some crowd control measures for Sawyer's coffee house. We can't have the paparazzi crowding out the paying customers." He glanced at me and asked, "You alright with me taking the lead on that, Bonny?"

"Absolutely. Thanks Ro," I said, raising a toast to him with a teacup.

"No worries, mate." Roger turned to Alastair next. "Your office building is secure, though that narrow, one-way street out front might become an issue if it gets snarled with paparazzi waiting for a shot of you. Could you work off-site while I figure out another way to get you in and out of the building?"

"Sure, no reason why not. In fact, I could set up an office in the flat I recently bought. From what I hear, it's in a very high-security building." Alastair turned to me and asked, "Will you move in with me, Sawyer? That's not just because you'll be a lot safer there, but because I love you, and I want you to live with me."

I smiled at him and said, "Of course I will."

Mark asked, "What do you mean, you hear it's in a secure building? It sounds like you have no idea what you bought."

"I don't," Alastair said. "I sent a real estate agent out with my list of wants, and when she told me she found the perfect place, I purchased it sight-unseen."

"Seriously?"

"Well, yes. I bought it primarily to throw my family off my scent, so they wouldn't realize I was spending every night with my boyfriend. And you know I've had way too much on my plate to give house-hunting any time at all."

Mark said, "That's true."

Alastair told me, "If you and I don't like it when we go to take a look at it, we can put it right back on the market and find something else. I want a place that will feel like home to both of us."

I pulled him into my arms and kissed him, and then Bertie got up from the table and said, "You're daft, the whole lot of you. Buying multi-million-pound flats without even looking at them!"

"Hey, that was Alastair's doing, not mine." I looked around and asked, "Bertie, do you have an espresso machine? Not that tea isn't enjoyable, but I need something higher octane to start my day."

"I've got a Mr. Coffee and a can of something or other in the pantry. I think I bought it during the Thatcher era, but you're welcome to it. And Alastair, if you were serious about wanting to learn to bake, I'll give you a lesson right now. I could use a nice blueberry scone myself."

Alastair said, "Fantastic! What about you, Dad, want a baking lesson? You might find it relaxing. That is, assuming you don't need to get right back to London."

"I believe I'll make a day of it, and baking lessons sound delightful," his dad said as he took off his suit jacket and tossed it over the bench. "I might even spend the night and call for a car in the morning. That is, if it's alright with you, son. This is your house, after all."

Alastair rested his hand on his father's shoulder and said, "I'll begin the paperwork to revert ownership back to your name first thing Monday, if that's what you want. It was never my intention to take Wordsworth from you, not if you still want it, and I only brought it up today to keep Mum from firing my second family."

"I know, and I don't want it. I've always found Wordsworth to be a bit garish, to be honest. No offense, son. I know you adore it, and I'm glad it's been passed on to someone who'll appreciate and care for it. That's exactly what my great-great-granddad always wanted, and I dare say you're the first Penelegion since old Bernard to see it the way he did."

While I found the coffee maker and the can of coffee that was older than I was, Alastair and his dad went to work on Bertie's scone recipe while she supervised and called out instructions. They were pretty terrible at it, which resulted in a lot of laughs and some much needed father-son bonding. When the scones went into the oven and the novice bakers left the kitchen to change their flour-spattered clothes, Bertie came over to me and draped a pretty, silk scarf around my neck. "Present for you, laddie," she said.

"Thank you, Bertie," I said as I ran my fingers over the delicate, royal blue fabric and admired the tiny white flowers and vines printed on it. "What's the occasion?"

She tied a loose knot in the scarf and draped one of the ends over my shoulder as she said, "You looked fantastic in those tabloid photos. What I wouldn't give to have legs like yours! I'd be wearing miniskirts every day of me life! But I realized just now that you'd dressed down to come here, like maybe you weren't sure if you'd be accepted if you turned up in a frock. So, this scarf is a way of welcoming you to the family, and it's to let you know you can be yourself here. It was me mum's, and now it's yours. I hope you wear it with pride, because you should never have to hide who you are, Sawyer. Not for anyone." I had to swallow a lump in my throat as I gave her a big hug.

When Alastair returned a couple minutes later, dressed in a pink polo shirt and white shorts and looking like all that was good about summer, he took my hand and said, "Fancy a bit of a stroll while the scones bake?"

"Sure." I ran a fingertip along the tortoiseshell frame of his glasses and said, "I'm glad you didn't switch these out for your contacts. You look so cute in them."

He grinned as he led me to the door. "As I've said before, I look like a primary school mathematics champion. But I'm among family here, so I can just be my dorky self."

We strolled through the vegetable garden, and as we circled to the right, toward the back of the house, I said, "So, when we arrived last night, you neglected to mention the fact that you personally own Hogwarts."

"That's because I haven't quite come to grips with it. I mean, on one hand I'm thrilled, because it means no one can sell her, and I can ensure she's properly cared for as long as I live. On the other hand though, it's a bit surreal. I'm not going to make any drastic changes, because it's also very much my family's home. Both families, as a matter of fact. But over time, I have a few plans for this place."

"Like what?"

"Some of the furnishings and artwork belong in museums. I'd like to donate extensively, and replace them with things like a couch one can actually sit on. I've never liked that fussiness. I also want to slowly replace the formal garden and let Mark do whatever he wants back here." He gestured at the geometric precision of the plants and paths at the back of the house. "Plus, I plan to build an observatory."

"That's terrific!"

"It won't be as big as the one I left behind at Saithmore, but it doesn't have to be." Alastair smiled like a kid on Christmas morning and said, "I'm looking forward to shopping for a telescope."

When we reached the center of the lawn, halfway between the formal garden and the woodland, Alastair paused and pulled out his phone to check the time, then returned it to his pocket and grinned at me. "You're up to something, aren't you?" I said.

"As a matter of fact, I am." He took my hands in his and looked into my eyes. "I love you, Sawyer. I've been wanting to tell you that for some time now, and I wanted it to be special. I knew how much it hurt you to never hear it from your ex while you were together, so I thought, don't just tell him you love him, show him! Make it big! Big as the sky. So that's exactly what I did."

He tilted his chin upward, and I burst out laughing and exclaimed, "Oh my God!"

He'd hired two old-fashioned biplanes to write 'I love you, Sawyer' in plumes of white smoke in the cloudless, blue sky, and as they looped around and declared Alastair's love for me in giant letters, he said, "I stole my own thunder earlier. I was waiting for this moment, but then it just popped out."

I kissed him and said, "I love you, Allie. You amaze me, every single day. Thank you for being completely over-the-top, and going to all that trouble, and for making me feel special. I'm so incredibly grateful for you."

"I'm every bit as grateful for you, love."

As the planes flew off, the words slowly began to dissipate, becoming a part of that perfect summer sky and soon disappearing all together. I was sorry to see them go, but then, they weren't really necessary. All I needed to do to know Alastair loved me was look in his eyes.

Epilogue

Four Months Later

I shook the snow from my black wool coat, stepped into our apartment, and hung it on a hook in the foyer before unzipping my thigh-high black boots. They definitely had 'hooker' written all over them, but I didn't care, because they made me happy. I left the boots beside the coat and wandered into the living room, looking for Alastair. He was usually at his desk, but since the apartment had an open floor plan, I had a clear line of sight to his office, and it was empty.

I paused in the middle of our home and looked all around me, which made me grin. We'd been decorating it slowly over the last four months, buying pieces of furniture or artwork or random odds and ends whenever we found something we liked. The few walls and the marble floor were white, and so were the bigger pieces of furniture, like the leather couches that faced each other in front of the free-standing modern, steel-clad fireplace (a terrible design, actually, because it got too hot to touch when you actually made a fire in it, but we'd decided it was too beautiful to tear out).

What kept the modern space from looking austere were the framed photos of Alastair and me, and our friends and family, which were clustered on many of the surfaces. I adored those pictures. I also enjoyed the big, bold pops of color in the artwork, the bright red dining room chairs, the yellow area rug beneath the coffee table, and currently, the ten-foot Christmas tree, which was lit with a thousand white lights. It was decorated with dozens of colorful ceramic ornaments, which we'd found the month before on a weekend getaway to Barcelona, and amazing lead crystal snowflakes, which I'd found in Penelegion's while taking a break in the grand department store. It had been years since I'd had a Christmas tree. The last one had been when my dad and Sherry were still married. Every time I looked at it, the towering pine brought a smile to my face.

After a moment, I spotted Alastair outside and crossed the apartment. I kept a pair of sneakers beside the glass door and slid my feet into them before stepping onto our rooftop garden. I shivered a little. My black mini-kilt, wool tights and long-sleeved T-shirt weren't enough protection from the weather, and I wished I'd kept my coat on. But I forgot all about being cold as I watched Alastair's face light up at the sight of me. He held his arms out and said, "Hi, love. I'm glad you're home."

So was I. I joined him at the railing on the edge of the roof, slipped my arms inside his camel-colored wool overcoat, and nestled against him. Then I actually found myself sighing with contentment as he put his head on my shoulder. All around us, the lights of London were coming on as sunset turned to dusk.

Our home was basically a glass and metal rectangular box on the rooftop of a high-rise apartment building, and the view of London's skyline was phenomenal. Even Allie had to admit it gave the view from his apartment in San Francisco a run for its money. Basically, that real estate agent who'd been sent off with a wish list had totally nailed it. As soon as Alastair and I saw the place, we knew we were home. The fact that my boyfriend had always been drawn to rooftops and we now actually lived on one delighted us both to no end.

I kissed him, then ran my thumb over his lower lip as I said, "You're cold, Allie. How long have you been out here?"

"Half an hour maybe? It rarely snows in London, and it'll all be gone by the time we return from our holiday, so I wanted to enjoy it." He tilted his face up and stuck his tongue out to catch a flake, and I chuckled before doing the same. Then he said, "I love that hush when the snow is falling, don't you? It feels as if all the world is pausing to pay its respects to the wonder of nature."

"That's a nice way to put it."

I kissed him again, deeper that time, and then he smiled at me and said, "I know one way you can warm me up. How much time do we have before Roger arrives to accompany us to the airport?"

"Not long."

He ran his fingers through my short hair and said, with a mischievous glint in his eye, "In that case, what are your thoughts on joining the mile-high club on our flight to California?"

"Absolutely! But will we have enough privacy on the plane? I don't want to traumatize Roger."

"I reserved a plane with private bedrooms, since this is an overnight flight."

"Perfect. Since we can't fool around yet, I know what else we can do to warm up."

He knew what I meant without asking, and played Time After Time from his phone, which we'd officially proclaimed as 'our song' at some point. We danced in the snow and took turns leading. Both of us threw in a few awkward but fun dips and spins, which made us laugh. Alastair pulled me close and asked, "Have I told you lately that I adore you?"

"You did, as a matter of fact. You texted me twice while I was finishing my Christmas shopping, then video-chatted with me when I was on my way home and told me twice more. My driver Lenny thinks we're a couple saps. He told me to tell you that."

"Lenny's a fine one to talk. I've heard stories from when he was courting his wife. Ask him sometime about the Michael Bublé flash mob he organized to try to impress her."

I burst out laughing. "Tell me you're kidding." He shook his head, and I said, "That's awesome."

Roger let himself into our apartment just then with his key and called, "Are you both decent? Please say yes. I'd love to make it through today without an encore performance of the Bonny Barebottom show." He didn't knock, because he was family, and normally that was no problem, because he always let us know when he was on his way over. But the week before, I'd forgotten he was dropping by and completely mooned him, because I'd been cooking in just an apron.

We went inside and locked the door behind us as I said, "Yup, all dressed and ready to go. Did you say goodbye to your mum?"

"I did, and I promised yet again that we'd all be home for Christmas dinner. But right now, we need to get our arses out of this flat and onto a plane. Come on, then."

"Well, someone's certainly eager to get to San Francisco," I said as I swapped my sneakers for my hooker boots. "That wouldn't have anything to do with a certain beautiful brunet who happens to be living in Alastair's apartment, now would it?"

"What? No, of course not." Roger looked flustered, which I thought was cute.

"I told Gabriel you're coming, Ro, and he's excited to see you."

Roger stared at me with wide eyes, then spun on his heel and said, "Just come on. You're keeping your driver and the usual contingent of paparazzi waiting. Of course, the latter can stand out in the snow and freeze their todgers off for all I care."

I put on my coat and applied some red lipstick, then said, "Show time," as I turned to Alastair and took his hand. It was annoying that we were followed around and photographed, but the paparazzi's numbers had been dwindling steadily over the last few months. It was just a matter of time before we became old news, so we were just waiting it out.

*****

A couple hours later, Alastair and I were stretched out naked in bed. Our small but fully appointed bedroom had reached cruising altitude at just about the same time that we inaugurated each other into the mile-high club. As he caressed my thigh, I ran my gaze down his beautiful, naked body and said, "The last time I was on a transatlantic flight, it was that redeye to London. I was crammed into an inhumane seat and hoping you'd be happy to see me. That feels like a lifetime ago."

"You had to know I'd be thrilled to see you. You give my life meaning, Sawyer. It might have looked like I had everything before, but that wasn't even remotely true. None of it mattered, not until you came along and I got to share it with you."

I grinned at him and said, as I gently ran my thumb along his jaw, "I think the holidays are making you sentimental."

"Oh they are, no doubt about it. Our first Christmas together! I haven't been this excited for the holiday since I was a child. No, scratch that. I've never been this excited. I know for a fact this one will be magical."

I grinned as I thought about the dozen beautifully wrapped Dunford Racers hidden away back in our apartment, one for each of the twelve days of Christmas. I could hardly wait to give them to him, along with the probably overdone pile of other treasures I'd been buying and stashing for the last month. For a man who had everything, Alastair was remarkably easy to shop for, probably because I knew him better than I'd ever known anyone.

He pulled a blanket over both of us and settled into my arms. I breathed in his clean scent, and listened to the low, steady hum of the jet engines, and after a few minutes, I whispered, "Thank you."

"For what?"

"For loving me, and sharing your life with me, and always treating me like I'm something special. You make me feel cherished, every day. I had no idea what that felt like before you came along." I added, "I guess I'm getting sentimental, too. I'm going to blame it on the season." Alastair pulled me even closer.

*****

The fact that Sherry's and my dad's duplex was all one color had to be progress. They'd painted it a crisp white with purple trim, a compromise of sorts, and pots of pansies and violas graced both sides of the wide staircase. Three months earlier, Dad and Sherry had begun dating. They were proceeding slowly, cautiously, and still lived on their own sides of the house, but I had high hopes for them.

"Well, isn't this fancy," Sherry said as she hoisted up her long, pink dress and climbed into the back of the limo. She then leaned over, kissed my cheek and said, "I'm so happy to see you, sweetie. You, too, Alastair." I'd introduced them over Skype at one point, and the two had bonded instantly.

Once my father climbed in the limo, I did a round of introductions. Gabriel and Roger were seated beside Allie and me and kept shooting shy smiles at one another. Dad dropped onto the bench seat across from us, looked around and said, "A limo? So, I guess you're a big shot now."

"He is, as a matter of fact," Gabriel chimed in. "Sawyer's business is booming, and he just opened his own coffee roasting facility in London. Now he's looking for a place so he can open a second location here in San Francisco. Just watch, Sawyer MacNeil Coffees is going to become the next Starbucks!"

"Seriously not the goal," I told him as Alastair draped his arm around my shoulders and the limo rolled forward.

Sherry put her beaded purse on her lap and picked up my father's hand. "I think it's fantastic, both your success with the coffee business and that you were nice enough to rent us a limo. I haven't been in one of these since senior prom. There are some stories from that night, don't ya know! We'll just save those for another time, though."

I was pleasantly surprised when my dad cracked a smile at that. It was also nice that he didn't feel the need to say anything about the fact that I was wearing lipstick and spike heels with my tux. I'd given him a heads-up about the way I was dressing these days, and all he'd said was, "Nothing you do surprises me anymore." I'd almost come back with, "Challenge accepted," but instead, I'd decided to just be mature about it.

When we pulled up to the firehouse a few minutes later, Allie smiled and said, "Will you look at that! The place looks grand! Now if only we could cut through all that red tape and actually let the kids move in here."

The licensing process was still dragging on, despite everyone's best efforts to get the shelter doors open. In the meantime, Nana Dombruso had begun finding homeless LGBT+ teens around the city and letting them live in her house. I admired her dedication.

She and Alastair had decided to host a big holiday party at the firehouse, since it wasn't being used for anything while the paperwork was going through. The place was decked out in a riot of Christmas lights, with big wreaths on the red bay doors. Nana was dressed like an elf, complete with a tall, pointy hat and even pointier ears, and she grabbed Alastair and me in a slightly choking hug when we got out of the limo. "It's been too long! I hear you're going to start jet-setting back and forth between here and the UK though, and that's fantastic news! I don't like going too long without seeing my boys," she said. When she finally let us out of the headlock, she took a good look at us, then proclaimed, "Being in love certainly agrees with you. You both look fabulous!"

I said, "So do you, Nana."

"I know. Now come on inside," she said. "There are a hell of a lot of people waiting to see you! We also got River catering the shindig for us, and Ash the DJ is laying down some sick beats. Let's party!"

We barely made it through the door before Kai nearly tackled me in a hug. Jessie and Izzy took turns next. The little girl was decked out in the most recent princess dress I'd sent her, and she looked radiant. "I'm so happy to see you, Izzy," I told her. "I see you opened your Christmas present already."

She looked worried. "Is that bad? I couldn't wait, because I knew it'd be something pretty and I wanted to wear it to the party."

"I'm glad you didn't wait. This way, I get to see how beautiful you look in your new dress."

Izzy beamed at me. "You look pretty, too. I love your lipstick and your Barbie shoes." I loved how it was a total nonissue for her.

Elijah pushed through the crowd a minute later and gave Allie and me quick, self-conscious hugs before saying, "I'm so happy to see you. Are you really going to start splitting your time between San Francisco and London? Please say that's actually happening."

"It is," Alastair told him. "I can work remotely most of the time, and Sawyer intends to open a branch of his coffee house here in San Francisco and let his employees handle the one in the UK. So, in just a few weeks, you'll be seeing a lot more of us."

"Best news ever." Elijah turned to me and said, "Hey, I've been meaning to ask, are you still taking online classes?"

"Yup, just two at a time, because work keeps me busy. At this rate, I'll get my bachelor's degree when I'm forty, but that's alright. How are things going at Saithmore?"

"Last quarter was so much better, since I was out of the dorms and staying in that quiet, private, beautiful house," he said. "Thank you again, Alastair. Jed's around here somewhere too, and he also wants to thank you."

"I'm happy to help."

Gabriel was standing nearby, adjusting the sleeve of a knitted black tunic, and he looked up at us and said, "I should clear out of the apartment. I'm a total squatter, I've been there for months. I'm sure you'll want it to yourselves whenever you're back in the city."

"You're a wonderful roommate, Gabriel," Alastair said. "Please stay. Not only do we enjoy your company, we'll feel good knowing the apartment is in good hands when we're in London." Our friend looked a little like he might cry as he thanked us.

Darwin and his boyfriend Josh were the next to reach us. As Darwin grabbed me in a hug, I said, "There he is! Jack the Giant Slayer. Great job on getting that transphobic asshole Huntington to withdraw from the mayoral race."

Our night of putting up posters and exposing Huntington at his fundraiser had lit a fire in Darwin. He'd spent the months leading up to the November elections volunteering with grassroots political organizations to help the better candidate get into office. He'd also been posting videos online talking about politics, discrimination, and his experiences as a transgender teen, and he was developing a significant following.

He studied the floor shyly when he let go of me. "It wasn't just me. A lot of people saw Huntington for who he was. I think his campaign was doomed from the start."

443

"You helped, though. And I've seen all your videos, way to make yourself heard."

"As much as I dislike being in the public eye, I realized it's important to be a voice for others like me, the kids who can't speak for themselves."

He looked genuinely happy when I said, "I'm so damn proud of you, Darwin."

*****

A couple hours into the party, I noticed a tall figure hovering in the doorway, and I told Alastair, "Tracy's here. I was pretty sure he'd blow off my invitation."

"I thought he would, too."

"Want me to introduce you?"

While Alastair seemed to mentally weigh the pros and cons of that, Rollie chimed in, "You can introduce me! That guy's a fox! Is he gay and single? Please say yes." I told him he was and that I'd be happy to introduce him, but then Rollie noticed Alastair's grave expression and said, "Um, maybe you could just send that hunk my way later on. It looks like there's a little unfinished business between your then and now."

Alastair's brows were knit as we crossed the ground floor of the firehouse. When we reached Tracy, I said, "Hey. I'm glad you came."

He shifted uncomfortably from foot to foot and looked at anything but me as he said, "Yeah. I, uh, wasn't going to. I figured the invitation was just a pity thing. But then, I also figured, I don't know anyone in California, so why not just show up and give it a shot?"

"It's good you did. So, um, there's someone I want you to meet."

I braced myself as I introduced Tracy and Alastair, remembering some comments Allie had made once about wanting to inflict bodily harm on my ex. They muttered hellos, and then he and Alastair just sort of appraised each other for a long moment. I thought they were just going to leave it at that, but then Tracy blurted, "I hope you know how lucky you are. Sawyer's one in a million."

"I know. Thank God you were dumb enough to let him go, so he could end up where he belonged: with me."

"I was an idiot, and he definitely belongs with you. You can give him things I never could, and I'm not talking about all the shit you can buy him because you're filthy rich. It's obvious you make him happy, and he's free to be himself with you. That's what matters."

445

Alastair watched him for another moment, then said, "I hope you find what you're looking for." Tracy nodded and didn't look at either of us.

I lightened the mood by saying, "Come on, time to stop hovering in the doorway. Let me introduce you to some of my friends, starting with that fantastic little lady right there." I gestured at Nana, who'd lost one of her elf ears and was twerking enthusiastically on the dance floor. Tracy looked more alarmed than I'd ever seen him, but then he pulled up his game face and let me lead him into the crowd.

*****

"Oh man," River said. "I just got this total déjà vu, like we've all been here before."

Yoshi told him, "That's because a few months ago, we were all sitting around just like this at another party."

"Nothing ever changes," River muttered.

I looked at Alastair, who was curled up against my side, and said, "Except when it does. Your whole life can change in the blink of an eye. One minute, you're single and sure you'll stay that way forever. The next, you're following a trail of mini-muffins which, unbeknownst to you, are leading directly to your future. And then you reach the end of the trail, and you have a choice to make. Do you keep your feet on the ground, or do you go out on that ledge? Be safe or take a chance, that's the question. And the answer should always be, take that chance! See what happens. Because maybe, just maybe, you'll find everything you were ever looking for."

Alastair smiled at me, and River said, "Super weird mini-muffin analogy, dude."

"It's not an analogy," Yoshi said as he got to his feet. "It's their origin story. Come on, River, dance with me. Maybe we'll accidentally find an origin story of our own."

River thought about that for a moment, then got up, took his friend's hand and said, "Stranger things have been known to happen." Murphy and Rollie exchanged an awkward series of looks and gestures, which they somehow must have understood, because they both got to their feet, and then they too headed to the dance floor.

"It'd be weird if they ended up as couples," I said as Alastair nuzzled my cheek with his.

"Wouldn't it, though?" After a moment, he sat up and looked at me with a sparkle in his eye. "Hey, how do you suppose we access the firehouse roof?"

"I know exactly how to do it. I found out when I was working on the renovations."

Getting up there wasn't difficult. We took a back staircase and emerged on the roof through a door that we kept propped open with a box, to make sure we could get back in later. I took Alastair's hand, and we stepped around some infrastructure and headed toward the back of the building.

He looked around us and said, "I'm going to bring in a landscape architect and turn this into a garden for our future residents. An expert could hide all the vents and things and create something usable and beautiful up here. I think the kids might like an outdoor space, and I know they'll enjoy this." We'd reached the edge of the roof, and he gestured at the beautiful view of San Francisco's skyline.

"Great idea."

"I'm so glad we're finding a way to split our time between San Francisco and London. I've missed this and all those fantastic people downstairs."

"Me too."

I studied his profile as he took in the panoramic skyline, and after a moment he said, "My God, that's beautiful."

"The most beautiful thing in the world," I murmured, still not looking at the view.

"Are you glad to be home?"

"San Francisco isn't home, Allie," I told him gently.

He glanced at me and asked, "It isn't?" I shook my head.

Alastair took me in his arms, and I pulled him even closer and whispered, "Now I'm home."

The End

#####

Thank you for reading!

The series will continue in 2017. Next up is a novella narrated by Dante Dombruso, which brings the arson investigation introduced in The Distance to a close. Additional Firsts and Forever novels will follow. As always, old friends will make appearances, new characters will be introduced, questions will be answered, and love will win.

A Firsts and Forever Series Family Tree is located at the end of this book.

For more by Alexa Land,
please visit her Amazon author page,
find her on Facebook,
or on Twitter @AlexaLandWrites

And visit her blog at
alexalandwrites.blogspot.com

The Firsts and Forever Family Tree

Who's Who and How They're Related

The Dombruso Family:
Sicilian-American family with roots in organized crime
Dante, Vincent, Gianni and Mikey Dombruso (in order from oldest to youngest) are brothers.
They were raised by their grandmother, Stana Dombruso (Nana), after their parents were killed.
Nico Dombruso is their cousin (one of many).

Dante is married to Charlie
Vincent's husband is Trevor
Josh is Vincent and Trevor's adopted son; they also have twins.
Josh is dating Darwin.
Gianni is dating Zan Tillane
Mikey is dating Marie. He's a widower with three sons.

Nana also had three sons: Paulie, Alberto and a third I have yet to name.
Paulie was Dante, Vincent, Gianni and Mikey's dad. He was killed when they were little.
Alberto is Nico and Constantino's father. They also have a sister.
Nana's third son was married twice and had several children, including Jerry and Carla.

Jessie worked for Nana as a chauffeur/assistant. She considers him family.
Nana is married to Ollie.

The Nolan Family:
Irish-American family, many of whom are in law enforcement
Kieran and Brian Nolan are brothers
Shea and Finn Nolan are brothers (Kieran and Brian are their cousins)
Jamie Nolan is also their cousin

The Friends:

Christian and Skye are best friends. They went to Sutherlin art school with Christopher Robin.

Christopher is friends with Hunter Jacobs (Storm), and with Charlie

Skye's half-brother is River.

River's ex-boyfriend is Cole.

Cole and Hunter were a couple years ago

Chance and Christian are friends.

Zachary is Chance's friend.

Alastair and Zachary are friends.

Alastair used to race with Jessie and Kai (his racing name was Six)

Gabriel is also Zachary's friend.

Yoshi is friends with Gianni and River

Charlie is Jamie's friend and ex-boyfriend.

Sawyer is Kai's best friend. Kai is married to Jessie

.

More family ties:

Zan Tillane (Gianni Dombruso's boyfriend) is Christian's father.

TJ Dean is Trevor's father.

Tony is Chance's father.

Tony's adopted son is named Cory.

Chance's kid brother is Colt.

Colt's ex-boyfriend is Elijah.

Luca's brother is Andreo.

The Series in Order, and the Couples:

1. **Way Off Plan**: Jamie Nolan and Dmitri Teplov

2. **All In**: Charlie Connolly and Dante Dombruso

3. **In Pieces**: Christopher Robin Andrews and Kieran Nolan

4. **Gathering Storm**: Hunter Jacobs/Storm and Brian Nolan

5. **Salvation**: Trevor Dean and Vincent Dombruso

6. **Skye Blue**: Skye and Dare

7. **Against the Wall**: Christian George and Shea Nolan

8. **Belonging**: Gianni Dombruso and Zan Tillane

9. **Coming Home**: Chance Matthews and Finn Nolan

10. **All I Believe**: Nico Dombruso and Luca Caruso

10.5 **Hitman's Holiday**: Andreo and Connie (Constantino)

11. **The Distance**: Jessie and Kai

12. **Who I Used to Be:** Zachary and TJ

13. **Worlds Away**: Sawyer and Alastair

The series will continue on from here. Thank you again for reading!

Made in the USA
San Bernardino, CA
11 March 2017